Empe

Alex Gough is an author of Roman historical adventures. The Carbo Chronicles, including *Watchmen of Rome* and *Bandits of Rome*, was written as a result of a lifelong obsession with ancient Rome, and the culmination of a lot of research into the underclasses of the time. He has also written a collection of adventures following Carbo and other characters from *Watchmen of Rome*, where you can learn more about their rich lives.

For reviews of Roman fiction, and articles about Roman history go to www.romanfiction.com

Also by Alex Gough

Carbo and the Thief
Who All Die

Carbo of Rome

Watchmen of Rome
Bandits of Rome
Killer of Rome

The Imperial Assassin

Emperor's Sword
Emperor's Knife
Emperor's Axe
Emperor's Spear
Emperor's Lion
Emperor's Fate

ALEX GOUGH
EMPEROR'S
FATE

CANELO

First published in the United Kingdom in 2022 by

Canelo
Unit 9, 5th Floor
Cargo Works, 1–2 Hatfields
London SE1 9PG
United Kingdom

A CIP catalogue record for this book is available from the British Library.

Print ISBN 978 1 80032 903 4
Ebook ISBN 978 1 80032 902 7

Cover design by Stephen Mulcahey

Cover images © Shutterstock, Arcangel

Look for more great books at www.canelo.co

Printed and bound in Great Britain by Clays Ltd, Elcograf S.p.A.

1

To Abbie and Nome

To all my readers for getting this far through Silus' journey

And to little Ivy, constant companion, still going, against all odds, like Issa

Chapter I

Alexandria, December 215 AD

Silus squinted at the piece of graffiti scratched into the plaster on the side of the Temple of Isis, the distance of an arrow flight from the Great Harbour of Alexandria. He tilted his head to one side, trying to work out exactly what two figures were doing with each other. He traced his fingers over the angular writing beneath the picture, and his lips moved as he deciphered the Greek letters. Then his eyes widened, and he whispered, 'Fuck!'

Now he knew what the words said, the intention of the unknown artist became clearer. It was a cartoonish depiction of a man and woman in a sexual position, the quality about the standard of a child's scribble. But the inscription clearly read, 'Tarautas and Jocasta.'

A couple of young Alexandrian lads saw him examining the image. One nudged the other and wandered over to Silus.

'Pretty life-like, huh?' said one in Greek, a sneering smile on his face.

Silus raised an eyebrow. 'You think? If that's what you believe sex is like, you have clearly never taken a woman to bed.'

The young man puffed his chest out, put his shoulders back.

'I've had plenty of women.'

'Sure, I bet your mother had plenty of nannies for you, to keep you out of her way while she screwed some good Roman men.'

The Alexandrian stepped forward, but his friend put a hand on his shoulder, holding him back.

'He's just trying to provoke you. Leave him.'

'I'm not afraid of him.'

'I know, but look, he's clearly Roman. Touch him, and the legionaries will beat you black and blue.'

The first Alexandrian glowered at Silus, then turned and stalked away, his friend hurrying behind.

'Tell your mother I said hello,' Silus called after them, but they didn't turn back. Silus shook his head. Oclatinius would have been disgusted with him. He was meant to be keeping his head down. But something in the cocky boy's demeanour, and his clear approval of the disparaging artwork, had riled him. And it wasn't because of righteous indignation on behalf of Caracalla, he realised. It was because of the insult to Julia Domna.

Tarautas was a gladiator, as famous for his bloodthirstiness and recklessness as he was for his hideously ugly visage and short stature. There had been a joke going around the Empire for some time comparing Caracalla to Tarautas, and it was even possible to purchase statuettes outside the Flavian amphitheatre of a stunted Caracalla dressed as a gladiator, his handsome features twisted unkindly. As for the reference to Jocasta, even Silus' meagre literary education informed him this referred to the mother and lover of the unfortunate Oedipus.

If Caracalla saw it, of course, he would explode like Vesuvius.

And Caracalla was due to tour Alexandria the next day. Currently he was resting with his men in the Roman camp to the east of the city, having marched many hundreds of miles from Syria. He had left his stepmother, Julia Domna, the graffitist's Jocasta, in Antioch, in charge of the administration of the East, while he turned his attention to Egypt. It was another step on the ladder that reached up to the invasion of Parthia, his ultimate aim. Having pacified Britannia and Germania, consolidated his position in Rome, and defeated the barbarians of the Danube, he simply needed to deal with a belligerent Armenia and a grumbling Alexandria, and the invasion could proceed.

Armenia was a technically independent vassal state of Rome, but bordering Parthia, it was a constant bone of contention, shifting from the influence of one Empire to the other depending on who was on the throne. It would have to be dealt with before the operation against Parthia could begin.

Alexandria was a different proposition, however. Since the reign of Augustus Caesar it had been an Imperial province, and though in all that time it had never been in outright rebellion against Roman rule, it was constantly simmering, and often boiling over into open riots. Caracalla had resolved to ensure the passivity of this vital part of the Roman Empire prior to continuing his adventure, and also, Oclatinius had informed Silus, to raise funds which were running dangerously low, despite his liberal bleeding of the richest of the Roman elite.

The city had a feel of unrest now, Silus thought, as he strolled nonchalantly into the agora, the wide meeting place and market that was the Greek equivalent of the Roman forum. Philosophers and prophets stood on the steps of temples and sermonised to passers-by with threats of doom if they didn't turn from their evil ways or delivered unsought advice on how to live a fulfilled life. Stallholders cried out for custom, advertising their fresh fish, fruits, perfumes, shoes, jewellery and slaves. Prostitutes propositioned lone males, and in some cases accompanied males, much to the disgust of their partners.

But there were others hanging around with less clear purposes. Groups of men skulked, looking sullen, leaning against walls, carving inscriptions, throwing stones, with occasional fights breaking out between them. Women and old men shot them concerned glances and rushed to complete their business, so they could hurry home, ushering oblivious children and grandchildren before them.

Silus had been in Alexandria before and had found himself in the midst of a full-blown riot. He knew how easy it was for this city to explode, and the presence of Caracalla with his army outside the city was more like pouring oil on a fire than on troubled waters.

But that was not Silus' problem at that moment. He had been tasked with keeping tabs on an Imperial freedman called Eugenios. Formerly, Eugenios had worked closely with Festus, the late Commander of the Sacred Bedchamber and head of one of Caracalla's spy organisations. His successor was the freedman eunuch Sempronius Rufus, who had already been the Head of the Bureau of Memoirs, and Oclatinius was suspicious of the man's increasing power and the trust shown in him by Caracalla. Eugenios was now in Rufus' employ, but an informer had passed intelligence to Oclatinius that Eugenios was conspiring against Caracalla. Whether he was involved with the conspirators who had supported

Festus and were never found, or was acting under orders from Rufus, or there was some other conspiracy brewing, Oclatinius did not know, and he had tasked Silus with finding out.

Eugenios was a short man, which was irritating when it came to tailing someone. He disappeared in and out of the crowd, and Silus had to stick closer to him than he liked to avoid losing him completely. Silus had cut his teeth tracking wolves and deer in northern Britannia under his father's cruel and judgemental tutelage and graduated to hunting barbarian Caledonian and Maeatae. Tracking a man through a city had obvious differences, but the basics were the same, and, besides, Silus had had much experience since he had joined the Arcani.

So he was able to follow Eugenios from the Roman camp, through the Canopic Gate, down the Canopic Way and past the gymnasium and the Temple of Saturn to this spot. Eugenios occasionally stopped abruptly, took a random turn or loitered at a market stall. But his craft was clumsy, amateurish, and he showed no signs of noting his tail.

Silus followed him through the agora and out of the southern side, and up the hill to where the magnificent Serapeum overlooked the city. The temple complex dedicated to Serapis held bad memories for Silus, the site of the culmination of Julia Soaemias' plot to make her son Avitus ruler of the East. But that had had a happy ending, more or less, and he put it from his mind as he slipped through the colonnaded garden, keeping Eugenios in sight the whole time. The Imperial freedman gave one final glance around him, then knocked a complex rhythm on a wooden door in a small temple dedicated to Anubis, which was situated in the Serapeum complex. The door

5

opened just enough to admit Eugenios, and he squeezed inside.

The temple had no ground level windows and only the single entrance. Silus didn't like the idea of climbing up to the openings under the rafters to enable him to observe what was happening inside. Clambering up temple walls was hardly the best way to stay inconspicuous, and, besides, Eugenios could leave and be away before he could get back down. So instead, he took up the position of a meditative worshipper at a nearby altar, kneeling so he could keep the temple entrance in view.

A seller of sacrifices approached Silus, dragging with him a small menagerie. Despite the fact that Silus was clearly in the middle of an act of worship the sacrifice-seller started to harangue him in native Egyptian accented Greek.

'Doves, sir? Pure white, no marks. I personally guarantee the liver will be free of lesions.'

Silus half-closed his eyes and pressed his hands together before him.

'New-born kid? Pure white. The best price, sir.' The kid bleated on cue, and a caged dove let out a coo.

'Go away,' hissed Silus.

'Something more impressive to honour Serapis? I can get you a full-grown bull, best price in Alexandria, healthy. I can even get you the priest to do the sacrifice, good omens or your money back.'

Silus pulled aside a fold of his tunic to reveal his blade, and the sacrifice-seller backed away hurriedly.

The door to the temple opened and half a dozen figures emerged, Eugenios among them. The others were typical Greek Alexandrians in appearance, complexions lighter than the native Egyptians, apparel finer in quality than the poorer indigenous peoples. Silus kept his head bowed until they had passed, then scurried over to the temple. He eased the door open quietly and peered in. The interior was dimly lit by the few lofty apertures allowing in the sunlight. The air was cool and thick with the scent of incense. But there was nobody inside, so he hurried to catch up with the group who had left a moment before.

The men walked, deep in muttered conversation, glancing around them furtively as they processed back down the hill towards the city centre. It was much harder to avoid detection by an alert group than an individual because of simple mathematics – at any one time someone was more likely to be looking in the pursuer's direction. So Silus had to hang back a lot further than he would have liked, unable to hear their words, and frequently losing sight of them.

When they reached the busy crossroads of the Aspendia Avenue and the Canopic Way at the south-west corner of the agora, they halted. Silus turned to face a wall where more graffiti was inscribed, and studied it, keeping the group at the edge of his vision. It was another uncomplimentary message directed at Caracalla: 'Go home Caracalla, brother killer.' Not much subtlety there. The anger in the city was palpable. Silus thought it would take even less provocation than usual for it to boil over, and he had witnessed a riot after Atius accidentally kicked a cat.

The group of men split, heading in pairs south, east and west. Silus followed Eugenios and his new partner, a tall, skinny man with a shaven head, wearing a priestly robe, maybe a celebrant of Isis or Serapis. They walked east down the Canopic Way. The avenue was wide, lined with olive trees and cedars, carts, wagons, litters and chariots passing each other in a seemingly chaotic fashion that

7

nevertheless succeeded in keeping the vehicles moving. Pedestrians dodged in and out of the traffic, and the busy throng allowed Silus to approach his quarry much closer.

He was curious now. Oclatinius had clearly been right, as always. Eugenios was definitely up to something, and this furtiveness suggested whatever it was, he shouldn't be doing it. Of course, it might be something illicit that had nothing to do with Caracalla, or conspiracies against the Imperial person. He could be attending a meeting of a banned or secret cult, conducting some shady business deal, arranging a theft. But Silus doubted if he would be that lucky. It was bound to be something worse.

Pockets of restless men were gathered along the roadside, and Eugenios and the priest stopped several times to talk to them. Silus couldn't hear the words, but he saw angry nods and clenched fists. The uneasy feeling in Silus' guts intensified.

A pregnant woman jumped out of the way of a grain wagon that had veered to avoid a cat. She bumped into Silus, then fell onto her backside, spilling her basket of loaves into the dirt. Silus blurted out an apology and bent to help her up.

'Go home, Roman,' she spat, batting away his proffered hand. Silus was taken aback. He was hardly wearing a toga and spouting Latin speeches, but neither had he dressed as an Alexandrian. He had supposed there would have been enough Romans in Alexandria that he wouldn't stand out, and certainly the last time he had been in the city, he had attracted little attention. The mood towards Romans had clearly changed. Maybe it was fear of Caracalla's army, anger at his announcement to tax them heavily to pay for his war, or maybe it was just typical Alexandrian volatility. But Silus had clearly miscalculated.

8

As he stepped back from the woman uncertainly, an old man waved a stick at him, and cried out, 'Leave her alone, Roman. Can't you see she is pregnant?'

Silus turned to him to protest his innocence, stepping forward and spreading his hands wide.

'Look, he is harassing that old man now,' shouted a plump woman.

Three young men who had been lounging against a wall, throwing pebbles at a sleeping dog, nudged each other and wandered over to him, shoulders rolling, arms away from their sides in a way subconsciously calculated to exaggerate their bulk.

'Hey,' called out one. 'Want to pick on someone who can fight back?'

'No, listen,' said Silus desperately, glancing towards Eugenios and the priest who were a score of yards down the road, talking to a stallholder who was selling kitchen knives. 'It was an accident. She slipped.'

'They all say that,' said another youth, and pushed him hard in the shoulder. 'Oh look, did you slip?'

Silus clenched his jaw.

'I don't want any trouble.'

'You should have thought of that.' The youth drew his fist back, swung a punch aimed at Silus' temple.

Silus caught the fist in his hand, twisted, slammed down with his elbow and broke the lad's arm.

The scream cut through the hubbub of the street, and everyone nearby stopped and stared. Silus looked across to Eugenios who was looking in his direction and frowning.

Maybe if Eugenios hadn't recognised him, he would have dismissed it as simply another street brawl. And there were very few people in the extent of the Empire who would know Silus, and what he did. He gave no public speeches, there were no busts of his likeness, he appeared on no coins. But those in the Emperor's inner circle knew well exactly who he was, and Silus saw the realisation of his identity hit Eugenios.

'Run,' yelled the freedman to the priest, and they both broke into a sprint.

The uninjured youths tried to grab Silus, but he brushed them aside and charged off after the fleeing men. The stallholder that Eugenios had been talking to threw a wooden crate into Silus' path as he passed, but Silus hurdled it and continued uninterrupted.

Eugenios and the priest passed another small group of idle men and yelled to them, 'Help, the Roman is trying to rob us!'

The men, four of them, stepped across Silus' path, jaws set, fists enclosed in palms.

Silus leapt onto the back of a cart full of watermelons. His feet sank into the juicy fruits with a squelch, and he almost tumbled headlong. Windmilling his arms, he kept his balance, stepped up onto the side of the cart, then onto the yoked ox's back. The driver yelled a protest at him, and the ox let out a long low, then Silus jumped back down, bypassing the men obstructing him. They shouted curses at him as he left them behind.

Eugenios looked back, eyes wide in alarm, and urged the priest to a greater speed. The priest gestured to an alley between two residential buildings. They took the corner and disappeared momentarily from sight. When Silus reached the alley, it was empty.

He ran on for a moment, thinking maybe they had reached the end and turned another corner before he had got there. But he soon realised that they weren't that quick. He stopped, looked around.

There were entrances to the buildings on either side of the alley. On one side the door was shut and barred. On the other side the door was open, with a chained dog inside the vestibule, fast asleep. There was no way two men had run past the canine without waking it, unless it was deaf, or dead.

He took a few steps back, then barged into the locked door with his shoulder.

The wooden door burst apart and Silus flew through. A startled porter in the vestibule raised his hands in protest but did not have time to stand before Silus had clamped a hand around his throat.

'Which way did they go?'

The porter's wide eyes darted left and right, seeking help. Silus squeezed. The porter gurgled and pointed through the atrium towards the peristylium. Silus let go and ran through. The porter slid off his stool, clutching his neck and breathing hard.

A startled slave girl who was polishing a marble bust screamed at the sight of him and knocked the bust off its pedestal so it fell to the ground with a crash. It didn't matter, Silus had sacrificed stealth for speed.

The peristylium had a central garden of short ornamental shrubs, a colonnaded walkway around the perimeter and half a dozen closed doors leading to small rooms. There was no way out of the little garden without a ladder to scale the clear walls. A couple of the doors were open, and Silus could see they were empty. He picked the nearest closed door and kicked it in. The room beyond was a simple store, containing a small number of amphorae and storage jars of various sizes.

He smashed open the next door. Two child slaves cowered in a corner, clutching each other in terror.

'How dare you enter my home!' came a loud, indignant voice from behind him.

Silus turned to find himself looking into the red face of a portly man wearing a fine, gold embroidered tunic, smelling of powerful perfume and wearing a gold necklace and gold earrings. Silus gave the man a hard shove, and he toppled backward into a bush with a cry, the small branches breaking his fall and tearing his tunic.

Eugenios and the priest were behind the third door. They stood with their backs to the wall, defiant expressions on their faces.

Silus paused a moment to recover his breath. There was no escape for them – there were no other exits from the room, and there was no way they were getting past him.

'Silus, isn't it?' said Eugenios. 'To what do we owe this pleasure?'

'Shut your mouth,' said Silus. 'You can talk to Oclatinius when he is having you tortured.'

Eugenios paled. 'I don't know what power you think you have, but I work for Sempronius Rufus.'

'I'm aware of that. And I'm sure you will be telling us the extent of his involvement in whatever this is, at the same time you give us every single detail of your plot.'

'Listen,' said Eugenios, spreading his hands placatingly. 'There is no need for violence and torture. I will tell you everything you need to know. In exchange for immunity from any punishment. And of course, a cash consideration. I will need to go into hiding after I have spoken to you. You understand, I'm sure.'

Much as Silus wished to beat a confession out of the slimy man, he knew that Oclatinius would jump at the chance of getting the information voluntarily. He always said that anything obtained under torture was unreliable

– the victim saying whatever they thought the torturer wanted to hear. It was for this reason that Oclatinius detested the law that said a slave's testimony in court was inadmissible unless it had been extracted under torture, the assumption being that all slaves lied all the time. Silus' objections to that law were based much more upon consideration for the slave's welfare, unlike Oclatinius' more pragmatic reasoning.

'Fine,' said Silus. 'I'll take you and your friend here to Oclatinius, and you can make the same offer to him. It's his call. But first, for my curiosity and as a sign of goodwill, tell me. Were you acting on the orders of Sempronius Rufus?'

Eugenios opened his mouth, and the point of a knife emerged from it, followed by a gush of blood. Eugenios stiffened and sank to the floor. The priest kept his grip on the knife hilt, and it slid out of the back of Eugenios' neck as he fell, coated in gore. Silus was impressed, he hadn't even seen the priest move. Oclatinius would be furious and would berate him for underestimating his prisoner.

Well, it wasn't the end of the world. They could still interrogate the priest. He was sure he would know just as much as Eugenios.

The priest glared at Silus, pressed the tip of the blade between two ribs, and plunged it in. He slumped to the floor beside Eugenios.

Silus looked down at the two corpses lying in a lake of blood and said, 'Fuck.'

–

Caracalla barely acknowledged Oclatinius and Silus when they entered his presence. He was flanked by his most

13

trusted advisors, Macrinus the co-praetorian prefect, Ulpius Julianus, Julianus Nestor and Sempronius Rufus. Of Caracalla's innermost circle, only Epagathus and Theocritus were missing. These were freedmen who had been elevated to positions of supreme praetorian commanders by Caracalla more through favouritism than merit – Epagathus had been Caracalla's dance teacher! But Theocritus was in the East gathering resources for the campaign, and Epagathus was in Rome, helping keep order while the Emperor was absent. It felt strange not seeing Julia Domna by Caracalla's side, but she had remained in Antioch to oversee the civil administration of the East. Silus had no doubt this was the prime reason for her to have been left behind, highly skilled administrator as she was, but he wondered too whether Caracalla had decided to spare her the lengthy journey to Egypt on account of her illness. There was also their disagreement about finances. When Domna had warned him they were running out of money, and there was no longer any source of revenue available to them, just or unjust, Caracalla had unsheathed his sword and said that as long as he held this weapon, they would have no shortage of money.

All Caracalla's attention was focused on the bizarrely dressed man in the centre of the room. Tall, hook-nosed, with a long white beard that reached to his waist, Kemosiri the astrologer wore a black robe with various zodiac signs and other mystical symbols stitched into the cloth. He pranced around, seemingly unaware of the Emperor's intent stare fixed upon his antics as he tossed coloured sand around in the air, swung incense burners around his head in circles and chanted in incomprehensible tongues.

Silus was no stranger to superstition. He always said a prayer or made an offering to the relevant god in time of uncertainty, whether it was a god of war, or the sea, or health, or luck. He was careful to spit on his right shoe before putting it on, and to say Bonus Salus after someone sneezed. He didn't know whether these rituals made any difference, but why take the chance?

But equally, he knew a charlatan when he saw one, and this man oozed showmanship over substance. Silus caught sight of Oclatinius, whose mouth was pursed in a straight line, a sign, Silus knew, that he was trying not to laugh out loud.

Eventually Kemosiri cast some knuckle bones and bent down over them, examining them intently. Caracalla seemed to hold his breath, like a defendant waiting for the jury's verdict.

'Victory over the Parthians is assured,' said the astrologer finally, and Caracalla exhaled in relief.

'And my own personal safety?' he asked.

Kemosiri drew out a scroll from a fold of his robe and unrolled it dramatically. Silus could see it was covered with more astrological symbols, star charts and mathematical equations. It looked impressive, and completely impenetrable. The astrologer scrutinised it carefully for a long period, then looked Caracalla straight in the eye.

'You will reign for many years, until old age bears you away.'

Caracalla's shoulders slumped in relief, while Silus suppressed a contemptuous tut. What else would the astrologer say? Predicting the Emperor's death could be construed as treason – a dangerous path to tread. Assuring him of long life was risk free – a dead Emperor would not come back to complain about the inaccuracy of the prophet.

Still, if it soothed Caracalla's anxieties and made him calmer and more stable, maybe it was all to the good.

Caracalla waved the astrologer away, and the dismissed trickster gathered his paraphernalia and retreated backward, bowing as he left. Caracalla turned to Macrinus, his mood lightened.

'How is the grain harvest in Egypt this year? Will we have a good surplus for the army?'

'I'm assured it has been a good year,' said Macrinus.

'And the new taxes? How have they been received?'

Macrinus hesitated. 'I think it's fair to say there has been some disquiet.'

'Outright defiance, I would call it,' interrupted Sempronius Rufus.

Caracalla raised an eyebrow. 'Really? In what form?'

'Protests. Small outbreaks of civil unrest.'

'I see,' said Caracalla. 'Anything to be concerned about?'

'I'm sure not,' said Macrinus, 'although I can't rule out the need to use the legions for some sort of police action.'

Oclatinius let out a polite cough, and Caracalla turned to acknowledge him for the first time.

'You have something to add?'

'Augustus, I think the situation may be more serious than Macrinus admits. The unrest is real, and widespread. But more than that, it appears to be organised.'

'Organised? By whom?'

Oclatinius kept his eyes away from Rufus as he spoke, but Silus watched the new spymaster closely. There was no trace of a reaction. Either he knew nothing of Eugenios' actions, or he was a great actor. Silus thought both alternatives equally likely.

'The conspiracy seems to have originated in the Temple of Serapis and the surrounding Serapeum. But I'm afraid to say that a man in your service was implicated. His name was Eugenios, and he was an associate of Festus.'

The plot in which Festus, the late Commander of the Sacred Bedchamber, and Rufus' predecessor, had been a major participant, had come as close to a successful assassination of Caracalla as any to date, with the possible exception of the attempt against him by his own brother. Silus thought it had shaken Caracalla considerably, much more than he admitted, increasing his paranoia as it shortened his temper.

Oclatinius clearly didn't want to implicate Rufus directly at this stage, although Caracalla would be able to make the connection that if Eugenios had been working for Festus, he might now be in Rufus' employ. Rufus had performed a purging of anyone suspicious in the office of the Keeper of the Sacred Bedchamber after Festus had been revealed as a traitor, but he had been fairly light-handed, giving the benefit of the doubt to many. The generous explanation for this was that he wanted to keep the spy organisation intact and functioning as much as possible. It would diminish his power considerably if he cleared out all his useful operatives at the start of his tenure. The cynical explanation was that he had been complicit with Festus, and his purges had been cosmetic only. Silus hadn't made up his mind which possibility was most likely yet, and he thought neither had Oclatinius.

'You speak of him in the past tense,' said Caracalla.

'He was apprehended but murdered by his Alexandrian associate before he could be questioned.'

'I see. And the associate?'

'Suicide, Augustus.'

Caracalla threw his hands up in despair. 'Sometimes I feel I need to do everything myself. What do you think, Oclatinius, Rufus? Should I be a spy?'

'You would undoubtedly be excellent in the role, Augustus,' said Oclatinius, 'but I fear you might be too recognisable to carry out the duties inconspicuously.'

'Maybe you are right. Very well. At least tell me what you know.'

Oclatinius took a moment to gather his thoughts, stepping forward into the centre of the room, fist pressed to his mouth like a lawyer in a courtroom preparing to speak.

'Augustus, my intelligence and the actions of this Eugenios suggest a conspiracy to incite a riot in Alexandria.'

'To what end?'

'That I don't know. For Alexandrians, a riot is an end in itself. But those who wish to provoke it? Maybe it is local protest against the new taxation. Or maybe it is something aimed more directly at your Imperial person.'

'What makes you say that?' asked Caracalla sharply.

'Just because Festus is dead, doesn't mean that his conspiracy died with him.'

Caracalla frowned, and Silus was surprised to see it was possible for the furrows in his brow to become even deeper than usual.

'But the astrologer prophesied I would live long.'

'And it is my job, and the job of others, to ensure that prophesy comes true.'

'But the Alexandrians don't wish me harm, do they? After all, everyone has to pay their taxes. Even that Christos fellow who seems so popular these days told his followers to pay Caesar his dues.'

'I'm sure the common people love you, Augustus,' said Oclatinius carefully, 'but they are easily led.'

'Pah,' spat Sempronius Rufus.

'What was that, Rufus?' asked Caracalla.

'Oclatinius is hiding the truth from you, Augustus. He fears your anger. But you should be told the facts by your advisors. The people of Alexandria hate you.'

Silus swallowed reflexively. What was Rufus doing? Feeling left out by Oclatinius' more detailed intelligence report? Or trying to prove his loyalty after the treachery of his subordinate was revealed? Whatever the reason, he was poking the wasps' nest, and the results would be messy.

'What makes you say that?'

'My sources. The mood on the streets. The speeches in the Serapeum and the philosophical schools. The graffiti.'

'What graffiti?'

Don't say it, prayed Silus.

'Many examples,' said Rufus affecting an offended air. 'Slogans against you personally. Caricatures. One particularly egregious example I have seen involved a cartoon of a man and woman having sex, with the caption reading "Tarautas and Jocasta".'

He said it. Fuck.

Caracalla's good mood after his favourable horoscope evaporated like a splash of water on a hot stove. His face reddened, his nostrils flared like an angry chariot horse, air whistling in and out as he breathed hard.

There was going to be an explosion. But not right then. Caracalla had a fearsome temper, but even these days, with his psychological state increasingly fragile, he was able to control and direct it.

'Oclatinius,' he said. 'Inform Athaulf and the legionary commanders. Tomorrow, we enter Alexandria. I will take an honour guard of a dozen Leones, and a century from the Second Parthica. I will visit the Serapeum and see for myself what they think of their Emperor.'

'Augustus,' said Oclatinius diffidently. 'Might I suggest a larger force? Alexandrians are so unpredictable, and with the evidence of a plot...'

'Nonsense,' interrupted Caracalla. 'I told you. Kemosiri said I would live long. I have nothing to fear.'

Oclatinius bowed his head. 'It shall be as you command.'

Silus and Athaulf rode just behind Caracalla, who was in full military regalia, at the reins of a gold quadriga, progressing majestically down the Canopic Way. Delicatus trotted proudly behind in perfect time, his gait elegant, clearly in possession of an acute sense of occasion. Silus had polished his uniform as best he could, though some battle-damage was hard to conceal, and his pristine mount always made him feel slightly ashamed of his appearance. Not that Delicatus was a show pony – he had proven himself on more than one occasion in battle with Silus on his back. Behind came Oclatinius and Macrinus, then more Leones, including Maximinus Thrax the giant, and a century of legionaries from the Second.

Alexandrian children, Greeks and natives, strewed flowers, wreaths and garlands in the path of the Emperor, and the avenue was lined with locals, the foremost of whom were cheering and clapping and singing hymns of praise and adulation. But it was obvious to Silus that these were all planted by the local dignitaries trying to make a good impression, maybe paid or otherwise coerced to appear delighted at the Imperial visit. One didn't have to look far back into the crowd to see sullen faces, tight lips, clenched jaws and hunched shoulders. Whatever this looked like superficially, this was not a triumphal procession such as Silus had witnessed in Rome, nor an Emperor honouring an adoring provincial city with a visit. This felt more like a march through recently conquered territory, for all that Egypt had been part of the Roman Empire for a couple of centuries.

Caracalla was either oblivious to the undercurrents, or chose to ignore them. After all, they were not outright hostile, at least not yet. Silus noted a number of freshly painted walls, no doubt hastily covering up the most obvious and most insulting graffiti, although some could still be seen if he looked hard enough, either escaping the cover up, or newly scrawled.

At the Agora, the procession turned left onto the Serapic Way, ascending the hill towards the Serapeum, the same route along which Silus had tailed Eugenios. The Serapeum stood atop the hill, its vast structure staring impassively out over the city. The whole complex was bounded by a wall, colonnaded on the inside, and a large number of steps led up to the main entrance. Caracalla alighted from the chariot and passed the reins to a slave. The members of the entourage on horseback dismounted, and Caracalla, Oclatinius, Macrinus and the Leones entered the temple complex while the legionary century drew itself up in three ranks across the main gate.

A delegation of Alexandrian dignitaries awaited Caracalla, but he ignored them, and made his way to the main temple. The Alexandrians watched him pass in puzzlement, but stayed where they were as he went inside, with just Athaulf and Silus accompanying him. As soon as they were inside, Athaulf told the priests and other attendants to get out, so they could be alone, and the various religious personnel hurried out.

Silus had been inside the enormous temple before, but he didn't think it would ever fail to impress him, with its enormous marble columns, its ornate carvings and wall paintings, its strange mechanical contraptions and its colossal statue of Serapis. Even Caracalla looked suitably impressed, pausing inside the entrance and gazing around him while taking in a deep breath that swelled his barrel chest.

But the Emperor had visited the temple for a reason, it transpired. He strode to the altar, the same altar on which a fanatical Julia Soaemias had prepared to witness the sacrifice of her own son. Fortunately, Caracalla was unaware of that crazy episode, and even more fortunately, Soaemias had come to understand the horror of the crime that Silus had prevented and had repented of her behaviour.

Caracalla unbuckled his belt, drew his sword, and then offering it with both hands before the great statue of Serapis, prayed aloud.

'Lord Serapis, ancient protector of the city of Alexander, I come to you as an earthly ruler and the son of a god, to ask for your blessing. A heavy weight hangs on me, and I ask that you lift it. This is the very sword with which, in my own defence, I slew my brother. Accept it as my offering to you, O Great One.'

Silus stared in surprise. Not only had Caracalla kept the sword with which he had committed fratricide, he had carried it from Rome, and borne it all this time. And now, he was admitting his guilt, albeit not accepting liability.

Caracalla placed the sword reverentially onto the altar and bowed his head. Silus saw a tear form in the corner of his eye and roll down his smooth-shaven cheek to splash onto the marble floor. Silus felt himself moved to the verge of tears as well. Caracalla's relationship with his brother had always been tempestuous, but this was evidence hidden from the world that the gruff, rough Emperor had really cared for him, and felt genuinely sorry for Geta's death at his hands.

Caracalla stayed in this position long enough for the shadows to move noticeably across the walls. Eventually, he got stiffly back to his feet. He wiped his tears on the back of his hand and glared at Athaulf and Silus, daring them to comment. They both looked at the floor, avoiding eye contact. Then he straightened his back, rebuckled his belt and now empty scabbard, and strode back out into the bright light of the courtyard, to greet the delegation.

All of them were drawn from the Greek ruling class of course – native Egyptians had held no positions of responsibility in Alexandria since the city was founded by Caracalla's hero, Alexander the Great. The vice prefect, Aurelius Antinous, headed the delegation. His late superior, Marcus Aurelius Septimius Heraclitus, had been executed after disappointing Caracalla for his failure to quell previous episodes of unrest in Alexandria, and his successor had not yet been named. Others represented the various important offices and interests of the city, the Greek-style city council known as the boule, the priests of Serapis and Isis, the philosophers and teachers of the Aristotelian school.

Antinous bowed low before the Emperor, and then gestured slave girls forward who presented him with more wreaths and garlands. Dancers, cymbal players and flautists accompanied them as Antinous ushered Caracalla and his trusted advisors to a set of tables bearing a sumptuous feast of local delicacies. Silus was offered a plate of morsels of a sweetly seasoned meat by an Egyptian serving boy. He took a piece and bit down on it, finding it succulent and delicately flavoured but chewy.

'What meat is this?' he asked the slave.

'Cameleopard, master.'

Silus nodded his head appreciatively. Not a common dish in northern Britannia, he reflected, although the Egyptians probably had less access to squirrel than he had had back home, so these things balanced out.

The leader of the boule, an Alexandrian Greek called Chares who sported a ruddy birthmark down one side of his bald pate, presented Caracalla with a beautifully painted black and orange vase in the traditional Greek style, sporting scenes from the Trojan war. He seemed pleased, admiring it from various angles before passing it to Athaulf for safekeeping. Then Chares spoiled the moment by launching straight into a complaint in an irritatingly whiny voice, drawing out each vowel as if to make the most of each word.

'Augustus,' he said. 'Most noble ruler. Our ancient city, second only in your great Empire to Rome itself, is highly honoured by your visit. We pledge our deepest loyalty to Rome and to you personally, and we support and applaud your efforts to pacify and expand the borders of this vast Empire. But, too, we beseech you, have mercy on our beloved home. Here gather the finest minds, the best rhetoricians and philosophers and students of the mysteries of the universe. It is a place like no other in the world, and it must be cherished. We beg you therefore, to spare us the heavy burden of taxes, that empty our grain stores and drain our treasuries. It can only lead to an exodus of the wondrous talent that has flocked here since the times of the Ptolemies. We know how much you admire our founder, Alexander the Great, and we implore you to consider how he would have felt to see his most magnificent creation looted in this way.'

Caracalla was in the process of eating a succulent piece of foie gras, and he savoured its full flavour as Chares droned on. When the leader of the boule had finished speaking, Caracalla took a deep draught of wine from a silver goblet, then belched loudly. Chares blinked but maintained a respectful demeanour.

Caracalla put an arm around Chares' shoulder in a friendly, informal manner, and Chares' eyes opened wide in alarm at the unexpected familiarity.

'Chares, Alexandria is indeed a wonder. But no part of the Empire is more important than the Empire as a whole, save perhaps Rome itself. It is a sad fact that the Empire is besieged on all sides, and even from within. Since I was first promoted to co-Emperor with my father, I have worked tirelessly to keep the Empire's borders safe, in Britannia, Germania, Dacia, never wishing any reward for myself, only that our great commonwealth and its people will survive and prosper. So is it such a big thing that I ask for some money and men to keep us all safe?'

'Well, no Augustus, but…'

'Is it so terrible that I ask Alexandria to provide its fair share to the effort?'

'Of course not, Augustus, I only…'

'Is it not fair that Alexandria contributes resources that ultimately lead to its own protection?'

'No, Augustus,' said Chares, and bowed his head, defeated. Glares from the other Alexandrians suggested they thought he had given up too easily, but Silus didn't know what they expected. Did they really think an argument that rich and sophisticated Alexandria should be exempted from war taxes would receive a sympathetic hearing with the bluff, militaristic Emperor?

'I'm so glad we concur,' said Caracalla. He raised his voice so the whole delegation could hear him clearly. 'Chares has agreed on behalf of Alexandria to increased monetary contributions to the Imperial war chest, and to contribute men to the fight.'

A number of Alexandrian heads swivelled towards Chares, sending dagger stares in his direction.

'I didn't exactly...' stuttered Chares, 'I mean... oh dear.'

'So to take full advantage of this generosity,' continued Caracalla, 'I am announcing today the formation of a new unit in my army, a phalanx organised in the style of Alexander the Great, with men drawn from this great city. A true Alexandrian phalanx in every sense.'

The philosophers and council members looked at each other with expressions of anger and incredulity, but Caracalla ignored them.

'Tomorrow, all the young men in Alexandria will meet in the gymnasium area. They will be enrolled into the new phalanx, with excellent pay and conditions, and they will serve their city and Empire with honour and glory.'

The announcement was greeted with silence. Caracalla turned his back on the Alexandrians, took a cake from a waiting slave, and bit deeply into it, putting his hand out to catch the crumbs as they fell.

Sounds of shouting came from beyond the complex wall. Silus cocked his head, trying to make out what was being said, but the voices merged and blurred. He caught Athaulf's eye, who was also listening, Athaulf jerked his head towards the gates, and Silus went to investigate.

The main double gates were barred shut, but there was a small side door. Silus lifted the bolt and slipped through. Outside the walls a large crowd had gathered. But this was not the superficially adoring throng that had cheered them through the city earlier. This was an angry host, waving fists, chanting slogans. Silus heard the names Tarautas and Jocasta shouted out, along with yells of 'Romans out' and 'No new taxes.'

The legionary century stood in rigid ranks before them, shields to the fore, spears held tightly, pointing upright. Their faces were set, lips pressed into narrow lines, eyes straight ahead. Their centurion, who stood to one side, exhorted his men to stay calm and maintain their position, glancing nervously at the growing crowd.

Silus was still gauging the size of the mob when the first object was thrown. He had just concluded that the crowd outnumbered the century at least five to one when an over-ripe orange flew through the air and exploded in a sweet, gooey mess on the shield of one of the legionaries. For a moment, no one moved, and everyone seemed to hold their breath expectantly. Who would react first, the soldiers or the crowd?

'Centurion, what's your name?' barked Silus in the most authoritative tone he could muster.

'Centurion Caius Cassius, sir.'

'Order your men to hold their positions. Do *not* retaliate.'

'Hold!' roared the centurion as the legionaries began to fidget.

Then more missiles arced out over the crowd. Fruit, vegetables, hard loaves. Then stones, the rattle of the solid objects impacting the shields contrasting ominously with the softer splats of the foodstuffs. The legionaries and the centurion ducked down behind their shields, hoping to weather the storm. But Silus could see this was no spring shower. He darted back inside the door, bolting it behind him, and rushed over to where Athaulf and Oclatinius were standing.

'It's getting ugly,' he said, interrupting their polite conversation. Athaulf was instantly on alert, head up, shoulders back, hand dropping reflexively to the hilt of his sword. The only visible change in Oclatinius was a narrowing of his eyes.

Athaulf waved a hand towards the Leones who had been holding a wide perimeter around the gathering, and they moved in towards Caracalla, not crowding him, but making sure they were in reach if there was trouble. Though their actions were not too overt, Caracalla noticed them. He turned away from the philosopher who was in the middle of delivering a monologue about Aristotelian Virtue Theory and approached Athaulf, leaving the mid-sentence philosopher nonplussed.

'What's happening?' Caracalla asked Oclatinius and Athaulf. They indicated Silus should explain.

'There is a large crowd gathering outside the gates, Augustus,' said Silus. 'Well, more of a mob. They look angry.'

Caracalla looked towards the gate and gave his characteristic scowl.

'Well, I suppose I should see what they want.'

'No, Augustus,' said Athaulf. 'I cannot allow it.'

Silus was impressed at Athaulf's self-confidence, to contradict the Emperor and even forbid him something. He half-expected an angry retort from Caracalla. But his relationship with the head of his personal bodyguard was strong, and Caracalla would always listen to Athaulf's advice, even if he didn't always heed it.

'Thank you for your concern, Athaulf, but you know it is not in my character to hide from a confrontation.'

Athaulf bowed his head in acquiescence – even in his privileged position there was a limit to how much defiance was sensible. Athaulf gestured to Silus and Maximinus Thrax to fall in behind him and the three Leones accompanied the Emperor to the gate. Unwilling to sneak out through a side door, Caracalla bid them to open the main double gates. Athaulf and Silus exchanged a glance, then Athaulf nodded. Silus and Maximinus lifted the heavy bar free, then hauled on the handles. The thick wooden gates opened and revealed chaos.

The steps leading up to the main gate were stacked with angry Alexandrians hurling abuse and bricks at the besieged legionaries, who had not yet drawn their swords, but were brandishing their spears and using them to fend off the nearest of the protestors. Centurion Cassius looked terrified, and Silus heard him calling out an oath to Jupiter Optimus Maximus that he would dedicate him an altar if the great god saved them.

Caracalla marched straight to the top of the steps behind the legionaries and lifted both arms in the air.

'Alexandrians!' he called out, and his deep, booming voice cut through the noise and commotion. The rain of missiles and the struggles of the crowd ceased momentarily.

'I understand you have complaints,' said Caracalla. 'I am willing to hear them. But this is not the way.'

The crowd seemed to listen for a moment, which stretched out, and Silus thought that maybe Caracalla had achieved the prodigious and calmed an Alexandrian mob.

But for all that his father was now deified, Caracalla could not perform miracles. With shouts of 'Tarautas,' and 'brother killer,' and 'go fuck your mother!' a hailstorm of stones, bricks, roof tiles and pots launched through the air, forcing Caracalla and the Leones to duck down behind the shields.

'Augustus, let's get back into the compound,' said Athaulf. Caracalla growled, a non-verbal animal sound. In front of them a legionary toppled backward with a cry, bleeding from a gash in his forehead. Athaulf put a hand on his elbow. 'Augustus, please. There is nothing wrong with a tactical retreat, to withdraw in the face of superior odds in order to marshal your forces.'

Caracalla hesitated, and Silus prayed reason would triumph over fury. Another legionary staggered back, clutching a broken wrist.

'Fine.' He stood and turned his exposed back on the mob and strode back through the double gates. More projectiles followed him and would surely have hit him if Silus hadn't grabbed a shield from the fallen legionary and protected him in his rather too leisurely walk back to safety.

'Centurion,' called Athaulf. 'Have your men draw swords and push these criminals back by any means necessary. Then return to the compound and bar the gates.'

The legionaries drew their swords with a vicious pleasure, and on a command from Centurion Cassius, stepped forward, thrusting and stabbing into the unprotected foremost rioters. Angry shouts changed to screams and howls as blades found soft parts and vital organs. Those further back yelled their outrage, but those at the front panicked to escape the slaughter, and they slipped in blood and entrails and tumbled backward down the steps, upsetting others behind them.

For a moment there was a clear space in front of the legions. Cassius drew breath to order a charge, but Athaulf shoved him hard in the side to forestall him.

'Get your men inside. The priority is to protect the Emperor.'

The centurion nodded and issued the commands. The well-drilled legionaries made an ordered retreat, keeping their shields and weapons to the fore, taking one careful step after another until they were through the gates. More missiles followed them, some potentially lethal such as slingshots and even the odd javelin, maybe a souvenir or the property of an old veteran. One legionary suffered a broken collarbone from a pebble fired from a sling, and another fell and twisted his ankle to the extent that he had to be carried to safety by his colleagues, but they were able to slam the gates closed and bar them before there were any fatalities in the century.

Cassius leant his back against the gates, closed his eyes, and mouthed a silent prayer of thanks.

Caracalla looked ready to explode. The Alexandrian delegation were flapping about like panicked sheep, uttering denials of complicity and distancing themselves from the mob while eyeing the armed and angry century of legionaries that was now in their midst. The Leones were spoiling for a fight, not least Maximinus Thrax, who was having to be restrained by three of his colleagues from throwing himself out of the gates and into the mob. Athaulf was issuing orders to his men. Macrinus seemed paralysed with fear and indecision.

It was Oclatinius that took charge, with his character-istic calmness.

'Augustus, there are tunnels beneath this complex that lead to a safe exit outside the city walls. I strongly suggest we avail ourselves of them, so that we can regroup and you can consider your response to this outrage.'

Silus only fleetingly wondered how Oclatinius knew about secret tunnels. Of course he knew. This was Oclatinius.

Caracalla looked to the Leones and the century of legionaries, and Silus suspected he was weighing up their numbers and resolve against the mob outside. The instinct of a military commander was to attack. But a good leader also knew when to listen to his advisors, and both Athaulf and Oclatinius had recommended he withdraw, to link up with the main force of his army. Rioting civilians, no matter how numerous, were no match for even a single legion.

Caracalla turned to Chares and pointed a white, trembling finger into his face. 'Tomorrow, all of Alexandria's young men. At the gymnasium.'

'Of course, Augustus, it will be done without fail,' babbled the council leader, maybe daring to believe that he was not about to be slaughtered on the spot.

'Show me these tunnels,' snapped Caracalla to Oclatinius. Oclatinius bowed respectfully and led the way. The ruler of the Roman Empire sneaked out of an Alexandrian temple, while behind him a mob bayed for his blood.

Chapter II

The gymnasium complex in Alexandria was situated by the Canopic Way that led from the east, and the Canopic Gate by the hippodrome to the Moon Gate in the west. The set of buildings stood out even in a city full of architectural marvels. Its porticoes, which were extended as colonnades, were over two hundred yards long. The vast courtyard was lined with neat rows of trees that cast a welcome shade on sunny days. There was a changing room, baths, covered walkways in which races could be run in inclement weather and other covered spaces where philosophers could give public speeches.

Gymnasia were thoroughly Greek inventions, as ubiquitous in Greek cities as amphitheatres were in Roman equivalents. An intricate political hierarchy organised the workings of the gymnasium, and the complex was integral to the life of Hellenistic communities, acting as a place of assembly for citizens, entertainment, sporting contests and learning. However, they always remained true to their original function, to give physical training to the Ephebes, the young Greek men aged between eighteen and twenty years. Gymnasia throughout the Greek-influenced world were daily filled with youths engaged in running races, wrestling and boxing matches and all forms of exercise so important to honing the youthful body.

On this warm, sunny morning, the gymnasium at Alexandria was filled with more than the usual collection of young men. Part cajoled by their elders who were trying to keep the visiting Emperor happy, part persuaded by the promise of money and excitement, the overwhelming majority of the Alexandrian Ephebes had gathered to sign up for the new Alexandrian phalanx. Though in many parts of Alexandrian society Caracalla was detested, for his fratricide, for his harsh tax regime, or just for being a Roman occupier, many grudgingly or openly appreciated his admiration of Alexander of Macedon, and many of the young men had jumped at the chance of joining a unit drawing so heavily on the glorious history of Alexandria and its founder.

So the young men in the gymnasium courtyard joked, laughed, wrestled and sung good-naturedly, awaiting the arrival of the Emperor to whom they would pledge their fealty.

Silus stood beside Caracalla on the other side of the Canopic Way on the steps of a temple dedicated to Anubis, a handful of Leones in close attendance. His heart was heavy with foreboding. Was Caracalla really going to induct these troublesome youths into his army? True, he had taken barbarians from the frontiers of the entire Empire and turned them into loyal soldiers, not least his devoted Germano-Celtic bodyguard, the Leones. But those peoples had not personally insulted him or the Empress, nor forced him into a humiliating retreat.

And Caracalla was making sure he left a pacified Empire behind him before his Parthian campaign. Silus doubted he would leave Alexandria, with all the importance the city and the province held for the Empire in terms of wealth and grain supply, before he had checked any hint of rebellion.

Silus had witnessed Caracalla's brutal machinations before, particularly in Germania, and he was sure he was about to see something similar. Oclatinius had told Silus to accompany him that morning but was tight-lipped about Caracalla's plans. He had simply told Silus he should bear witness to the day's events.

And Silus' worst fears were confirmed when he heard the heavy tramp of hob-nailed boots marching in time down the Canopic Way. The pedestrians on the streets fled at the sight of the approaching legionaries. Carts, wagons and litters were abandoned, and shunted to the side of the road or destroyed where they stood by the vanguard of the legion. Silus watched the Second Parthica legion at full strength, in full battle array, its mounted legate and standard bearers to the fore, march up to the gymnasium and halt.

At an order from the legate, the legionaries arrayed themselves around the gymnasium, encircling it on all four sides. They turned inwards, interlocking their shields on command. A ripple of unease washed through the gathered youths as they became aware of the soldiers. Silus could imagine the confusion going through their minds. Was this how recruitment worked? Was it some sort of test?

Their doubts were resolved as the soldiers drew their swords as one and advanced. Silus closed his eyes and balled his fists tight by his sides. Behind his eyelids flashed images of a slaughter on a field in Germania, a betrayal of allies in the name of strategy. And here it was, happening again. But while last time the massacre had a military purpose, Silus couldn't help feel that this was personal.

Maybe Caracalla had genuinely intended to recruit these men into a phalanx, before the unrest and the threat to his life the previous day. Or maybe this was what he had always planned.

The first cries of pain and terror forced Silus' eyes open. The soldiers were among the Ephebes now, their encirclement closing like a noose. Young men were down already, howling, clutching mortal wounds, or lying still. The legionaries worked with brutal and methodical efficiency. Step forward, thrust, twist, withdraw. Step forward again. Each stab met unprotected, undefended flesh.

Some of the youths fought back with whatever was to hand. Some had swords or knives, though they were useless against the shielded and armoured soldiers. Some picked up stones and rocks and hurled them desperately at the advancing troops. One even picked up a heavy haltere, a dumbbell used for weightlifting and the long jump, and had some success bashing it against shield and helmet before a thrown pilum took him through the chest and pinned him to the sand.

Some of the young men dropped to their knees and pleaded for their lives. They were killed on the spot. Others tried to flee, but there was nowhere to go, and as the soldiers closed in they turned on each other like rats in a sack thrown into a river. Soon they were packed into a dense mass, and the extermination became a repetitive chore, like butchers working their way through a herd of pigs.

Caracalla looked on with a faraway, dispassionate look on his face. The bodyguards around him shifted from foot to foot uncomfortably. The Leones had not been formed at the time of the massacre in Germania, and this was their first experience of a slaughter of undefended innocents. Silus wondered if it would change their view of their adored leader. A little acrid fluid came up from his stomach and burnt the back of his throat.

To kill a large number of men, even unarmed and unresisting, was time-consuming and hard, physical work. The legions laboured for the best part of half an hour, working up a sweat, taking it in turns in the front line to complete the chore. Silus tried to imagine what the soldiers were thinking. Surely some were detesting their orders, feeling sick for what they were commanded to do? But Roman discipline was iron, and none was prepared to let down his comrades or the Emperor. So the work continued with grisly efficiency.

Before the massacre began, there had already been a small crowd in the streets around the gymnasium, relatives and sweethearts proudly and tearfully waiting to see their young men join the army. At the start of the attack, their screams of horror and despair mingled with the death cries of the Ephebes, the whole terrible cacophony summoning other citizens. Soon a large, angry crowd had formed, hurling abuse and some missiles. But there were plenty of legionaries to see them off, and a couple of charges into their number was enough to keep them well at bay, where they witnessed the death of the pride of their citizenry in helpless horror.

When the screams of the youths were stilled, the legate came to report to Caracalla that the duty had been performed. He accepted the report with the equanimity of a commander receiving a message about a delivery of caligae.

'Very good, legate. Now assign two centuries to my direct authority. The city now belongs to the legions.

Send a message to Macrinus to summon the praetorians and the auxiliaries. Gather the treasures from the temples and schools. Order all citizens to remain indoors. Kill anyone you find in the streets.'

'At your command, Augustus.'

The legate efficiently detached two centuries, and Caracalla greeted them, and marched them up the hill to the Serapeum.

The large temple gates were barred against them, but the legionaries used a marble statue as a ram and soon battered them open. Caracalla marched through at the head of his Leones and the two Second Legion centuries.

A collection of local dignitaries cowered in the temple courtyard, where they had retreated when the killing started. Silus recognised Chares, but unlike his previous meeting with the Emperor, he was trying to make himself inconspicuous among the boule members, priests and philosophers.

Caracalla bid the gates closed and set a guard on them, then marched into the great temple, ordering the dignitaries to be ushered in behind him. He approached the altar, where the sword he had used to kill his brother still lay undisturbed. He raised his hands and prayed aloud.

'O Lord Serapis, your city does not honour you. Its citizens riot against legitimate authority. It denies aid and taxation to the Empire that protects it. I pledge to purify Alexandria of its rebellious, disloyal elements, great Lord, and I offer you these sacrifices as proof of my devotion, and my earnest desire to return your city to its former glory.'

Silus looked around for sacrificial animals, then his gaze fell upon the dignitaries herded into a group.

Shit.

Silus stepped back, slipping behind a statue of Isis. He didn't want to be part of this. But he couldn't help watching.

Chares was first. Two legionaries grasped him by each arm and pulled him forward to the altar.

'Augustus,' he gasped. 'What are you doing? You can't think me guilty of any disloyalty?'

Caracalla regarded him with a cold stare, then nodded to one of the legionaries. 'Kill him.'

The legionary stood behind him, put a hand on Chares' forehead and pulled it back, exposing his neck. He raked his sword deep across the council leader's throat. Blood fountained forward, spurting over the altar. Chares gurgled, eyes wild in disbelief, then sunk to the floor in a crimson pool.

One by one, the other noble Alexandrians, mostly old, grey-bearded and bald-headed, were dragged forward by the legionaries. Some cried, some pleaded, some, particularly the Stoic philosophers, accepted their fate without protest. All died by the sword at Caracalla's feet.

When the killing was done, Caracalla walked out of the temple, his feet sloshing through a lake of blood. Few remained within the Serapeum, most of the priests and philosophers who had not been sacrificed in the temple having fled, only the slow and stubborn left. The legionaries cut these down, and Caracalla made his way to the communal dining area of one of the Aristotelian schools in the complex. There he sat down and ordered food and drink for himself and the men. Terrified slaves hurried to carry out his orders, bringing him the finest delicacies and wine they could find at such short notice. He waved them away, and told them to bring him bread and water, and when it arrived he consumed the simple fare with relish.

Silus took his expected place as bodyguard behind Caracalla, but refused all offers of food, only taking a cup of water to try to wash the sour taste from his mouth. It didn't help.

When he had finished eating, Caracalla stood and announced he was going to visit the tomb of Alexander. Athaulf tentatively suggested he might want to wait until his soldiers had finished their work on the city streets, but he ignored the head of his bodyguard and strode out of the temple complex and down the steps, the Leones and the detached centuries hurrying to keep up.

Silus walked beside him and to his left, hand on the hilt of his sword, wary at all times for threats to the Emperor. Surely someone would make an attempt on his life? A bereaved brother or father of one of the murdered Ephebes, a priest outraged at the looting of a temple, a citizen who had had everything taken away and had nothing more to lose.

But this perpetually rebellious, restive city seemed completely cowed for a change. They marched through city streets in a state of chaos. Although the men had been commanded to leave those within their homes alone, this was a tough, battle-hardened army let off the leash to pillage at will. So of course they broke into any premises they wished, to loot, to kill, to rape.

Silus saw women, young and old, dragged out of humble dwellings, assaulted and cast aside. He saw men and boys beaten and tortured for sport, hacked to death, beheaded. Even the sacred cats and ibises were targeted by those soldiers who knew how cherished they were by the Alexandrians. The sandy streets drank in the blood with a thirst as insatiable as the soldiers' lust for killing.

Caracalla marched through the chaos and savagery, barely glancing to the left or right, even when an elderly man ran into his path and dropped to his knees, hands pressed together in desperate supplication, before the legionary who had been pursuing him ran him through with his spear. Silus gritted his teeth, feeling his gorge rise, and anger too. He had seen plenty of slaughter in his time, in Caledonia and Germania and Dacia. And though he had hated all of it, he had usually seen the necessity, or at least the logic. Even in Caledonia where entire villages of innocents had been wiped out, or Germania where an allied army had been betrayed and destroyed, Silus had understood the military logic of ruthlessly removing a threat. But this just smacked of revenge, a petty retaliation for insults and riots, taken to catastrophic extremes.

The mausoleum of Alexandria, known as the Soma, literally 'the body,' had housed the body of Alexander the Great since the first Ptolemy had hijacked it when it was on its way back to Macedonia for burial. The prestige of being in possession of the mortal remains of the great conqueror helped establish the Ptolemaic dynasty and bring Alexandria to such a pre-eminent position among the cities of the Hellenistic world.

Since Egypt had been brought into the Roman Empire, Alexandria had been visited by many of the Empire's rulers. Caesar had famously wept when he read the life of Alexander in his early thirties and saw how little he had achieved compared to the Macedonian at that age. By the time he visited the Soma, he must have been much more satisfied with his place in history. Cleopatra had plundered gold from the tomb to help in her war against Octavian Augustus, and when the first Emperor of Rome, victorious in that fight had made his own visit to pay his respects to the conqueror, he had placed flowers on the tomb, a golden crown on Alexander's head, then accidentally broken off his nose. Caligula and Caracalla's own father, Septimius Severus, were among the other Imperial visitors to the Soma, and now Caracalla was following in their footsteps.

For Caracalla though, this was more than just a touristic visit, or an idle wish to see the corpse of history's greatest conqueror. Silus knew that Caracalla felt a much deeper personal connection with the great Macedonian. Over the last couple of years he had changed his dress to a Macedonian style, shaved his characteristic beard to match the busts of Alexander and formed an army unit in the style of an ancient Macedonian phalanx, which some thought was a clever tactic to counter the Parthian cavalry, and others thought was a crazy vanity project.

So Caracalla entered the mausoleum with an air of supreme reverence, taking only Athaulf and Silus in with him.

Silus looked around him in wonder. Despite some of the previous visitors to the mausoleum removing some of its riches, others had added to them, and the impression of wealth was overwhelming. The walls were gold plated, there were marble and gold statues of different gods, and the sarcophagus was gold. Caracalla approached with a slow step and laid his hand on the sarcophagus which was moulded to Alexander's body. He closed his eyes and mouthed a few silent words of prayer, then lifted the lid to reveal the corpse inside.

Silus couldn't help staring. Egyptian embalmers were almost supernaturally talented, and Silus found himself confronted with Alexander's boyish face, framed by a mop of curly, light brown hair. The eyes were closed, the cheeks pale and smooth, though with a hint of leatheriness about them. Only the missing nose marred the beauty of the figure. Silus looked to Caracalla and saw the rough general was weeping openly. Silus glanced to Athaulf, but the Leones leader kept his eyes fixed straight ahead, determined not to witness the display of emotion.

From outside the mausoleum came the sound of a child crying and a woman screaming. The woman's screams were abruptly cut off. The child's wails crescendoed, then stopped. Silus squeezed his eyes shut. Here he was in a tomb with the corpse of one of history's most famous men, together with the ruler of the Roman Empire, while just outside the door innocent men, women and children were being murdered. Silus felt his face flush, his temples pound. This wasn't right.

Caracalla was kneeling in front of the sarcophagus, tears flooding down his face, his back to Silus. Athaulf was watching the entrance to the mausoleum, alert to threats from without. Silus found his fingers were gripping the hilt of his sheathed sword tight, the knuckles turning white. He suddenly realised he could end this. One thrust from his spatha would finish this increasingly monstrous man.

Silus' breathing quickened, and a pressure seemed to build up inside him. Could it really be so simple? It would mean his death – Athaulf would try to kill him and if he didn't succeed, Silus would be executed anyway. And Tituria would be killed by that vile slave who watched over her. But what were two lives, when weighed against all the death and suffering that this man was inflicting on the world? He took a deep breath, readying himself.

Caracalla stood. Athaulf turned from the door at the sound and gave Silus a curious look. Silus smiled weakly at him.

Caracalla removed a ring from his finger, a gold band inlaid with small blue jewels, and laid it reverently on Alexander's chest. Then he closed the lid, bowed his head briefly, and strode from the mausoleum. Athaulf followed close behind. Silus leant over, hands on his knees, struggling to breathe. He had come close to death many times, but that was the nearest he had been to suicide. What had he been thinking?

But as he walked out into the bright light of the day and the scenes of the ongoing massacre, he knew it was not a moment of madness. Something had to be done.

—

'Something has to be done.'

Cassius Dio looked at the man who had spoken, seated opposite him in his tablinum. He had a long grey beard, and gold earrings dangled from his pierced ears. They were both members of Caracalla's council, though Cassius Dio was perpetually ignored and overlooked. He would have his revenge though. Writing a history of Rome was slow going, and he was currently working on the reign of Tiberius. But when he reached Caracalla – then there would be a reckoning. Posterity would see him for the monster that he was.

'That has been apparent for some time,' said Dio. 'And yet nothing changes.'

'The killing is still going on,' said Dio's colleague. 'Though they are running out of victims. Alexandria has almost the population of Rome, and his men are systematically slaughtering them. The scale of the massacre is hard to understand.'

'Yes,' said Dio. 'And I bet that even after he has robbed them of their wealth, he will continue to come to us senators for more. As if we have anything left to give.'

The man gave Dio a calculating stare, and Dio wondered if he had come across as insensitive, caring more about his wealth than the death of thousands. But Jupiter, he was suffering too. He had had to sell some of his vineyards in Campania to pay the taxes that Caracalla had imposed. And some of those vineyards produced damn good grapes.

'So, what should we do?' asked the man.

Dio threw his hands in the air in exasperation. 'What can we do? He is the Emperor. We must do his bidding. This isn't the Republic any more.' More was the pity he thought. He had written about those heroic times when the Roman Republic had fought off threats and expanded its borders. When Cincinnatus had laid down his plough, defeated the invading Aequi, then returned to his farm. When Scipio Africanus had defeated Hannibal. When Cicero had saved Rome from Cataline. None of them had grabbed supreme power for themselves. And then those fools Pompey and Cato and all the rest had played into Caesar's hands, and the Republic was gone, replaced by a king in all but name. He longed for those days, when an important man like himself, who had been a consul and a proconsul, would be respected and admired, would be sought out for his wisdom and advice. Not bled dry of every last sestertius, then cast aside.

The man regarded Dio steadily for a long, silent moment. Then he said, 'And if there was a way? If enough like-minded people decided that enough was enough, that Rome needed a new ruler?'

A fine cold sweat broke out over Dio's forehead. 'But that is treason. Just talking about it risks death. If anyone should overhear...'

'I can assure you that no one can hear us at this moment. Even my slaves are out of earshot.'

'Still, to even contemplate such a thing. Look at poor old Festus...'

'Festus was careless,' said the man. 'But he did not work alone. Some of us still feel there must be a way to bring about change. But there must be enough support. The Senate would be needed to ratify and legitimise a new Emperor.'

Dio was shaking his head as the man spoke. 'No, no, no. I won't listen. It's just too dangerous. And it's quite impossible. Even buying the praetorians is not enough these days, now he is protected day and night by those fanatical barbarian Leones.'

The man's bushy eyebrows drew together, and he fiddled with one earring.

'You are right, of course. We aren't ready yet. But the time will come. And when it does, are you with us?'

'Well,' said Dio, attempting to equivocate. 'It will obviously depend on all the circumstances at the time...'

The man leant forward, grasped his hand firmly, and looked him straight in the eye.

'Are you with us or against us?'

Dio swallowed, wishing he was anywhere else, weighing up the risks of conspiring against the tempestuous and vengeful Caracalla, versus opposing the man who wished to replace him.

'I'm with you,' he whispered.

The stench of decay hung over the city, inescapable. The buzz of flies, normally less numerous in the wintertime, though still omnipresent in the hot country, was incessant. Bodies lay in deep trenches dug throughout Alexandria, and the Nile was choked with corpses, too many for the crocodiles to consume. Dogs tore and rended at limbs and torsos that a few days before had belonged to living, breathing citizens, going about their daily lives in the bustling streets.

The killing had still not finished but was more targeted now. Caracalla had given orders for whole communities to be wiped out. Thousands had fled into the countryside, boats full of people heading south down the Nile to perceived safety, the prows pushing through bloated cadavers.

Silus sat outside a tavern on the street with his stew untouched in front of him. Bluebottles wandered across the surface of the bowl, stopping to sup, then flying off to be replaced by others from the hovering swarms. He lacked the willpower even to wave them away.

Oclatinius ate slowly and methodically, like a man who knew he needed to fuel his body even if he had no real desire to do so. Silus wondered if Oclatinius had seen anything like this in his long, long career. He doubted it. Oclatinius had joined the legions when Marcus Aurelius was emperor, and that profound, revered ruler would never have behaved like this. His useless son was mad in his own way, but there were no massacres associated with his name and, as far as Silus knew, the violence of the year of five emperors that had brought Caracalla's father Severus to the throne had not targeted civilian populations. So this level of brutality against Roman citizens was outside living memory.

Not much shook Silus. And he had never seen Oclatinius affected like this before. But they were both silent, lost in their thoughts. Silus wondered what Atius would make of this. Surely it would test his unshakeable faith in Caracalla. But maybe not. If Atius was anything, he was loyal. He only struggled when his loyalty was divided.

Silus and Oclatinius both tried to speak at the same time.

'I don't know...'

'I want...'

They both stopped.

'You first,' said Oclatinius.

'No, you,' said Silus.

'I insist,' said Oclatinius, and Silus could see from his expression that this wasn't just a polite turn of phrase.

Silus swallowed hard. What had Caesar said when he crossed the Rubicon? The die is cast. The Rubicon was by all accounts a tiny stream, but highly significant nevertheless. What he was about to say was just a few words, but when they were said, they couldn't be taken back, any more than Caesar could uncross the Rubicon.

'I want to kill the Emperor.'

Silus detected no discernible change in Oclatinius' facial expression, just a slight dipping of his shoulders as he breathed out. The silence extended.

Eventually Silus couldn't stand the tension, and blurted out, 'Say something.'

'Not here. Walk with me.'

Oclatinius threw a couple of coins onto the table to pay for their barely touched meal and rose. They walked westwards through the city, no words passing between them.

A huge trench had been dug along the side of the road, a mass grave. It had not yet been covered up, since more bodies were being added to it every day. Silus glanced down and saw tangled corpses, tossed carelessly one on top of another, rich and poor, woman and man, adult and child, mixed together in a macabre melange. Clouds of flies coated them and buzzed around, and torsos twitched where rats had burrowed within. The stench was powerful enough to make Silus gag, so he had to breathe through a cloth pressed over his mouth. Here and there upturned faces among the dead stared at him out of sightless eyes, expressing confusion and horror.

He gritted his teeth and walked on, sidestepping occasionally to avoid patches of gore in the road, blood or rotting entrails. A large wall was being built across the centre of the city, teams of labouring slaves working on the foundations, while others brought in cart loads of bricks and the lime and ash needed to make the cement. Caracalla had decreed that all foreigners and native Alexandrians, except the merchants, be expelled from the city, and this wall be constructed to enable the city to be more easily kept pacified. Maybe the wall would have been simply a prudent measure given the history of Alexandrian unrest, prior to the events of the last few days, but now it looked like an instrument of oppression and control. He had also closed down all the communal areas of the museums and philosophy schools and banned all public events. Alexandria would not be rising up again any time soon. Silus wondered how those people who had made jokes at Caracalla's expense and taken part in the riots felt now. Though they could not have foreseen this response, they must be feeling profound guilt at the consequences.

They left the city through the western moon gate, into the fresher air outside the city walls, and into the necropolis. Oclatinius led him past the tombs and monuments, to the entrance to an underground tomb. The heavy doors were locked, but Oclatinius had a key, and the doors opened easily. Silus didn't bother to ask why Oclatinius had a key to a tomb in Alexandria. He presumed that at some point a family member had owed the spymaster a favour, or something similar. Oclatinius had been around a very long time and had accumulated a lot of debtors of one form or another.

A long spiral staircase descended deep into the earth, and they wound their way downwards. Little slits in the part of the shaft above ground provided some meagre illumination, but Oclatinius lit an oil lamp to improve the light levels. At the bottom was a vestibule with two niches cut into the wall, containing stone benches, presumably to allow those visitors to the tomb to rest after the long descent. The vestibule led to a circular hall, in the centre of which was a shaft leading down to a lower floor.

Oclatinius led him to a chamber dug out of the bedrock, supported by four pillars. Three benches were cut into the rock wall, arranged like the couches in a triclinium. Oclatinius sat on one and gestured to Silus to make himself comfortable on another.

Silus sat, feeling the cold stone chill his backside through the thin material of his tunic. The air was musty, stale, cool, but infinitely preferable to the tepid atmosphere of decay that permeated the city. Silus looked around him. The walls sported carved images, heads of various deities, abstract patterns, and a pair of winged serpents. He was aware that within this underground complex were the resting places of a number of prominent

Alexandrian families. And in normal circumstances, that would have chilled him, and he would have been whispering incantations and making signs against evil and bad luck. But after the sights of the city, a few ancient, entombed corpses no longer felt particularly unsettling.

He looked at Oclatinius, who was regarding him steadily.

'So, why have you brought me here?'

'What is my job?' asked Oclatinius.

Silus shrugged. 'Servant of a mass murderer?'

Oclatinius' mouth narrowed. 'I am the head of the Arcani. I am the chief spy for a paranoid Emperor. But I am not the only intelligence gatherer. Sempronius Rufus is looking like he is ably taking over Festus' role as head of the Sacred Bedchamber. Ulpius Julianus and Julianus Nestor are in charge of the frumentarii, who carry the Emperor's private messages. Macrinus has his own sources among the praetorians. And there are others. Caracalla is loath to put his trust in any one man, which means we all spy on each other.

'But we are all cautious. All of us appear to be completely loyal to the Emperor. Where our true loyalties lie, though, is a much more closely guarded secret. I genuinely don't know whether the other military and intelligence heads are loyalists, traitors, or are happy to follow whoever seems to be in the ascendancy.'

Silus was largely aware of this, though he wondered if Oclatinius had a greater insight into the mindsets of the men he had mentioned than he was letting on. Little was as it appeared with the old man.

'So you brought me to a freezing cold underground tomb to tell me this.'

Oclatinius sighed. 'The only others here who could overhear us are dead. Where else in the city could we be sure of having a conversation that would remain confidential?'

Silus nodded. It seemed like overkill, but Oclatinius hadn't lived to the age he had without being highly cautious.

'So, now, in private, rather than outside a tavern in a busy Alexandrian street, would you like to repeat what you said?'

It suddenly occurred to Silus that maybe Oclatinius had brought him here to kill him. Silus had a gladius at his belt, but it would be of limited use in this cramped environment. If Oclatinius was carrying a small blade, he would have the advantage. And being honest, Silus wasn't sure he could take Oclatinius in a fair fight in the open. The old man had ways of fighting that Silus, with all his experience, had yet to master. The walls seemed to close in on him, his heart raced, his breathing became tight in his chest. His eyes darted left and right, searching for the exit in the gloom.

'Calm down,' said Oclatinius. 'If I was going to kill you, I wouldn't have bothered dragging you all the way out here. A knife in the back as we walked would have been far more efficient.'

Silus felt his buttocks unclench a fraction, and he got his breathing back under control.

'Speak,' said Oclatinius.

'I know I'm putting my life in your hands here,' said Silus. 'And maybe that is foolish. But I can't do this any more. I can't serve a ruler who does this, who is capable of this. I know I have walked away before, and you have dragged me back. But I don't feel that leaving is enough now. Something has to be done.'

'I agree,' said Oclatinius.

'You're probably going to hand me over to the executioners now, or have me quietly done away with, but I don't care. He is a danger to the Empire, and to every man, woman and child within and without its borders.'

'I agree,' said Oclatinius.

'So, do what you have to do, but I had to… What?'

Oclatinius sighed. 'How many times must I say it? I agree.'

'You… agree? With me?'

Oclatinius inclined his head. Silus' mouth dropped open, and when it was obvious he could find no more words, Oclatinius continued.

'I was tasked with founding the Arcani by the Emperor Commodus. He was a man of many faults, but he knew he was not as intelligent or capable as his father, Marcus Aurelius. He knew he needed an organisation that would protect him from threats from those he was close to as well as others who bore him ill will or wished to usurp him for their own ambition.'

'And yet he was murdered by the praetorian guard.'

'He was. But not before I had saved him from many previous attempts on his life. I am not infallible. He alienated so many powerful men. He disregarded both the Senate and the military, and it is hard to survive without the support of at least one of those bodies. He had many killed, on the merest suspicions. And he was foolish enough to let a list of targets for execution fall into the wrong hands. Someone was bound to succeed in the end.

'He was a bad Emperor, a bad ruler, a poor military leader, and he was vainglorious, cruel and cowardly. And yet I remained loyal to him to the end. By contrast, Caracalla is capable, brave, intelligent, and in certain devious ways, militarily brilliant.'

He paused. Silus prompted him. 'But?'

Oclatinius just gestured in the general direction of the city.

'Every man has a limit. Every loyalty breaks if pushed hard enough. Maybe you could argue that the Alexandrians provoked him. Maybe you could say that he does what he has to to make Rome strong. But I saw the eyes of a child yesterday, a small girl. In one hand she held a doll. With her other hand she held the hem of the stola of her pregnant, dead mother. It was... too much.'

And to Silus' amazement, Oclatinius began to cry. Not uncontrolled sobbing; not howls of grief. Just an overflow of tears, streaming down his cheeks. Silus leant forward and patted his arm awkwardly, finding the back of his own throat swelling with emotion.

Oclatinius swallowed, regained control, though he did nothing to dry his eyes, maybe refusing to acknowledge the tears, maybe leaving them in plain view on purpose.

'I have stuck by Caracalla through everything, always loyal to him and his father. But I have drawn the same conclusion as you. He has to go.'

Silus nodded firmly. 'So, what do we do? I get him alone, cut his throat? Poison? An accident?'

Oclatinius shook his head. 'No. Even though you are part of his bodyguard and well-trusted, you could not kill him and survive.'

'I'm not afraid to die,' said Silus firmly, though that wasn't strictly true.

'We will not rush. Nor will we act alone. The Leones are fanatically loyal. They don't care about this slaughter, nor about whether the Empire is being well ruled. They love him as a soldier who behaves like them, and who rewards them well. We will need allies.'

'That won't be easy. How do you approach someone to join you in a conspiracy without risking being betrayed?'

'You don't,' said Oclatinius. 'You join one that already exists.'

Silus sat back, and donked his head against the hard, curved stone wall.

'But we don't know who the conspirators are.'

'True,' said Oclatinius. 'But we know one exists. We know it involves powerful people, maybe senators, maybe one or more of Caracalla's innermost circle. And I know who would know. We couldn't approach him if we were trying to destroy the conspiracy. But if we were trying to join it? Well, if I know this man, I think he might just give us what we need.'

Chapter III

The opportunity did not arrive for several weeks, during which Silus waited in Alexandria, dutifully carrying out his role as bodyguard of a man he had come to despise. Not that he had ever been a huge fan of the Emperor. The duties he had forced him to carry out had often been repugnant, and in most cases it was only the threat to Tituria that had kept Silus loyal.

That threat remained of course, and Silus had not yet worked out how to nullify it. He knew that Juik was the slave tasked with murdering Tituria if anything happened to Caracalla, but if Silus killed her, Caracalla would just replace her with someone else. He supposed he could desert, rush back to Rome and hustle Tituria off to some hiding place in a remote part of the Empire. Britannia for example. But what life would that be for a young noble Roman girl, aspiring to be wed, have children, and take her place in society?

Caracalla would have to be dead before Tituria was truly free, but Caracalla's death would mean the death of the young girl. It was a conundrum that kept him awake at night.

But there were other steps to take first. Oclatinius may be able to play a game of latrunculi in his head so he was four moves ahead of his opponent, but Silus was only really able to deal with what was in front of him. And his first task was to find out who was already conspiring against Caracalla so he could join them.

Silus had suggested to Oclatinius that if there was already a group of people plotting to kill the Emperor, maybe Silus and Oclatinius could just sit back and let them complete the job without taking any risk themselves. But Oclatinius seemed to have little faith in anyone else's ability to get the task completed. The past record of failed attempts on the Emperor's life would seem to give credence to this view, although Silus was personally responsible for saving the Emperor's life on more than one occasion – together with the hostage status of Tituria, it was the main reason Caracalla trusted Silus so much. Silus speculated that if he merely stood by and didn't exert himself on the Emperor's behalf, the conspiracy would be far more likely to succeed, but Oclatinius scoffed at this arrogance. Besides, the Leones were a more formidable and loyal bodyguard than any Emperor had had for generations, and Silus' position within that organisation might be essential for any plot to succeed.

At last, Silus was meeting with the man that Oclatinius hoped would give them access to the movement. Silus had gone on ahead to make sure that no surprises were waiting for them, and to ensure he wasn't seen with the suspected conspirator. Oclatinius had arranged to escort his contact there and meet Silus an hour later.

So Silus sat in the pitch dark now, oil lamp extinguished to save on fuel, conscious of the rock walls in the catacombs close around him. In the blackness, his hearing was sharp, and he could hear intermittent drips of water, creaks of wood as beams warped with changes in temperature, the scamper of tiny feet, rodents or lizards that had somehow found their way inside. Other noises he hoped were just figments of his imagination, groans, cries, sighs, just at the limit of his hearing. The spirits of the peacefully resting dead, or the restless lemures of a brutalised city.

The sound of footsteps on the staircase was as loud as a thundercrack in the stillness, and he actually let out a little yelp of surprise, before clamping his hand over his mouth in embarrassment. Shortly after, Oclatinius appeared in the little triclinium-like room, bearing a small oil lamp. He was ushering Cassius Dio in front of him.

Silus could tell, even in the dim, flickering light, that Dio was pale and trembling. He did not seem to have come of his own free will, though Oclatinius did not appear to be applying any physical force.

'Sit,' said Oclatinius, gesturing to one of the empty stone benches, and when Dio did so, Oclatinius took the remaining one.

'There is no need for this,' said Dio, his voice wavering and high.

Oclatinius cocked his head on one side, like a bird listening for the movement of grubs to pounce on. Dio glanced to Silus for help, and when none was forthcoming, he gabbled on. 'I don't know anything. You can torture me, and it will be useless. But please don't kill me. I still have so much to give. My epic history is not complete...'

Oclatinius held up a hand to stop the flow of words.

'Dio. Dio. Calm yourself. We aren't here to kill you.'

Dio breathed out through pursed lips, and Silus could see the relief flood through him.

'Then why...?' He waved a hand at the surroundings.

'We have some matters to discuss. Private matters.'

'I see,' said Dio. Now that the imminent threat of death had been removed, he seemed a little more self-assured. 'I'm not sure if I have any matters I wish to discuss with you.'

'Well, let's see shall we?'

Dio looked from Oclatinius to Silus, then shrugged.

'Tell me, what is your opinion of Caracalla?' asked Oclatinius, as if the question was of no importance, like a query about the weather.

Instantly, Dio was on his guard. 'He is our Emperor. No further opinion is needed.'

'Come now,' said Oclatinius. 'Everyone has their own thoughts about the man. I'm just asking you to share them.'

'Well,' said Dio, searching carefully for the right words. 'He is a strong man. The soldiers love him.'

Oclatinius nodded. 'Go on.'

'Some may think his methods are a bit... forceful.'

Oclatinius looked pointedly upwards in the direction of the city. 'Do you think forceful is a sufficient description of what is happening now?'

Dio spread his hands. 'What is it you want me to say? What do you want from me?'

Silus had found himself growing increasingly frustrated at the cautious sparring, and now he blurted out, 'We want to know who is conspiring against Caracalla.'

Immediately, Dio clammed up, his mouth shutting firmly.

'Silus,' snapped Oclatinius in exasperation.

'Let's stop tiptoeing around. Dio, we know you hate Caracalla. We know you associate with conspirators, maybe you are one yourself. We want you to put us in contact with whoever is in charge.'

'Are you mad?' Dio seemed genuinely surprised. 'Even if any of that was true, which it isn't, why would I give that information to the Emperor's chief spymaster and a trusted member of his bodyguard?'

'Because we want to join the conspiracy.'

'Silus! For Jupiter's sake, will you shut your mouth!'

Dio stared at Silus in disbelief, then looked across to Oclatinius.

'You're serious, aren't you?'

Oclatinius glared at Silus, but Silus ploughed on. 'Deadly serious. What he is doing is unacceptable. Barbarous.'

'I... agree.'

Silus sat back, satisfied that he had got a concession from Dio, and waited for Oclatinius to take over.

'Mithras' hairy arse,' muttered Oclatinius. 'Fine. Dio, we are disillusioned with the Emperor, and want to make contact with the leadership of the conspiracy that we know exists, and that we know you are aware of.'

Dio stroked his beard thoughtfully. 'I'm not saying I know anything about anything,' he said carefully. 'But it might be I know someone who knows someone who could put out feelers for you.'

'That would be appreciated,' said Oclatinius. 'And of course you will be discreet.'

'Of course,' said Dio. 'This is my life in danger too.'

Oclatinius nodded, then rose. 'Thank you for your time, Dio. Silus, wait here another hour. I will escort our new friend home. And Dio, needless to say, if word of our conversation reaches anyone it shouldn't, you won't live to see another sunrise.' He put his arm around Dio's shoulder, who had started shaking again.

Silus listened to them receding up the stairs and out of the tomb, leaving him alone again, with the dripping, the creaking and the scampering.

Aprilis to Iulius 215 AD

The march from Alexandria, the second largest city in the Empire, to Antioch, the third largest, would take around three months. A journey undertaken by a single person would have taken maybe a month, even quicker if travelling by sea. But a vast army, no matter how efficiently organised, did not move with the speed of a solo traveller. Caracalla departed Alexandria in the late spring, with the intention of arriving in Antioch by the end of the summer. He left behind him a city in shock, its population devastated and cowed. Silus was relieved to get away from the oppressive atmosphere, the air of death and mourning that clung to the place, not to mention the stench of decay that seemed to permeate every space, infiltrate every item of clothing.

As they progressed northwards up the Levant, Caracalla continued to visit shrines of healing, with Silus and Athaulf invariably chosen to accompany him. But the visits seemed more dutiful, less hopeful than before, like he had lost faith in their potency. He still consulted mystics and astrologers, but he was more dismissive, more quick to temper than before. When Silus was on guard duty outside his tent or bedchamber, he often heard cries or shouts in the night, though the Emperor slept alone. Silus was glad the man didn't sleep soundly.

There were many opportunities for Silus to draw his sword and put an abrupt end to Caracalla's reign. But none that he would have a chance of surviving. Cassius

Dio had not yet come back to them with word from the conspirators, and Silus was growing restless. Dio was often present at the larger council meetings, and Silus would try to catch his eye, but Dio would completely ignore him, as he would a slave pouring him wine. Silus wanted to grab him and shake information out of him, but Oclatinius' counsel to be patient prevailed. For the time being.

When they were just a couple of weeks' journey from Antioch, they reached the city of Emesa. As they neared, excitement grew within Silus to see Atius once more. He had received a few letters from his old friend, but they had been short on detail, not much more than, 'I am well, the weather is good, how are you?' Silus doubted he was a threat to Pliny or Cicero when it came to preserving his correspondence for posterity.

Emesa had been ruled by the Priest-Kings of Elagabal before the Romans had occupied Syria, and even after Rome had absorbed Emesa into the Syrian province, ending the reign of the Emesene dynasty, the royal family remained immensely rich and powerful in the area. And it was from this family, of course, that the Empress Julia Domna and her sister Julia Maesa, mother of Julia Soaemias and grandmother of Avitus, were descended.

So Caracalla had great respect for the city of Emesa, and he entered in a peaceful procession with fulsome honours being bestowed upon him by the city's great and good. At the head of the delegation that greeted him were Julia Domna, who had been left behind to administer the eastern half of the Empire, Julia Soaemias and the current chief priest of Elagabal, young Avitus. Silus stood respectfully behind and to one side of the Emperor as the Empress's niece and her son bowed deep and offered him gifts of gold jewellery and fine perfumes. Silus scanned the crowd, ostensibly for threats, but also hoping to catch a glimpse of Atius.

At first he couldn't find him, but then he saw him, just behind Gannys, his eyes too darting around. When their gazes met, Atius broke into a huge grin, and he waved manically. Silus tried to keep his face straight and fought down the impulse to wave back. Even if Caracalla didn't notice, Athaulf would have his balls if he showed him up that way.

When the meeting broke up, Caracalla accepted an invitation to dine at Soaemias' luxurious estate within the city, and Atius and Silus were both expected to attend as respective bodyguards of the host and the chief guest. Despite being in a room together for the first time in over a year, they were unable to exchange a word, on silent duty on opposite sides of the triclinium.

Soaemias was gushing in her praise of Caracalla, his victories and his magnificent rule of an expanding Empire, while at the same time pushing forward Avitus for his attention.

'How alike you are,' she commented at one point, holding Avitus' smooth chin in her hand and turning his head to one side, while looking from her son to Caracalla. The Emperor did not seem impressed, and Julia Domna changed the subject quickly.

After the dinner had finished and Caracalla and Domna had retired, Atius asked Soaemias if he could be spared for the rest of the night, and Silus asked the same of Athaulf. When both had permission to go off duty, they charged into each other's arms to give a crushing hug, then headed off to the nearest tavern.

They seated themselves at a table on the street, and Atius ordered two cups of wine. 'Something decent, mind you,' he said. 'We're celebrating. And get us something to eat.'

'Anything in particular, master?' asked the serving slave.

'Surprise us,' said Atius, which Silus felt was foolhardy in a strange venue in a foreign country. The platter of dried meats and fruits fortunately seemed innocuous, though Silus still muttered a little prayer to Hygieia that they didn't hold some sort of surprise for them. He didn't want to spend the rest of the week sitting on the latrine.

'So,' said Silus after they had toasted each other's good health, clinked their cups together and taken a deep drink. 'How's the posting?'

'Well,' said Atius, then paused to belch. 'Well,' he continued. 'I have to say at first I wasn't thrilled about the prospect of travelling to the other end of the Empire to babysit a weird kid and his mad mother.'

'At first?'

'Let's say, the assignment grew on me. Pleasant weather, light duties, agreeable company.'

Silus sighed, put his cup down, and fixed his friend with a stern gaze. 'You're fucking her, aren't you?'

Atius' eyes opened wide, his face reddening as he summoned his best semblance of affront. Then he cocked his head on one side and gave Silus a disarming grin.

'Christos, Silus, but she is hot.'

Silus let out a long sigh that whistled through his bent nose.

'What did I say to you before you left? Specifically, what did I expressly tell you not to do?'

'Listen, Silus, you don't know what it is like. There is no action here. Every day is the same. The boy leads the worship of that black stone, and they all dance around it

65

and chant and sing like they have been drugged. The rest of the time he meditates, goes to his lessons with his tutor, or plays with his mother's make-up and dresses. Soaemias stomps around the palace like a caged lion. And Gannys just mopes and gets drunk. Honestly, if I didn't have some distraction, I would go out of my mind.'

'I thought Soaemias and Gannys were an item. Does Gannys know about you and her?'

'I think he might suspect. But they haven't been bedfellows since Marcellus died. I think maybe if her husband had lived, she would have been rid of him anyway. But now he is gone, she needs to be associated with an influential man, one she can dominate, but who can keep the local military and authorities under control.'

'And you can't be that man?'

'Me? A lowly centurion? I'm just her bit of rough.'

Silus shook his head and took a drink, thinking through the implications of the revelation. Not that it was a shock or that he hadn't considered this possibility already. But would it cause problems, for Atius or for himself? He narrowed his eyes and worked through the potential outcomes if the relationship became public. How would Caracalla respond? Julia Domna? Oclatinius? He had no idea. That sort of insight into people's psyches was not one of his talents, which is why he supposed he would remain a lieutenant in the Arcani and not a general. And in any case, it was done now. Whatever resulted from Atius' actions was out of his hands.

Atius was watching Silus carefully, gauging his reaction. When there was no eruption of outrage, he clearly made the decision he could safely change the subject.

'And you? You told me Festus was dead, but you didn't tell me how and why.'

'It's not safe to put some details in writing,' said Silus. 'You can never be sure who is intercepting and reading the mail. The frumentarii carry most of it, and they report to Ulpius Julianus and Julianus Nestor.'

'Well, fortunately, Soaemias filled in a lot of the gaps you left out. She hears most things that go on from her mother and her aunt, you know. But what's all this about Alexandria? Some pretty bad stories are coming out of there from merchants and refugees.'

Silus passed a hand across his face, thumb and forefinger stretching his lower eyelids and the corners of his mouth downward so his face unintentionally gave the appearance of a tragedy mask for a moment. A corpulent black fly landed on a curled, desiccated slice of ham. He watched it take a few jerky steps, reorienting itself a couple of times before sticking something fleshy out of its face and sucking at the meat. He suddenly had an image of a dead youth lying on his back, sightlessly staring at the sky, a cloud of flies buzzing around his exposed, drying intestines. He squeezed his eyes shut, but the image was inside his head, and the darkness behind his lids just made it seem more real. He inhaled sharply, and suddenly felt there was not enough air, that he was suffocating, as if he was in a sealed sack.

He sat back and gripped his cup, examining the decoration baked into the clay in the classic Greek style of black and orange. A huntress with one breast exposed was shooting an arrow at fleeing boar. It wasn't top quality, but he was no art expert, and it seemed well enough executed to him. The distraction was enough to bring his respiration back under control, and a deep breath settled his anxiety, at least partially.

Atius was regarding him with concern and when Silus opened his mouth to speak, Atius held up a hand to forestall him.

'There's no need to say a word,' he said. 'I can read it all on your face.'

Silus nodded gratefully and took a further moment to compose himself.

'It was so unnecessary,' he said when he was finally able to talk without his voice breaking. 'You know how I felt about the slaughter of the Alemanni, but even I could see there was a military justification for it, though I hated how it was carried out. But the Ephebes were barely more than kids. And as for the other innocents, the women and children...'

'He was making an example of the city, wasn't he? That's what Soaemias told me. Making sure that their dangerous behaviour was punished thoroughly, so that no city or province would be tempted to rebel while he is away fighting the Parthians.'

'Dangerous behaviour?' Silus spat the words contemptuously. 'Some off-colour jokes and chucking a few stones. I always knew Caracalla had no sense of humour but saying this was an over-reaction is like saying you quite like women.'

Atius grinned, looking relieved to see his friend recovering his equilibrium. But the light-hearted comment did not detract from Silus' profound underlying sorrow, and he did not return the smile. Atius flicked the fly away and rolled up the slice of ham, popping it whole into his mouth.

'Well,' he said, after swallowing. 'He is the Emperor. We may not like his decisions. We may even not like him personally. But it doesn't affect our jobs, to serve and protect him.'

Silus said nothing. Atius looked at him quizzically. 'You don't agree?'

Silus worked his lips, trying to find the right words, but they eluded him.

'Silus, what is it? You're worrying me now.'

'What if,' began Silus. 'What if you couldn't do it any more?'

'My injury is all but healed—' said Atius, but Silus cut in.

'I don't mean that. What if something… inside you, couldn't let you do these things any more? Couldn't serve someone who orders these things, and still sleep at night, still live with yourself.'

'What are you saying?'

'If you had been there, Atius…'

'If I had been there, it would have changed nothing,' said Atius firmly. 'I took an oath, and I will not break it, no matter my personal feelings. I'm no traitor, Silus. Surely, after all this time, you know at least that one thing about me.'

'Forget I spoke,' said Silus. 'I'm just in a bad mood.' He attempted a smile, despite the crushing disappointment he felt. He knew it had been the slimmest of chances, to persuade Atius to join him. But he had had hope, until that moment. He wasn't scared. If Atius now suspected that Silus was not fully loyal, he would not betray him, their friendship was too deep for that.

But he couldn't reveal any more of his plans to him. It would strain their relationship too much, and, besides, it would put Atius in an unfair position, his allegiances tearing him in two.

'Tell me about Avitus,' said Silus. 'How is our little oddity?'

Atius gratefully accepted the change of subject and proceeded to tell a story about when Avitus had burst into Soaemias' bedchamber, forcing Atius to hide in a cupboard while the young lad had a deep and lengthy discussion with his mother about what it was like to be a woman, with Atius' unemptied balls aching like they had been kicked. Silus nodded and chuckled in all the right places, but his mind was elsewhere.

–

Silus met Oclatinius in the secluded temple dedicated to Belus, the chief god of the city of Palmyra, which was situated a couple of hundred miles to the east of Emesa. The temple was modest, and located a short distance outside of Emesa, since Elagabal dominated the worship within that city. But it was still beautiful despite its diminutive stature and its loneliness, mixing the familiar Greco-Roman architecture – porticoes and Corinthian columns – with the eastern and exotic – shrines and altars decorated with mystical symbols representing the zodiac and the planets, carvings of women wearing flowing robes and veils, and lines of camels.

The sun was fierce, and Oclatinius was seated on a marble bench in the shade of a tall wall in the courtyard. Silus tied up his ass to a tree outside the temple beside Oclatinius' camel – he tried not to ride Delicatus in this draining heat – and joined the old man. He took a waterskin from his belt and drank deeply, swishing the liquid around his mouth to wash away the dust before swallowing. He offered it to Oclatinius, who waved it away.

'I can't stand this climate,' said Silus, thinking back wistfully to the cold and rain of northern Britannia.

'I don't seem to feel the heat so much now I'm older,' said Oclatinius, and Silus noticed that he was wearing a cloak over his tunic. Silus shook his head. How did old people not simply roast to death in these conditions?

Silus watched a lizard bask in the full glare of the sun, before suddenly dancing into action to chase down a scuttling insect.

'How was Atius?' asked Oclatinius.

'Still Atius. He is unchangeable.'

'Including his loyalties?'

'Apparently.'

Silus took another sip of water and wiped away a trickle of sweat that was running into his eye.

'Is he definitely coming?'

Oclatinius nodded. 'He is being understandably cautious. He did not want to appear to be meeting us, so he took a more circuitous route.'

By the time the awaited guest arrived, Silus' waterskin was nearly empty, and he was beginning to wonder where he could go to get it replenished.

Cassius Dio appeared on a fine-muscled grey, trotting with the well-practised seat of a noble taught how to ride from a young age. The horse was entirely unsuited to the heat, however, and was sweating heavily, its head drooping, ears down. He tied it to a tree near Silus' ass and Oclatinius' camel and joined them on the bench. Silus offered him his waterskin, hoping he wouldn't empty it, but Dio shook his head and drew out a flask of wine. He pulled the cork, took a delicate sip, then recorked it and replaced it back in his pack.

'You weren't followed?' asked Oclatinius.

'One benefit of these vast expanses of dirt is that you can see for miles,' said Dio. 'There was no one.'

Oclatinius nodded, satisfied.

'Well?' demanded Silus impatiently. 'You have arranged a meeting for us?'

'Not exactly.'

Silus folded his arms and sat back, rolling his eyes in exasperation. 'This is a waste of time,' he muttered.

'Not exactly?' prompted Oclatinius.

'I was given this to pass onto you.' Dio took a wax diptych from his pack and handed it to Oclatinius. The old man turned it over, inspecting it carefully, then broke the seal on the opposite side from the hinge and opened it. He read, lips moving as he deciphered the cursive stylus marks. When he finished, he used his thumb to smooth the wax page flat, erasing the message. He handed it back to Dio.

'Do you know what the message said?'

'No,' said Dio. 'Nor do I want to know.'

'Then I suggest you get back on your horse and leave. Silus and I have matters to discuss.'

Expressions warred on Dio's face, irritation that a man of his senatorial rank be dismissed by this low-born spy, and relief that his task had been accomplished so simply. He rubbed the wax surface firmly to ensure no trace of the message remained, though Silus knew this was superfluous if the careful Oclatinius had already done this. Then he put the diptych away, strode back to his horse, which groaned when he mounted it, and rode away.

As soon as the senator was out of earshot, Silus grabbed Oclatinius' arm. 'So come on. Who was it from?'

'It was unsigned,' said Oclatinius.

'But you recognised the handwriting?'

'No. It is not in the hand of anyone I know. In fact, it was in several styles. I think the author got different scribes to write a line each, with the previous line hidden, so none knew the full message.'

'Fine, very clever. So what did it say?'

'Unsurprisingly, the author doubts our sincerity. Who can blame him? Or her.'

'Her?'

'Never rule anything out. There are some strong-willed women in Caracalla's inner circle.'

Silus had to agree with that, having met the Julias Domna, Maesa and Soaemias, though he had no inkling any of them wished harm on the Emperor.

'The message?' urged Silus.

'They require a deed that will prove our loyalty beyond doubt.'

'Anything in particular?'

'Yes. They want Athaulf dead.'

Chapter IV

Atius attended the ceremony before the black stone without compunction. Though he was a follower of the Christos, he lived in a multi-faith society, and he was used to the worship of a diverse pantheon, from the ancient Olympian gods of Greece and Rome, to deified emperors, the lares and manes, the eastern religions of Isis and Serapis, the secretive soldiers' religion of Mithraism, Judaism – the foundation of his own beliefs – as well as the vast assortment of minor gods, spirits, demi-gods and local syncretisms that he had encountered on his travels. He had no problem with remaining loyal to his own god, or the Trinity of gods – he was still a little vague on that concept – while accepting that others believed differently. It was not dissimilar, he supposed, to his loyalty to Caracalla, which remained firm, despite his closest friend's misgivings over the years, not to mention the outright treasonous slant of their last conversation.

The Imperial procession had moved on with suitable fanfare a month previously, en route to Antioch. Atius wondered when he would see Silus again. And hoped his friend was not planning anything stupid.

The worship of Elagabal, the mountain god of Emesa, was strange, mystical and very alien. It had some things in common with other eastern mystery cults, the dancing and music and states of ecstasy of the worshippers. It was the centrepiece that made it stand out. A huge, solid, conical black rock, it seemed to suck the light out of the temple. Some projections and markings on one side were supposed to represent the sun, though Atius had cocked his head on one side and squinted and couldn't see it himself. The rock was supposed to have fallen from the heavens in ancient times, and though it was not claimed the stone was the god Elagabal himself, Avitus had told Atius it gave privileged access to the deity, and that touching the stone with reverence could lead to visions and revelations.

A large crowd was in attendance that day as young Avitus led the celebration. Atius always thought the young lad was most comfortable, most at home, when he was in his role of high priest. The androgynous robes were maybe part of that, the boy being forced to express neither masculinity nor femininity, but Atius thought that Avitus was genuinely devoted to his god. As he leapt, twisted and gyrated around the stone in time with the drums, cymbals and pipes that accompanied his dance, his face wore an expression of rapture. Whenever he witnessed this trans-formation, Atius wished he could experience something similar. He knew that some followers of Christos spoke of these sorts of experience, but they had always eluded him. Maybe if he changed his ways, god would speak to him. But even as the thought occurred to him, he caught sight of Soaemias' legs, and his mind wandered to the previous night, when they had been wrapped around him.

Avitus was oblivious to the congregation, swaying to the music, the majority joining in wholeheartedly in the worship, unlike the crowds attending the formal religious rituals in Rome who were present purely out of duty. Soaemias, on the other hand was always fully aware of an audience. She was adept at manipulating a crowd and used her son's innocence and naivete to great effect.

As the worship drew to a close, she approached Avitus, and knelt at his feet, arms raised, looking up at his face.

'Varius Avitus Bassianus, high priest of Emesa,' she cried in a voice loud enough to carry around the large temple auditorium. 'Thank you for leading us ever closer to our Ba'al, the mountain god, ruler of heaven and earth, the Lord Elagabal.'

Avitus inclined his head indulgently and placed a gentle hand on his mother's head.

'The blessing of Elagabal, of the sun and the moon and the mountains and the sea, be upon you, most devoted daughter.'

It always bemused Atius how mother and son could effectively swap familial positions when Avitus was in his role of high priest. But it clearly seemed natural and normal to them, and who was he to question it? There were certainly some strange relationships in Roman mythology, not to mention the Old Testament, as Christians had recently started referring to the Hebrew bible.

Soaemias slowly rose to her feet and turned to address the congregations, standing behind Avitus with her hands on his shoulders.

'Let us all give thanks for his leadership to Varius Avitus Bassianus, son of Septimius Bassianus. Let us pray for his glorification, for Elagabal to uplift him, until one day he takes his rightful place as the ruler of mankind.'

The crowd cheered, clapped, sang praise, and Atius clapped too, while his mind slowly processed what he had just heard. Septimius Bassianus? Wasn't that the name the

Emperor had gone by, before he had been elevated to Augustus by his father? So she was saying that he was Caracalla's son? And because of that, he should be his successor?

Soaemias had clearly decided the time had come for a power play, to put Avitus forward as Caracalla's heir. He knew from her past that she was ambitious and impulsive. But surely this wasn't wise.

Despite the heat, Atius felt suddenly cold. If this got back to Caracalla, it would not go down well.

–

'And then,' Sempronius Rufus announced, wearing an expression of righteous indignation, 'she said, "Let us all give thanks for his leadership to Varius Avitus Bassianus, son of Septimius Bassianus!"'

'She said what?' exclaimed Caracalla.

'Yes, Augustus. And then, I am told she said that one day he would take his rightful place as the ruler of mankind.'

Those present only numbered Caracalla's innermost circle, the likes of Oclatinius, Macrinus and Domna, as well as Athaulf and Silus. But the audible gasps sounded like a gust of wind.

Domna, seated beside Caracalla, looked down at her hands, which were clasped in her lap, her face pale. Oclatinius shook his head sadly. Macrinus muttered, 'That's treason.'

Caracalla merely stared in disbelief.

'This cannot be true,' he said eventually. 'She wouldn't... Who has been spreading these lies? I want them caught and put to torture...'

'They are no lies, I'm sorry to say,' said Rufus. 'It was given to me directly by one of my operatives who was present. A man of unimpeachable honesty and loyalty, who I had tasked with keeping Soaemias under surveillance.'

'You have been spying on my niece?' asked Domna curtly. 'On whose authority?'

'Forgive me, Domna, but on my authority as Keeper of the Sacred Bedchamber. There has been gossip about Soaemias' activities and beliefs. It is my job to keep the Emperor safe from all threats, and I felt it my duty to investigate the lady myself.'

Domna gave Caracalla a challenging stare, but he ignored her.

'Is she plotting?' asked the Emperor, his voice taut. 'She seeks my overthrow?'

'That I cannot say,' said Rufus. 'I merely report what I know.'

'Of course she is plotting!' interjected Macrinus emphatically. 'Augustus, you of all people know that family ties are not enough to guarantee the loyalty of those around you. She must be dealt with.'

'This is my sister's daughter you are casually condemning, Macrinus,' said Domna fiercely. 'I recommend you think more carefully about your suggestions, at least until we know more.'

'You're sure?' Caracalla asked Rufus.

'Certain,' said Rufus.

Caracalla's jaw clenched and unclenched, and he sat, fists balled, staring into the middle distance. Now he was shorn of his characteristic beard, it was easy to see his face flushed with the blood of a high rage.

Attempting to forestall the storm, Domna appealed to Oclatinius.

'What do you think?' she asked him. 'You know my niece is careless with her rhetoric. Does this count as treason?'

Oclatinius spread his hands, not looking particularly comfortable to be drawn into the discussion.

'I'm no lawyer, Augusta,' he said, 'just a plain old military man. It is for my colleague Macrinus to make judgements about matters of jurisprudence.'

Domna pursed her lips in exasperation, then turned to Silus. 'You, Silus, you are familiar with my niece. Please inform Sempronius Rufus that she is incapable of treachery.'

Silus flushed as all eyes turned towards him, and his mouth worked as he tried to formulate a response. To outright say Soaemias would never betray Caracalla was clearly a lie given her past escapades, although Domna was not aware of the true extent of her previous conspiracy.

'I found Julia Soaemias to be a loving mother, who cares for her son, and like any mother is proud of him and wants the best for him. That is very different from saying that she is a traitor.'

Domna stared at Silus, and he felt her willing him to say more. But before he could think of anything to add, Caracalla stood abruptly.

'Nobody is above suspicion,' he announced. 'No one may utter words of treachery against the Imperial person. Rufus, come to my private chambers.' And with that he strode out of the throne room, Rufus hurrying after him.

–

'You don't need to know,' said Sempronius Rufus.

'Dear Rufus,' said Oclatinius, employing his most persuasive tone. 'We are on the same side. Though there was always rivalry between our respective organisations while Festus was Keeper of the Sacred Bedchamber, that time has passed. Now, more than ever, we should be co-operating to keep the Emperor safe, not competing with each other.'

'I appreciate the verbal olive branch, Oclatinius,' said Rufus. 'And I totally agree. There seem to be threats against the Emperor from all sides.'

Silus glanced at Oclatinius, a sudden chill coming over him. Were Rufus' comments aimed at him? Did he know something?

Oclatinius continued unperturbed.

'Quite. So we should make sure we work closely, don't you think?'

'Absolutely. Within certain constraints of course.'

'Constraints?'

'Well, there are some things that have to remain confidential. Highly sensitive matters, such as the identity of well-placed spies. I'm sure a man of your experience understands how vital it is to restrict the number of people privy to these sorts of secrets.'

Silus bridled on Oclatinius' behalf. The old man had forgotten more about spying than Rufus would ever know. But Oclatinius would not rise to the bait.

'Of course. But that doesn't restrict you from sharing details of any ongoing operations that might affect missions being undertaken by my own people.'

'Do you have any missions currently under way that might affect my plans?'

'How can I tell, if I don't know what your plans are?' Silus detected a note of irritation creeping into Oclatinius' voice now. 'Why don't you just say what the Emperor ordered you to do?'

'I'm sorry, he gave me instructions in confidence. I couldn't share them with you, even if I wanted to.' Silus understood the implication that Rufus had no desire to share secrets with Oclatinius. It was frustrating, but he had to acknowledge that it was good spycraft.

'Well, I can see we are getting nowhere,' said Oclatinius. 'It's a shame. I had been looking forward to an era of great harmony when you replaced Festus.'

'I'm sure we will be harmonious,' said Rufus. 'But we will remain discrete. As well as discreet. Good day to you.'

When Silus was sure Rufus was out of hearing range, he said, 'What do you think? What would Caracalla have told him?'

Oclatinius shook his head. 'He has kept his orders closely guarded, even within his own people. Of course I have sources in his organisation, as he does in mine.'

'He has spies in the Arcani?' asked Silus surprised.

'Not actual Arcani, no, just people I use for intelligence. I know who they are, but it suits me to leave them in place so I can feed false information when the need arises.'

'So what is your best guess?'

Oclatinius stroked his chin thoughtfully. 'Caracalla certainly looked pretty unimpressed, I have to say. And I have no reason to doubt that Rufus' source is telling the truth.'

'You think he gave orders for Soaemias' murder? Just as he sent me to kill his wife?'

'It does seem most likely.'

'But Atius is with her!'

'Yes. Atius would be a target too, as her bodyguard, and as a loose end with suspect loyalties.'

'Oclatinius, I have to warn him!'

'No. You must stay here. You have your task to perform for the conspirators.'

'To Tartarus with that! Atius is more important.'

'If you leave now, the conspirators will think you are acting on Caracalla's orders, or that you are acting to save Soaemias, both of which would shake their trust in you. And you would be blatantly disobeying both Caracalla and Athaulf. You would lose Athaulf's confidence, and with it the chance to carry out your mission. Or worse, Caracalla would have you executed for desertion.'

'But what if Soaemias is part of the conspiracy we are trying to join? We need to warn her.'

'If she was a conspirator, I doubt she would have made this play with her son. No, she clearly believes that by making this public, the heirless Caracalla would have to acknowledge Avitus as his own, maybe even elevate him to Caesar. She doesn't realise how badly she has miscalculated.'

'Then let me go to her.'

'No. I'll deal with it. I'll get a message to Atius. And don't worry. That lad can look after himself.'

Silus glowered, unsatisfied.

A thought suddenly occurred to him.

'Does this mean Rufus is not one of the conspirators against Caracalla?'

'Perhaps. Just because his man was involved in starting the riots in Alexandria, doesn't mean he was acting on behalf of Rufus himself. On the other hand, he may be trying to get Caracalla to trust him more by exposing

Soaemias. Then he would be better placed to strike when the moment presented itself.'

'These fucking spies,' spat Silus contemptuously, thoroughly fed up of all the treachery and double crosses.

'Silus,' said Oclatinius. 'You are one of these fucking spies.'

Chapter V

Azemilcus rode swiftly along the broad Roman road that was the main military route from Antioch to Emesa. He bent low over the cantering bay mare, which kicked up clouds of dust behind it. Oclatinius had given him a certificate so he could utilise the mounts at the stations of the cursus publicus. Being able to exchange a tired mount for a fresh one at regular intervals halved the journey time, but he still figured that after the best part of two days' hard ride, he was still an hour or so away from Shaizar, the small town that marked the approximate halfway point of his journey.

The September sun was still fierce, but Azemilcus was used to the heat. His ancestors came from the Phoenician city of Tyre, but he had spent his childhood as a slave working in the stables of a rich merchant, and he had been given the responsibility of caring for and exercising some of the estate's fine chariot horses. Fortunately, his master had no heirs, and his will stipulated the manumission of all his slaves, so Azemilcus found himself on the cusp of manhood, a freedman, but with no family, friends or money.

He had managed to find employment as a groom in the stables of one of the local chariot teams in Antioch, which provided him with accommodation and food but little else – after all, they had equally skilled slaves who could do his job without pay. So he made a side living as a thief in the Antioch markets, until one day he chose the wrong target. Though he thought he had some skill as a pickpocket, his mark, who he later discovered was an Arcanus, detected him as easily as if he had announced his presence by ringing a bell. He had thought, too, that he was swift on his feet, but the Arcanus had run him down without breaking a sweat and dragged him into a side alley.

Azemilcus had thought his life was at an end that day, but the Arcanus had seen something in him. When the man discovered he had a talent for riding, as well as some amateur skill in thievery, he had recruited him into the Arcanus organisation. Recently, he had been introduced to the old man himself, Oclatinius, who had regarded him with an approving eye, and told him that he might become an Arcanus himself one day, with the right mentoring, and enough dedication to his training.

For the first time in his life, Azemilcus felt valued, and from then on he wanted nothing more than to become an Arcanus, and resolved to work as hard as it took to become one. A few months of toil and labour commenced, with the Arcanus who had discovered him introducing him to the artistry, the science and the trickery of the assassin and the spy. He learnt lockpicking, how to follow someone without being detected, how to kill silently with garotte or blade or poison. He learnt to fight with dagger and sword and bow. His progress was slow, steady, frustrating and he had begun to wonder if he would ever make the grade. But his greatest strength was on horseback. He was a better rider than any man he had met. He could outpace anyone, turn his mount on a denarius, make it dance. Riding was his gift and his joy.

Then Oclatinius had come to him, with his first mission. An urgent message, to be conveyed to one of his operatives in Emesa. He was to leave immediately. He had accepted the order without question, and now here he was, the wax tablet onto which had been scratched the message feeling heavy in his pack to a degree well beyond its actual weight.

He encountered a number of fellow travellers on the road. Ox and donkey carts taking goods from the farms and workshops to the nearby towns and to Antioch itself. Military units, some small detachments, the occasional full century, sweating heavily as they marched in full uniform, and every so often another military messenger, although none of these seemed to possess his sense of urgency.

He wondered if he should have taken a more circuitous route to avoid detection, stay off the main thoroughfare. But Oclatinius had impressed on him that speed was of the utmost importance, so he had judged the risk of being seen was outweighed by the shorter travel time of taking the road. And he was supremely confident in his riding ability, should anyone try to chase him down.

The thought of pursuit prompted him to turn and look behind him. Just normal traffic. No one in a particular hurry. No signs of clouds of dust on the horizon, which might have been kicked up by a racing steed. He turned his attention back to the road in front of him as the path passed through a landscape of dirt, scrubby bushes and rocks. His backward glance had meant it took him a moment to refocus on the road ahead. So he nearly missed the rope stretched between two rocks on either side of the road, taut, about half the height of his horse's leg off the ground. His mount hadn't spotted it either, and they would be on it in two strides. He knew immediately that contact would be a definite leg-breaker for the horse, and probable neck breaker for himself.

Time seemed to slow as his senses were heightened by fear. He threw himself backward in the saddle, yanked on the reins, dug his heels into the mare's flanks, yelling, 'Leap, you bastard.'

Another step. No change in gait. Almost no time left. But enough for half a dozen thoughts to flash through his head. Thoughts such as, was there enough distance to clear the rope if the horse responded? Were horses of the cursus publicus even trained to jump? Who was trying to kill him?

He felt the mare's backquarters sink down, the immense musculature flexing and tensing. The forelegs came up, and the saddle forced up through his spine with the tremendous power of the horse's leap. They soared upwards in a perfect arc like a stone shot from a sling. The front hooves cleared the rope. The chest, the belly.

One iron-shod hind foot snagged the rope, checking the horse and throwing Azemilcus forward. He grabbed her neck, clinging on tight as she recovered her footing. Then she was racing onwards, and he urged her to a gallop, keeping the reins short, bent low, knees gripping her side so he could raise his backside and smooth out the forceful undulations as her back flexed and extended with each stride.

When he was sure she had regained her balance, he risked a glance back. Three men had been lurking behind the rocks, and he could see one cursing at the other two for their failure. But as he watched, they leapt onto their own horses and began to pursue him.

Who were they? Bandits was the obvious answer, looking for cash or jewels or something else they could sell or trade. But no, the increased military presence in Syria since the arrival of Caracalla's forces had suppressed banditry, forcing them into the hills and mountains to prey on rarely frequented routes and isolated communities. And wouldn't it be too much of a coincidence, to pick out him, instead of all the much easier targets ambling carelessly along?

So, they were after him, specifically. They must have known about his mission and set out in advance, waited for him along his obvious path. There was no way they could have departed Antioch after him and got ahead of him – no one was that fast. Did Oclatinius have a mole in his organisation? It was the only explanation. He would have to make sure he warned his boss.

But first he had to get out of this situation.

He was scared, his hands white from gripping the leather reins so hard. He had never been in danger like this before, fleeing for his life. But he was steeled by a firm confidence in his riding abilities. He had a swift mount, still relatively fresh. He had a head start. And he was a better rider than them. Of that he had no doubt.

His horse devoured the yards, smoothly curving past other road users without losing any pace. He mentally calculated how far he would have to go to reach the safety of another cursus publicus station. It would be many hours ride, but long before then, the race would be over, as his pursuers' horses tired and were unable to continue the chase, or his own horse fatigued first and he was overtaken.

He looked back again. They were at least two hundred yards behind, and though their horses were a little fresher, they showed no signs of gaining. He gave a grim, satisfied smile and rode on.

After half a mile, he eased back. Neither his horse nor his pursuers could keep up that pace for so long, and a slower speed was now required for endurance. Besides, it would be better to conserve some energy in case a sprint was needed later. The pursuers urged their horses to close the gap, but they too had to slow down or risk their horses collapsing, and the distance between them, after shortening a little, remained constant. It had turned into a contest of staying power. Exciting riding, trickery and sprint speed were no longer of use. But knowledge of how to get the best out of your mount was, and Azemilcus remained confident they would not catch him. Not unless something disastrous happened.

The disaster occurred two miles further on. A sizeable lizard scuttled across the road in front of them, startling the mare. She took an awkward sideways step, then over-reached with one of her hind feet, so it made contact with the back of the front foot. The tip of the hind foot shoe caught the hindmost lip of the front shoe, and ripped it clean off.

Azemilcus heard the ominous noise and looked back to see the shoe bouncing and rolling down the road. He knew instantly what it meant, even as his horse began to limp. In normal circumstances he would have pulled her up straight away. But these weren't normal circumstances.

He urged her to keep up her pace, a steady canter, while his mind furiously worked through his options. Stop, dismount, stand and fight? He would be cut down in moments. Keep riding? Even if she didn't break down completely, her pace would be impeded too much by having to adjust to the uneven footing, and the pursuers would rapidly gain on him. Or should he fight them, but on his terms?

He eased back on the reins, subtly reducing her speed further, making it look like she was struggling more than was the case. His pursuers rapidly gained ground. The sound of their combined hoofbeats crescendoed, and he could soon hear their excited shouts, pointless calls for him to stop, encouragement to each other and their horses.

Fortunately they weren't armed with bows – they had clearly been expecting to finish him off hand-to-hand after the ambush, and besides, it took a highly trained rider to shoot from horseback with any chance of accuracy. Azemilcus himself could have done it, turned and shot back at them like a Parthian, but sadly he had no bow either.

His mare was breathing hard through flared nostrils, but she wasn't overexerting herself, so she had plenty of energy in reserve. She would need it for what was to come. He reached down for the spatha sheathed at the side of the saddle and slid it out.

They came within a length of him, the head of the lead rider's horse almost level with his mare's tail. The other two flanked him, one on each shoulder. Any moment they would be on him.

He yanked on the reins hard, sawing them into his mare's soft cheeks in a violent movement he would never usually inflict on his mount. But she reacted instantly, pushing her legs out to check her pace abruptly. The horses behind swerved instinctively to avoid her and raced on. As the last rider careered past him, Azemilcus slashed down with his spatha. The blade bit deep into the horse's hamstrings, and with a heart-rending whinny, it went down, crumpling from its hind legs to lie on its side, kicking feebly, rider tossed aside. Azemilcus gritted his teeth. It hurt to inflict such injury on an equine, but he knew he had no option.

The other two riders wheeled their horses a score of yards down the road and kicked their flanks, spurring them to charge back towards Azemilcus. He flicked the reins, urging his mare back into motion, and she obeyed as if they had been riding together for years. They raced towards each other, accelerating all the time. Azemilcus aimed for the small gap between his two attackers, and they prepared to skewer him from either side. But at the last instant, he swerved to the left, so only one of the aggressors could reach him. The tip of a blade scored his upper arm, a skin wound only, though deep enough to immediately bleed profusely. In turn, he slashed at his opponent's shin, his spatha biting deep. It wasn't a disabling blow, but it would impede the man's ability to steer.

Once again they wheeled around, but the injured man was slower, so they came on one at a time. Azemilcus could see the look of fury in the assassin's face as he bent low over his horse's neck, his sword held high.

As they passed, Azemilcus ducked under the side swipe and stabbed out himself. His sword sank deep into his opponent's mount's chest, and the horse cried and fell. But it ripped his spatha from his hand, and moreover his opponent was able to roll clear of his fallen horse without injuring himself.

The second rider was upon him, and Azemilcus swerved his mare sideways. But her unshod hoof let her down, the uneven gait causing her to twist her fetlock. Her leg buckled, and then she began to hobble, barely able to touch her foot to the floor. Desperately, knowing it was hopeless, he urged her round to confront the last remaining rider. She responded gamely, attempting to trot, ducking her head low every time her injured leg touched the ground. The last mounted assassin saw her problem straight away, and with a cry, spurred his horse into a gallop.

Azemilcus held his sword up to try to fend off an incoming blow, but that was not the assassin's intention. He rode straight into Azemilcus' horse's shoulder on the opposite side from the injury. The impact caused her leg to collapse, and she rolled, a slow, almost majestic tumble.

Her full weight landed on one of Azemilcus' legs, shattering the thigh bone and trapping him underneath her. The pain hit him a moment later, unlike anything he had felt before, and he screamed. In the periphery of his vision, he saw the rider dismount, and his fallen but uninjured colleague joined him. They walked purposefully towards him, long swords held loosely.

Azemilcus felt for the backpack, and screwing his face up against the agony, fumbled with the strap. He opened it, drew out the wax tablet, and used his thumb to erase the message, smoothing the wax flat, so nothing legible remained. Then he tossed it aside, and lay back, staring at the sky.

It was unfair, he thought. Bad luck had been his undoing. If not for that, he was sure he would have had a great career as an Arcanus.

When the two assassins reached him and together raised their swords high, he closed his eyes, and waited for the final blows to fall.

—

The moon was on its way to full, and it illuminated the frescoes in the bedchamber with a pale light that brought out a different palate than the sun. Bright colours became more pastel, shades softened, hues altered. Atius lay on his back, one arm behind his head, and examined the ornate paintings. Sleep would not come to him easily that night, and though he had no reason to feel anxiety, nevertheless there was something bothering him, something that didn't seem right.

Maybe that feeling emanated from the woman beside him, but the sounds of her gentle, rhythmic breathing were, if anything, relaxing, even if she was the woman he was supposed to be guarding, a woman who believed that her son had been fathered by the Emperor. And no one seemed to care about her liaisons, especially now her husband was dead. Atius had liked Marcellus and was glad that he had not made a cuckold out of him, since Marcellus had died before Atius had first slept with Soaemias. Gannys of course had played that role, but he seemed content enough with his lot, having found himself the daughter of a local dignitary to keep himself amused.

Soaemias was an enthusiastic lover, if somewhat demanding, and it took all his vigour to keep up with her sometimes. It was fun and exciting, but he knew it wouldn't last. She would get recalled to Rome, or he would be reassigned, and their time together would end. But for now, he was perfectly content in his twin roles of protector and paramour.

The bedchamber was on the upper floor of Soaemias' palace, situated on a walkway raised above the peristylium, with a single inward-facing window, the shutters of which were currently thrown wide open to allow the cooling night air in. It was a pleasant room in which to be unable to sleep, since Atius could listen to the sounds of the night birds and the cicadas, and the bark of the watchdog if something disturbed him.

The dog was quiet now, and Atius felt his breathing slow. His eyes drifted closed, and he found himself on the cusp of sleep. Disconnected images crowded his periphery, swirling as they attempted to organise themselves into full dreams – a barbarian warrior's face, a rounded female hip, a Christian church, the black rock of Elagabal.

Suddenly he was wide awake. He wasn't sure what had disturbed him, but he lay still as a marble statue, the movements of his chest barely perceptible, and he strained his ears to see if he could catch whatever sound his dozing senses had alerted him regarding.

Nothing.

He took in a deep breath through his nose and blew it out slowly through pursed lips, a technique he had found invaluable in easing tension. He was often tense, despite his idyllic posting, memories of past traumas frequently intruding on his peace and making him anxious and irritable.

There it was again. A footstep. Padded feet, maybe wearing slippers. Taking one very slow step at a time. Not the heavy tread of the night porter doing his rounds, or the scurry of a slave on a nocturnal errand. This was someone deliberately attempting to remain undetected.

Burglars then. Or worse. Atius eased the blanket back, and rolled to the edge of the bed, feeling underneath for his blade. He kept a small knife with him at all times. Though Soaemias didn't approve, he had over-ruled her in his capacity of personal protector, so she had told him to keep it out of her sight. As far as he knew, she was not squeamish about someone committing violence with a blade. He thought she just preferred to be the one with her hand on the hilt.

His fingertips brushed the knife, and he grasped it tightly, then rolled his body slowly, his legs sliding off the bed and his bare feet finding the floor. Soaemias muttered something incoherent and turned over.

Atius was barely breathing, listening for any clues as to the intruder's intent. Would it be a stealthy entrance through the open window, hoping to catch them asleep, or a burst through the door, a clash of noise that would disorientate the newly awakened targets to give sufficient time for the intruder to finish his deed?

He heard the footstep at the door, a pause, then another footstep approaching the window. Atius flattened himself against the wall between the window and door, clutching his knife tight, hoping to be able to stab at whatever showed itself first, or at least grab a limb and catch them by surprise. He could hear his heartbeat pounding in his ears like a drum and wondered that it didn't wake Soaemias.

There was a blur of motion. A small figure dived head-first through the window, rolled and noiselessly regained its feet. Without pause, it rushed towards the bed, raised blade glinting in the moonlight. Atius urged his body into motion, his bulk an impediment to rapid acceleration. But as the figure prepared to plunge their knife into the sleeping Soaemias, Atius leapt and hit them square in the back with his shoulder.

He grappled for the intruder, but his tackle had thrown them clean over the bed. Despite the surprise, they landed elegantly, turned and whirled, knife still in hand, and Atius realised the assassin was a woman, slight and wiry, eyes blazing in fury. He was suddenly, stupidly conscious of his own nakedness, but the assassin didn't spare a downward glance. Soaemias was sitting bolt upright, clutching the bed sheets to her body, staring in disbelief.

The assassin moved with the speed of a cat, stepping up onto the bed, then leaping into the air so she could bring her weight into the downward swing of her knife. Atius had no time to move out of the way, but blocked the blow, forearm to forearm. Though he was clearly the heavier of the two of them, the force of the impact shuddered through him, and even as he was grimacing, she followed up with a strike from her free hand, a jab that sent extended fingers deep into his shoulder joint. His hand spasmed open and his knife fell to the floor. He took a step backward, and she advanced on him, backing him into a corner.

Atius felt a sudden lack of confidence, an unfamiliar feeling. Despite his vast experience and his superior size, this small woman seemed in total control. Her gaze was fixed on his eyes, and when he feinted one way or the other she adjusted her position instantly, the knife always between them. He tried a lunge towards her, but she took a step back and flicked the point of her blade across the back of his arm, slicing the skin wide and nicking the underlying muscle. He had a sudden terror that her blade might be poisoned, but although the wound hurt, he couldn't detect the sting or tingle that might suggest any toxins were working their way into his bloodstream.

He clutched his arm, the blood tricking between his fingers, and was at a loss. She wasn't toying with him, he thought, but she was confident in her position, so all she needed to do was wait for her opportunity to finish him. He thought about attempting to back himself round to the window, so he could throw himself out of it, and find a weapon to redress the balance. But that would leave Soaemias at the assassin's mercy.

And suddenly there she was, mother of the chief priest of Elagabal, niece of the Empress, rearing behind the assassin like a cobra ready to strike, Atius' knife in her hand.

The assassin saw Atius' involuntary widening of his eyes, but before she could turn, Soaemias thrust the blade into the base of her neck and buried it deep in her brain. The assassin's entire body stiffened; her eyes rolled up into her head. Soaemias twisted, withdrew the knife and stepped back, watching the corpse fall lifeless to the floor with a contemptuous sneer.

She looked at Atius, dripping blood onto her fine mosaic floor.

'Some bodyguard you are,' she said.

Atius gaped at her. 'I saved your life!' he protested.

'It looked to me like I saved yours,' she retorted. 'But that is a pointless argument. Who is she?'

Atius shook himself, then knelt down to inspect the dead assassin. No tattoos. No jewellery. A plain, eastern complexion. She could be anybody, work for anyone.

'I don't know. But I can tell you two things. The first is that she was highly trained. This was no thief, or ordinary citizen with a grudge.'

'An Arcanus?' asked Soaemias.

'It's possible. But the Arcani are not the only secret organisation the Emperor employs.'

'The Emperor? You think...?'

'That's the second thing. I'm no follower of politics, but even I know it's not prudent to announce that your son is the Emperor's bastard and heir. Paranoid rulers mistrust anyone who says they have a claim to the throne.'

Soaemias put her hand to her mouth, and her face, already pale in the moonlight, whitened.

The door burst open, and Gannys came running in, breathless from sprinting from his bedroom at the opposite end of the house.

He looked from her to the naked, bleeding Atius, to the body on the floor, mouth open. When he could speak, he blurted out, 'Soaemias, are you hurt?'

'Completely unharmed, thank you, Gannys.'

The night porter, woken by the guard dog's barking, who in turn had only been alerted to the intrusion by the sounds of fighting, pushed into the room behind Gannys. He stared around him, looking like a man who thought he was still dreaming.

'Psellos, take this rubbish away,' said Soaemias. 'Be discreet. Throw her in the River Orontes, but don't let anyone see you.'

'Y... yes, m... mistress,' stammered Psellos. He grabbed the body by the heels and dragged it away, leaving behind a trail of gore emanating from the wound at the back of the head.

'And send someone to clean up this mess,' called Soaemias after him.

'Who was behind this?' asked Gannys when Psellos was out of earshot.

'Gannys, you may not have noticed but both Atius and I are in a state of undress. Would you wait for us in the peristylium, and we will join you shortly?'

Atius wondered if Soaemias wanted to speak to him privately, but she did in fact merely want to get dressed, which she did unhurriedly, but efficiently, donning a modest stola. Atius pulled a tunic over his head, blood from his arm smearing across it in streaks. Soaemias picked up her palla and ripped a length of material from it. She used it to bind his arm, firm but gentle, and he nodded his thanks.

'Come, let us check on Avitus, and then join Gannys,' she said.

Young Avitus was sound asleep, undisturbed by the commotion, so they left him alone and went down to the peristylium, from where they were able to see the door to the boy's bedroom. They found Gannys reclining on a pillow-softened bench, being served a cup of wine by a slave girl, with whom, Atius suspected, he had been spending the night. He was affecting nonchalance, but Atius could see the worry in the lines of his face and was sure his own expression looked the same.

When the slave had served wine to Soaemias and Atius and been dismissed, Soaemias spoke.

'Give me your thoughts,' she said.

Atius looked to Gannys. He was her bodyguard, not her political advisor. But Gannys merely took a sip of wine and looked back at Atius.

Atius sighed. 'I have told you what I think. I believe this is an assassin sent by the Emperor. I think it was done without the knowledge or involvement of the Arcani, or else Silus or Oclatinius would have warned me. Not a frumentarius or speculator, they don't have these sorts of skills, and, besides, they are all men.'

'So who is left?' asked Gannys.

'There are a few other fringe organisations that report intelligence to the Emperor, but if I had to make an educated guess, I would see the hand of the Keeper of the Sacred Bedchamber in this.'

'Sempronius Rufus?'

'Yes,' said Atius. 'But not without orders.'

'Caracalla,' said Soaemias, and the name was a whisper. Atius said nothing.

'I'm doomed,' said Soaemias, struggling to keep her voice even. 'If he wants me dead, he will succeed, sooner or later. We cannot be lucky against assassins every time.'

'And if he wants you dead, then he won't leave Avitus alive,' said Gannys.

A tear sprung at the corner of one of Soaemias' eyes and rolled down her cheek.

'What have I done?' she whispered. 'Too soon. Too soon.'

'I'm afraid he will send for your head too, Gannys,' said Atius. 'You are widely seen as Soaemias' consort and Avitus' guardian.'

Gannys tried not to react, but Atius saw the tremor in his hand as he sipped his wine.

Atius thought for a moment. He was no Oclatinius, but he was not without wits. They were all alive, so they had options.

'This is what we are going to do,' he said.

—

The small Syrian village owed its survival in the arid landscape to a tiny tributary of the River Orontes, which the villagers used to water their goats and irrigate their lands. An elderly man, with wrinkled, sun-browned skin, leant on his staff and watched them approach the small settlement along the dusty track that had long since led away from the main Roman road. When they reached him, Atius dismounted and approached.

'Do you speak Greek?' he asked.

The man inclined his head.

'Are you the village headman?'

Again, a slow nod.

'I am… Lucius,' said Atius. 'This is my familia.' He gestured to his sole companions, Soaemias, Avitus and Gannys. 'We are travellers, looking for shelter and food. We can pay.'

'We have little to offer,' said the headman.

'We require little,' said Atius. 'Do you have a place we can stay? Is there a tavern?'

The headman's face split into a gummy smile, revealing a solitary brown upper eye tooth.

'We are too small for that sort of thing,' he said.

Atius looked beyond him. Indeed, there were around a dozen huts, wattle and daub walls, flat roofs made from palm branches. There would be no amenities. This place was set up for subsistence only.

'One of those huts, then? Is that possible?'

The headman looked around him. A small gathering of young children and women, some pregnant, some with toddlers on their hips, one elderly like the headman, regarded the newcomers with open curiosity. He spoke to the old lady in some incomprehensible local dialect, and she jabbered back animatedly, making what looked like insulting gestures towards Atius.

Atius reached slowly for his belt, being careful not to make any threatening moves. He drew out a purse that jangled with coins and selected two silver denarii. He passed one to the headman, and one to the old lady. The flow of her words stopped instantly and she held up the coin so it gleamed in the sunlight. Her mouth was open, and he wondered if she had ever seen such riches.

'A hut?' prompted Atius.

The headman nodded ponderously. 'My wife's sister died last week. Last of her family. In time it will pass to one of the lads, the first to take a wife and make his own little ones. But for now it sits empty. You may use that.'

'I thank you. And food and drink?'

'It shall be brought such as we have and can spare.'

'Would someone be able to feed and water our mounts, as well?'

The headman sighed but nodded. Atius called back to his companions. 'We're staying here. You can dismount.'

Gannys looked most relieved to be getting off his horse's back, and he walked over stiffly.

'Which is our luxury accommodation?' he asked.

The headman did not understand the words or the irony, or he chose to ignore the little barb. He pointed to a small hut a little further down the track. It probably had the footprint of a top floor Suburan apartment and was in about the same state of repair. The wattle was crumbling, and the palm leaf roof was threadbare. One of the door's hinges was broken, so it swung loose from the door frame, attached at a single point. Still, the surroundings were more picturesque than the Subura. And they were less likely to get mugged. Or at least he presumed so.

'How long are you planning to stay?' asked the headman.

'Is there a limit to your hospitality?' asked Atius.

'Is there a limit to your coin?' asked the headman.

Atius smiled. 'You need have no worry on that score.' Indeed, the treasure they had brought with them for safe-keeping in the saddle bags of the horses could have bought every one of these villagers as slaves many times over.

Atius helped Soaemias unload her baggage, and led her to the hut, Gannys and Avitus struggling behind with their own loads. He gingerly opened the door, taking care not to rip it off its one remaining hinge, and went inside.

It smelled of stale bread and old lady's urine, and Atius didn't think anyone had attempted to clean it since the death of the headman's sister-in-law.

Soaemias came in next and put the back of her hand over her nose. She took in the dirt floor, central firepit leading to a hole in the roof to serve as a chimney, the beams of sunlight from the only window making the dust motes dance.

'Very well,' she said. 'We don't exactly have a lot in the way of choice.'

'Oh there's always a choice,' said Atius. 'But good choices. They can be harder to find.'

Gannys came in next, sniffed, and exclaimed, 'By the mountain god's hairy…' and then bit back the expletive as Avitus pushed past him.

'It's wonderful, isn't it, Mother?' he said. 'Can I sleep under that hole in the roof so I can see the stars?'

'If you wish, dear,' said Soaemias with a sigh. They put down their packs, fished out rolled-up mattresses and blankets and set out their beds. After a while the headman returned with three small boys bearing clay plates holding a few loaves of bread and some dates and a jug of water. They handed them round, and Atius gave his thanks. The headman looked at him expectantly, and Atius passed him another silver denarius. The headman paused, clearly considering whether to ask for more, then deciding not to press his luck, nodded and backed out of the hut, taking the boys with him.

That evening, when the men and women without childcare duties returned from the fields, the headman invited the newcomers to dine with them around a communal fire in the centre of the village. Though few of the villagers spoke Greek, Avitus and Soaemias understood a smattering of the local dialect, and they were able to make some simple conversation. After the meal, Avitus danced and sang for the villagers, and they clapped and cheered with delight. He even led them in a prayer to Elagabal, and it seemed they were familiar with the mountain god and quite happy to worship him.

Afterwards, when Avitus had gone to bed, followed shortly after by a grumpy Gannys complaining about the lack of wine, Atius sat next to Soaemias on a log by the fire. Sparks drifted up into the dark sky, floating towards the bright stars that sparkled with a clarity he never saw in the polluted cities or the hazy northern climes.

'I leave tomorrow,' said Atius.

'I thought you would,' said Soaemias. 'What will you do?'

'I need to make contact with Silus. And Oclatinius, if Silus tells me it is safe to do so. But I will have to be discreet. I was ordered by the Emperor to protect you, and now he has changed his mind in that regard, he will probably view me as suspect, and wish to be rid of me too.'

Soaemias took his arm and rested her head on his shoulder. 'You could stay here,' she said. 'Would life here with me be so bad?'

'It can't last,' he said. 'Caracalla is still young; he will be on the throne for many years unless illness or assassination intervene. And one day, a villager will talk to the wrong person when travelling to the nearest market town, or Avitus will chafe at being cooped up in the backwater. No, this is just for now, to keep you safe, while I work out what to do next. Or Silus does.'

She kissed him softly on the lips.

'Then we have one last night together. Let's make the most of it.'

Chapter VI

'I'm not sure it can be done,' said Silus. 'At least not in a way that allows me to get away with my life.'

Oclatinius stroked his beard thoughtfully. They were sitting in a large public garden in Antioch, keeping a close eye on passers-by, making sure none paid them too much attention, changing the subject smoothly to innocuous matters if someone came too close. They had been talking for an hour already, chewing over scenarios by which Silus could kill Athaulf, but none ended with a good chance of both success and survival.

They had talked about poison, but Athaulf invariably ate in the communal mess with the other Leones and getting to only his food or drink was all but impossible. They had talked about stealthy assassination at night, but he slept in the Leones barracks, and it seemed unlikely that even Silus could dispatch him without raising the alarm. Oclatinius had mentioned the possibility of killing him while he was on duty but assassinating the head of the Emperor's bodyguard while he was working seemed as monumental a task as killing the Emperor himself. Then they had discussed arranging an accident, but they had not yet come up with a plausible method.

'So we wait,' said Silus. 'See what presents itself.'

'I suppose we must,' said Oclatinius. 'But our time is not unlimited.'

'You think the conspirators will give up on us if we don't follow through with this promptly?'

'That is possible,' said Oclatinius, 'but not only that. I'm talking about the ultimate plan, the reason why we are doing this in the first place.'

'I'm aware there is a point to this.'

'But there is also another reason for urgency. The deed must be done before the invasion of Parthia.'

'Why?'

'Two reasons. Firstly, the invasion of Parthia will probably be a disaster.'

'You think so?'

'Nothing is certain in war. But look at the history of our conflicts with Parthia. It is not a happy story. When Crassus invaded, Rome had had two hundred years of military success, since the defeat of Hannibal. A legion was considered the finest fighting unit in the world, and the only power that could stand against it was another legion. The two Scipios had destroyed Carthage, Marius had beaten the Gauls and conquered North Africa, Sulla had been victorious in the East against Mithridates, Pompey had conquered Spain, and Caesar had taken all Gaul. Crassus wanted his turn and led a force against Parthia that should have been unstoppable.

'But the Parthians used every advantage they had, not least their highly skilled horse archers, who the unmounted legionaries could not get near. Bad generalship, bad luck and some Parthian trickery played a role too, but ultimately their units and tactics were too good for Crassus, and the battle of Carrhae was the worst defeat for Rome since Hannibal's victory at Cannae.'

Silus listened to the history lesson grim-faced, aware of the disaster but not the detail.

'Of course we don't know how Caesar would have fared if he had led his legions against Parthia, as he was planning when he was assassinated. Better generalship might have made the difference. Or it might have been his humiliation, which his untimely death spared him. Certainly his deputy, Mark Antony, barely escaped with his life when he attempted an invasion. Even Trajan and Septimius Severus have only had limited success in conflicts with Parthia.

'So, if we don't stop Caracalla before he invades Parthia, we could see another defeat in the East that might destabilise the Empire. Caracalla has repressed the border tribes in Britannia, Germania and Dacia, but there is always someone new ready to rush in and fill a space created by failure. A serious defeat in Parthia could conceivably lead to the fall of the eastern part of the Empire.'

Silus let out a low whistle. He had become used to Severan success in battle, and generally took it for granted now. But he hadn't really thought through the consequences of defeat, and the way Oclatinius set them out was stark and unsettling.

'You said there were two reasons we needed to stop him before he invades Parthia.'

'The second is an even more disastrous scenario – that he wins.'

Silus raised his eyebrows in surprise.

'That would be a bad thing?'

'It depends on your viewpoint. But if you had determined, as we have, that Caracalla is a bad Emperor, and must be disposed of, then a victory in Parthia might put that out of reach. Until now, his victories can be dismissed as border skirmishes. He hasn't added any new territory to the Empire, just suppressed the barbarians that threaten the Empire's boundaries. But a decisive victory over the Parthians would bring him massive acclaim in Rome, not to mention the vast riches that would pour out of the Parthian Empire and into Caracalla's treasure chests. The legions and the people would adore him, and even the Senate would come back into line, knowing he had achieved something truly great, and opposition would be futile.'

'And then he really would be free to rule how he pleased.'

'No check on his worst impulses, except maybe from Domna, and only the gods know how long she has left.'

Silus nodded morosely.

'So his position would be unassailable if he wins in Parthia,' he said.

'Free to do whatever he wants. To whoever he wants.'

Silus shuddered, thinking again of the dead in Alexandria, and then of Tituria, innocently growing into a noble Roman matron in a respectable household in Rome.

'Before Parthia then. And when is that exactly?'

'Not yet,' said Oclatinius. 'He is still making preparations. He may not even be ready to start in the spring and may elect to wait another year. If Caracalla is brave and tactically aware on the battlefield, he excels in the strategic planning of an operation. It's his genius, and it is what makes a victory in Parthia possible for him where so many others have failed.'

'So we still have some time, but we shouldn't dawdle.'

'That about sums it up.'

'Very well. I'm going to find something to eat. Do you want to join me?'

Oclatinius shook his head. 'Too much work to do for leisure. I'll be in touch soon.' He got up and hobbled away with a stick, an affectation that Silus thought was at least four-fifths for show, to encourage people to underestimate him, physically and mentally. A sudden thought occurred to Silus. Was he, too, underestimating Oclatinius? Or misjudging him? Oclatinius, who had served several emperors in various roles with complete loyalty over many decades. He was now going to betray one? Or was this all part of some game by Oclatinius, maybe a test of Silus' loyalties, or a plan to flush out the conspirators? Oclatinius always seemed to be so many steps ahead of everyone else. Silus knew that if Oclatinius had indeed turned against him, he was finished. He could not hope to outwit the cunning old man. He watched him go, then headed off in the opposite direction, towards the centre of Antioch.

Though he was deep in thought, his subconscious was always alert for threat. So after a while a feeling formed, somewhere around the base of his skull, that he was being followed. Followed too by someone with some skill in surveillance without detection, since whenever he stopped to look at a market stall, or changed direction without warning, he couldn't spot his tail.

Who would want to monitor him or, worse, kill him? Was it one of Rufus' men? Surely he can't have learnt about Silus' change of loyalties already? Could Cassius Dio have given them away?

He fingered the hilt of his sword, loosened it in its sheath, then turned a sharp corner into a dark, deserted alley. He flattened his back against the wall nearest the corner and listened intently.

When his tail turned the corner, Silus reached out and grabbed the collar of his tunic, pulling hard to jerk him off balance. As the surprisingly bulky man jerked forward, Silus drew his sword, ready to place the tip against the surprised man's neck and start demanding answers.

Instead, the man, tall, muscular, wearing a long tunic and a scarf wrapped over his head, pirouetted away, allowing himself to check his forward momentum by bouncing off the far wall. Silus stepped forward, sword out. He would like to keep them alive for interrogation if he could, but he would prefer to prioritise his own safety, and if that meant skewering this possible assassin from back to front, then so be it. He drew back his weapon as the man turned.

'Silus, stop! It's me.'

Silus peered through the dim alley light, beneath the head scarf, into the unmistakeable face of Atius. He let the tip of his sword droop as he stared in disbelief.

'Saturn's poor balls,' said Silus. 'What the fuck are you doing here?'

'Good to see you too.'

Silus laughed and stepped forward to throw his arms around his friend, crushing him in a firm hug. When they broke apart, Atius said, 'Is there somewhere quiet we can go? I have some things to tell you. I don't know if you will like them.'

Silus was instantly on his guard. Much as he trusted Atius, he didn't know how things would turn out between them if they ended up on opposite sides.

'We definitely have some things to talk about,' said Silus. 'I'm not sure if you will like what I have to say, either. Come on, I know a tavern with a private backroom where we can catch up away from prying eyes.'

'Give me directions and I'll meet you there,' said Atius. 'It's probably best we aren't seen together.'

This alarmed Silus as much as anything, but he didn't argue. He told Atius where to find their rendezvous, then left him behind.

The tavern would not have been out of place on the streets of Rome, a low-fronted wall dotted with depressions containing large bowls full of soups and stews, benches and chairs outside, a small room inside, and another more private room out the back, useful as a meeting room though more commonly a convenient place for one of the serving slaves to take a customer for an intimate half an hour.

He sat on the stone bench with a cup of well-watered wine and waited for Atius to arrive. Uncomfortable scenarios ran through his overactive mind. Had Atius really meant to kill him, and when Silus had caught him out, thought up this ruse so he could corner him with reinforcements? Would Atius appear at all, or would some group of frumentarii burst in to arrest him?

He didn't have long to speculate. Atius entered, alone, a half-eaten sausage dripping oil in his hand. Silus breathed out his tension and gestured to a seat.

'Still not dead then,' noted Silus.

'Observant as ever,' said Atius.

'Well I spotted your amateurish attempt to tail me easily enough.'

Atius spread his hands in acknowledgement. He took a bite of his sausage and then said, with mouth half-full, 'So why did you think I might be dead?'

'Didn't you get the message? The warning?'

'The first indication I had that there was a problem was the assassin climbing through my bedroom window.'

Silus whistled. 'I'm sorry, friend. Oclatinius said he would get a message to you.'

'Never arrived.'

Silus shook his head. 'I'm sure Oclatinius would have done as he promised. The messenger must have been intercepted. I wonder if his organisation is as secure as he thinks.'

'So who sent the assassin?' asked Atius.

'Sempronius Rufus.'

'On Caracalla's orders?'

Silus nodded. Atius pursed his lips, then took a deep drink of his wine.

'Hold on, I don't understand,' said Atius suddenly. 'I know your feelings towards Caracalla are ambiguous, to say the least, but Oclatinius has always been staunchly loyal. Why was he trying to warn me about Caracalla's orders?'

Silus looked into his friend's eyes, wishing he could read his thoughts. But this was Atius. Even if they had disagreed, they could trust each other. Surely.

'Before I answer that, how are your feelings towards our Emperor now?'

'Well, seeing as he tried to kill me and the woman I am sleep... I mean, the woman I am guarding, then I would say that right now I'm pretty fed up with him.'

'Atius, some things have changed. I've changed. Oclatinius too.'

Atius sat back, eyes narrowed, waiting for Silus to go on.

'You weren't in Alexandria. You can't imagine how bad it was.'

Atius put a hand on Silus' forearm and squeezed reassuringly.

'You implied as much last time we met. And you also implied you were having doubts.'

'It's gone beyond that now. Atius, you know I trust you. You have saved my life countless times, as I have saved yours. We are more than brothers. But I have to ask you, what I am about to tell you, you must swear on your Christos not to reveal. Even if you don't like what you hear.'

'You shouldn't need to ask me that. But if it makes you happy, I swear by Christos and his mother Maria that I will not betray your confidence.'

'Thank you, Atius. I'm sorry.'

'These are strange times, friend. Don't be sorry.'

Silus reached out and grasped his friend's shoulder. Then he took a breath and blurted out his secret.

'Oclatinius and I are joining a conspiracy to assassinate the Emperor.'

There, it was said now. He couldn't take it back, pretend it was a joke. He had put his life in Atius' hands.

Atius went very still, so all that could be heard was the sound of their breathing, and the noises from the tavern beyond the door, and the street beyond that. A dog barked somewhere, a deep, booming sound, and a woman's voice yelled at it to shut up. Two men were singing out of tune. A couple of children let out a peal of high-pitched giggles. Then the big Arcanus walked out of the room.

–

Silus stared at the wall of the small, dark room, not knowing what to think. Was Atius going straight to Caracalla? Was he going to flee back to Soaemias? He couldn't believe he had misjudged him. He had always expected

Atius to be there for him. Had he asked too much of his best, his only friend?

Atius strode back in with a large cup of wine in his hands. He slumped down in his chair and drank deeply. Silus looked at him intently.

'Sorry. You took me by surprise with that comment. I really needed a drink. I take it you aren't joking?'

'What do you think?' replied Silus.

'I think,' said Atius, then paused and took a sip of his wine. 'I think I need to join you.'

Silus let out a long sigh of relief.

'You don't know what that means to me,' said Silus.

'I think I do. You see, I came to Antioch for your help. I'm in trouble, and I didn't know what to do. I thought you would have an answer for me, and you do. Admittedly, I didn't expect it to be that answer.'

They both chuckled, more from released tension than appreciation of any humour.

Atius shook his head. 'So. What's the plan?'

'Ah. Well, that is still a work in progress.'

'You've got nothing?'

'I wouldn't say nothing.'

Silus explained Oclatinius' suggestion they join the existing conspirators to strengthen the chance of success of both parties, and the deed that Silus had to commit to prove his credentials for admission into their circle.

'But the trouble is, we haven't figured out how. And the shadow moves around the sundial, whether or not we want it to hold still.' He outlined the difficulties that Oclatinius and he had enumerated earlier that day.

'Well, that's easy,' said Atius.

'It is?'

'Of course. I kill him.'

Silus thought for a moment. 'How would that help?'

'Well, you can't do it, because you would be suspected straight away. Even if you lured him somewhere with just the two of you, it would be difficult to ensure no one saw you together. Me, on the other hand. No one even knows I am in Antioch. I am supposed to be hiding, in fear of my life. So I kill him at a time when you have an alibi. All sorted.'

'But…' Silus worked through the ramifications. Could the solution really be that simple? And would it work? There would still be the problem of getting Athaulf alone, or at least in a known location at a known time when Atius could get the job done. But Silus thought he could probably engineer that. Would it matter if it wasn't Silus himself that killed him? He didn't think Cassius Dio had specified how Athaulf should die, just that it be done.

'Oclatinius can help with the details, make sure we haven't missed anything,' said Atius. 'But in principle, do you think it might work?'

Silus smiled. 'I'm glad to have you back.'

October 215 AD

The opportunity had still not arisen though a month had passed since his conversation with Atius. He kept in regular, discreet conversation with his friend, who was staying in the back room of a dingy tavern and not venturing out during the day. But he had not spotted an occasion that would be suitable for an attempt yet. And in the meantime, he had to work with Athaulf, all the time knowing he was planning his death. Although the tough, shaggy-haired, half-blind German was a stern boss, Silus had come to respect and even like him. He was loyal, honest, brave and a skilled fighter. He could also be witty and intelligent, and when, on a rare impulse, he insisted on buying Silus a drink after their shift guarding Caracalla finished that day, Silus found himself laughing and chatting, almost able to forget the fate he had planned for the Leones commander.

A few other Leones had joined them, including the taciturn giant, Maximinus Thrax. Silus wished it had been that big brute he had been tasked with ending. The two of them had never got along, and that didn't seem likely to change. Thrax resented Silus' position in the Arcani and preferential treatment in the Leones, while clearly believing himself superior in combat. Silus disliked Thrax personally, as well as hating the fact that he was intimidated by him physically, for all that he thought he could probably better Thrax in a fight. So they acknowledged each other when they had to and generally kept out of each other's way.

That didn't stop Thrax from goading Silus when he got the chance, however, and that night was no exception.

'How did you like Alexandria?' Thrax asked Silus.

'A beautiful city,' said Silus, dismissively.

'Not the city,' said Thrax. 'The people. The ones we killed.'

Silus' jaw clenched, and he forced himself to relax.

'It was unfortunate they gave Caracalla the cause to be punished.'

'Unfortunate? It was magnificent! We killed for days. Traitors and rioters and criminals. I slaughtered scores of them myself.'

Traitors, rioters and criminals, thought Silus. And old men, women and children.

'I didn't see you taking part in the killing, Silus,' said Thrax. 'Don't like getting your hands dirty? Worried a bit of blood might make you puke your guts up?'

Some of the other Leones laughed, and Silus looked down at the table, his hand tight on his cup so his knuckles whitened.

'You know that's not true,' said Athaulf. 'And besides our orders were to protect Caracalla, not carry out the massacre. That was the legions' and auxiliaries' job. I only let you off the leash, Thrax, because I know that if you don't satisfy your blood lust from time to time, you will roam the streets looking for babies to eat.'

The laughter turned on the giant now, and he flushed red.

'You imply I have no honour,' said Thrax, his voice low.

'Thrax,' said Athaulf warningly. 'You are drunk. Don't say anything you will regret.'

'You think just because I have Getae blood in my veins, that I will prey on innocents. No innocent ever died by my hand!' His voice was a roar, and he stood up and overturned the table, sending drinks and dice flying through the air. One of the Leones reached out a hand to restrain him, and Thrax shrugged him off, hurling him to one side. He took a step towards Athaulf. For a moment, Silus wondered if Thrax might do the deed for him and kill Athaulf without the need for any subterfuge. He was sure he could claim credit somehow.

Thrax aimed a roundhouse punch at Athaulf's head, and such was the power behind it, that firm impact would have clubbed Athaulf unconscious.

But this was Athaulf, and it was not for nothing that he had been chosen to be leader of the Leones. He ducked under the blow, and as Thrax was momentarily off balance, he punched Thrax in the throat.

And just like that the fight was over. Thrax went down on one knee, clutching his neck and gasping. The hoarse noise he made showed that Athaulf had not collapsed the windpipe – he must have drawn the force of his punch for he could easily have killed the giant that way if he wished. Athaulf gestured at two of the Leones. 'Take him back to the barracks.'

The two bodyguards groaned. They were not small men themselves but dragging the half-incapacitated giant home would be no easy task, and they had just settled themselves for a night's drinking. But they did as they were told without questioning, helping Thrax to his feet and carting him away.

And then there were just four of them, Silus, Athaulf, and two subdued-looking Leones.

'Come on, let's not let that idiot spoil our evening,' said Athaulf. 'The night is young, and we aren't on duty until noon. We can get properly drunk before we head home. Slave, more drinks.'

And then Silus realised, could there be a better time than this? Four drunk Leones staggering home together in the early hours of the morning. A random mugging. One man left dead.

But this had been a spontaneous party. He had had no chance to alert Atius. Well, nothing was without risk.

'I need a piss,' announced Silus, and got up, exaggerating the effect of the wine with a sway as he walked – in reality he had drunk little. The other three Leones didn't even look up, engrossed as they were in the game they had resumed after righting the table and finding the dice in separate corners of the tavern.

When he got outside, he leant against the wall with one hand and let out a stream of urine, while looking up and down the street. He spied what he was looking for, and when he was finished, went over to a street urchin, sitting in a shop doorway, dirty-faced and ragged clothed. He held out his hands reflexively but without much hope as Silus approached, his mournful eyes looking up at him. Silus reached into his purse and drew out a denarius.

'This is for you,' said Silus, 'if you do something for me.'

'Anything, master,' said the child, his eyes fixed on the coin that could feed him for a week.

'Do you know the tavern with the sign of the goat and wolf, in the south of the town?'

The boy nodded.

'Go there, find a man called Lucius,' – Lucius was the name Atius was going by – 'and tell him the name of this tavern, and how to get here. That's all. Can you do that?'

The boy nodded even more vigorously. Silus handed over the coin. He hoped the boy wouldn't take it and run. He thought not. It was a simple low risk task for the lad to perform, and if he did well, he might think there was a chance of more lucrative work for little output. The boy scurried away, and Silus made his way back to the tavern. He hoped the message to Atius was clear – this was the ambush point. No time given in the message meant now was the time. Hopefully Atius was in his room, not out drinking or fucking. But his friend seemed to have put that behind him, at least for now while he was on this mission. Maybe Soaemias was a good influence on him. That was a surprising thought.

Silus wandered into the tavern, sat down and picked up his drink.

The way back to the barracks led through windy unlit streets with insulae crowding in from each side. The four men sang drinking songs loudly enough to draw some shouts to shut up and go to bed, from behind shuttered windows. The other two Leones were completely inebriated, arms around each other's shoulders, still drinking from a jug of wine.

Silus and Athaulf walked behind them, talking inconsequentially and enjoying the good humour of their comrades. Silus thought the whole thing unreal. Could this really be about to happen? Maybe Atius wouldn't get the message. Maybe he wouldn't understand. Maybe he wouldn't find them.

But Atius was far from incompetent, and Silus, looking out for him, caught a glimpse of him following a score of yards behind.

What was his plan? He would have to make something up on the spot. And there were three Leones – no ordinary soldiers – against Atius' one Arcanus. Silus couldn't be seen to aid him either, and in fact would have to make it look like he had tried to stop him or apprehend him. He felt the familiar nervous feeling grow inside.

As the two leading Leones turned a corner, Atius approached swiftly from behind. He was quiet, but it was hard for a big man to be noiseless. Athaulf must have heard something, for he hesitated, cocking his head on one side. Atius was still too far away to strike. If Athaulf turned, the moment could be lost, and Atius would have to fight the four of them or flee with his mission unaccomplished and his target alerted.

Silus pretended to entangle his wine-addled feet, and stumbled sideways into Athaulf with some force, pushing him into the nearest wall.

'Steady there, Silus,' said Athaulf, catching him. Then suddenly he stiffened, let out a groan, and slid down the wall. Atius and Silus looked down into his face. The sudden loss of colour made Silus think that Atius' long knife stuck into Athaulf's back had made it all the way to his heart. Athaulf looked up from Silus to Atius, surprise, pain, shock all mingling. And at the last, the dying man seeing Atius and Silus there together, Silus thought maybe he understood Silus' betrayal. He hoped not.

He reached down and rested a hand on Athaulf's head for a moment, then yanked his coin purse from his belt.

'Take this,' hissed Silus. 'And run!'

He gave Atius a dozen yards head start before he started to yell.

'Murder! Help!'

The two Leones came blundering back round the corner and froze like statues when they saw Silus leaning over the body of their commander. For a moment, they were unable to comprehend. Then Silus pointed at Atius' fleeing figure.

'Don't let him get away.'

Silus joined the two men in the chase. But Leones were not built for speed, characteristics of strength and bulk being preferred in the selection process.

Unfortunately, Atius suffered from the same hindrance, and only slowly did he draw away from his pursuers. If this chase went on too long, others could get involved, patrolling soldiers, helpful civilians. Atius might be caught, or someone might see his face and give a description.

'Come on,' Silus urged the Leones. But they were already at the limits of their endurance, puffing and panting, not helped by the large quantities of wine in their bellies.

'We can't,' gasped one. 'Go on without us. Catch that bastard. For Athaulf.'

Silus nodded, and put his head down, pumping his arms and legs. The Leones gave up the chase, but the distance between Silus and Atius began to close, and the Leones could see that Silus was gaining on him. What was he supposed to do when he caught him? Damn it to Tartarus, Atius. Hurry up!

Atius turned a corner, out of sight of the other Imperial bodyguards, and Silus raced after him. Atius looked back, and when he saw only Silus behind him, he stopped and put his hands on his knees, breathing heavily. Silus caught him up, and rested one hand against a wall, taking deep gulps of air.

'Couldn't you run a bit faster?' complained Silus when he was able to speak again.

'I did my best. Have you been training?'

'Always. It looks like you have been putting on weight, living a life of luxury, though.'

'Cheeky bastard. Right, what now?'

'Hit me.'

'What?'

'Hurry up. The others will come soon. They will be expecting me to have you, or for you to have incapacitated me and escaped.'

'Right.' Atius drew back his fist.

'Not the...'

Atius' punch hit Silus square in the middle of his face, and Silus felt his already wonky nose break again. He slumped backward against the wall, hands clamped to his face as blood spurted between his fingers. The pain was excruciating. Atius peered over him.

'Not the what? Oh, the nose, right? Sorry about that.'

Silus mumbled vicious curses at him. 'Can't quite make that out, but you're right,' said Atius. 'I'd better be off. Get a cold flannel on that.'

Atius trotted off down the alleyway, and Silus lay back, letting the blood flow down his tunic, and feigned unconsciousness while he waited for the arrival of the other Leones.

Chapter VII

Athaulf's funeral was well attended. A large honour guard of Leones stood to attention as his body was carried in all solemnity to the bier. Caracalla was the chief mourner, and he wept openly at the loss of the man he had trusted with his personal safety. Silus stood at the front of guard, sweat dripping into his eyes, feeling profoundly sad at the loss of his leader, and profoundly guilty that he was the cause, even if it hadn't been him wielding the blade.

The funeral was a traditional Roman one, but with elements of Germanic ceremony added to pay respect to Athaulf's origins as well as the Empire he served. So as well as the usual offerings to the ancestors, the spirits of the underworld and the Roman pantheon, sacrifices were also made to Wotan and the goddess Hel, who ruled the German version of Hades. He lay on the funeral pyre with his sword on his chest, with an expression that Silus couldn't help read as thoroughly angry.

Caracalla gave a lengthy speech about what a loyal servant Athaulf was, what a fine man and what a warrior, and he continued to talk about loyalty and faithfulness. Silus bowed his head as he listened, hoping his face wasn't showing any signs of guilt.

Maximinus Thrax had taken over as temporary commander of the Leones, and he kept casting sideways glances at Silus, looking away when he gave him a challenging stare back. After the funeral, the council would advise Caracalla on a permanent replacement for Athaulf. Silus hoped to all the gods that Thrax wouldn't be confirmed in the role. They had never seen eye to eye, and not just in a physical sense, given the giant was more than a head taller than Silus. They hadn't taken to each other from the start, and now Thrax seemed to have some suspicion that Silus was involved in Athaulf's death. He couldn't really understand why, beyond Thrax not liking him, and wanting him to be a traitor.

After, there was a feast in the grounds of the palace. Silus attended as both mourner and bodyguard – he was after all still one of the Leones, and, apart from Thrax, no one thought Silus had anything to do with Athaulf's murder. It had in fact officially been put down to an opportunist mugger, although most people thought this unlikely, given how stupid the mugger would have to be to take on four Leones, when there were much easier pickings in the city.

Still, Silus' task, unpleasant as it was, was completed, and now he had to wait. His wait was shorter than he expected. Although technically on duty, Caracalla had allowed all but two of his Leones to take the food and fine wine and pay their respects to their fallen leader. Silus stood in a shady corner by a life-size marble statue of Diana, sipping from a cup containing no doubt some expensive vintage and failing to taste it at all. It was a sizeable gathering, with Imperial family, council members, senators and important local nobles. Silus was checking the position of the sun in the sky, wondering what time it was and when he could leave, when Cassius Dio wandered over, nibbling at delicacies from a silver plate. The senator bent over, pretending to examine Diana's bow. Silus tried not to look at him.

'They want to meet you,' said Dio under his breath.

Silus kept his face neutral as his heart raced. He said nothing.

'Tomorrow, dusk, the house of Bryaxis. Bring Oclatinius. Don't be followed.'

Dio straightened up and, without looking at Silus, wandered back to the party.

—

The house of Bryaxis was a nice-sized domus on the west of the city, with a shop either side of the main door, leading into the vestibule. Bryaxis, Oclatinius had told Silus, was a well-off merchant who claimed descent from a famous sculptor who had worked in Antioch several centuries previously. He had vacated his building for the night, lending it to whoever they were about to meet. Oclatinius had gone on ahead, thinking it was better if they arrived separately. But Silus, on an impulse, had decided to bring Atius. After all, Atius was the one who had killed Athaulf, so they would have no reason to distrust him.

An aged porter ushered Silus and Atius past the chained guard dog into the vestibule, and from there a slave led them through the beautifully painted atrium, lined with bronze and marble statuettes, and from there into the triclinium. The room was lit with numerous oil lamps, and the last of the evening sun was shining through the open windows that backed onto the peristylium.

Oclatinius was in place already, reclining on one of the couches. He raised a cup to salute Silus and Atius as he entered. Silus looked around at the others, who stared back at him with expressions of suspicion, anxiety and hope.

Ulpius Julianus.

Julianus Nestor.

And Macrinus.

Silus couldn't decide whether to be surprised. Or whether to be pleased.

At least these were heavyweights – quite literally in the cases of Ulpius Julianus who was short, broad and muscular, and Julianus Nestor who was spindly-limbed but with a voluminous pot-belly. If he had gone to all this effort just to join the ranks of a couple of minor senators or junior military officers, he thought he would have cried. Nestor and Julianus were the commanders of the frumentarii, the messengers and intelligence officers of the military. Macrinus was co-praetorian prefect with Oclatinius, and though they were both nominally under the command of the supreme praetorian prefects Theocritus and Epagathus, the titles for those men seemed to be purely honorary, something to give them authority while they roamed the Empire doing Caracalla's bidding. It was Oclatinius and Macrinus who actually commanded the praetorians. Having the leaders of the frumentarii, the praetorians and the Arcani allied seemed on the face of it a formidable threat.

But were these men capable of carrying through a conspiracy that resulted in the assassination of the Emperor? If they had been trying already, they hadn't had much success, although he had to concede they had come close. But then, much of what they had attempted so far had been planned by the late Festus, hadn't it?

'Take a couch, Silus,' said Macrinus. 'And your friend. Atius, isn't it?'

'At your service, prefect,' said Atius with a bow.

'Might I ask,' said Macrinus, 'why you brought an uninvited guest to our secret meeting? Are you under some misapprehension as to why we are all here?'

'Atius is the one who put the knife into Athaulf,' said Silus bluntly.

Macrinus looked at Atius with renewed interest. 'I see. Your reputation has you unswervingly loyal to Caracalla.'

'All loyalties have a breaking point,' said Atius. 'Mine was when the Emperor sent an assassin to kill me and the family I was protecting.'

'Yes,' said Macrinus. 'I was aware of that command to Sempronius Rufus. I presume your friends in the Arcani warned you?'

'Apparently they tried, but the messenger never arrived. I had to deal with the situation as it arose.'

Macrinus nodded, impressed, then frowned. He turned to Oclatinius.

'Why didn't your messenger get through? Is there a spy for Rufus within the Arcani?'

Oclatinius shook his head. 'In this murky world, nothing is impossible. But there are numerous ways Rufus could have found out about the messenger without the need for an Arcani traitor. An intercepted message, an overheard instruction, or it might even have just been bad luck on the road, a bandit or a fall.'

'You're usually too thorough for that sort of mistake, Oclatinius.'

'No one is perfect, Macrinus, and nothing is certain.'

Macrinus pursed his lips and didn't reply. Silus and Atius settled themselves onto couches, and Atius helped himself from a platter of delicacies left on the table – there were no slaves present.

Ulpius Julianus spoke up. 'Cassius Dio said you wanted to meet us.'

'Yes, where is he?' asked Silus.

Julianus Nestor laughed mirthlessly. 'He is nowhere to be seen when there is any danger involved. He hates Caracalla but fears him too. So a bit of behind the scenes message bearing is his limit. He won't be involved in any move against the Emperor. When Caracalla is dead, it will be another matter though. It will be fascinating to read his history when it reaches Caracalla's reign. I can't imagine he will have too much good to say.'

'Well, the rest of us are all here now,' said Atius. 'So tell us your plans, and how we can help.'

Macrinus, Nestor and Julianus exchanged glances.

'Our plans?' asked Macrinus, fiddling with one of his gold stud earrings.

'Your plans,' agreed Oclatinius. 'You know. The ones you have spent all these years cooking up to finish off our Emperor. I know you have had setbacks along the way, not least due to the actions of these two fine men here. But now they have changed sides and are no longer opposing you, but in fact assisting you, your plans should be much easier to set into motion. Just tell us what they are, and what you need us to do.'

None of the three conspirators spoke for a moment. Finally, Macrinus said, 'We… don't have any plans.'

'You what?' exploded Silus. 'Then what is the point of this meeting? Did we kill Athaulf, a good man, for nothing?'

'Athaulf needed to go,' said Julianus. 'He was too good at his job. We need him replaced with someone either incompetent, or even better, in debt to us. To have you kill him, Silus, was like – what was it Daedalus did to get the feathers for Icarus' wings? Hit two birds with one rock?'

'Your classical Greek education is impeccable as always, Julianus,' said Oclatinius. 'You have a replacement in mind?'

'Aelius Decius Triccianus.'

Silus knew the man well. He had come from poor origins, it being said that he had once been the doorkeeper for the legate of Pannonia but had worked his way up through the ranks to become the prefect of the Second Parthian legion. He had been co-opted into the Leones when part of the cavalry of the Second Parthians had been incorporated into the newly formed Imperial Bodyguard unit and would seem a reasonable choice to both the rank and file Leones and to the Emperor.

'Why him?' asked Oclatinius.

'Let's just say,' said Macrinus, 'that I have had the opportunity to have had a number of private conversations with him, and he is thirsty for advancement, and willing to be loyal to anyone who can aid him in his career path.'

Naked ambition, thought Silus. As common a reason as any for betrayal and backstabbing.

'I see. Well, having the commander of the Leones on board could certainly make all the difference. But that is far from having any strategy to be rid of Caracalla.'

'We thought you had a plan!' blurted out Nestor, earning himself rebuking glares from Macrinus and Julianus.

'Mithras help us all,' muttered Silus under his breath.

'Silus, this is a waste of time,' said Atius. 'We don't need these idiots. Let's go.'

'Stop,' said Oclatinius, holding up a hand, his authoritative voice brooking no argument. 'Maybe this is no bad thing. We have a blank wax tablet to start. We can come up with a brand-new scheme that avoids the mistakes of the past.'

'Mistakes?' bristled Julianus.

'If you failed, there was a mistake, even if it was only obvious with hindsight.'

Julianus grumbled and took a sip of wine.

'Is this genuine, Oclatinius?' asked Macrinus suspiciously. 'I mean, you did as we asked with Athaulf, but I know you. Maybe you thought that was a price worth paying to penetrate our circle.'

Silus' own mind was not entirely at ease on this matter.

'It's a fair point, and yes, if I was still siding with Caracalla, I would have been prepared to sacrifice Athaulf to get to you. But the fact is I am no longer with Caracalla. Nor is Silus. Nor is Atius.'

'Atius has given his reasons,' said Macrinus. 'What about you, Silus?'

'Plautilla, Titurius and his family, Cornificia, Helvius Pertinax, Papinianus. Need I go on?' Caracalla may have given the orders, Silus reflected, but the blood of all those he listed was on his own hands. Saying their names out loud seemed like reciting a curse, and he shuddered in sudden fear that their lemures were stirring in the underworld as they were called out.

'You don't mention Geta,' said Nestor.

'He was as bad as his brother,' said Silus. 'I don't feel any sorrow for his passing.'

Macrinus' jaw clenched at this, but he took a breath and relaxed.

'The murders you mention all happened some time ago,' continued Macrinus. 'Why did you stay loyal all that time, and why have you changed your mind now? If it's money or personal advancement, say. There is nothing wrong with that – in fact it is easier to understand and trust someone with base motives than noble ones.'

'It's not money,' said Silus contemptuously, 'and I have more responsibility than I ever desired.' He sighed, sipped his wine, and continued. 'I saw brutal massacres in Caledonia, but that was a war, against an enemy that had attacked Britannia province. I believed that war was justified, for the defence and glory of the Empire. Germania too, I thought was a just war, until the betrayal of the Alemanni. But Caracalla has always had a hold over me that meant I could not turn on him.'

'Ah yes, the girl Tituria,' said Macrinus.

Silus opened his eyes in surprise, and glanced at Oclatinius, wondering if he had already told the conspirators about his Achilles heel.

'No, it wasn't Oclatinius that let that little secret out. Festus long ago told us about your father-like feelings towards her, though we never worked out how to turn that to our advantage. Talking of protective feelings, why don't you and Atius explain a little more about what Soaemias and Avitus mean to you.'

Silus turned to Atius, but he was uncharacteristically shy, and just shrugged. Silus took that for assent to go on.

'Atius has formed something of a romantic attachment to the Empress' niece. Likely temporary, knowing my friend, but that isn't why he has joined us. He is on Caracalla's death list now, so has no reason for loyalty to the Emperor.'

'And you, Silus? When we aided Soaemias in her plan to split the Empire and put Avitus on the throne in Alexandria, you stopped us. You didn't know our names, or even Festus' involvement at that point, but you could have turned Soaemias and Avitus over to the harsh mercy of the Emperor.'

Silus looked down for a moment. Then he met Macrinus' curious gaze with a challenging stare of his own. 'I lost my family. I was the cause of Titurius losing most of his family. I couldn't do it again. Besides,' and he gave a half smile here, 'the lad is kind of endearing.'

'That's one word for him,' said Macrinus. 'But they are out of the way? They aren't going to stir up any trouble for us? What's with all this nonsense about Avitus being Caracalla's son?'

Silus didn't believe it was nonsense, but he said, 'They are in hiding, and will likely remain there until there is a new Emperor.'

Macrinus nodded. 'And you, Oclatinius? What are your motivations?'

'I simply do the best for the Empire,' he said. 'Given Caracalla's military prowess, for a long time I believed he should remain in power. The Alexandrian massacre and this obsession with Parthia and the potential for ruin if he fails have led me to change that view. But what about you three? Why have you tried for so long to bring him down, despite the risk to yourselves?'

Macrinus looked at his two colleagues, who gave him a nod of assent to speak on their behalf.

'I've had my doubts since the death of Plautianus,' he said. 'He was my friend and mentor. But I respected Septimius Severus, and I liked Geta. Once they were both dead, I feared for the future of Rome.

'We believe in the Empire,' he continued when no one interrupted. 'A strong Empire that rules the world, as it should. That keeps everyone in the place they belong. The Constitutio Antoniniana giving everyone in the Empire citizenship will be a disaster in the long run, even if it temporarily increases taxes, you mark my words. We need a strong Emperor, yes, but one who heeds the wisdom of his advisors and the Senate. And as you say, we need to end these foreign wars that are draining our treasury and bleeding the wealthy dry and strengthen our borders to protect what we already have.'

It wasn't the most stirring call to arms Silus had ever heard – join us so the rich can stay rich, the poor can stay poor, and everything can carry on just as it is. But the alternative was the increasingly murderous Caracalla remaining in power.

'Very well,' said Oclatinius. 'We know each other's motivations. We have some degree of cautious trust that we have the same goals. We don't have a plan, but we can work on that. Now you have the benefit of my wisdom and cunning to call on, I think a strategy will be forthcoming soon. But before that, I have one pressing question. A dead Emperor needs a replacement. He has no heir. Who will be the next Emperor?'

Macrinus blinked, looking surprised. 'I thought that was obvious,' he said. 'Me.'

–

The next day, Silus met Oclatinius at Atius' hideaway at the back of the tavern known throughout the quarter for its sign of a goat being dragged down by its hindquarters by a ferocious-looking grey wolf. Atius already had a round of wine cups and some snacks, and he greeted Silus the way a dog did whose owner has left the house and returned moments later for having forgotten something important, giving him an over-enthusiastic hug considering the short time that had elapsed since their last meeting.

'By sanctified Petri and Pauli, it's boring here,' he said. 'Care for a game of dice?'

'Maybe later,' said Silus. He waved a perfunctory greeting to Oclatinius who nodded back, then slumped down on a wooden stool, resting his back against the rough stone wall.

'So what do we all make of it?' he asked. It was the first occasion they had had a chance to talk in private since their meeting with the conspirators, although Silus had had plenty of time to try to think things through in the meantime. His conclusions hadn't been promising.

Atius shrugged noncommittally and looked to Oclatinius. The spymaster rubbed a tired hand over his face.

'It isn't exactly what I hoped for, I must confess,' he said.

'What were you hoping for?' asked Atius.

'Ideally, Sempronius Rufus and all his spies with a ready-made plan, and not much for us to do beyond cheer him on.'

'But Sempronius Rufus is loyal, you think?' asked Silus.

'Yes,' said Oclatinius. 'Before you arrived yesterday, I asked them about that Eugenios character I had you following in Alexandria. He was one of Rufus' men, but he had previously worked for Festus, and Ulpius Julianus had used that, and a considerable bribe, to turn him to their cause. But it was a clumsy attempt to stir up trouble, and hard to see what it would achieve. Which brings us to the main problem.'

'Which is?' asked Atius.

'These idiots are incompetent.'

Silus and Atius were silent for a moment, but they couldn't bring themselves to disagree.

'Festus was the intelligent one among them,' said Oclatinius when no one else spoke. 'And with him gone, they are like a ship without a rudder in a stiff breeze, panicking and going in circles.' Silus grimaced. He wondered if Oclatinius was going to suggest they abandon the whole enterprise.

'On a more positive note,' Oclatinius continued, 'between Julianus, Nestor, Macrinus and myself we have the commanders of the praetorians and the frumentarii in our group. That is quite formidable. But it is not enough on its own. Caracalla is too popular. We couldn't, for example, just command the praetorians to depose him. They would mutiny and hack us to pieces before we had finished giving the order.'

'So it's down to us,' said Silus. 'We need to work out a way to bring Caracalla down.'

'And please can it involve a sharp blade,' said Atius fervently. 'No collapsing ships, or inciting riots, or trying to get him to walk under a precariously dangling block of marble on a construction site.'

'I agree,' said Silus. 'The next attempt has to work and putting a knife through him is the only way to be sure.'

'That is death for anyone who attempts it, successfully or otherwise.'

Silus took a deep breath.

'I'll do it.'

The words hung in the air between them like a dark cloud.

'No,' said Atius. 'No way. I'll do it.'

'You can't get close to him like I can. You're already on a slate for assassination. It has to be me.'

'Or me,' said Oclatinius, and they both looked at him.

'I'm an old man, not a useless one. Silus, you have much more life ahead of you. I don't have many years left to lose.'

Silus shook his head. 'That won't work.'

Oclatinius raised an eyebrow. 'And why not?'

'Come on, you're the clever one. Think it through. Who takes over when Caracalla is dead?'

'Macrinus,' said Oclatinius. 'We have established that.'

'And who advises him?'

'Ulpius Julianus and Julianus Nestor,' said Oclatinius, starting to see what Silus was getting at.

'Is there anyone else with sufficient seniority who is trusted by Macrinus, who could help steer the Empire in the turbulent time following the murder of an Emperor?'

'No,' said Oclatinius heavily.

'So you would leave the Empire to be run by those three?'

Oclatinius' shoulders slumped. 'Gods of Olympus,' he muttered. 'You're right. I'm going to have to steady the ship, or it will surely founder.'

'Well,' said Silus. 'That settles it. It has to be me.'

The other two opened their mouths to disagree, but no words emerged. Silus nodded.

'I guess it just remains for me to look for an opportunity. It shouldn't take long, it will be easy enough if I'm not expecting to survive the attempt. I'll need you both to make sure Tituria is safe, though. Remember, there is a slave in her household called Juik who has orders to kill her should anything happen to Caracalla.'

'This isn't right,' said Atius. 'This isn't how we do things.'

Oclatinius was shaking his head. 'There must be a better way.'

'No one has found one yet, not Festus, not us.'

'At least let us bide our time. I know I said there was some urgency, that it must be done before he starts the Parthian war, but it is late in the year, there will be no campaign this side of spring, and he still has more preparations to make in the East, more diplomacy and trickery, so it might not even be next year. We may think of something else. Something may present itself. Or maybe he will die by another's hand, or by the hand of Fate.'

Silus frowned. He didn't like the thought of waiting, with his impending death hanging over him. He would much rather be done with it.

'Please,' said Atius. 'Silus, don't do anything unless we are sure it is the only way.'

Silus sighed. 'Fine. I'll wait. But no promises. If the perfect opportunity presents itself, I will take it.'

Atius looked beseechingly at Oclatinius, but the Arcani spymaster was stone-faced.

Silus took a big gulp of wine, swilled it round his mouth, then swallowed, feeling the warmth fill him. He sat back and looked at the other two, brimming with resolve.

—

The council was in sombre mood, Athaulf's funeral still fresh in everyone's mind. Caracalla's face, stony at the best of times, now looked like it had been hewn from pure granite. Beside his throne sat Domna, looking pale and somewhat thin, and behind them both and towering over them stood Maximinus Thrax, acting head of the Leones. The usual inner circle was present, Oclatinius and Macrinus, Julianus and Nestor and Sempronius Rufus, standing a little apart from the others. Suspicious eyes constantly darted left and right, buried in Rufus' plump, rounded eunuch face. Silus stood guard by the door together with another of the Leones called Skylurus, a tall, broad Scythian, although nowhere near Thrax's stature – but then, who was?

'We will be overwintering in Antioch,' Caracalla was saying in a tone that allowed no room for argument. 'Julia Domna will continue with her admirable task of civil administration of the city and such Imperial duties with which she will lighten my load. I will remain focused on the forthcoming campaign in Parthia. However, I have had word from Theocritus that Armenia is unsettled.'

Silus glanced at the faces in the room at the mention of the Supreme Prefect of the East. None of them apart from Caracalla and Domna were nobly born, but at least they had all worked their way up to their current positions, Oclatinius, for example, through the legions, Macrinus through his education and the law courts. Theocritus, however, owed his position to the fact that he was a favourite freedman of Caracalla, having taught him dancing and other physical arts, and that had been sufficient to have him promoted way beyond what many considered his ability. Nevertheless, Caracalla considered him loyal and had tasked him with gathering resources from the East for his campaign. Still, everyone's faces remained impassive at the mention of Theocritus' name. Anyone who graced Caracalla's court who had not learnt extreme tact and diplomacy was long dead, Helvius

Pertinax for one. So no one made any reference to Theocritus dancing around the East, for example, but all nodded gravely as Caracalla spoke.

'Armenia is our last obstacle before we can take on King Artabanus of Parthia. So at a later stage we will have a council of war with the military commanders present today and some of the senior legates to discuss strategies there.'

Macrinus failed to prevent an expression of discontent crossing his face, if only for a moment, since Oclatinius was, deservedly in Silus' opinion, the praetorian prefect responsible for military matters, while Macrinus with his training and experience was responsible for legal and judicial matters, and so tended to get left out of the nitty-gritty of strategy and tactics.

'But now, I wish to ask the council for their recommendations for a successor to noble Athaulf, cruelly slain while among his comrades.'

Silus felt the eyes of Thrax and Rufus on him, and he struggled to remain expressionless, though was unable to prevent a ruddy flush on his skin and a prickle of sweat on his brow.

'Maximinus Thrax here has most ably stood in as commander of the Leones, and few would doubt his physical ability to fight, nor his natural ability to lead, given his powerful presence. What say the council to appointing him on a permanent basis?'

Sempronius Rufus spoke first. 'There seems little need for discussion, Augustus. A man of undoubted loyalty and unsurpassed physique. Just think what impression you would make on barbarian kings, both allied and enemy, if you attended a parley with this man as the chief of your bodyguard. Not to mention the deterrent effect on any would-be assassins.'

Caracalla inclined his head and looked around at the others. For a moment, no one spoke.

'In that case...' said Caracalla, but Macrinus, who had been twisting one of his earrings between thumb and finger, interrupted.

'Forgive me, Augustus,' he said.

'What is it?' snapped Caracalla.

'I just wonder... I mean to say, no disrespect to the awe-inspiring man who guards your person at this moment. But, doesn't the leader of your guard need more than just long legs and big muscles?'

Caracalla looked sternly at him but gestured he should continue.

'Well, you have a whole bodyguard full of burly men. It's not the leader's job to be the strongest or the tallest or the ugliest.'

Silus had to fight down a smirk at this. Maximinus Thrax was certainly one ugly-looking bastard, and his face was slowly turning a violent shade of purple as Macrinus spoke.

'Shouldn't the head of the Leones have experience as a military leader, a proven ability to command, a steady, reliable, intelligent head on his shoulders?'

'You have someone in mind?' asked Caracalla.

'No, Augustus, I can't think of anyone immediately. Can anyone else?'

'How about Aelius Decius Triccianus?' suggested Ulpius Julianus, a little too quickly for Silus' liking.

'Triccianus?' Caracalla sought for a moment to place the name. 'The former prefect of the Second Parthica?'

'Yes, Augustus. A man of proven ability in battle, respected by his men, a born leader.'

Steady on, thought Silus, you are showing your hand a bit too clearly. And he wasn't sure if Caracalla would like the idea of appointing someone with leadership skills to high office. It didn't take too much to turn a good leader with ambition into a usurper. Caracalla seemed uncertain and addressed Oclatinius.

'What do you think, prefect?'

Oclatinius appeared to consider deeply, though Silus knew it was all for show.

'I am, of course, aware of Triccianus' career, and my sources have never given me any cause to doubt his absolute devotion to yourself, Augustus. He is well liked by his men, although not to the extent that they would idolise him before other loyalties. And he possesses excellent skills on horseback, too. Something else that would impress barbarian kings.'

'Rufus?' Caracalla prompted.

'I... know little of this Triccianus,' he said, looking like a schoolboy who had not learnt his Greek conjugations and was expecting a caning from his tutor. 'But I still think Thrax possesses every quality you need.'

Caracalla looked at Domna enquiringly, who gave a little nod. Silus didn't know if this meant she was agreeing with Oclatinius or Rufus, but Caracalla clearly understood the Empress in ways that only lovers did.

'It is decided. Triccianus will be the next commander of the Leones. Thrax, thank you for your excellent service. You do of course retain your rank and privileges as a Leones centurion. You are dismissed.'

Thrax, to his credit, merely blinked once, then bowed low and said, 'It is always an honour to serve, Imperator.'

And he made a slow, dignified exit from the room, not sparing Silus a sideways glance as he passed him. Silus couldn't help but feel relieved. Though he knew the conspirators wanted Triccianus in place for their own purposes, Silus had had no desire to serve under that brute of a man who clearly despised him.

'Julianus, summon Triccianus immediately. The rest of you may go.'

All bowed deeply, and left Caracalla alone with Domna.

Chapter VIII

Silus had drawn a late shift, and consequently had been standing on guard at the doorway to Caracalla's tablinum for what felt like half the night. Of course he had nothing by which to gauge the passing of time, except for the frequency with which the slaves topped up the oil in the numerous lamps that illuminated the office, and his increasing fatigue, which was dragging his eyelids downwards. Skylurus was his companion again – they seemed to be on the same shift pattern, but he hadn't really got to know the Scythian bodyguard. When they were on duty, they couldn't talk, and when they were off duty, Skylurus retreated to the barracks, preferring to keep himself to himself.

Despite the sword of Damocles hanging over him in the form of his determination to carry out a suicidal assassination attempt on the Emperor, his life had become very boring. Oclatinius was giving him no missions in the Arcani, except, as the old man put it, for this, the most important one of his entire existence. So his working life consisted of training with the Leones and long, seemingly endless spells of hanging around, ensuring the safety of an Emperor he wanted to see dead. Even his time off duty was tedious. Indulging in wine, women and fine dining held little attraction for him when he could only see his execution in the near future. Atius had returned to his hideaway in his village somewhere near Emesa. He was able to stay in touch with Oclatinius by an intermediary in the city of Emesa itself, but even Silus and the spymaster did not know the exact location where Atius had secreted away Soaemias and Avitus. Not because he didn't trust them, he hoped they understood, but he knew from experience that there was only so much bodily harm you could endure before you were prepared to tell your torturer absolutely anything.

So he hung around the Leones barracks, dicing with the other bodyguards, keeping fit, biding his time, and trying not to dwell too much on his fate. Although Oclatinius was still counselling patience, he hoped his opportunity to strike arose before he went completely mad.

Caracalla was muttering to himself while he pored over a large map which was unrolled on his desk, the corners weighted down appropriately enough by a set of statues depicting the four Venti, the gods of the winds, North, South, East and West. Silus had long since stopped trying to make sense of the words the Emperor was uttering, although some names and territories were repeated often enough that he got some idea what Caracalla was puzzling over.

Vologaesus was one name Silus recognised, formerly Emperor of Parthia. He had lost the throne to his brother Artabanus in a civil war, but still ruled in the neighbouring kingdom of Seleucia. Vologaesus, if Silus recalled correctly, had sued for peace before even meeting the Roman forces in battle, so impressed was he by the size of the army Caracalla had gathered.

Tiridates was another name, the former King of Armenia, whom Vologaesus had handed over to Caracalla as part of his peace proposals, and Khosrov, the son of Vologaesus and current King of Armenia, came up more than once. Armenia was a client kingdom of Rome, part of the Empire in all but name, but with the locals responsible for their own laws, taxation and defence. A nice deal for Rome, helping them keep their borders secure without committing too much manpower.

Everything Silus knew about the politics of the East came from conversations with Oclatinius, and he was certain he hadn't yet got the whole thing straight in his head. From a distance it looked like one big family feud, brother against brother, uncle against nephew.

It was no wonder Caracalla was concentrating so hard as he worked through his military and political options in the constantly shifting sands of desert diplomacy. Silus wished that there was no need for these underhand methods, that everything could be decided in a fair fight. But he knew that Rome's enemies outside its borders were so numerous and powerful that even the vast might of the Roman legions could not take them all on at once. He reflected also that much of his own work for the Arcani was underhand and treacherous, and, he had to concede, that made it all the more exciting.

Caracalla's finger traced a road to the edge of the map, then stopped.

'Where's Pontus?' he said. 'This useless piece of garbage doesn't have Pontus on it.'

Silus and Skylurus exchanged a glance, but said nothing, presuming Caracalla was not expecting a response.

'Well?' he demanded of the two guards.

'Um,' said Silus as Skylurus pressed his lips together tightly. 'I'm sorry about your map, Augustus.'

'Don't be sorry. Go and find one of the freedmen who looks after the library and tell him to fetch me a map that has Pontus on it.'

Silus looked at Skylurus and nodded to him.

'At once, Augustus,' said Skylurus, and hurried towards the door. Then he hesitated. 'What if he is asleep?'

Caracalla's thunderous expression was enough to send Skylurus fleeing. Caracalla returned to glaring at the map, marking out distances with his thumb as a measure, talking to himself.

'Two legions here, supported by auxiliaries. The Macedonian phalanx here to counter the Parthian horsemen. Osroene mounted archers, where to place them?'

And suddenly Silus realised he was alone with the Emperor. Silus, armed with a freshly sharpened gladius. Caracalla, unarmed and distracted. Would a better chance than this ever present itself?

His mouth became instantly dry, while his palms and forehead grew damp with sweat. His heart raced, seeming to beat higher in his chest than usual, and louder, so loud that he thought Caracalla must hear it pounding. He moved his hand slowly to the hilt of his sword, his motions slow so as not to attract attention.

Was he really going to do this? He couldn't quite believe the moment had come. That he was finally going to get a chance to finish off Caracalla, not for punishment for all the harms that the man had inflicted on individuals and entire nations, but to prevent him bringing more harm down on the world, those within and without the Empire's limits.

How long did he have until Skylurus returned? Some time, he figured. Skylurus would struggle to locate a librarian, who would then have to locate the required document. But he shouldn't dawdle. He took a tentative step towards Caracalla.

The Emperor didn't look up.

Another step.

He was maybe ten feet away now. When should he draw his sword? The instant he was in reach, and not a moment before. He took another step forward. Caracalla grunted, swivelled his head, surveyed the furthest part of the map. Silus froze, but Caracalla, deep in his internal deliberations, had not noticed his bodyguard had come nearer.

Would he survive this? It seemed unlikely. It would be obvious that Silus was the assassin, so his only chance would be to do the deed and flee for his life. But where in the world was remote enough, obscure enough, for the murderer of an Emperor to hide and live out his days? And that was assuming Caracalla didn't manage to cry for help before he died, so Silus would be hacked down before even getting a chance to run. Or even, might he fail to kill the Emperor at all? Caracalla was muscular, fit, well-trained. Silus, usually so self-confident of his own skills, marvelled at the self-doubt that made him think he might not be able to kill the unsuspecting, unarmed man before him.

He swallowed hard, took in a deep breath, let it out slowly, then took another step forward. He was nearly there. One more step, and he could strike. Slowly, inch by inch, praying to all the gods that it would not stick and make a noise, he slid his sword from its sheath.

The door flew open, the wood crashing back into the plasterwork. Silus whirled, drawn sword pointing towards the intruder. Sempronius Rufus stood there, framed in the doorway, red-faced and breathing hard. The eunuch's eyes, which had immediately sought the Emperor, now flicked to fix on the tip of Silus' blade. How had he known what was in Silus' mind? Was it some sort of magic, sorcery? What had given him away?

Silus gripped his sword, weighing up his options. Did he make a lunge for Caracalla, ignore Rufus and let him raise the alarm? Or dispatch Rufus, and then have to fight an angry and forewarned Caracalla?

As he hesitated, Caracalla's voice boomed out. 'Rufus! What is the meaning of this?'

'Augustus, I humbly beg your forgiveness for the interruption. But I have just received news that can't wait.'

'You didn't think to ask for entry?'

'There were no guards outside the door, Augustus, and I thought...'

'Silus,' said Caracalla, and his voice was low and dangerous. 'Why is your sword drawn?'

For a moment, Silus couldn't find his voice, and perhaps if that had remained the case, it would have meant the end for him. But then inspiration arrived, in the nick of time.

'I heard the footsteps outside, and the door thrown open unannounced,' he said, aware he was speaking too quickly but unable to slow down. 'My first instinct, and my foremost duty, is to protect you, Augustus. I thought he was an assassin, and if I hadn't recognised Sempronius Rufus as quickly as I did, I'm sorry to say he would be dead at your feet right now. There is no time to ask questions when your Imperial person might be in danger.'

Caracalla let out a dry chuckle. 'He's right, Rufus. That will teach you to be more cautious in future. That blade of his could be in your guts as we speak. He knows how to use it, you know.'

Rufus flushed and bowed his head.

'In any case, you can put it away now, Silus.'

Silus hesitated. Was there still a chance? A thrust to Rufus' chest, pull the blade, turn, slash to Caracalla's neck, finish him, run. It could be done.

The sound of hurrying footsteps from the hallway beyond the tablinum reached him. Skylurus, returning promptly with the librarian. The opportunity was lost.

Silus sheathed his blade, bowed to the Emperor and took up his post by the door.

Skylurus and the librarian entered moments later, the librarian still in his night clothes, but bearing a bundle of scrolls under one arm.

'Augustus, I have brought with me all the maps I could find of the region around Pontus, and anything that shows Cappadocia, Galatia, Armenia and Asia.'

'Yes, yes,' said Caracalla impatiently. 'Put them down on my desk and get out.'

The librarian did as he was told and hurried away.

'Now, Rufus, out with it. What was so urgent?'

'A messenger just arrived from Theocritus, Augustus. Armenia is in revolt.'

—

'It seems,' said Oclatinius, 'that Theocritus has gone a little beyond his orders.'

'How so?' asked Caracalla.

The others in the council meeting looked at Oclatinius with interest. Theocritus wasn't particularly popular among the rest of Caracalla's closest advisors, who disliked his, in their eyes, unjustified advancement. Hearing about him messing up was always going to be heartwarming for the others, Silus reflected as he stood at attention by the throne room entrance.

'My sources tell me that he made some demands for money, food and soldiers that King Khosrov found unacceptable. So Theocritus arrested him and put him in chains.'

Julianus and Nestor both quickly suppressed the smirks that crossed their faces on hearing about this stupidity. Domna pursed her lips, Macrinus shook his head, and Rufus looked down at his feet.

'I see,' said Caracalla, clearly struggling to keep his voice even. 'And what is the situation now?'

'Well, as you know, Augustus, we have had a kind of fudged agreement with Parthia over Armenia that dates back to the time of the Emperor Nero. We choose the Armenian king, so we can claim Armenia as a client kingdom. But we always choose someone from the Arsacid Royal House, which is also Parthian royalty, so they too can consider Armenia a satellite.'

'But Artabanus of Parthia appointed Khosrov when Valarash was killed on campaign with Theocritus, and he did it without my permission. That's a declaration of war, right there!'

'Indeed, Augustus, or at least a casus belli when you launch your campaign. But unfortunately that may have to be delayed until Armenia is pacified.'

'Give me numbers.'

'Well, Augustus, it is a little hard to be accurate. Armenian society has three layers, rather like our senatorial, equestrian and lower ranks. They have nobles, priests and commoners. The nobles are semi-independent and rule vast areas, so the king rules by consensus among the nobles. For that reason, Armenia is often little threat to Rome, since their internal squabbles keep them busy. But if something unifies them...'

'Like putting their king in chains...' put in Macrinus.

'For example, yes, then they can draw on vast reserves of manpower. Our estimates are that they are able to field a cavalry in the region of sixty thousand horses, plus more from client states and allies like the Alans, and maybe another sixty thousand infantry.'

Caracalla slammed his fist into the side of his throne.

'Curse them to Tartarus,' he growled. 'This means diverting even more resources to Armenia. This could set the Parthian campaign back by a year.'

'I'm sorry, Augustus,' said Oclatinius, though Silus doubted he meant it. A delay to the invasion of Parthia meant more time to prevent it completely, and to do away with Caracalla. Silus realised how pointless it would have been throwing his life away prematurely, when Fate had not yet finished rolling the dice.

'Well. What forces do we need to send to Theocritus?'

'To... Theocritus?' asked Macrinus in surprise.

'Yes. Theocritus is in charge in Armenia.'

'He is retaining his command?'

'Whyever not? He is a competent general, he is on the spot, and he knows the situation. Besides, this is his mess, he can clear it up.'

'Of course, Augustus,' said Macrinus.

'He has, what, five thousand men with him at the moment. Against a possible one hundred and twenty thousand. Fine, send him another fifty thousand legionaries, auxiliaries and cavalry. That should be plenty given most of their army consists of levied commoners. Ulpius

Julianus and Julianus Nestor, look through the lists and work out where we will draw those numbers from, then bring them to me for approval. No praetorians or Leones, though, and don't touch the Macedonian phalanx. They all stay with me.'

'Yes, Augustus,' the two frumentarii commanders chorused.

'Now, as for the Parthians, we will have to wait to engage them head-to-head. But you all know my ways by now. Wars are not just won on the battlefield. I have made a decision. I am going to marry the Emperor of Parthia's daughter.'

The silence around the room was so profound Silus could hear his blood pumping in his own ears. Mouths dropped, eyebrows raised. Even Oclatinius, usually so accomplished in his imperturbability, could not keep the surprise from his face.

Julia Domna stood.

'Excuse me, Augustus, I feel a little unwell. The heat, you understand…'

'Of course, Augusta,' said Caracalla, standing and taking her hand. 'I'll accompany you.'

'No, no, my maids will take care of me. You continue your meeting.'

As she swept out of the room, past where Silus still stood stiffly on guard, he could see her eyes glistening with tears.

'And if Artabanus agrees? What then?'

The man speaking was Marcius Agrippa, a broad, shaggy-bearded man with the slightest hint of a Gallic lilt, despite his careful, formal Latin pronunciation. Oclatinius had made sure Silus knew all about the latest addition to the conspiracy, prior to this meeting in the house of Cassius Dio (who was of course absent, on very important business elsewhere in Antioch). Also present in Dio's triclinium, some lounging nonchalantly, some sitting upright with hands clasped and brows furrowed, were Macrinus, Nestor, Julianus, Oclatinius and the new head of the Leones, Triccianus.

Marcius Agrippa, according to Oclatinius, was a fascinating man, but Silus wasn't sure how thrilled he was to welcome him into their ranks. The more people that knew a secret, the more chance it had to leak out, with disastrous consequences for them all. Still, his background intrigued Silus. Born a slave, he served in Gaul as a beautician of all things. Somehow, he was granted his freedom. Oclatinius suspected that he had been able to blackmail his master somehow, since he was unlikely to have been able to afford to save up enough money to purchase his liberty – beauticians were skilled and hence valuable slaves.

For most slaves, emancipation and a new life as a freedman would be enough, but Agrippa was more ambitious than that. He pretended to be far richer than was the case and claimed to be a member of the equestrian rank. With this, he was able to obtain a job as fiscal advocate in the treasury. When his deceit was discovered – someone who had known him as a slave recognised him and reported him – the then Emperor Septimius Severus had ordered him exiled to a remote island off the Greek mainland. Caracalla must have seen something he liked in the man though, since when he became Emperor, he had recalled Agrippa, declared him ingenuitas, giving him the rights of a man born free, and promoted him to the

Senate. His current role, like his near namesake at the battle of Actium, was commander of the fleet.

Silus wondered if they were wise to have a man of his character among them, but perhaps his abilities in the fields of treachery and subterfuge would be useful. Macrinus, who had invited him into the conspiracy, clearly believed so, not that Silus thought much of Macrinus' judgement. It was Macrinus who now replied to Agrippa.

'It changes nothing. We move ahead.'

'It changes everything,' said Triccianus. 'If Caracalla is married to the Emperor of Parthia's daughter, and we... you know, murder him, then we will be at war with Parthia – the very thing we are trying to avoid.'

'We can defeat Parthia, should it come to that,' said Macrinus.

Triccianus and Agrippa exchanged glances.

'You are so sure of your military leadership that you are confident you can defeat the Parthians?' asked Agrippa. 'Despite the fact that we fear Caracalla will lose against them, an Emperor who, for all his faults, is an excellent strategist?'

Macrinus opened his mouth to protest, and hesitated. Silus saw his dilemma. If he dismissed the Parthian threat as trivial, then the need to be rid of Caracalla was greatly diminished. But if he accentuated the danger from Parthia, then Triccianus' point of provoking their eastern rivals was valid.

Macrinus folded his arms, maybe trying to look decisive, although Silus just thought it made him look defensive. 'Then he must die before the wedding,' he pronounced.

And then everyone in the room turned to look at Silus.

Chapter IX

The gecko clung to the vertical wall in the palace gardens, absorbing the early morning rays of the sun, heating itself to be ready for the day's work. Silus stopped his pacing to watch it for a moment. He too felt the sun on his back and tried to enjoy the warmth. But the overwhelming sense of doom weighing him down made it difficult to take pleasure in anything.

As the only member of the conspiracy with both the skillset and potential opportunity, it had fallen to him to be the designated assassin of the group. There had never been any question of anyone else attempting the task, nor was there any discussion on Silus' chances of survival. For all that he was at the heart of the group, and possibly its most vital component, he was clearly considered expendable. Not even Oclatinius had talked to him about an escape plan after the deed. He thought maybe his mentor was too embarrassed to bring the subject up, knowing that it was futile, and that Silus would know that any attempt at reassurance about his survival chances would be patronising at best, insulting at worst.

A small black fly buzzed too close to the lizard. It flicked its tongue out almost too fast for Silus to follow and the fly was gone. Silus wished his task was so easy.

Or indeed, any killing. Simple. Instant. No time for the victim to feel pain or fear, no time for the killer to think. And no remorse afterwards.

But no, he didn't really think killing should be like that. He had done so much of it. It should never be easy, and there should always be remorse. He would even feel sorry for killing Caracalla. For all the evil he had done, he was still a human, with feelings and emotions, virtues as well as flaws. Mark Antony famously praised Caesar at his funeral, though his actions in the Gallic and civil wars had led directly to the deaths of uncountable hundreds of thousands, barbarians and Romans, all sacrificed on the altar of his pride and ambition. Was Caracalla any worse than the first Augustus, who had ordered the proscription and slaughter of hundreds of innocent noblemen for financial gain, or Trajan, who had overseen the death of a reputed eleven thousand in a three-month orgy of killing in the Flavian amphitheatre to celebrate his victories? For that matter, how would Silus' heart weigh against the Feather of Truth on the scales of Osiris if he ended up in the Egyptian afterlife? Would he be accepted into Atius' god's heaven? He doubted the good he had done outweighed the bad. Maybe the best he could hope for was oblivion, the fate that some of the philosophers believed awaited everyone, virtuous or wicked.

Suddenly, with tears pricking his eyes, he wished with all his soul that he was in his hovel in northern Britannia with his wife and daughter. That he had never killed that damned barbarian chief and set his life on this unalterable course of loss, suffering and fear. He wished that somebody, anybody else, was standing in these sandals of his. Then he felt shame for his cowardice.

He remembered a story Atius had told him from the life of the Christos he revered. The Christos was supposedly the son of a god, and when he knew he was to die in some sort of human sacrifice ritual – Silus hadn't been fully paying attention so was a little hazy on the details – he had prayed to his father to spare him his fate. If the son of a god could have such doubts, maybe he was being too harsh on himself for feeling the same.

A touch on his shoulder jerked him out of his morbid reverie, surprising him so he let out a yelp. He whirled, hand instinctively seeking the hilt of his sword.

Julia Domna's kindly eyes looked into his.

'Apologies, Silus. I didn't mean to startle you.'

'Augusta,' said Silus, taking his hand hastily away from his weapon and bowing his head.

'You appeared to be in a reverie.'

'I just finished a night duty on guard, Augusta. I'm tired, and I thought I would walk in the gardens before I took myself to bed. I got lost in my thoughts.'

'May I ask what their subject was?'

Silus flushed, hoping she couldn't see into his mind and read the plots and plans regarding her stepson and lover that were written there.

'Life and fate, Augusta,' he said with what he hoped was sufficient vagueness.

'Much the same that consumes my own deliberations,' said Domna. 'I'm sorry, I am being intrusive. Will you walk with me? An arm to support me is welcome these days.'

'Of course, Augusta.'

He offered his arm, and she took him by the elbow. They walked together along the gravel path between the topiaried hedges, punctuated with ornate fountains and bronze sculptures and lined with beds of colourful flowers with delicate scents – roses, lilies, geraniums, violets, daisies and buttercups.

'What do you think of my stepson?' asked Domna.

Silus turned to stare at her, before remembering himself and setting his eyes back on the path ahead.

'The Emperor is a great man, strong, brave, intelligent…'

'Don't worry,' she said with a light laugh. 'I'm not going to report back to him. I'm sick, Silus. You are one of the few people in the world who know that. Only you, Antoninus, a small number of my personal slaves, a couple of Greek physicians like Galen, oh, and a host of mystical healers that Antoninus has sought out on my behalf.'

'It must be very difficult for you,' said Silus, not really knowing how he should respond.

'Sometimes there is pain. Sometimes I lose my desire, for food, and other things.'

Oh, no. She wasn't going there, was she? Silus kept his eyes fixed on the gravel.

'Antoninus no longer desires me either. Maybe it's my illness, or just my age. Or maybe he fears to hurt me. But there is more distance between us now than ever before. That distance does give me perspective. I see him more clearly, I believe. It's why I ask for your opinion of him.'

Silus shook his head.

'All great men do bad things,' he said as diplomatically as possible. 'I don't believe it is possible to become great without doing some evil.'

'He killed my son,' said Domna. 'His own half-brother. And I forgave him, because Geta was trying to do the same to him. He had no choice. And also I forgave him because I loved him.'

Past tense noted Silus. For a moment he had a crazy idea, that Macrinus had somehow induced Domna to join the conspiracy against Caracalla. He dismissed it immediately, it was nonsense. Still, here was Domna now, complaining to him about the Emperor. Maybe she suspected that he too was dissatisfied with Caracalla's rule.

'I have served Caracalla through good and bad,' said Silus carefully. 'Through brilliant victories in Caledonia and Germania.' He took a deep breath and ploughed on, 'And through shameful betrayals and massacres of the Alemanni and the Alexandrians.'

Domna didn't seem taken aback, but just nodded silently. 'He has always had it in him, I think, to behave that way. His father was able to keep it in check. But after Geta's death, and even more when I became ill, he has just become more... angry. And sad.

'I'm not making excuses for him. I just think I am the one who is closest to understanding him. And even I do not know him, sometimes.'

She stopped to sniff at a rose and Silus paused his walk, waiting dutifully for her, and waiting too for this excruciating conversation to end. But Domna was not finished.

'Is she very pretty, do you think?'

'Who, Augusta?'

'This daughter of Artabanus that Antoninus plans to marry.'

'Ziyanak, Augusta. I don't know. I have never seen her, or even her picture.'

'She is young I suppose.'

'Far from a child, Augusta, but not yet thirty years of age I believe.'

'I have seen fifty-six winters now. I don't think I will see many more.'

'Come now, Augusta…'

'I mean it. The physicians have offered to cut my tumour out, burn it with caustic substances, apply poisons to it. But they don't believe it would help. They say it would cause a lot of pain, and then it would come straight back. So I just wait for it to take its course. As I wait to see what fate has in store for Antoninus.'

Again, Silus wondered if she was referring obliquely to his plans for the Emperor. Surely he was being paranoid. But Domna was exceptionally intelligent. And well-informed.

'It's just diplomacy,' said Silus, bringing the subject back to safer ground, the forthcoming nuptials of the Emperor. It had taken some persuasion on Caracalla's part to persuade Artabanus that the offer was genuine. The Parthian King of Kings' first response had been to humbly submit that a barbarian bride was not suitable for a Roman Emperor. Caracalla had dismissed this as nonsense, praised the great Parthian civilisation, pointed out that with the Roman infantry and the Parthian cavalry they could rule the entire world, promised an alliance against Artabanus' rebellious brother Vologaesus, and thrown in some generous gifts for good measure. Artabanus had finally agreed, the alliance against Vologaesus probably being the deciding factor, and consequently, Caracalla, accompanied in great pomp by the Senate and his military, was due to leave Antioch the next day, and progress to meet Artabanus near his capital at Arbela in Parthia.

Silus was still looking for his opportunity, hoping against hope something would present itself that did not involve him throwing away his life. He prayed he would get his chance when they were travelling. But in the worst case, he would do the deed right before the wedding, and take the consequences.

Domna was, of course, being left behind in Antioch. Even if very few knew the truth of her relationship with her stepson, there were enough rumours to make her presence at the wedding uncomfortable for all. She was being left in charge of civilian administration in Antioch, as when Caracalla had gone to Alexandria, and she excelled at this.

Silus wondered what would become of her when Caracalla was dead. He was fond of the Empress and wished her no harm. But he had a bigger duty, to Rome and its people. Despite his fears, his doubts, his resolve had not altered in any material way. Caracalla still had to die.

'I'm quite fatigued,' said Domna. 'Will you escort me back inside?'

She did indeed look a little weak. Making sure to support her surprisingly slight weight, Silus accompanied the Empress back into the palace, and handed her over to the care of her maids, who fussed around her, and scolded Silus for tiring her. He bowed and made his exit, feeling exhaustion creeping up on him as well, and he made his way to the barracks, and to a sleep filled with vivid nightmares.

—

The differences between an army marching to war, and an army marching to accompany its Emperor in a ceremonial role such as a triumph were subtle, but obvious if you had fought in earnest before. It mainly came down to polish. Legionaries that expected to fight spent their free time polishing and sharpening their weapons. Taking the whetstone to the spatha blade, checking the heads of the javelins, that their shafts were true. They spent time too patching holes in shoes, making sure that endless hours of marching would not leave them crippled when it came to the battle.

Legionaries that expected to be on display spent more time polishing the boss of their shields, their helmets, their chestplates, so they gleamed as if fresh from the armourer. Boots were attended to as well – there would still be plenty of marching involved en route to the ceremony, but they also made sure their boots shone like a fine lady's bronze mirror.

As Silus rode behind Caracalla, he noted the polish, the exceptionally fine presentation of the legionaries and their officers, the auxiliaries, their servants and mounts and beasts of burden. Even the Leones had smartened up for the occasion, shaggy barbarian hairstyles combed or tied back, beards untangled, undertunics washed for the first time in months.

And yet, these men had not neglected their arms. Just as much attention had been paid to their swords and spears as their belt buckles and the feathers in their helmets. Silus had seen the centurions in the evenings walking around the barracks in the marching camps, admonishing the men not to forget that they were soldiers first and foremost, and no soldier marched into enemy territory unprepared. He shouldn't be surprised, he supposed. Caracalla was nothing if not thorough, and it was a rare day that would see the Emperor taken by surprise by anything. They were after all going to be deep in Parthia, and Parthian treachery was not unknown to Rome. Crassus himself had been murdered by the Parthian general Surena after being lured to a peace conference after the disaster at Carrhae.

Caracalla would never allow himself to be caught out that way, especially since that sort of a betrayal was a favoured tactic of his own.

Caracalla rode his finest grey stallion at the head of the procession. Silus had wondered if he would have preferred an elephant, a suitably eastern mount, but he had Aureus, his now fully grown lion, complete with impressive mane, padding along beside him. Caracalla's horses had been trained not to take fright at the predator, as had all the horses of the Leones. Elephants were harder to acclimatise to lions despite their greater size, since they came from the same geographical areas, Silus supposed.

Still, even without an elephant, Caracalla at the head of his army was a sight to inspire awe surely even in a King of Kings. Artabanus was lucky Caracalla was coming in peace, not war.

The journey would take around two months. An army on campaign could move faster, maybe twice or three times the speed, but were limited by the pace of the baggage train, the oxen pulling carts laden with weapons, food and animal fodder. So Silus had plenty of time to make a move against Caracalla. Plenty of time but no opportunity. Several Leones were in close attendance on the Emperor at all times. He could still think of no better plan than to strike him down when they reached their destination and accept the consequences.

They had passed near to the city of Carrhae, the approximate halfway point of their journey, around ten days previously but had avoided the old battlefield. It would not have done for the superstitious soldiers to march over the sand-covered bones of their forefathers, and it would have been a poor omen for the upcoming nuptials, to visit the site of Rome's greatest defeat in the

East. Each day brought Silus, and Caracalla, nearer to their intertwined fate at the Parthian capital.

Off duty that evening, Silus strolled inside the perimeter of the marching camp, nodding to the sentries who came to attention as he passed. Sleep was becoming harder to find, and when he did manage to doze, he often jerked awake in a cold sweat, images of violence and doom receding with his somnolence.

A figure stepped out from the shadow of the palisade in front of him and he started, momentarily alert for threat until he recognised the old man.

'The stars are bright tonight,' said Oclatinius, nodding to the dark sky. Silus glanced upwards and shrugged. He cared as little for the stars as they cared for him. 'Don't let me interrupt your walk.'

Silus continued on his way and Oclatinius fell in beside him, matching his step as if they were soldiers on a very slow march.

'You were just out to take the evening air as well?' asked Silus.

'Of course not,' said Oclatinius. He never did anything just for the sake of it, every action had a purpose.

'Then I guess you have something to talk to me about.'

Oclatinius looked hard at Silus for a moment, but Silus didn't return the look, just keeping his eyes fixed straight ahead.

'You've given up, haven't you?'

Silus pursed his lips but didn't reply. Oclatinius continued anyway.

'You can't see a way out, so you are resigned to throwing your life away in order to complete your task.'

'It's what everyone wants of me, isn't it? It's what I am good for. The sacrifice that will renew the Empire.'

'Snap out of it,' said Oclatinius. 'This maudlin demeanour doesn't suit you.'

'What do you want?'

'Listen, I don't want you to make your move yet. There's something wrong, but I can't work out what.'

'What are you talking about?'

Oclatinius shook his head. 'This wedding, this whole diplomatic approach. It's not Caracalla's style. But it's more than that. Subtle things seem out of place, but I can't really put my finger on it. I'm not a great believer in intuition, but there is an itch at the back of my head that I can't scratch.'

'Well I doubt there are any lice living on your bald pate.'

Oclatinius ignored him. 'And I'm sure Sempronius Rufus is holding out on me. When I challenged him, told him to make sure he keeps me fully informed, he just smiled enigmatically and said, "Of course, just as you do for me".'

It was a fair point, thought Silus. Oclatinius was hardly generous with his secrets. But he didn't see what any of this had to do with him, and he said so. A pair of sentries, patrolling in the opposite direction, approached. One held up a torch to peer at their faces, then saluted, and they marched on. When they were out of earshot, Oclatinius said, 'Just keep your sword sheathed for now. Of course, if the opportunity arises to complete your mission without undue risk to yourself, do it. Otherwise, do nothing, until the last possible moment.'

'When is the last possible moment?' asked Silus.

'When Caracalla is about to make his vows.'

Oclatinius had given Silus a sliver of hope, and his mood lifted enough to enable him to eat and sleep better. But as the days passed, and they neared the city of Arbela, he saw his chances fading again. He managed to meet Oclatinius alone on several more occasions, on walks, in a small temple they had passed, even sitting next to each other on the toilet at one point. But Oclatinius had found out nothing knew, for all his protestations that he was squeezing every source he knew. Sempronius Rufus wouldn't admit that there was even anything amiss, let alone tell Oclatinius what it was.

Silus had also pressed Oclatinius to tell him how he was going to care for Tituria when both Caracalla and Silus were dead. Oclatinius informed him that there were plans in place to protect her, but he wasn't reassured. He had asked Oclatinius to dispose of Juik, the assassin slave planted to kill Tituria if anything happened to Caracalla, but Oclatinius had said that would be foolhardy as the assassin would be replaced by someone else unknown, and therefore harder to stop. Silus then wondered if they should move Tituria into hiding, but Oclatinius grew impatient, telling Silus that any moves to protect Tituria would alert Caracalla that Silus believed the Emperor was in danger. Silus had sulkily agreed, though every fibre in his body screamed at him to flee, run to Rome, take Tituria to a village in northern Britannia and live out their lives as humble sheep farmers, in peace if not in prosperity.

And then time ran out.

They had camped for the night within an hour's journey of Arbela, and Silus disconsolately accompanied Caracalla as he strode around the grid-pattern streets of the encampment, looking in on his men. There was a buzz around the camp, excitement at the prospect of the ceremony and what it would mean for the soldiers' beloved Emperor, and the Empire itself, for Caracalla to be married into the powerful Parthian royal family. Excitement, too, at the entertainment that was being lavishly prepared by both parties – gladiatorial games, wild beast hunts, feasting. Something more too, just a feeling. An expectation of some sort, maybe? Silus couldn't put his finger on it.

Caracalla, accompanied by Thrax and Silus, paused at a brazier where a contubernium of eight legionaries were sitting, just outside their communal tent. Two were polishing their armour, one was sliding a whetstone along the edge of his sword, then holding the weapon out before him so he could check its edge for nicks or dents. The rest were playing knucklebones for a small pile of copper coins and eating stew out of their bronze mess bowls.

'It should be a fine day for a wedding tomorrow, shouldn't it, lads?' said Caracalla, his deep, gruff voice managing to be both authoritative and familiar.

The soldiers all jumped to attention as they caught sight of him, but he motioned to them to be seated, and sat down with them. Thrax remained standing, his powerful presence a warning to the men that they should still treat their Emperor with all due respect. Silus was weary and wanted to sink to the floor next to Caracalla, but that would be a liberty too far. Besides, despite the imminence of his own death, he was feeling tremendous guilt about his impending treachery to this man he had served, more or less loyally, for so long.

'Well, aren't you going to share your pottage with a hungry man?'

One of the legionaries hurriedly refilled his bowl with a ladle and passed it to Caracalla. Caracalla took a large spoonful, blew on it, and swallowed it down.

'Not bad. Were any of you with me in Caledonia?'

Two of the men hesitantly raised their hands.

'Do you remember that mutton the quartermasters got for us then? Tough as caligae that had marched a thousand miles, and about as much flavour.'

The legionaries grinned. One of the older ones, looking like he was nearing the end of his twenty-five-year term of service, said bravely, 'Your father used to say an army hungry for food was hungry for battle.'

The others paused, watching Caracalla closely to see how he would take this.

'My father was a great general, but on this I'm inclined to disagree. You need a full belly for a hard day's fighting.'

'But there will be no fighting for us tomorrow, will there, Augustus?' said another soldier. 'Just a day of feasting and celebration.'

Silus' own belly clenched at the thought of the next day. Damn Caracalla, why was he making himself likeable, now of all times? His overactive imagination ran through how he thought the day would pan out. A sleepless night. A morning of absolute panic. The futile hope that something would happen that would mean he wouldn't have to go through with it. Waiting outside Caracalla's tent for him to emerge. Then the fatal moment, the knife thrust, the look of pain and betrayal in Caracalla's eyes. And finally, the vengeful swords of his comrades, hacking into his own body. He shuddered.

'And hopefully the Parthians put on a better spread than our cooks, eh lads?'

The soldiers laughed and one put on a show of eating his stew as if it was a great delicacy, which drew more chuckles.

'Well, I had better be on my way, brothers. I need a good sleep before a heavy day of partying.'

'And then a heavy night of—' one of the bolder soldiers began to say, then broke off abruptly, scared he had gone too far.

Caracalla fixed the soldier with a stare that made him quail. But then he said, 'Don't worry, I'll give her one for you.'

They all gave an overly hearty laugh, relieved that the brave joke hadn't landed them in hot water. Caracalla rose, knees creaking audibly as he stood.

'Just hitting forty years of age, and my joints sound like an old man's already,' he commented. 'That's what you get for hanging out with you lads on the training grounds and battlefields instead of spending my days reclining and feasting like some of my predecessors.'

The soldiers laughed and made some polite comments about Caracalla's fitness and physique.

'Enjoy tomorrow, men,' said Caracalla. 'It is going to be a memorable day.'

And with that he wandered on, Thrax and Silus in tow, looking for another contubernium to chat with as if he was a low-ranking soldier like them.

Chapter X

As he had expected, Silus had slept little the night before. He had gone off duty when Caracalla retired, but had lain on his back, listening to the snoring of his fellow Leones, his guts clenched and his breathing tight. Now he stood, bleary-eyed, back on duty outside Caracalla's tent. His sword was loose in its sheath, ready to be drawn in one smooth motion, to aid him in performing the last act of his eventful life.

He looked to the east, where the sun was just casting its first beams between the low hills on the horizon, illuminating stripes of the plain on which they were camped. He supposed it was beautiful, but it was impossible to find beauty in anything that morning. When was the last time he had even felt relaxed, at peace? He couldn't remember. There was no joy any more. No happiness, no contentment. All that remained was duty.

Skylurus stood the other side of the tent flap. He scratched an insect bite on the back of his neck, looked across at Silus and gave him a nod. Silus nodded back, then returned to staring into the distance. Not long now.

Low voices came from within the tent, too quiet for Silus to hear. Caracalla had not yet emerged that morning. Presumably his attendant slaves had already begun making him ready for the wedding, combing and trimming his hair, oiling him down and scraping him clean with a

strigil, perfuming him, dressing him in his finest cere-
monial uniform. But, to Silus' surprise, he had also
summoned his council to his tent. One by one they had
trickled in, in various states of preparation, some wearing
only half their uniforms, some clearly unwashed and only
recently roused from their beds. Sempronius Rufus was
first, with Oclatinius soon after. Then came Macrinus,
Ulpius Julianus, Julianus Nestor and Aelius Decius Triccianus, as well as the legates of the First, Second and Third
Parthican legions and the Second Adiutrix. Presumably
Caracalla was going through the arrangements for the day
with them, where their units were to be stationed, when
they would be expected to parade, some comments about
expecting a certain standard of behaviour from the men
in front of their new allies.

Silus wondered what sort of world it would become,
if he allowed Caracalla to live, to marry this princess and
forge an alliance with the only Empire to rival Rome's in
the four hundred years that had elapsed since the Punic
wars. Well, no one would ever find out. He itched to put
his hand on the hilt of his sword, to feel the comforting
solidity of its grip against his palm. With an effort he
let his arm hang loose at his side, trying to give the
outward appearance that he was calm and relaxed, though
he noticed Skylurus give him an occasional puzzled sideways glance.

He heard some voices raised from within the tent,
which surprised Silus a little. What could they be arguing
about, the type of flowers on display, or the vintage of
the wine on offer? More likely it was some jockeying for
position in the ceremony, a dispute over rank. He couldn't
see Oclatinius indulging in that sort of nonsense, so more

likely it came from the legates, though Silus doubted Caracalla would tolerate the argument for long.

As predicted, Caracalla's voice snapped out, loud and clear enough for Silus to hear.

'Enough. It is decided. You know your roles and duties today. Carry them out.'

And then the tent flap swept open, and Caracalla strode out, looking neither left nor right.

Silus was taken unawares by the abruptness of the Emperor's departure, but he was still an Arcanus, with all his training and experience, and he was soon in motion. He stepped in behind Caracalla, noting that Skylurus was slower to respond, and matched the Emperor step for step so he was positioned directly behind him.

He swallowed hard. Took a deep breath. Reached down and grasped the hilt of his sword, began to withdraw it slowly and quietly from its sheath.

A firm hand clamped on the top of his own, and pushed the sword back into its home, while at the same time an arm wrapped around his shoulder and steered him to one side. Silus turned, startled to find himself looking into the stern face of Oclatinius. The spymaster gave Silus a little shake of the head, waited to be sure that Silus had acknowledged him, then clapped him on the back and moved away.

Skylurus caught Silus up.

'What was that about?'

Silus was staring after Oclatinius in disbelief.

'I haven't a fucking clue.'

—

The two Empires met in the vast plain before the city of Arbela. The Parthian Empire was around four hundred and fifty years old, and Parthia was the successor to one of the world's largest ever Empires, the Persian Empire, and so could trace its origins back over seven hundred years. Rome had been founded according to the traditional date nearly a thousand years earlier. The Parthian Empire at its height encompassed a million square miles of territory, stretching as far as Syria in the west and India in the east. The Roman Empire, possibly at its greatest ever extent when taking into account Caracalla's father's conquests in Africa, boasted territory of around two million square miles. Rome had a population of around ninety million. Parthia did not carry out a census, but its population was estimated by the philosophers and mathematicians to be between ten and twenty million.

These vast figures had been impressed upon Silus by Oclatinius, who had been wishing to emphasise the astounding significance of a merger of these two super-powers. Surely the whole world would tremble at the prospect, from the desert lands south of the province of Africa, north to the Germanic lands, and east to India and the mysterious faraway land of Sinae, from where silk was reputed to come.

Silus sat on Delicatus in Caracalla's honour guard, sweating heavily, and not just because of the mid-morning heat. His mind was whirling. Just an hour before, he had been on the verge of ending Caracalla's life and accepting his own fate. Then, bafflingly, Oclatinius had stopped him, then left, without explanation. A violent tremor had seized him, and he had had to fight it down to avoid anyone else noticing. Even now he felt like the fear and excitement remained with him, and he was trying hard not to vomit, while his body dealt with the comedown following the predicted and unexpectedly averted violence.

He watched the approach of the Parthian wedding party in complete confusion.

The Parthian King of Kings, Artabanus, rode an immaculately groomed, pure white horse, its bridle decorated with gold medallions, the leather saddle embossed with religious and astrological symbols. The King of Kings wore a flowing robe of fine silk inlaid with gold thread, and as he neared, Silus could see he was a slim, middle-aged man with a long pointy beard. Like Caracalla, he was accompanied by a mounted bodyguard, stern-looking men with bows on their backs and javelins and quivers bulging with arrows at the sides of their saddles. At the back of the guard, with head bowed, face veiled, riding side saddle on a dappled, dish-faced pony, came what Silus presumed was the bride, Ziyanak. Silus wondered briefly what she thought about this, being taken from her homeland and passed as some sort of gift to seal an alliance to a rough foreign man that she had never met. He supposed it was how things were done among the nobility. Where Silus came from, you found someone you liked the look of, and if she and her father agreed, you married her, and if she survived the child-bearing years, you lived out the rest of your lives together.

Behind the immediate wedding party, Artabanus had brought his army, as a show of strength as well as respect. A much higher proportion were mounted than the army at the back of Caracalla, reflecting the importance Parthia placed on cavalry, and horse archers in particular. But there were foot soldiers too, a variety of nationalities drawn from all over the Parthian Empire, just as Caracalla's men came from places like Britannia, Mauretania,

Macedonia and Syria. If this had been two armies meeting for war, they would have been evenly matched in terms of numbers, and there had surely been few times in history when two such vast bodies of fighting men had met in peace.

The civilian population of Arbela had turned out too. Men, women and children flocked behind the Parthian military, waving palm branches, cheering loudly for the Emperor Antoninus and the Parthian King of Kings Artabanus, and singing hymns of praise to Ahura Mazda, the Zoroastrian deity, as well as Jupiter Optimus Maximus.

Artabanus gently reined his horse to a halt, then dismounted, as did his bodyguard. He reached behind him and was passed a large skin of wine. He removed the stopper and tipped it up, pouring the contents into the sand, intoning in a loud voice some ritual words in the Parthian language.

Caracalla half-turned to the men behind him. 'Be ready,' he said to them quietly. 'Stay mounted.'

Be ready? Silus' heart lurched. Be ready for what? Why did they need to stay mounted? He looked at the other Leones, who appeared equally confused, except Triccianus, who was tight-lipped. Silus looked back at the legions behind them, who were drawn up in cere-monial uniform, alert but relaxed. Some movement in his peripheral vision caught his attention, and he saw Roman cavalry moving forward on both flanks, like the extended wings of an eagle.

Caracalla dismounted and took several large strides towards Artabanus. He spread his arms giving a broad grin of welcome.

'Artabanus, King of Kings, we meet at long last.'

'Antoninus, Augustus, Emperor of Rome, we are well met.'

They shook hands, then Caracalla drew Artabanus into a close embrace. A vast cheer went up, from the Parthian soldiers and civilians, and from the Roman legionaries and auxiliaries behind Caracalla. The Parthians threw down their bows and javelins, drew out wine cups and following the example of their king, poured libations into the sand, then drank deeply, raising their cups and cheering and singing.

Later, Silus understood that the embrace had been Caracalla's signal to his cavalry. On edge, nerves jangling, he heard the order and the sound of trumpets when to most others, especially the Parthians, the sound was drowned out by the musicians and singers and cheering crowds. He whirled and saw the cavalry that had advanced beyond the line between the two armies break into a trot, wheel inwards in a perfect manoeuvre from both flanks, and then break into a canter.

At the same time, commands rang out among the legions behind Silus. Confused legionaries, nevertheless, drilled to obey orders without hesitation or question, came to attention, then formed up into ranks, drawing their swords.

How had he been so stupid? How many times had Caracalla done something like this, since he was first prevented from slaying the Caledonians at a peace conference by his father? The betrayal of the Alemanni, the slaughter of the Ephebes in Alexandria. Now this. Why hadn't it been obvious that this was what Caracalla planned all along?

Maybe it was because Caracalla himself had been so secretive that he had kept it from almost everyone until that very morning. Domna clearly hadn't known, grieving as she was for the loss of her lover to a nubile young eastern princess. The conspirators hadn't known, or they would have told Silus and Oclatinius. Maybe Sempronius Rufus was aware, he seemed to be the Emperor's closest confidante these days. Silus presumed that Artabanus had spies and informers in Caracalla's camp, the way they did in the Parthians'. And if Artabanus had got the slightest hint of this treachery, he could have drawn the Romans into a counter-ambush and massacred them. So the extreme secrecy made sense.

At least Silus now knew the content of Caracalla's early morning meeting with his commanders. But why had Oclatinius prevented him from killing Caracalla before the wedding? He wondered if Oclatinius hadn't had enough time to work through the consequences of what he had just heard, to work out what plans were already in motion. A half-executed betrayal of the Parthians, with Caracalla dead, could lead to an absolute disaster for the Romans that would dwarf Cannae and Carrhae.

It took a long time for the Parthians to become aware something was wrong. They had been completely taken in by Caracalla's assurances, his bonhomie and his openness. Even now he was clasping Artabanus' hand, talking loudly about the honour the King of Kings was doing him by allowing him to marry his beautiful daughter, the great military alliance the two Empires could now enter into. Murmurs rose among the Parthians as the first of them noticed the cavalry, and the anxiety spread as more heard or felt the thunder of hooves, turned to see the heavily armoured horsemen charging into the unarmed, unprepared, unprotected flanks of the Parthians.

One of Artabanus' bodyguards called out a warning, and Artabanus tried to turn. But Caracalla kept a firm grip on the King of King's hand, kept him facing towards his still fiercely grinning face.

'Augustus,' gasped Artabanus.

Caracalla held up his free hand. 'To me, Leones,' he called. And then he reached to his belt to draw a knife concealed beneath the folds of his cloak.

Silus spurred Delicatus forward. For all he wanted Caracalla dead, now was not the time. For better or worse, the Romans were engaging the Parthians in bloody combat, and if they didn't follow through ruthlessly, with all their strength, and their leadership intact, it could go very badly for them. So Silus raced forward as the Parthian bodyguard, dismounted and unprepared, did the same.

Artabanus wrenched his hand out of Caracalla's grip and staggered backward as Caracalla slashed his knife between them. The Parthian King of Kings stared in disbelief at the Roman Emperor who moments before had been embracing him in friendship and was now trying to kill him. For a moment, he seemed frozen, and Caracalla advanced purposefully on him.

But Artabanus' bodyguard was not slow. Four bulky Parthians converged on the position of the two combatant rulers. The first was unarmed, the second had picked up a javelin, and the third and fourth had grabbed swords. Another further back had retrieved his bow from where he had discarded it on the ground, and was desperately restringing it, straining muscles as he used his foot to bend the wood.

Silus heard other Leones behind him, starting belatedly into action. But none had his reflexes and quickness of thought, and Silus knew for a few moments he would be facing down the Parthians alone.

Caracalla slashed across Artabanus, and the king put up his forearm to ward off the strike. The blade bit deep into the muscle, down to the bone, and Artabanus cried out in pain, shock and outrage. Caracalla, wearing the grin of a feral dog, grasped Artabanus by the collar of his priceless silk robe, a fistful of long beard caught up in his grip, and drew back his arm ready to thrust the killing blow through Artabanus' eye socket and deep into his skull.

The first Parthian bodyguard arrived, and threw himself at Artabanus, arms spread. He caught him round the chest, tearing him from Caracalla's grip, and the two, king and guard, thudded heavily into the ground, the air leaving Artabanus' chest with an audible whoosh. Caracalla growled in frustration and holding his knife in both hands, thrust downwards, all his weight behind the blow. The knife penetrated deep into the guard who was covering the king with his body, and the guard cried out, back arching.

Caracalla put a foot on him to pull the blade free, and as he did so the Parthian with the javelin drew his arm back. Only ten feet away from the Emperor, he couldn't miss.

Delicatus barrelled into the javelin thrower just as his arm came forward. The missile flew wide, and the guard disappeared under Delicatus' hooves, the prissy, noble horse seeming to take great delight in trampling the body below him.

But now the last two Parthian guards arrived, and Silus' charge on Delicatus had taken him momentarily beyond the ability to help. He yanked on Delicatus' reins, desperately bringing him round, watching helplessly as

Caracalla faced down two swordsmen, armed only with a knife.

Caracalla was a muscular man, in his prime. He exercised regularly, both with the troops and in the gymnasium. Most importantly, he knew how to fight, and had done so in practice and on the battlefield. So, outmatched as he was in weaponry and numbers, alone until help arrived, he fought with a savage ferocity, his little blade parrying sword thrusts, while he kicked and punched, fighting both for his life and the opportunity to finish the supine Artabanus.

Delicatus was now facing the right direction, back towards the fight, and Silus kicked his flanks hard. The agile horse sprung into an immediate gallop, and Silus raised his sword high, roaring with all his might to distract Caracalla's attackers. They saw him, and saw too that the other Leones, further back and slower to start, were now converging on them. One of the guards broke off the fight and grabbed hold of Artabanus, dragging him from under the corpse of their comrade. The King of Kings cried out in pain, but the guard ignored him, and pulled him towards where Artabanus' white horse had been waiting patiently, a dozen feet away.

The other guard took up a defensive stance, angling his body so he held Caracalla at bay while bracing himself for Silus' arrival. Caracalla rushed him, growling incoherently as he saw his prize being snatched away. The guard parried and dodged, not attempting to counter, just buying time for his comrade to get the king to safety.

Silus flew in from the side, Delicatus at full speed, legs stretching out and throwing up clods of muddy sand behind him. He reached down and swung his sword, a blow that could have taken the head off the bodyguard with one strike. But Silus was not a natural rider, certainly no Parthian, and Artabanus' guard was no peasant conscript. The guard ducked the blow and slashed out, slicing a wound over Delicatus' ribs. The charge carried Silus on past the guard, but he had done enough. With his sword extended as he struck Delicatus, the guard's side was unprotected, and Caracalla thrust his own blade deep into his side, between the ribs and straight into the chambers of his heart. The guard stiffened and fell, and as Caracalla withdrew his blade, a gout of crimson spouted out of the rent in his torso.

Silus reined in beside Caracalla.

'Are you hurt, Augustus?'

'Of course not,' snapped Caracalla. 'He is getting away!' He pointed at Artabanus, who had just been helped into his saddle. As Silus watched, the guard slapped the fine white horse on its rump, and sent it charging to the rear, bearing away its royal burden to safety.

Now the first Leones arrived. It seemed like it had taken them an age to react, but in fact the whole fight had been over in moments. Triccianus and Thrax were at the fore. Thrax's face was red, but his eyes were alight with excitement. Triccianus looked more sober. 'Your orders, Augustus,' he asked.

'Get after Artabanus! Bring me his head!'

'Leones!' cried Triccianus. 'On me!' And when the mounted Leones had formed up behind their leader, he spurred his horse to the charge, heading into the ranks of the Parthians in pursuit of Artabanus.

But now the initiative had been lost, at least as far as this part of the battle was concerned. The Parthian bodyguard had had time to remount, regain their weapons, and form up to protect the escape of their king. Silus saw, behind the

Parthian horsemen, the fleeing white horse of Artabanus, and by his side his daughter, veil streaming behind her, as father and daughter rode for their lives.

Then he was in among the battle.

The front line of the Parthian bodyguard fought with long swords and engaged the Leones as the two bodies of cavalry crashed into each other. They slashed and hacked at the opposing riders and at their horses. Delicatus' first wound had been superficial, and he soon had a couple more to match it, but the fine horse fought on with grace and skill as if he was showing off his talents on a parade ground.

Silus took some blows too, a trio of nicks to his sword arm, and a bruised shin where a Parthian rider had kicked out. There was little difference in numbers, strength or martial ability between the two sets of bodyguards, although the Leones had been slightly better prepared, having remained mounted, unlike the Parthians. But on the rest of the field it was a different matter.

With a Parthian horse spooked into bolting before him, Silus found himself in a lacuna in their fight and had a moment to look around. The Roman cavalry charge that had begun the battle had devastated the unprepared and unarmed Parthian foot and dismounted horsemen. Routed before they had even had a chance to fight, most of the Parthians turned to flee, especially when they saw the distinctive white horse of their king disappearing in the direction of the mountains.

But their escape was choked by the large number of civilians from Arbela who had come to witness the wedding and take part in the feasting and entertainment. The Roman heavy cavalry rode among them, slaughtering at will, civilian and military alike. Light cavalry was skirting around behind the fleeing Parthians, cutting off their escape. And the Roman infantry was marching forward now, purposefully, terrifyingly, pilums protruding from between interlocked shields.

The Parthian cavalry bodyguard saw the danger, too, saw their window of escape rapidly closing. A command rang out and was taken up by other Parthian horsemen. Silus didn't understand the words, but he knew an order to retreat when he heard one. With great skill, the Parthians disengaged, and rode to the rear.

The Leones chased after them, but the Parthian body-guard was an elite unit, highly trained and experienced, and it did not flee in disorder. With a skill that took Silus' breath away, they retreated before the Leones, then feinted a charge, then retreated again while firing arrows over their shoulders, the famous 'Parthian shot'. Several of the Leones went down each time they performed this manoeuvre, and it stalled the Leones' charge. Before long, the Parthians had opened up a gap betweenthemselves and their pursuers, and when they were comfortably out of javelin range, they turned and galloped away. The lighter Parthians with their smaller horses easily outstripped the sturdy Leones' chargers bearing their bulky riders, and when it was clear the pursuit was now futile Triccianus ordered them to halt.

Silus leant down to pat Delicatus on the neck. The horse's agility and skill had saved Silus during this fight, and not for the first time. Blood was trickling down his flanks from multiple wounds, but none looked deep, and provided they got adequate attention from the veterin-arius, they would not prove fatal. The beautiful horse would sport some impressive scars after today's work, however, and Silus wondered whether the vain animal would wear them with pride or shame.

Much like his own scars, he reflected. How many of them could he be truly proud of? Looking out across the plains before the city now, and watching yet another massacre unfold, he knew today was another day of which to be truly ashamed. The air was filled with screams, soldiers, men, women and children, as the legions got in among them, and fulfilled their deadly orders, not caring to distinguish between combatant and non-combatant, warriors and innocent bystanders. It was certainly a dramatic way to declare war. There would be no forgiveness from the Parthians for this treachery. Silus wondered if this time, Caracalla had poked a nest of hornets that would rise up in a swarm to sting him to death.

He sat astride Delicatus, breathing heavily, staring in dismay at the slaughter. Could he have prevented it by killing Caracalla when he intended? What would the consequences of that deed have been for Rome, and for Parthia? Worse? Better? Maybe Janus, able to look forward and backward in time could tell. Silus didn't know.

What he did know was that he had expected to be dead by now. He knew that he could have killed Caracalla. And he knew that thousands upon thousands were being massacred before him, and that soon the legions would be unleashed on the villages, towns and cities of Parthia.

He suddenly felt as if he couldn't breathe, as if there was no air left in the world despite being out in the open on this vast plain. He opened his mouth, gulping in mouthfuls of breath, trying vainly to master the sensation. Then he leant forward, took hold of Delicatus' neck in his arms, and broke down, deep, uncontrollable sobs. Weeping for the people of Parthia, of Alexandria, of Germania and Britannia. Weeping too for his own losses.

His wife.

His daughter.

His soul.

–

'Well that's it then,' said Marcius Agrippa. 'There is no point continuing.'

'What are you talking about?' snapped Macrinus. The conspirators were ensconced in a private mansion that Macrinus had commandeered to be his own temporary residence. The noble family to which it had previously belonged had not contested this, and Silus presumed they were lying dead on the plain before Arbela in any case, even now having their soft parts pecked away by scavengers, after their valuables had been looted.

The house was an old one, built in the Seleucid fashion, Macrinus had told them proudly before their meeting began, pointing out the Ionic columns at the front, testament to Ancient Greek influences, although the interior had been redecorated over the centuries in Parthian styles, with the figures on the wall frescoes characteristically gazing forward towards the viewer rather than at each other, to give a quite disconcerting effect. Silus stared into the eyes of a lion-headed person who was regarding him steadily and shivered. The argument around him continued, but he was only half-paying attention, his weariness and dejection making it hard to concentrate.

'I'm talking about the point of our plot,' replied Agrippa. 'Wasn't it to prevent a war with Parthia? I think we can safely say we failed.'

'That was not our only goal,' said Macrinus forcefully. 'This treachery on the battlefield demonstrates even more why we must be rid of this tyrant.'

'The soldiers love him more than ever now, though,' said Triccianus. 'He has inflicted a massive, maybe decisive defeat on the Parthians, for next to no loss. What's more, he has allowed them to pillage freely, so they will greatly enrich themselves, and the state will benefit far less.'

'Exactly,' said Macrinus. 'His fiscal irresponsibility has squandered all the wealth that his father built up, to the point that Rome is on the verge of bankruptcy.'

'He will no doubt devalue the coinage,' said Julianus Nestor.

'And what does that solve?' asked Ulpius Julianus morosely. 'Nothing.'

'It's not a decisive defeat,' put in Oclatinius in the silence that followed.

'What do you mean?' asked Macrinus.

'You have to understand how vast the Parthian Empire really is. If it wasn't so disunited, it could crush Rome's forces in the East. But its territory and population are truly enormous. Artabanus escaped alive, and though Caracalla will lead the legions on a mission of destruction and pillage through the Parthian territories, Artabanus will retreat and regroup. He won't offer us a fight until he is ready to meet us, but he will harass our supply lines and our isolated detachments, much like the Caledonians and Maeatae did in the early stages of Septimius Severus' war in northern Britannia. But unlike that war, Parthia is too vast to completely suppress, or even to annex, without some degree of consent from the local population.'

'He still has Vologaesus to ally with, hasn't he?' said Triccianus.

'He does. But that is just taking one side in a civil war, and we all know how protracted they can be.'

Sombre nods all round greeted this remark.

'What news from Rome?' Macrinus asked Nestor and Julianus, the frumentarii commanders. 'You are still able to read Caracalla's correspondence that your men deliver, before you present it to the Emperor?'

'Nothing untoward,' said Nestor. 'Flavius Maternianus grumbles about the finances of the city, but the people are not restive. There is going to be no uprising to overthrow the Emperor from that direction.'

'If you hadn't stopped Silus doing his job, we wouldn't be in this situation, Oclatinius,' grumbled Macrinus.

Silus, on hearing his name, looked up, and saw Oclatinius sit up a little straighter, his expression become a little colder.

'And what situation would we be in instead?' he asked, his voice even in a way Silus recognised as dangerous.

'Well. I don't know. A different one.'

'You don't know. I don't know. I had moments from finding out about Caracalla's treachery to decide whether I should let Silus proceed. What might have happened that day if Silus had killed Caracalla before the wedding? Would the legions have rioted, fallen into disarray before the Parthian army? Would false rumours have caused them to blame the Parthians, and make them attack, without Caracalla having lulled the Parthians into disarming themselves?'

'Even so, if Silus hadn't lost his courage...'

Silus stood up. He was not a tall man. He was muscular, but not bulky like a gladiator. Nevertheless, everyone fell silent. He looked around the room, staring each man in the face, even Oclatinius, one by one.

'Is there anyone here, who doubts my courage?' he said quietly.

No one spoke.

'I'm done here.' He made towards the doorway.

'Silus,' said Oclatinius.

Silus paused.

'Macrinus is right about one thing. This isn't over. The massacre at Arbela changes nothing. We must still be rid of Caracalla, sooner or later. And you are still the one to do it.'

Silus didn't nod, didn't do anything to acknowledge agreement. He continued out of the doorway, onto the streets of Arbela, which were full of the stench of smoke and decomposing flesh.

August 216 AD

The Roman siege equipment had done its work. Ballistae had peppered the thick mud-brick walls with great stones, knocking the tops off the turrets protecting the main gates. Two siege towers, iron-clad to protect them against fire, were wheeled up to the wall, heavily armed legionaries pouring out of the top onto the battlements to engage in hand-to-hand fighting with the defenders, while simultaneously a huge battering ram, protected within a shed called a tortoise, was slammed into the city gates.

Rayy was a big city, not on the scale of Rome or Alexandria, but nevertheless one of the biggest in the Parthian Empire. It was technically in Median territory, which was claimed by Vologaesus, Artabanus' brother, who was currently at peace with the Romans, and Caracalla had carefully avoided pillaging Media to avoid provoking

Vologaesus. Rayy, however, boasted that it was one of Artabanus' several capitals and so was fair game.

But despite its size and its formidable defences, the defenders had no chance. Abandoned by their king and his army, their resistance was doomed from the outset. Still, it was fierce. They knew what had happened at Ganjak and Tabriz, two cities to the west that Caracalla had already sacked. Ganjak had resisted and been utterly destroyed, and its sacred Fire Temple, dedicated to Media-Atropatene, was looted and desecrated, to the horror of all Parthia. Tabriz had surrendered without a fight, but that had made no difference to its fate, suffering an orgy of pillaging and destruction by the rampaging Roman troops. So the people of Rayy knew they must hold out or die.

On their long march through Parthian territory, Caracalla's armies had slaughtered the livestock, burnt the crops, razed every settlement, village and town they came across, destroyed every dam, water well and orchard. Caracalla insisted to his council that the wanton and brutal destruction served the dual purpose of weakening the enemy and provoking Artabanus to meet him on the field. Reports from various spies, including some within Vologaesus' camp, suggested that Artabanus was gathering a vast army in the mountains beyond the Tigris, and Caracalla wanted to draw it into a pitched battle before he ran out of supplies for his legions, and the men became weary and wanted to return home.

Meanwhile Artabanus had continued to engage in guerrilla tactics, targeting wagon trains, supply dumps and smaller detachments. Each individual skirmish counted for little, but the cumulative effect of the little cuts were turning into a significant bloodletting for the legions.

Rayy was a big prize, however, and would be the last target of the year's campaign, since it had become clear that Artabanus was not ready to face Caracalla that year. So Caracalla had spared no effort in bringing it to its knees.

The gates buckled and the walls shook with each crash of the ram. Defenders rained hot oil and fire arrows down on the protective cover, but the ballistae and the attackers already on the walls limited their effectiveness. Before long, the gates burst open and a huge cheer rang out around the legionaries. The soldiers manning the ram pulled it out of the way, and the first units of heavily armoured legionaries charged forward with a roar.

The city defenders were for the main part light militia, armoured with a padded curaiss at best, and armed with a hotchpotch variety of swords, spears and agricultural implements such as scythes and hoes. The legionaries advancing in formation, shields to the fore, short swords stabbing out at any foe near enough, brushed the Parthians aside with ease, and in that moment the defence collapsed, and the city was open.

The army flooded in like the inundation of the Nile, swamping the citizens of the city who were soon drowning beneath the rampaging soldiers. Caracalla watched with satisfaction from horseback as another city was crushed beneath his heel. Silus, mounted on Delicatus, who had recovered fully from his injuries except for some pale, hairless scars along his flanks, looked on, face impassive, innards churning. It had all been so predictable, all this death and destruction, and the knowledge that he could have prevented it burnt deeply.

Even now he wondered if he should just turn and thrust his sword deep into Caracalla's bloody heart. But the chances of him successfully assassinating the Emperor were becoming ever more slim. Silus wasn't sure if Caracalla had genuine reasons to suspect there was a plot against his life, or whether it was just paranoia, but he had become increasingly careful in recent months. He now wore a thick linen breastplate at all times, in battle, in council or at rest, and always went armed. There were always at least two Leones with him at all times, and more often than not, one of his pet lions, who had a tendency to lash out at anyone who approached too close. Silus thought, though didn't know for sure, that he could best Caracalla in a one on one fight, especially if he had surprise on his side. But he knew he now had next to no chance of delivering a killing blow before he was stopped. And much as he wanted Caracalla dead, and was prepared to die in the process, he was not prepared to throw his own life away for nothing. He had told the conspirators this, and though some had grumbled, Oclatinius had firmly backed him, telling the others that it was important that Silus remained in his privileged position as one of Caracalla's closest bodyguards. His actions at Arbela had at least increased Caracalla's trust in him, even as he became more mistrustful of everyone not a member of the Leones.

'Silus, Skylurus,' said Caracalla after he had watched the last of the legionaries and auxiliaries disappear through the broken defences. 'Get into the city, see what's happening, and report back to me.'

Silus' heart sank. Could he not catch a single break? He had hoped he could remain with Caracalla outside the city until the worst of the brutal work was done, but no, he was ordered to go in among the horror and look upon it anew. How much savagery could one man witness and remain sane, he wondered, even as he said, 'At once, Augustus.'

Skylurus and Silus spurred their horses to a slow canter and followed the army into the dying capital. When they first passed through the destroyed wooden gates, Silus thought maybe it wouldn't be as bad as his imagination had told him it would be. Yes, there was blood soaking the sand, yes there were dead bodies bearing catastrophic injuries, yes, there were wounded men crying feebly for help, many of which would not see the sunset. But they were all soldiers, fighting men. The battle had been one-sided, but many battles were. Silus could handle that.

But as soon as they had passed the site of the initial fight just inside the city walls, the picture changed. It was no longer a battlefield, but a butcher's shop. Helpless victims were being sacrificed in every direction Silus looked. To his right, a pair of Gallic-looking auxiliaries were taking it in turns to kick an old man in the head. To his left a wiry Egyptian or Syrian was dragging a woman down an alleyway by the hair, ignoring her screams for pity. Some way ahead of him was a small pack of dogs fighting over some scraps which, as he approached and shooed them away, turned out to be a small child.

He glanced at Skylurus. His fellow guard's mouth was compressed into a tight line but was not otherwise visibly perturbed. He seemed neither to want to join in the depravity, nor condemn it. Silus wished he possessed that equanimity to suffering. His conscience, in fact his entire life, would have been much easier. But then, wouldn't he have been a different person, someone other than Gaius Sergius Silus?

He was distracted from his philosophising by the sight of a pair of praetorians marching out of a temple with a sack full of silver and gold. Silus could see offering cups, statues and ornate lanterns spilling out, and the two men, their clean uniforms showing they had not taken part in any serious fighting, laughed together. An old man dressed in a striped blue robe with a priestly hood rushed out after them. He fell to his knees, grasping the hem of one of the praetorians, and babbled in words incomprehensible to Silus, yet with clear meaning. Please don't steal the sacred treasures of my gods.

The praetorian half-turned, a look of annoyance passing across his face, and kicked out, sending the priest sprawling backward. But he was not to be put off, his duty to his gods outweighing fears for his own safety. He crawled forward again on all fours, weeping, begging, then he grabbed the leg of the praetorian and hung on tightly. The praetorian exchanged an exasperated glance with his comrade, drew his blade, and skewered the prone priest through, from front to back. The priest gasped, gurgled, twitched, and was still. The praetorian shook his leg free, made some sort of joke to his comrade, and they both laughed.

Silus and Skylurus reined in their horses beside the praetorians and looked down at them. The praetorians looked up, and with the sun behind the Leones, they had to shield their eyes to look them in the face.

'What do you want, barbarian?' said the one who had killed the priest, a short, thick-set, bearded man with features suggestive of a Roman or Italian native.

'Quite a haul you have there,' said Silus, ignoring the jibe about his origins. Particularly since Caracalla had awarded citizenship to every free man within the limits of the Empire, where a Roman came from should be of no consequence. But the Leones were drawn almost exclusively from the Germanic and Celtic races, and the praetorians had a history of being drawn from upstanding

Roman citizens since the time of the Republic. Of course, they had been dissolved after their shameful behaviour in selling the Empire off to the highest bidder, and replaced by men drawn from Septimius Severus' own army, but that had been over thirty years prior, and all those Severan loyalists had long since retired. The praetorians had never fully recovered from the shame of that year, when five emperors had ruled Rome in quick succession, and the fact that Caracalla had created a new bodyguard in the Leones who received favourable treatment over the praetorians was a constant source of friction between the units.

'Not bad. What business is it of yours?'

A half-naked woman ran screaming down the street, pursued by three long-haired auxiliaries who were treating the chase like some wild beast hunt.

'Planning on sharing any of that with the treasury?'

The praetorians frowned. 'Why would we? The Emperor gave us free rein to do what we want when the city fell, just like everywhere in Parthia. Old Caracalla is making his soldiers rich, just like his father told him to on his deathbed.'

'There is more treasure there than even a couple of praetorians could blow on whores and dice, surely. Why not donate it to the Imperial coffers? It would go down well with the Augustus Antoninus.' Silus wondered if they would notice his use of Caracalla's formal name and title, but from the smell of wine coming from them, he guessed they were half drunk already, and even sober he doubted they were much for subtlety.

'Fuck that,' said the praetorian. 'We'll share it out among the lads, maybe, but that's it. This is spoils of war.'

Silus looked up and down his pristine uniform pointedly. 'Did a lot of fighting to earn it, did you?'

'Listen you little barbarian shit. Just because you and those long-haired, uncivilised lions are the Emperor's darlings right now, doesn't mean you can talk to a praetorian that way. If you want to make something of it...' He whipped up his sword, which until then had been hanging loosely by his side, the blood of the priest still dripping from the tip.

Silus reacted quicker than the praetorian could move. He leapt from Delicatus' back, both arms spread, neatly twisting his torso to stay clear of the blade, and flattened the praetorian, using the soldier's body to break his fall. The praetorian grunted loudly and his sword flew from his hand. Silus straddled the winded man and grabbed him by the throat, fist drawn back, ready to pummel him in the centre of his face. But there was no fight remaining in the praetorian, who just closed his eyes, waiting for the blow to fall.

Instead Silus hauled him to his feet. In the corner of his eye, he saw that Skylurus had the tip of his spear resting under the chin of the other praetorian who was standing very still and keeping his hands well away from his sword.

'Who are you?' asked Silus.

'Martialis,' said the praetorian, breathing fast and shallow. 'Julius Martialis. This is my brother Titus.'

Silus pushed him away. 'We aren't your enemies. Try to remember that.'

He remounted, and Delicatus shifted his weight from foot to foot, ready to be away.

'You aren't going to take the treasure?'

Silus shrugged. 'I've no use for it. But maybe if you presented at least some of it to the Emperor as a gift, it would do you some favours. Maybe you would make centurion one day, get that transverse crest on your helmet, carry the vine stick to beat those under you into obedience.'

Silus watched a shrewd calculation come into the praetorian's eyes. The other praetorian said, 'But that treasure is going to buy me a farm in Campania.'

'Shut up,' said Martialis. 'You, lion, what is your name?'

'Gaius Sergius Silus.'

'I've heard of you. And now I have put a face to a name, I won't forget you.'

'Nor I you,' said Silus. 'Come on, Skylurus. I think we have spent enough time here.'

—

They spent as little time in the city as Silus thought they could get away with, before riding back to Caracalla's encampment. He supposed the Emperor would find a nice residence to occupy within the city walls once the killing had finished. Caracalla quizzed them about the situation inside Rayy and seemed satisfied with Silus' and Skylurus' answers. Although Silus had been planning to leave their encounter with the praetorians out, Skylurus, who was maybe smarting from their insults more than Silus had realised, told Caracalla the whole thing. Caracalla had frowned at the derogatory comments directed towards his closest guards but listened without interruption. Then the Emperor commented, 'Maybe I treat the praetorians a little harshly. They are after all well led now. On the other hand, I do not approve of rudeness to the Leones. I will think on it.'

He waved a hand to dismiss Silus and Skylurus. As Silus was about to depart though, a soldier came puffing up the hill towards them, carrying a heavy sack. To Silus' surprise, he made out the features of Julius Martialis as he neared.

'This is the praetorian I was telling you about, Augustus,' said Skylurus. Two of the other Leones guarding Caracalla stepped forward, presenting spears, points forward, to the newcomer. 'Shall we get rid of him?'

'Let him approach,' said Caracalla.

Martialis trotted forward, back bent under the weight of his burden.

'Augustus, I come to you with a gift.'

Caracalla gestured for Martialis to show what he had brought, and the praetorian upended the sack, and a huge quantity of treasures, gold and silver coins, jewellery, ornaments and more, spilled out at the Emperor's feet. Caracalla raised an eyebrow, waiting for Martialis to explain.

'I know you said we could keep what we looted, Augustus,' he said. 'But I thought, there is too much here for one man to spend, even if he likes his whores and his dice.' He gave the Emperor a half-grin but was not rewarded by it being returned. He pressed on. 'I know you have the wealth of Empire at your disposal, Augustus, but who doesn't need a little extra? So I thought, who better to present this treasure to than yourself, Caracalla, I mean Antoninus, Augustus, sir.'

Caracalla regarded him for a long moment, then said, 'I thank you for your gift, praetorian. You are dismissed. Silus, escort him out.'

Martialis bowed deeply and let himself be led out of the Emperor's presence by Silus. When they were out of earshot, the praetorian hissed, 'I thought you said he would make me a centurion?'

Silus sighed. 'I said it might help. He doesn't know you. You need to prove yourself to him.'

'How do I do that?' grumbled Martialis. 'The praetorians are never first into a fight, we only ever mop up, so I can't prove myself in battle. And only the Leones are trusted as bodyguards at the moment, so I can't get close to him that way.'

'Well, you know how he loves his sporting contests. Maybe you could show him your skill in the discus or javelin or something?'

'I don't know about that,' said Martialis doubtfully. 'But I can run fast.'

'There you are then, get yourself in training, and show the Emperor you are worthy of that vine stick.'

'Thanks, Silus. I will. And, I'm sorry about earlier. You're alright, you know.'

'It's forgotten,' said Silus. He clapped him on the back and left him to report back to his unit, hoping that was the last he would ever see of Julius Martialis.

Chapter XI

Decembris 216 AD

Caracalla had chosen Edessa as his winter headquarters. The old city had been built on the banks of the Scirtus river by Alexander's general, King Seleucus Nicator, founder of the Seleucid Empire, and had changed hands between Seleucids, Armenians, Parthians and Romans a number of times over its existence. Situated a couple of hundred miles north-east of Antioch, from where Julia Domna still headed the civil administration of the Empire, it was an ideal location for Caracalla to marshal his strength, reprovision, rest and train his troops, and plan for the spring campaign.

Numerous spies controlled by both Oclatinius and Rufus had reported Artabanus' gathering army in the East, but with each new snippet of information detailing Artabanus' growing might, Caracalla became ever more animated and excited. He boasted in his council meetings how his actions at the mock wedding to Artabanus' daughter, and their subsequent harrowing of the Parthian cities and countryside, were insults that no king could ignore and hope to remain in power, and so he had cleverly forced Artabanus into a full confrontation.

Silus had to concede he was probably right from a purely military point of view. Parthia was too vast to conquer and occupy, unless their forces could be decisively defeated once and for all. It was the tactics of Fabius Cunctator, the delayer, that had finally defeated Hannibal, since that great general, with all his resources, was never offered a battle on Italian soil after Cannae, and eventually had to return home, undefeated and yet unsuccessful. From his own personal point of view, of course, he wished he had never set foot in this parched, baking land, nor for that matter ever left Britannia for which he pined more and more. Still, cutting off a barbarian chief's head can dictate which path you are forced down in life.

Although some of Caracalla's forces were distributed across the wider area to make accommodating and provisioning the enormous army easier, the bulk of his forces remained with him in Edessa. To keep morale up and keep his men fit, he arranged for hunts, spectacles in the arena such as gladiatorial bouts and executions, and athletic and other sporting competitions.

It was at one of these that Silus encountered Martialis again.

They were taking part in a foot race in the city gymnasium, a two-hundred-yard dash, once down the track and then back again. It was one of a number of athletic competitions that Caracalla had organised that day, including javelin throwing, discus, long jump and wrestling. A dozen athletes from the ranks of the auxiliaries and legions lined up at the start. Silus stood behind the seat that Caracalla occupied by the start line, waiting for the competition to get under way.

One of the competitors caught his eye, and he had to think for a moment before he placed his face. Julius Martialis, naked like the rest of the athletes, his well-oiled body bulging with muscles. Beside him was his brother

Titus, slapping him on the shoulder and giving him a last-minute pep talk. Martialis noticed Silus looking at him, and gave him a nod, before turning his attention back to the length of track before him.

'Who is that?' asked Caracalla, indicating Martialis.

'He is Julius Martialis of the praetorians, Augustus,' said Silus. 'The one who presented you with that treasure after the sacking of Rayy.'

'Ah yes, the one who doesn't like the Leones, right?'

Silus was impressed with Caracalla's memory – the incident had happened some months before, but Martialis' derogatory comments towards his hand-picked guards obviously still rankled in the Emperor's mind.

'I'm not sure he dislikes us, Caracalla.'

'No matter. Do you think they look ready enough to start the race?'

The athletes were all lined up expectantly now, and their comrades and trainers had left to line the track and cheer them on. A sizeable crowd, mainly soldiers, but civilian men and women, had gathered to watch.

'I believe so, Augustus.'

Caracalla lifted his hand and called out in a loud voice, 'Athletes, on the line. Ready. Go!' He brought his arm down and the runners burst into action and the crowd burst into spontaneous roars of encouragement.

The first twenty yards was a melee of pushing and shoving as the closely packed competitors jockeyed for position. Cries of 'foul' and 'cheat' came from the crowd, and one man nearer the front, deliberately tripped by the man behind him, tumbled to the ground and was trampled by those bringing up the rear. As they made their way down the track though, gaps began to open up, and by the time they had reached the far end, a long-legged Egyptian was in first place, with Martialis a close second.

Coming back down the track proved a challenge, since the frontrunners now had to shove their way through the rearguard, who, puffing and sweating, were in no mood to let them through easily. Martialis was buffeted to one side by a savagely placed shoulder, but retained his balance and pushed on through, into the clear.

The Egyptian was not so fortunate, and a badly timed jostle caused him to trip over his own feet and tumble to the ground. Martialis looked back at the fallen athlete with an expression of triumph, and sprinted on, arms pumping, grinning broadly.

But the Egyptian was agile, and he was up in a heartbeat, his long legs quickly eating up the gap that had emerged between him and Martialis. Martialis saw the threat, and his smile faded. He put his head down and pounded on, but he was blowing hard now, red cheeks puffing out. Twenty yards from the finish, the Egyptian was on his shoulder, with all the momentum on his side, getting ready to ease past Martialis to victory.

But Martialis was not one to give up so easily. As the Egyptian drew level, he threw out his elbow hard, catching his challenger firmly in the middle of the face. The Egyptian cried out, grabbed his nose as blood spurted, staggered for a few steps, then resolutely ploughed on.

Martialis had done enough, though. Although the Egyptian closed the gap again, it was too late, and Martialis crossed the finish line a foot ahead. The crowd erupted, split evenly between those who had bet on the Egyptian and were outraged by the unsporting tactics, and those who had bet on Martialis and thought everything had been perfectly fair.

Titus came over and embraced his brother, holding his hand high in the air. Behind them, the Egyptian with blood smeared across his face glared at them resentfully.

Martialis and his brother approached Caracalla, still seated on his folding chair from which he had watched the event with mild interest. Both the praetorians dropped to their knees before the Emperor and bowed their heads.

'Augustus,' they said.

'Congratulations. Julius Martialis, isn't it? The one who so generously donated to my treasury.'

'Yes, that's correct, Augustus.'

Caracalla reached a hand behind him, and one of his attendant slaves passed him a crown made of woven olive leaves. He placed it on Martialis' bowed head.

'Well done, victor,' he said then turned to the slave. 'What's the next event?'

'Augustus, if I might be so bold?'

Caracalla looked down at Martialis in surprise. 'What is it?'

'Augustus, I have served you loyally in the praetorians for ten years. I have gifted you treasure. I have won the olive crown for my skill in athletics. Would you consider this sufficient to warrant my promotion to the rank of centurion?'

Caracalla stared at him for a moment, and a sneer passed across his face.

'You? Just because you gave me some stolen trinkets, and cheated your way to victory in a minor contest? Get away from me you low-born mongrel.'

Martialis' face flushed bright red in embarrassment, and his brother Titus looked up, glaring angrily into the Emperor's eyes.

'We are not low-born, Augustus,' he said, his voice tight.

'Don't speak back to me!' snapped Caracalla. 'It wouldn't surprise me if you were both conceived in some alleyway in the Subura by a slave charging a copper coin a go.'

'Don't speak about our mother like that!' cried out Titus, and leapt up, seizing Caracalla by the shoulders and shaking him.

Caracalla was too amazed to react, but the Leones did not hesitate. Four of them, including Skylurus and Silus, leapt onto Titus, hurling him onto his back and pinning him to the ground.

Caracalla got slowly to his feet, visibly shaking, face white with anger.

'You dare to lay hands on your Emperor?'

'Augustus,' said Martialis, and the word was a high-pitched squeak. 'He didn't mean any harm...'

'This is treason,' said Caracalla, and his quiet words drew gasps from the crowd, which was looking on in amazement.

'No, Augustus, it's just our mother...'

'Thrax.'

The giant bodyguard stepped forward.

'Kill him.'

'Yes, Augustus.'

Thrax bent down and hoisted Titus to his feet, the other Leones releasing him as he did so. The terrified Titus looked up into Thrax's impassive face. Then Thrax reached out, grasped Titus around the neck, lifted him into the air and squeezed. Titus grasped Thrax's hands, tried futilely to prise them apart. No noise came from him, as no air could pass through his windpipe, but his feet kicked against Thrax's shins.

'Titus, no!' Tears were streaming down Martialis' face. 'Augustus, I beg you, spare him.'

Caracalla said nothing, just regarded the execution with cold eyes. Martialis was frozen in indecision, looking like he might try to intervene, but knowing that would mean his own death.

It was soon over. Titus' legs stopped kicking, his eyes rolled upwards, his head lolled. Thrax continued to squeeze until he was sure all life was gone, then he let go and stepped back. Titus' corpse fell to the ground in a crumpled heap.

Martialis rushed over to clutch his brother's body to his chest, weeping hysterically. Caracalla rose.

'The rest of today's games are cancelled.'

And he strode away.

—

'He's an idiot,' said Silus.

'But maybe a useful one?' replied Macrinus.

Silus kept the thought to himself that that was exactly how he felt about Macrinus. He was reclining with both praetorian prefects, Oclatinius and Macrinus, and the commanders of the frumentarii, Ulpius Julianus and Julianus Nestor, in Nestor's house in the richest quarter of Edessa. Now the threat of death was not quite so immediate for Silus, he had recovered his appetite, and was enjoying the succulent strips of pork meat and dates that Nestor's cook had served up. Little moments like that made him wonder if he really wanted to throw his life away, no matter how noble a cause. And now Macrinus was suggesting that there was an alternative.

'Maybe,' conceded Silus. 'What do you think, Oclatinius?'

Oclatinius stroked his beard thoughtfully. 'I've done some digging into Martialis' background. His mother was, as he and his brother asserted, from a moderately well-off merchant family, but she got herself pregnant by some sailor who then deserted her. When she gave birth to Julius Martialis, the embarrassed family shipped her off to live in the country, and eventually she married a craftsman of some sort, and bore him Titus, although she died giving birth. The craftsman raised them both in a rather absent way, and it was Julius who did most of the caring for his younger brother. They joined the legions at a similar time, and when the recruiting officer noted they were particularly fit and strong, he recommended them for the praetorians. But their careers stagnated there, mainly because of their quick tempers and disinclination to obey orders.'

'Well Martialis sounds ideal to join us then,' said Nestor sarcastically, but Oclatinius shook his head.

'He may not be perfect, but he is a man with a very strong motive to want Caracalla dead. If he was as close to his brother as my sources suggest, he may even be careless of his own life, if it means the end of the Emperor.'

An alternative sacrificial beast thought Silus. I like the sound of that.

'Fine, I'll talk to him, sound him out. I hope he doesn't blame me for his brother's death though – it was me that put the idea of becoming a centurion in his head, which led to last week's tragedy.'

'I'm sure you will be persuasive,' said Macrinus. 'Now that's sorted, Nestor, is there any decent vintage wine in this place?'

'I think I will be on my way,' said Silus, not particularly interested in spending more time in their company now their business was concluded. 'I bid you all goodnight.'

Oclatinius nodded to him, and the others gave him offhand waves as they turned to discussing viniculture in the East.

Silus emerged onto the darkness outside the house and looked up and down the street. Then he looked up, and saw a figure crouching on the roof, almost invisible in the darkness, but silhouetted against the stars behind. The man had been staying perfectly still until Silus caught sight of him, but as soon as he was spotted, he leapt up, and raced across the rooftop.

Silus called out after him to stop, then broke into a run, keeping his eyes on the figure above him, while trying not to stumble on the stones and uneven paving slabs under his feet. The intruder was able to cut diagonally across the roof while Silus had to run around the walls. But the house was detached, with no other buildings within leaping distance, and as Silus rounded a corner, he saw the man lowering himself to the ground from the lip of a gutter. When he dropped, Silus was only a dozen yards behind.

The intruder was quick, but Silus was no slouch, especially over short distances, and he started to gain on the fleeing figure, as he darted down an alleyway. At Silus' belt was a small dagger, and he wondered how well-armed his opponent would be when he caught him. Not that he was unduly concerned. It was a rare man who could best Silus one on one.

The figure disappeared down a cut-through between two houses, and Silus put his head down, legs pumping, straining to close the gap. He turned into the narrow passageway, and something heavy hit him full in the face. His legs kept running momentarily, even as his head snapped back, and he crashed to the ground heavily.

The stars overhead spun in slow circles, and new ones, little flashes of light, danced across his vision. He wasn't sure if he had blacked out, and if so, for how long. A face loomed over him. He fumbled for his knife, but his hand didn't seem to respond the way he wanted.

'Calm yourself, Silus.' Silus recognised Oclatinius' voice, just as his face swum into focus.

'Did he...?'

'I heard you shout, but by the time I got here, whoever you were chasing was gone.'

Oclatinius reached out a hand and helped Silus to sit up. A wave of nausea rose up inside him as the buildings rotated crazily around. Something on the middle of his face hurt, and he was having some sort of trouble breathing.

'Silus,' said Oclatinius. 'I think you broke your nose.'

Oh, not again. Fuck!

–

Sempronius Rufus sat back in his leather-cushioned chair and stroked his smooth, plump face thoughtfully.

'Triccianus wasn't present?' he asked. 'Agrippa?'

'I didn't see them, master,' said his spy. 'I cannot swear to their absence. But I was on the roof for some time, and I was able to observe everyone who arrived in the house after dusk.'

'It's a shame you weren't able to watch everyone leave too.'

'That Silus has good eyes, master. I thought I was well-concealed.'

'No matter. Tell me what you heard.'

'Little I'm afraid, master. The walls are thick, and their voices were very indistinct. But I heard the words "useful idiot" and also "the end of the Emperor".'

'It's hardly conclusive. But it does tally with my own suspicions. Macrinus covets power, and I'm sure he has been behind the conspiracies against Caracalla ever since the death of Severus. But Caracalla trusts Macrinus, even if he doesn't respect him much. Apparently, an astrologer cast Macrinus' horoscope for the Emperor and declared him to be no threat.'

The spy inclined his head, letting the Commander of the Sacred Bedchamber continue his musings uninterrupted.

'But the fact that the Arcani are involved – that is interesting. I can't say I haven't always had my doubts about Oclatinius. But he is so hard to read. Still, he can be predictably loyal to his own. Sending that courier to warn Atius about my orders to have Soaemias assassinated was so obvious, it was trivial to find his agent and ambush him. It's a shame my assassin in Emesa was less efficient.

'You know,' continued Rufus, 'I'm sure Oclatinius thinks I have a mole within the Arcani. I don't think his pride would let him believe that I simply outwitted him.'

'You are clearly his superior, master.'

Rufus frowned. 'You should know by now I don't approve of sycophancy. Leaders need to hear the truth, not what they wish to here. Especially in the field of espionage. Lives depend on it.'

'I didn't mean…'

Rufus waved the start of the apology away. He placed his hands together and pressed them to his face, deep in thought.

'I can't take this to Caracalla. The evidence is too weak, and the conspirators too powerful. I will need to make Caracalla come to suspect them himself.'

'How will you do that, master?'

'Hmmm. Caracalla is very fond of astrology, isn't he? There is a seer in Africa called Hiempsal that I recall the Emperor knew and trusted as a boy, when he was growing up there with his father. I had a report about him recently, that he had fallen into debt, and was in danger of being sold into slavery. I think he may be of some use to us.'

Rufus drew out a wax tablet and a stylus and started to write, scratching out neat cursive letters. When he was finished, he closed the tablet, melted a blob of candle wax onto the free edge and pressed the imprint from his ring into the soft wax to seal the message. He handed it to his spy, together with a small bag of silver coins.

'Take this to Hiempsal, he resides in Utica in Africa Proconsularis. When he has read the message, convey him to Rome, and make sure he gets into the presence of the city prefect Flavius Maternianus. He is a sound man and will know what to do.'

'Yes, master.'

'It's a long journey and this will all take some time. Speed is useful, but it is most important that the mission is completed. The timing is not critical, the success is.'

'I understand.'

The spy took the tablet and money, bowed and departed.

Rufus sat for a while in thought. So, Oclatinius. Once again, you are at odds with the Commander of the Sacred Bedchamber. But this time, you are on the wrong side.

—

'Let me buy you a drink.'

'Fuck off and leave me alone.'

Silus ignored the sullen reply and drew up a stool beside Julius Martialis. His nose still ached, and when he had looked at it in a mirror, he thought it resembled the track made by a drunken donkey cart driver. He had been proud of his nose once. Or at least, there had been nothing wrong with it. Still, there were worse injuries to have sustained. He always shivered when he saw the amputee veterans begging on the streets, one arm a stump at the elbow, or a leg cut off above the knee.

Silus signalled to the serving slave in the tavern, and ordered two cups of wine, not the cheapest, but not the best. He wished Atius was here doing this. Atius was the affable, charismatic one who people warmed to even when they didn't want to. But Atius was many miles away, guarding Soaemias and Avitus, and so it fell to Silus to sound out Julius Martialis.

The morose praetorian didn't look up, even when the slave put a cup of wine in front of him.

'I know how you feel,' said Silus.

'I doubt that,' said Martialis.

'I haven't lost a brother, true. But I have lost family. A wife and daughter.'

'And been denied a promotion?'

Promotion? Was that what he was so down about? But just as the unsavoury thought crossed Silus' mind,

Martialis burst out, 'He wasn't just a brother to me! I cared for him. I raised him. He was like a son.'

Tears began to roll down cheeks that already showed the smeary tracks of previous bouts of weeping. Silus patted Martialis gently on the arm, wondering what Atius would say at this point. Although he had a knack for inappropriate jokes, he could also be sympathetic and tactful on occasion.

'It was unjust,' said Silus tentatively. Those words alone could be construed as treason if they got back to Caracalla's ears. Silus hoped he had judged Martialis correctly.

It seemed he had.

'Of course it was unjust. I deserved that promotion. I have served loyally. I gave gifts, I won a prize. Why shouldn't I be made centurion? And Titus, he saw it too. Family was everything to him. So when Caracalla compounded the insult to me with an insult to our mother...' He shook his head. 'Even then, he never struck the Emperor. I know he shouldn't have touched him, but surely a dozen lashes or exile would have been enough. Even being sold into slavery as punishment – at least he would still be... alive.'

Martialis choked down a sob, then picked up his cup of wine and took a deep drink. Silus felt genuinely sorry for him, and a little guilty that he was going to use him so blatantly. But only a little guilty. His continual harking back to his denied promotion grated on Silus' nerves. Still, it was that grievance and the loss of his brother that made him valuable to the conspirators. Silus flicked his fingers for the serving slave to fill up Martialis' cup. Martialis accepted the refill gratefully and drank again.

Good, thought Silus. This was definitely going to be easier if the praetorian was drunk. He turned the conversation onto safer subjects while he waited for the wine to get to work, although it wasn't easy to find a topic that didn't trigger Martialis' sensitivities.

'Did you see the javelin competition? That winning throw was immense.'

'I bet he gets a promotion.'

'Where do you think Caracalla will send the praetorians when the campaigning season begins?'

'What do I care, I'll just be a foot soldier forever, until I get killed or retire with a pittance.'

Silus doubted that Martialis would be hard up when he retired, given the enthusiasm with which he had embraced Caracalla's offer to allow the soldiers to loot as they pleased. He suspected that Martialis had easily made up the gold he had donated to Caracalla in the rest of the year's campaign of looting and pillaging.

'I hear the brothel next door has some new Egyptian girls in. Very popular, apparently.'

'Not in the mood.'

He didn't become less glum as he became increasingly drunk, but he did become more talkative.

'And another thing, about that fucking Cacar... Caracaca... that fucking Emperor. He claims to be one of the lads, marching and fighting with us, but at the end of the day, which of us has a fucking palace to go home to? A villa by the sea in Capri?'

Silus was pining for a small farm in the cold and damp of northern Britannia, but he nodded agreement nonetheless. In fact, the more he had observed of the life of an Emperor, the less he liked the look of it, and he couldn't imagine why Macrinus or anyone would want that job. There was always someone that hated you, always someone trying to kill you, and the constant worries of legal, financial and military matters seemed to give no room for peace. He did know that some men liked power for power's own sake, even if he didn't understand it. But of all the powerful people he knew, Oclatinius was the only one whose job he could consider doing – valuable, worthwhile, but behind the scenes, quiet, not attracting attention. He wondered what his former self, slaughtering a barbarian chieftain for personal glory and provoking a war in the process, would have made of his ruminations now.

'Maybe someone will do something about him one day,' Silus said, judging Martialis was sufficiently inebriated to have his guard down and say what he really thought.

'I wish it was me that could do him in.'

Silus looked around him. He had made sure they were in a quiet corner of the tavern with no possibility of being overheard, but the flagrant treason spoken out loud was unnerving. Fortunately, the tavern was all but empty, just the serving slave, and a couple of tired-looking workmen dicing in the furthest corner.

'He is very well-protected these days,' said Silus. 'I should know, I'm one of his bodyguards. It would be almost impossible to kill him and survive the attempt.' In all conscience, if they were going to recruit Martialis for this, he wanted to make sure that the praetorian knew the risks.

'I don't care. I wish I was dead. I'd be happy to take him down with me. In fact…' Martialis stood up suddenly, putting his hand on the table to steady himself. 'In fact I'm going to go to see him right now, and I'm going to stab him in that stupid face of his.'

'Shhh, sit down, that's not the way.'

Silus looked around again, but the two workmen had not even glanced up from their game.

'Maybe an opportunity will come your way. Maybe, just maybe, I know some people who could make that opportunity come about.'

Martialis slumped back onto his stool.

'What are you talking about?'

'I've said enough. We can continue this another day, when you are sober. If you are serious, that is.'

'Of course I'm serious.'

'Fine, let's talk again soon. But, Martialis. Breathe a word of what we have said to anyone, whether it's your closest friend or a priest or whoever, if you mention this conversation, it will get out, and then you and I are both dead men, who have achieved nothing.'

The thought of achieving nothing seemed to resonate with Martialis, and he nodded solemnly. 'By Mithras' bull, I swear not to reveal your words to a soul.'

Silus nodded. It was unnerving, putting his life in the hands of this fool. But he believed his sincerity, and his earnest wish to kill Caracalla. That could just be the way ahead for them all.

Chapter XII

Flavius Maternianus looked down at the Punic seer with distaste. The man who had accompanied him from Africa had reported that the seer had vitally important information that he needed to give directly to the urban prefect, the official in charge of Rome in the Emperor's absence. Maternianus had dismissed the seer's chaperone, and now stood in his office, hands clasped behind his back, waiting for the seer to speak.

'Prefect, my name is Hiempsal. I am a holy man from Utica. I see things and hear things. I prophesy. Men and women come from many miles to hear my words. When the Emperor Antoninus was a boy, I used to visit his father's residence, and I used to give my wisdom to the deified Septimius Severus, as well as the young Antoninus. The Emperor will remember me well, with fondness I hope, as I remember the clever and strong young lad with affection.'

'Yes, yes,' said Maternianus, thinking about the pile of letters and documents on his desk that he needed to read. Engineering work was needed on the Cloaca Maxima, one of the aqueducts was leaking, and half the roads in Rome seemed to be in urgent need of repair all at the same time. The last thing he needed was some foreign mystic man spouting hocus pocus. But if he really was favoured by the Emperor, he couldn't ignore him. So he just waited as patiently as he could to hear him out. 'Get on with it.'

'Prefect, I have had a vision. One that fills me with fear, as the mouse cowers before the shadow of the swooping eagle.'

Maternianus sighed inwardly and bit the inside lip to stop himself commenting. He had decided it would be quicker if he simply let the man speak without interrupting.

'I saw the colour purple, and I saw a sharp edge, and I saw a lake of blood.'

Maternianus tensed. He really hoped this wasn't going where he thought it was.

'I saw the new Alexander, murdered by Seleucus, and Antogones, and Ptolemy, and Cassander.'

The successor generals of Alexander the Great, who divided his Empire between them after the young warrior died. And new Alexander? Did he mean…?

Hiempsal clearly didn't want to leave any room for his message to be misinterpreted. 'I saw the Emperor Antoninus, dead, murdered by those closest to him. And I saw Macrinus and his son Diadumenianus, wearing the purple and commanding the legions, while the Senate bowed before them.'

Maternianus went cold. This man had just prophesied the assassination of the Emperor by one of his closest advisors. Maternianus had mixed feelings about prophecy. It wasn't that he disbelieved the concept, as such. It was more that the world of prognostication was full of incompetents and charlatans – they could be hard to distinguish from each other – and when a prediction did turn out to be true in hindsight, it was often too ambiguous to have been any use prior to the event. This, however, was both specific, and highly dangerous. If this seer went about Rome, crying out his vision on street corners, and word got back to Caracalla that Maternianus had heard his words and done nothing, then Maternianus was as good as dead himself. So doing nothing was not an option.

Maybe the best thing would be to kill him on the spot, right now. His prophesy of doom would go no further then.

But what if he was right? Maternianus owed his position to Caracalla, and he had no major complaints about the Emperor's leadership. Yes, he had drained the treasury for his campaign, but he was winning victory after victory on the battlefield, and surely would bring back unimagined riches after defeating the Parthians. He had heard the stories of the massacres of the unarmed and the civilians in Alexandria, Germania and Parthia, but he had not witnessed the horrors personally, and from a safe distance he tended to applaud the actions as great victories with minimal loss.

He scribbled a note on a scrap of papyrus. 'Take this to my banker, it authorises you to withdraw five hundred sestertii from my account. Return straight to Utica. Do not talk to anyone about what you have seen. If you do, it will be the worse for you, do you understand? Leave it to me to alert the Emperor to the threat to his life that you have seen.'

Hiempsal took the note and bowed deeply in gratitude.

'I know you will do your duty by our great Emperor, prefect. I thank you for your time, and for this generous gift.'

'Be off,' said Maternianus. 'I have work to do.'

Hiempsal hurried away. When the door was closed behind him, Maternianus began to pace the room, long-legged strides, one hand on the opposite elbow, supporting the hand that stroked his chin. Even if Hiempsal was as good as his word and said nothing more about the matter, he had obviously already told enough people for the story to be out. The man who had brought him from Africa clearly knew the content of his vision already, for one. And the gods knew how many others had heard his words. So Caracalla had to be warned, that was clear. But what was the best way to get the message to him far away in the East?

Maternianus decided that a single letter direct to the Emperor was not sufficient. Bandits, shipwrecks, riding accidents and countless other intercessions of the gods could cause a message to fail to reach its destination. So he resolved to write two letters. One would go with the official messengers, the frumentarii, direct to Caracalla. The other would go to Julia Domna in Antioch, and one of his trusted freedmen clients would be the courier. That seemed to give the best chance of this vital message getting through.

It would mean death for Macrinus and his son, of course. Maternianus didn't have any strong feelings towards Macrinus, positive or negative. He seemed to be a competent lawyer, and Caracalla had no need of relying on him for advice in military matters, which was fortunate since Macrinus seemed to have little knowledge of experience in that field. He had never done Maternianus any harm, nor any particular favours. But sadly, he and the young Diadumenianus would be the casualties of this divination.

He sat down at his desk and drew out two blank sheets of papyrus, a bronze pen and a clay inkpot. He thought for a few moments, and then began to write.

Februarius 217 AD

Julia Domna stood naked before the mirror, alone in her bedchamber. One side of her body was admirably firm, rounded and feminine without any excess. She took regular walks and regular baths, ate healthily and did not overindulge in wine. If one only took into account that half of her, she would still be attractive to a man half her age.

But the eye of any prospective lover would be drawn immediately to the other side, and particularly the chest. The tumour was advanced now, an ulcerated, oozing red mass that took up about a third of the surface area of the breast. When she was brave enough to touch it, she could feel how deep it extended. And it smelled. Though her maids, with carefully neutral expressions, washed it gently, and perfumed her, she was constantly aware of an odour of putrefaction. She, who had been the adored lover of two emperors of Rome.

And it hurt. There was a constant ache from the mass, and a sharp sting when she moved her arm. Her physician had prescribed her poppy juice, but she had been reluctant to take it — it made her head fuzzy, and she had affairs of state to attend to.

Sometimes she cried, less from the pain and more from the loss of her womanhood, the deformation of such an essential aspect of her femininity. Most of the time though, she bore her affliction stoically, knowing that Caracalla depended on her.

Caracalla. She hadn't seen him for months, and when he had been in Antioch, he had spent little time with her. He certainly had no interest in her as a woman now. Not that she would let him near her. She couldn't bear to see that handsome face regard her with disgust.

There was a quiet knock at the door, and her most trusted slave asked to be admitted. Domna assented. She would not hide from her servants. They at least would see her body for what it had become.

'Would you like help to dress, Augusta?' asked the slave. Domna nodded. First the slave placed an absorbent wool pad over the tumour, held in place with a breast bandage. Without that, a bloody ooze would strike through her clothing, causing a shameful embarrassment. Then the slave swiftly but carefully helped her into her stola, expertly draping it to minimise the rubbing of the cloth against the sore tissue. After this, she attended to her make-up and perfume and pinned an ornate wig in place. In recent years, Domna had made the wearing of intricate, wonderfully styled wigs highly fashionable among the noble women of Rome, though she still had a fine head of hair of her own that the ornatrices worked miracles with.

When she was ready to face the world, she proceeded to her office, where one of her freedman advisors awaited her to discuss the day's itinerary and present her correspondence. As her clerk spoke in a monotone about the meetings taking place and the religious ceremonies to attend that day, she shuffled through the various scrolls and tablets that waited to be read. One caught her eye, a letter from Rome, from Flavius Maternianus. She cracked the wax seal with her thumb and unrolled it.

At the first words, 'Augusta, I write with news of a most dread and unwelcome nature…' she held up her hand for her clerk to stop speaking and quickly read through the whole letter. She read it a second time, then sat back.

He was in danger. Her stepson. Her lover.

The man who had killed her only son. A man who ruled Rome with an iron fist, who perpetrated massacres on vast numbers of people, within and without the limits of the Empire. Who had betrothed himself to someone else without thinking about how it would hurt her.

Who could no longer look upon her naked body, or even bear to be near her.

She closed her eyes. Her breast throbbed, pulsing in time with her thumping heartbeat.

'Augusta, are you well?' enquired the clerk anxiously.

She crumpled the letter into a ball, then tucked it inside a fold of her stola, opened her eyes, and gave the clerk a forced smile.

'Continue. What duties must I attend this afternoon?'

–

Macrinus re-read the letter in horror, hoping that the terrible words would somehow say something different on the second reading. But no, they remained the same. 'Augustus, it is my difficult duty to inform you of a prophecy that has come to my attention that pertains to the safety of your person.'

And there, in the scratchy handwriting of Maternianus, was his own name, Macrinus, accused of conspiracy to murder the Emperor. That it was true made it feel no less unjust. Damn Maternianus. What had he ever done to offend the prefect? And his son was named too, which chilled him. He saw little of the boy, who was currently safely in Antioch with Macrinus' wife, Hamia, whom he also visited infrequently. But still he was his flesh and blood and would become Caesar to his Augustus when Caracalla was gone, as Caracalla and Geta had been to their father when they were young.

But now all was in jeopardy.

He looked up at Nestor and Julianus, who were regarding him with open anxiety.

'When was this written?' he asked.

'Last month, according to the date,' replied Nestor.

'Has he written to anyone else?'

'We don't know. Obviously this was couriered by the frumentarii, so we were able to intercept and read it before it went to the Emperor.'

'It's a small consolation. It buys us some time at least. But if Maternianus hears nothing back, in due course he will send another letter. Allowing time for a message from here to Rome, then time while Maternianus decides what to do, then a further letter being sent, maybe by a different route, we have, what, three months?'

The frumentarii commanders nodded agreement with the calculation.

'Then within that time, Caracalla must die. If he doesn't, it will be our heads rolling in the sand.'

Nestor and Julianus looked at each other, faces pale at the thought. Macrinus fiddled with one of his earrings, knowing he would get nothing useful out of his two allies until they had finished panicking.

'We need to meet Oclatinius and Silus,' said Macrinus firmly. 'Arrange it.'

Chapter XIII

Sempronius Rufus swept the correspondence off his desk to the floor, the wax tablets housed in their wooden cases clattering, while the messages written on papyrus drifted down soundlessly. Why was there no news from Rome? He had had word from his agent that the seer had been conveyed as promised to Flavius Maternianus and had delivered his fake prophecy. Why had Maternianus not written, to him, or to Caracalla, or at least to Julia Domna in Antioch? Was he in on the conspiracy? He had no evidence to believe so, although it was difficult to know who to trust these days.

That was why he had wanted Maternianus to be the one to send the message to Caracalla that Macrinus was involved in a plot. For all Caracalla's current, and as far as Rufus was concerned, justified paranoia, he seemed to have some trust for Maternianus, or he wouldn't have left him in charge of Rome when he departed, with all the potential that position held for rebellion.

He wished Caracalla trusted him so much, he thought ruefully. If Caracalla would take Rufus' suspicions as fact, he could be done with Macrinus before he could do any damage. But Rufus had not been in his position long, unlike Oclatinius for example. And Rufus' imme-diate predecessor was a proven traitor. So while Caracalla seemed to put some store in Rufus' reports, he was not yet ready to believe him blindly. That would come, he hoped. When he had exposed Macrinus' conspiracy, and Caracalla had purged his inner circle, Rufus' prestige and power would be augmented many times. He would become the Emperor's right-hand man. Maybe he would even be entrusted with power himself, as Sejanus was by Tiberius.

For that to happen, though, he must prove Macrinus a traitor. He knew how superstitious Caracalla was, his trust in astrologers and horoscopes and the healing powers of mystics. That was why Rufus had engineered a prophecy from a faraway country as his evidence of Macrinus' wrongdoing.

But if that message was somehow being blocked from getting through, he would have to find an alternative. Someone local, who he could present to Caracalla in person. His organised mind began to sift through reports he had read about potential local troublemakers in Edessa, which always included prophets and seers. One leapt out at him, a flamboyant priest of Astarte, the ancient Syrian goddess associated with war, royal power and healing. The goddess' symbol was the lion, something dear to Caracalla's heart with his pets and his bodyguards. And this outspoken priest was also very fond of gold. He would do. He summoned one of his freedmen assistants.

'Bring me, Serapio, priest of Astarte. At once.'

—

Silus was on edge as he stood guard beside Caracalla, with Thrax and Skylurus also in attendance. When he and Oclatinius had met with Macrinus, Nestor and Julianus the day before, the news had been bad enough to give him a sleepless night. So they had the task assigned to him to make sure Caracalla was dead within three months. He understood the urgency, but what power did he have to make it happen, after all this time trying? It was extra pressure, but without any solutions.

The preparations for war were nearly complete now. Soon Caracalla would be marching out at the head of his army to meet the Parthians. They had decided the best time to do the deed was towards the end of the battle, when hopefully the Parthians were defeated. Silus would have to work on Martialis. He hoped the praetorian was self-disciplined and intelligent enough to do as he was told. Not least because if Martialis failed, the back-up plan was Silus himself. And unless he was exceedingly cunning and lucky, and could make Caracalla's death look like a result of enemy action, killing Caracalla would be the last thing he did.

So, maybe his reprieve had been short-lived.

Triccianus had finished giving a report to Caracalla about the strength and morale of the Leones, both of which were excellent. Earlier, Oclatinius and Macrinus had reported on the current status of the praetorians, and Agrippa on the fleet.

Now it was Sempronius Rufus' turn to speak, and Silus expected to hear something vague about intelligence reports regarding threats from the Parthians and threats from within the Empire. Instead, the Commander of the Sacred Bedchamber requested of Caracalla that he be permitted to introduce a seer into the Imperial presence.

Caracalla frowned, but nodded agreement.

Silus tried to avoid catching Oclatinius' eye, but Macrinus looked with alarm at the Arcani spymaster. Oclatinius' face remained unperturbed. But Silus' guts were clenching in fear. Had this Hiempsal been sent from Rome to report his prophecy direct to Caracalla?

Rufus called out, 'Send for Serapio!'

Serapio? That wasn't the name of the African prophet. What was Rufus playing at?

The doors opened and in swept a tall priest with fine cheek bones and a beard trimmed into a point beneath his chin. He wore a dark silk robe embroidered with images of the sun, the crescent moon, doves, bees, lotus flowers and palm trees. On his back he wore a lion skin, the head of the lion acting like a hood, so a fierce, bestial, snarling visage glared out from above Serapio's forehead.

'Augustus, may I present Serapio, renowned and respected prophet, and priest of Astarte, the ancient Syrian goddess. It has come to my attention that Serapio has had a vision. I don't personally know how much faith you can put in the accuracy of these sorts of prophecies, but I thought you were the best one to judge, knowing so much more about these matters than I.'

'What vision?' asked Caracalla, looking intrigued.

Rufus gestured for Serapio to speak. The priest closed his eyes and bowed, and the lion's head covered his face. He held that pose for a long moment, up to the point where the onlookers were starting to get impatient. Then he threw his head back and raised his arms to the sky.

'I saw blood,' he wailed, in a high-pitched, strained voice. 'I saw death. I saw betrayal. I saw you!' He extended a long, bony finger towards Caracalla. 'I saw a purple robe torn in two, a gold throne split in half. I saw you, Augustus, lying dead with your throat cut wide open.'

There were gasps from around the room. Caracalla was staring at the priest with a look of horror on his face. These were lethal words. Prophesying the demise of an

Emperor was always going to mean someone would end up dead. The only question was who.

'And I saw you!' The priest spun and this time, his accusing finger sought out Macrinus. The praetorian prefect blanched visibly and took an involuntary step back. 'Yes, I saw you, Macrinus, you and your son, receiving the acclamation of the Senate and the People of Rome, as they greeted you as their new Emperor, and your son as their Caesar.'

'This is preposterous!' exclaimed Macrinus.

'Augustus, my prophecy is true. Your reign will be short, and this man will succeed you.'

There was a stunned silence in the room. Silus prepared to move. He ran through in his head how things would play out. He would go for Caracalla first, ensure his first strike was mortal. Then he would have to protect Macrinus. That would mean taking on Thrax. There was no one else in the room who could possibly stand up to the giant. He hoped that Triccianus and Oclatinius could handle Skylurus. And then what? But there was no time to think any further than that. He tensed, ready to spring.

Caracalla rose to his feet slowly.

'When did you have this vision?' he asked quietly.

Serapio looked taken aback. He hadn't expected to be questioned. 'Um, last month, Augustus.'

'And you waited until now to bring this news to me?'

'I… was unsure what to do. It was a fearsome experience, Augustus, and I was afraid. But I knew my duty was to…'

'You believe in horoscopes? In astrology, how the fate of man can be read in the movements of the stars?'

'Yes, of course, Augustus. We are all ruled by forces beyond our control. Even emperors must bow before the will of Fate. If you like, I will cast a horoscope for you now, to confirm my vision.'

'There's no need,' said Caracalla. 'Only yesterday, Oclatinius presented me with three of the foremost scholars of the stars in the East, that he had summoned to Edessa for me. They read the movements of the sun and the moon and the stars and the wandering bodies and examined the birth dates of all those close to me, as well as my own. And do you know what they said?'

Serapio shook his head, uncertainty and trepidation in his eyes.

'They told me, firstly, that Macrinus was my loyal and dedicated servant. What say you to that?'

Oh, well played, Oclatinius, thought Silus.

'I hesitate to say that these learned men were wrong, but my vision was clear. Though I never said that Macrinus would betray you, only that someone would, and Macrinus would succeed you. Maybe in the same way that the Emperor Pertinax was betrayed, but it was your honourable deified father who ultimately avenged and succeeded him.'

'They also warned me that a false prophet would come before me, predicting my death and accusing those closest to me of treachery.'

Now it was Serapio's turn to pale. 'No, Augustus, I am no false prophet. I am a priest of Astarte…'

'You come before me, with lies about the praetorian prefect, with lies about my own murder!' Caracalla's voice was rising, louder and higher. 'You dare to come before your Emperor with these words?'

'Augustus, if I have offended, I apologise, I only thought it right that I…'

'Get on your knees.'

Serapio dropped to his knees, hands clasped together.

'I pronounce your words treason,' said Caracalla.

'No, Augustus,' squeaked the priest. 'I only wished to serve you.'

'The punishment is death. Silus, execute him.'

It was far from the first time that Silus had been forced to serve Caracalla as executioner. But it was the only time he was happy to perform the role. The priest had clearly been bribed or blackmailed by Rufus and did not care that his words would get people killed.

Silus stepped forward, and before the priest could say another word, Silus stabbed downwards, his blade going under the collarbone into the chest cavity, the same killing strike that was the fate of the defeated gladiator who did not receive the Emperor's mercy.

Serapio gasped, clutched at Silus, then toppled forward to lie on his face at the Emperor's feet, blood gushing from the wound. Caracalla looked down at the body with contempt, then up at his shaken advisors.

'This meeting is adjourned. Silus, go and clean yourself up. Thrax and Skylurus, with me.' Caracalla strode from the council room, leaving it strangely silent after the dramatic scene a moment before. Rufus glared at Oclatinius, who returned the stare steadily, unblinking. Then Rufus hurried after the Emperor, no doubt anxious to distance himself from Serapio's words.

The only people left in the room were the conspirators. Oclatinius and Silus, Ulpius Julianus and Julianus Nestor, Triccianus and Agrippa, and Macrinus who was trembling visibly. All knew how close they had come to disaster. But none spoke, nor even caught each other's eyes. They were in the Emperor's home, and anyone could be listening in.

With nods and handshakes, one by one, they all wordlessly departed.

–

'We must act now,' said Macrinus. 'Now subtlety has failed Rufus, he might just come straight out and denounce us to the Emperor.'

'Without evidence?' asked Agrippa, sceptical, but his tone holding a quiver of anxiety.

'He could fabricate evidence easily enough,' said Ulpius Julianus. 'A forged letter. A false testimony from someone claiming to have overheard us plotting.'

'Every day could be our last,' said Julianus Nestor. 'If we don't kill him right now, we are all dead men.'

Silus tutted to himself. The conspirators were talking themselves into a state of high panic. They were meeting in a secluded temple some way from the city, at night, not willing to risk another spy acting for Rufus or anyone else reporting on their movements and conversations. But the scared faces made more sinister by the flickering lamplight illuminating them, the creepy, dark surroundings, and the cries and hoots and chirruping and rustling of nocturnal animals, birds and insects accentuated everyone's anxiety.

Fortunately, Oclatinius was present, and as always he provided the serene voice of reason.

'Calm yourselves, friends. There is no urgency.'

'How can you say that after yesterday?' demanded Nestor.

'Precisely because of yesterday. Rufus' stock is too damaged to risk another attempt at exposing us right now. Especially with false evidence. There would be a strong possibility we could disprove whatever he presented, and that on top of yesterday's debacle would mean the end for him. Yes, our own stock is damaged too – Caracalla may have sided with us, but doubts will have remained. And we still have the words of the seer from Africa hanging over us like the sword of Damocles, ready to fall who knows when. So, we shouldn't be hasty, but nor should we delay unnecessarily.'

'What do you recommend?' asked Macrinus, clearly fighting to keep his voice steady.

Oclatinius looked around the group, making sure he had their full attention.

'I believe we have our assassin, in the person of Julius Martialis. Silus has sounded him out, and we think he will do as we ask, even if it costs him his own life. So it comes down to timing. The Parthians must be defeated, or in their fury at Caracalla's betrayal, they will storm through the Empire like a whirlwind, wreaking death and destruction everywhere they go. Maybe we could defeat them without Caracalla, but he is by far the best man to lead us in the field.'

Macrinus glowered at this but said nothing.

'So we make sure Martialis is stationed near to Caracalla during the upcoming confrontation with Artabanus,' continued Oclatinius. 'Triccianus here can request some praetorians as back-up for the Leones as bodyguards during the battle. When we are sure the battle is won, we give Martialis the signal, and he kills Caracalla. Then Martialis is cut down by the Leones – Silus will need to ensure this happens. We can't have him surviving to boast that he was working for us. Then Macrinus can plausibly distance himself from the assassination, and declare himself Emperor, since Caracalla has no heir.'

'You make it sound so simple,' said Agrippa.

'The best plans usually are. Are we agreed?'

There was a pause, then nods all around.

'Good. Silus, you need to speak to Martialis.'

Poor fellow, thought Silus. Still, rather him than me.

Chapter XIV

Aprilis 217 AD

Once again, Silus was privileged to witness the might of the Roman army on the march. And this was as big a mass of men as Silus had ever seen. Caracalla had gathered the units that he had dispersed to their winter quarters, and the sum of the parts, infantry, cavalry, artillery and supply train, was truly vast. What was more, this was an army of well-trained and experienced soldiers. Many of them had fought in Britannia, Germania and Armenia as well as the more recent skirmishes as the legions pillaged Parthia. Many would also have taken part in the massacres of the Alemanni and Alexandrians and the slaughter at Arbela, which, while not teaching them much about battle, would at least have got them used to killing. Given the length of service, a minimum of twenty years plus five years in the reserves, a good number of the legionaries in Caracalla's army would have served his father in Africa fifteen years before, and some would even have taken part in the civil wars that brought Septimius Severus to power twenty-four years prior. Few of the men in this army were green recruits, the majority being hard-bitten, scarred, calloused veterans.

Silus, now riding with the Leones at the front with the Emperor, had watched the army assemble with Oclatinius, the Arcani leader and praetorian co-prefect, who had pointed out to him the insignias on their shields that boasted to which legion they belonged.

The usual forces that habitually accompanied the Emperor were present, of course, the praetorians, the speculatores, the frumentarii and the Leones. The Leones and praetorians rode in the van alongside the Emperor, the appearance of the neat, highly polished praetorians contrasting with the rough, shaggy, barbarian Leones. The new Macedonian phalanx came next – this of all the forces had the least experience. Although Caracalla had experimented with tactics involving the unit during the last summer's campaign, there had been no pitched battles to truly blood them, even if many of the individual soldiers were veterans of the legions. After the Macedonian phalanx came the full strength of the First, Second and Third Parthian and the First and Second Adiutrix legions.

Other units in the army were drawn from across the Empire. Although Caracalla was too prudent to denude his frontiers to the point where they would be vulnerable, his previous campaigns had pacified the trouble spots sufficiently that he could withdraw large numbers of men from the Empire's border defences to augment his force. The army for the Parthian invasion therefore included detachments from legions stationed in Mesopotamia, Pannonia, Germania, Africa, Raetia, Arabia, Syria, Moesia, Palestine, Dacia and Italy itself, including a cohort of the Urbaniciani, whose main job was policing the city of Rome, but were often drawn upon for major campaigns. In addition to the regular legions were auxiliaries and allies from Armenia, Mauretania, Gaul, Germania and Britannia who served as light infantry, slingers and archers. The navy had provided some of its marines as infantry, and large numbers of barbarian mercenaries had been recruited from the parts of Germania and Scythia outside the limits of the Empire.

Behind the main fighting force came the artillery, mainly ballistae, the crossbow-like scorpions, siege towers and battering rams, and in the rear was a baggage train, wagons and carts pulled by oxen, mules and donkeys that seemed to go on forever. This contained all the supplies needed to sustain an army in the field for a campaign – food and drink for the soldiers, fodder for the cavalry horses and pack animals, the construction materials for the marching camps that would be built each night, the ammunition for the archers, slingers and artillery, javelins, spare caligae and gladii and shields. A significant force of legionaries brought up the rear to protect against a surprise attack from that direction.

It was hard, even for a society as detailed in its record keeping, to make an exact tally of the men in Caracalla's army. Not every cohort or century would be at full strength, where sickness, injury and death had not been compensated for by new recruitment. But Oclatinius reckoned the fighting strength that Caracalla commanded at around a hundred and fifty thousand men.

Despite his feelings about Caracalla, Silus had to be impressed by the dedication the man had shown to his goal of conquering the East. Years of preparation, recruitment, training, pacification of any threat elsewhere in the Empire that could interfere with his great plan. It was hard, knowing Caracalla's military prowess, the morale and experience of his men, and the truly enormous force he commanded, to believe anything except that Parthia would soon become another province of the Roman Empire, and that Caracalla would go down in history as the first man to conquer the territory of the ancient Persian Empire since Alexander the Great.

Yet, Oclatinius also sounded a note of caution. They had had word, via Artabanus' brother Vologaesus, who still opposed the Parthian King of Kings, of the size of the force that Artabanus had gathered. Infuriated by Caracalla's treachery which led to the deaths of many of his relatives, and even some of his children, Artabanus had gathered the might of the entire east of the Parthian Empire, ready to meet Caracalla in the field. Tribes and peoples that Silus had never before encountered, and in some cases never even heard of, had rallied to Artabanus' cause. He was reported to number Dahae, Medes and Arabs in his army. He had tribesmen from further east mounted on two-humped camels. And of course he had the fearsome Parthian cavalry, mounted archers as well as armoured cataphracts, in much superior numbers to the Roman cavalry. The result would be no foregone conclusion, and the only difference between the two armies on the day of the battle may be Caracalla's strategic and tactical prowess.

And then, when the battle was won, Martialis could do his job.

The talk had gone as well as he could have hoped. He had spelled out in detail what was required, and though Martialis had been loath to allow Caracalla to live long enough to experience the pleasure of victory, he admitted to understanding the importance of the Emperor to the battle, and how the safety of Rome depended on his survival just that bit longer.

But when the battle was won, Martialis was free to strike. The praetorian hadn't asked what would happen next, and Silus hadn't brought the topic up. They both knew that Martialis would likely not survive, even if he was successful. Caracalla was surrounded by too many adoring men to let his assassin live long. But Martialis seemed to accept this. Silus had told him that Triccianus, the Leones commander, and Oclatinius and Macrinus, the praetorian prefects, would ensure that Martialis was in close proximity to Caracalla at the right time. Then he had patted the praetorian on the back and left him with his thoughts.

Martialis was somewhere behind Silus now, riding with the mounted units of the praetorians. Silus wondered what feelings and emotions were whirling inside their chosen assassin. Very similar to how Silus himself had felt, when he was the one nominated to give his life for the cause, he supposed. Not that Silus was in any way relaxed himself. If Martialis failed, it would be Silus' task to finish the job properly. And if Martialis succeeded, Silus would need to fly to Rome, to outstrip the message of Caracalla's death, to save Tituria from Caracalla's agent that would kill her as soon as she heard of his demise.

He straightened his back on Delicatus, waving to the cheering crowds from Edessa who scattered petals and palm branches in their path, willing them on to victory. He imagined the onlookers could not comprehend the defeat of such a force.

To Silus, the future had never seemed more uncertain.

—

The camp had been broken down before the sun had risen over the distant hills, and the men had dressed and breakfasted and were ready to march. It was the sixth day before the Ides of Aprilis, what would have been a chilly day in northern Britannia, a pleasant one in Rome, and would likely be overwhelmingly hot here in the middle of Parthia, like most other days. Progress of an army of this size was not quick, since they could only proceed at the speed of the slowest elements, the baggage carts. Still, in the few days since they had left Edessa, they had covered sixty miles and were now deep in Parthian territory. In fact, they were near the town of Carrhae, close to which had been fought the disastrous battle which had seen one of Rome's worst defeats, and the death of the fabulously wealthy triumvir, Crassus.

On that day, over two hundred and fifty years before, Crassus had led seven legions of heavy infantry, around thirty thousand foot soldiers, and four thousand cavalry into battle against ten thousand Parthian mounted archers and armoured cataphracts. Though superior in numbers, he was helpless against the Parthian tactics. The archers rode up to the legions, then retreated, loosing their arrows behind them in Parthian shots. When the legions formed a tortoise with interlocking shields that were impenetrable to the archers, they lost mobility, and the armoured heavy cavalry charged them and inflicted more losses. Crassus and his son were both killed, and there was a story Silus had heard, which Oclatinius dismissed as apocryphal, that Crassus had had molten gold poured into his mouth as mockery of his wealth.

There was palpable tension among the army as they prepared to march near this scene of ill-fortune. Even the grizzliest veterans made signs to ward off evil, and whispered prayers to whichever god seemed most appropriate to protect them from the lemures, the wandering spirits that could find no rest because of their premature deaths, that no doubt inhabited this country. Silus himself was not immune to it, and mumbled brief prayers to Jupiter Optimus Maximus, Serapis, Mithras and even Atius' Christos to be on the safe side.

Caracalla, ever in tune with the mood of his men, also noticed their disquiet, and so before they started their day's march, he pulled up his horse before them and addressed them, his deep voice carrying far in the still dawn air, his words being relayed by others to those further back so that all the army received his speech.

'It is not beneath my notice through what lands we travel today. No one with any knowledge of the history of our great Empire can fail to have heard of the disaster that fell the legions near here, against the same foe that we march now to meet.

'But let me tell you, my comrades, my friends. We are not marching to a Carrhae, nor a Cannae, nor a Teutoburg forest. We are marching to a Zama, an Alesia. We will emulate Alexander the Great at Gaugamela and smash these successors to the Persians. Because I am no Crassus. I am no Varus. I am Alexander, reborn, to bring victory to Rome and death to its enemies.'

The cheers and roars from tens of thousands of men were deafening, rolling like thunder from the hills across the army as Caracalla's words reached each unit. Caracalla held his arms up and basked in the adulation. When the noise died down, he spoke again.

'But we must not forget the fable of the fighting cocks, the victor carried off by an eagle just as he crowed in triumph. Fate may bring us down if we are not respectful of the gods and our ancestors. For this reason, I am going to journey to the Temple of the Moon, to make offerings to the fallen heroes of our past, and to the gods of Rome, to ensure they look upon us favourably.

'The Parthians are marching towards us now, and soon we will hear the sound of their drums and the horses' hooves. But I have no fear. Because I know the might of your sword arms, and the strength in the hearts of each and every one of you.'

More cheers of approval and adoration rang out, and Caracalla soaked it all up, his grim face as close to content as any time Silus had seen it.

'I leave you now, taking with me just a small number of guards, so that I do not disturb your march. But I will return before sun down, and then I will lead you to victory!'

Caracalla waved and rode out, accompanied by a handful of Leones and praetorians, among them Silus, Thrax, Skylurus, Triccianus.

And Martialis.

—

'I'll be glad to see something green,' said Silus to Julius Martialis. They rode together, side by side, just as the other Leones and praetorians in the group were mixed up. It had been Triccianus' suggestion to integrate the praetorians and Leones further, his argument to Caracalla being that it was dangerous to neglect the feelings of the praetorians and show too much favour to the Leones. Bringing the praetorians back into bodyguarding work, and mixing them with the Leones, would reduce the resentment and the feeling of neglect that some of the praetorians were experiencing. Caracalla was hesitant, feeling much more comfortable around the Leones, and well aware of the role the praetorians had played in the demise of previous emperors. On the other hand, he also knew that snubbing them could be equally dangerous, so he had agreed to allow a limited number of praetorians to accompany the Leones, albeit well outnumbered by his favoured personal guard.

The real reason for Triccianus' request, of course, was to get Caracalla and the Leones used to the praetorians being around, and in particular to normalise Martialis being in close proximity to the Emperor, so when his time came at the end of the forthcoming battle, no one would question the assassin's presence until it was too late. Caracalla had made no comment at Martialis being included in the trip. Silus wasn't sure whether he hadn't noticed or didn't particularly care that a man whose brother he had ordered executed and to whom he had denied promotion was in his entourage. Maybe he was just too distracted by the imminent climax of everything he had been preparing for, for so long. And Martialis had not put a foot wrong since the death of his brother, acting every inch the loyal servant.

Still, Silus wanted to keep an eye on him, and so he stuck close, watching carefully for any slip in the mask, any signs of anger or hatred towards Caracalla that others could pick up on. But Martialis seemed to be a good actor, or genuinely in strict control of his emotions. He replied to Silus in an offhand manner.

'The eye certainly tires of sand and scrubby bushes. And even blue sky. The occasional cloud wouldn't go amiss.'

'Exactly,' said Silus. 'Where I am from, blue sky is a rare treat, and something to be treasured. Here it is like a fine delicacy that you are given so much of, it makes you feel sick.'

Martialis chuckled.

'And trees,' continued Silus. 'We have towering oak trees full of leaves from spring to autumn, and ash and elm and willow. And even in the winter, we have the evergreens to give us colour, holly and fir and yew. I miss trees.'

'I miss my brother,' said Martialis quietly.

Silus threw him a sidelong glance. Martialis' lips were pressed together, and he was looking straight ahead, focused somewhere in the middle distance. So, the emotions were in there, just well-locked down. He quickly looked around him, but none of the others were riding close enough to overhear.

'I know how it feels,' said Silus. 'I miss my family, every single day. But your time is very close. The battle can only be two or three days away.'

Martialis nodded.

'I won't survive, you know.'

It was the first time Martialis had come right out and acknowledged his fate. And it was true. His chances of seeing nightfall the day of Caracalla's murder were almost non-existent. Silus didn't know what to say. There was no point lying to the man, he wasn't stupid.

'But I think I'm fine with that. Half of me died with Titus. The other half will join him soon.'

Silus leant across the gap between them and patted him on the shoulder. They rode on in silence for a while.

An hour further down the road, still maybe an hour or so shy of their destination, Caracalla held up his hand for them to halt. The Leones and praetorians reined their horses in and waited patiently.

'I'll see what's happening,' said Silus, and urged Delicatus into a light trot towards the head of the small column.

'Caracalla has ordered a rest stop,' said Triccianus, when Silus reached him. Silus was surprised. They weren't far from their destination, and Caracalla was a man in his prime, with formidable stamina. Why did he need a rest?

But when Silus looked at the Emperor, he saw he was clutching his abdomen, bent forward, and he had a pained expression on his face. He dismounted gingerly and hobbled off the road into the scrubby bushes. Ha! Imperator Caesar Marcus Aurelius Severus Antoninus Pius Augustus, father of his country, consul, Pontifex Maximus, victor over the Germans and Britons, needed a shit. Not quite a god yet, then. Silus wondered if his habit of dining with the soldiers had caught up with him – a strong stomach was needed to digest some of the rations that were doled out.

'Men, dismount,' called out Triccianus. 'Take some food and water and see to your mounts.' And then, in a lower voice, he said, 'And avert your eyes. No one wants to be gawped at while they crap.'

Silus trotted back to Martialis, then slid off Delicatus, and gave his backside a rub. He took a swig from his waterskin and offered some to Martialis, who shook his head. Silus leant against Delicatus and closed his eyes, shutting out the bright midday sun for a few moments. He felt like he could almost sleep standing up. It was a rare moment of peace, and his body seemed to be urging him to take the chance to shut down, just for a short while.

'Who me?'

Silus opened his eyes. It was Martialis that had spoken, but he didn't understand who he was replying to. He hadn't heard anything.

'Of course, Augustus,' said Martialis, 'at once.'

The praetorian strode purposefully towards where Caracalla was crouching down behind a bush, grunting and straining. Silus frowned. Why had Caracalla summoned Martialis? Was he going to humiliate him by making him wipe his arse? But Caracalla was hidden from sight by the leafy shrub. How had he summoned Martialis from that position?

Silus looked around to see if anyone else had noticed, but all had their faces resolutely turned away from their Emperor in this intimate moment. Of course, the men were used to communal toilets, chatting to their neighbour while seated for nature's call. But the Emperor expected and deserved more privacy and respect, and Leones and praetorians alike afforded him this.

Except Martialis, for some reason.

Later, Silus blamed his slow response on his dulled state of mind, dozing as he was, although Oclatinius thought it a poor excuse for an Arcanus. But still, he was the first to realise something was amiss, and that was only because he knew Martialis and his hatred for the Emperor.

Silus started to walk quickly towards the praetorian, trying not to attract attention from the other bodyguards, desperate to break into a run. But to intercept Martialis before he had done anything wrong would raise all the wrong questions, would, in fact, ruin everything. On the other hand, if he didn't get to him in time, Martialis would do the deed way too early.

He wasn't going to make it in time.

Martialis disappeared behind the bush. Should he shout, warn Caracalla? Oh, Martialis. Couldn't you have waited just another couple of days for your vengeance?

Silus rounded the bush to see Martialis, dagger in hand, standing over Caracalla. The Emperor was squatting down, back to the praetorian, tunic pulled up around his waist, hairy arse on display. The noise of Silus' arrival, more hasty than Martialis had been, alerted Caracalla. He looked up.

Martialis brought the dagger down.

Despite his vulnerable position, despite being unarmed, Caracalla reacted like a snake, spinning, arm up, trying to knock the dagger from its path towards his heart. He succeeded in diverting the blow a fraction, and the blade sank deep under his shoulder. Caracalla let out a cry of absolute fury that would be heard for miles around. As Martialis drew back to strike again, Caracalla grabbed him by the wrist, and grasped Martialis' throat in a meaty fist. Maybe it was his fury, maybe there was something supernatural, god-like about the Emperor, but he shrugged off the deep wound as if it was a horse fly bite and began to strangle Martialis to death with his bare hands. Martialis gurgled, his face turning purple, and the dagger fell from his hand.

Silus looked on in horror, frozen into inaction. The possible futures played out before him, and all held disaster. If Caracalla's wound was not mortal, and Martialis survived, he would be held and tortured, and the name of every conspirator would be revealed. All of them, Silus included, would be executed in the most painful way imaginable, and Tituria and Atius too would die.

If Caracalla's wound was not mortal, but Martialis died, then maybe the conspirators would be safe. But there would never come a chance to be rid of Caracalla again. Paranoia multiplied, his ranks would be purged ruthlessly, while a victory over the Parthians would put him in unassailable good favour with people, army and Senate alike.

Still a young man, Caracalla might continue his savage rule for decades to come.

And if Caracalla died, the armies faced the Parthians without the Emperor's tactical genius, and they faced a military disaster such as Rome had maybe never experienced before.

Martialis sunk to his knees and Caracalla towered over him, blood pouring down his back, spittle at the corners of his grimacing mouth. Silus heard shouts of alarm, running feet.

It was time to decide.

Silus stepped forward and thrust his blade into Caracalla's back between the ribs, into the spot that Martialis had been aiming for originally. The long knife reached the chambers of the heart and ripped them open. Caracalla turned to stare at Silus and opened his mouth to speak. But no words came out, only a gout of blood. As he sank to the ground, he kept his furious eyes fixed on Silus, until the life went out from them, and they stared blankly into the distance.

Silus' hand loosened on his knife, almost dropped it. His knees went weak. The enormity of what he had done nearly paralysed him.

Yet he was an Arcanus. Picked for his innate abilities, highly trained, and highly experienced. Veteran of wars and deadly missions. And he had only a moment to save himself, and the conspirators.

Martialis had struggled to his feet, breathing heavily, holding his bruised throat.

'Silus,' he said, voice hoarse. 'I'm sorry. I saw my chance, and I worried it would never come again. I had to do it. For Titus.'

Silus shook his head. 'You're a damned idiot, Martialis. And I'm sorry too.'

And he thrust his knife up under Martialis' ribs, through his liver, lacerating vessels and puncturing his lung. Martialis gasped, grabbed onto Silus, stared into his face, wide-eyed. Then an expression of calm came over him. He gave Silus a single nod, then let go, and toppled backward.

The footsteps and shouts were nearly upon Silus now. He looked around for Martialis' fallen dagger, pressed it into his hand, then knelt down and grabbed Caracalla, cradling his body.

Those moments alone with the dead Emperor seemed to last an eternity, as if time stood still, though he knew looking back that the Leones would have reacted as soon as they heard the disturbance and would have covered the distance separating them at a sprint. He stared down at the clean-shaven face, still angry in death, brow furrowed and eyes narrowed as always. Had he done the right thing? Had he saved Rome or condemned it? What did it mean, for him, or Tituria?

Then the world jolted back into motion, and there was no more time for reflection, or planning. For everything that followed, he would have to rely on instinct. Instinct, and the training and experience of an Arcanus.

Skylurus arrived first, Thrax, surprisingly fast for his size, just behind, both Leones with swords drawn. They halted abruptly and stared at the tableau before them. Silus looked up at them, still holding the Emperor's corpse, and with Martialis dead nearby, the terrifying Caracalla lying dead in his arms, both of them murdered by his own hand, he did not need to feign a look of heartfelt anguish.

'What did you do?' demanded Thrax and though his voice was low, not much more than a whisper, the words hit Silus like a hammer. Others were arriving now, praetorians and Leones, their faces all mirrors of one another, shock and horror turning to fury. If Silus said the wrong thing now, they would rip him to pieces before he had finished speaking.

'Martialis,' said Silus, and his voice trembled. 'He killed our Emperor.'

There was an intake of breath. Though it was obvious Caracalla was dead, hearing the words out loud seemed to make the fact more true, more final.

'There's blood on your blade,' said Thrax.

'Martialis' blood, yes,' said Silus. 'I tried to stop him; I was too late.'

'Death seems to follow you everywhere, Silus,' said Thrax. 'How do we know it wasn't you that killed Caracalla, and killed Martialis too when he tried to stop you?'

An angry murmur went around the soldiers. Hands went to sword hilts. Blades were half-withdrawn. Thrax took a menacing step forward, holding no weapon, but his great hands lethal killing tools on their own. Silus closed his eyes, unable to summon any further argument, too tired to resist any more.

'Look,' said Skylurus. 'Martialis is holding a blade wet with blood. And Silus has no wounds upon him. It must be the Emperor's blood.'

Thrax paused, glaring at Silus.

'And I saw Martialis approach the Emperor first,' called one of the praetorians. 'Silus went after him.'

'Why did you follow him?' asked Thrax, voice still cold and dripping with suspicion.

'You killed the man's brother, Thrax! On the orders of the Emperor. I thought Martialis was going to argue with him, maybe even strike him and get himself in trouble like his brother did. I didn't expect… this.'

Thrax was silent. The others, Leones and praetorians alike, looked to him, as if waiting for a decision.

'Stand back,' came a firm, clear voice of command.

Triccianus strode forward through the onlookers and stood over Silus, looking down at Caracalla. Then he knelt and took the body from him, kissing it gently on the forehead, and laying it on the ground, arranging it in a dignified state of repose. Silus couldn't help notice the strong stench of faeces, the result of Caracalla's last action in this world.

'There will be time for grieving, time for anger and retribution,' said Triccianus to the men. 'But for now, our duty is clear. We must convey the Emperor's body back to the army and the council, so that wiser heads than ours can decide what happens next. Will you perform for our illustrious Antoninus this last duty, and escort him back to the bosom of his beloved army?'

The sombre bodyguards mumbled their assent.

'Thrax, Skylurus, wrap him in his caracallus and bear him back as best you can.'

'What about Martialis?' asked Skylurus.

Triccianus looked at the corpse of the praetorian, avenged for his brother, and reunited with him now, and then spat on him.

'Leave him. The wild dogs and vultures can clean that traitor's bones.'

—

257

A great commotion preceded them into the camp, as news spread like a fire in dry forest. One of the praetorians had been tasked to ride on ahead to the camp so they were forewarned, and it seemed the whole army had turned out to watch as the small group of bodyguards brought Caracalla's body back.

Oclatinius and Macrinus, as the two praetorian prefects the most senior military men present, stood at the front of the crowd. Oclatinius' face was like ice, and when he met Silus' eyes, Silus could read his thoughts like they were engraved on stone. 'How could you let this happen?' he was saying. Macrinus on the other hand was pale, and though he was trying to portray an air of grave sombreness, Silus thought he looked frightened.

Skylurus and Thrax carried the body with solemnity and laid it on a blanket that had been put out to receive it. Macrinus and Oclatinius advanced together, and while Oclatinius looked down in sadness, hands clasped before him, Macrinus threw himself to the ground and began to weep and wail loudly, tearing his hair and crying aloud how cruel the gods were, to take their Emperor from them, who everyone loved more than life itself.

It was an impressive display, thought Silus, and it seemed to do the trick of convincing the army of Macrinus' innocence. In fact, the only murmurings of discontent that were heard were that the traitor Martialis had got away so lightly with this heinous crime, that he should not have been afforded the mercy of a quick death. All acknowledged that he acted alone, and there was no talk of plots or conspiracies. Even Thrax seemed to accept that Caracalla's death was the act of a lone, suicidal madman with a grudge.

Only Sempronius remained suspicious. Silus could tell, from the way he gave long appraising stares in the direction of Macrinus, Oclatinius and himself. Silus ignored him and Oclatinius stared back. Macrinus, however, could not meet his eyes, and no doubt Sempronius was the only one outside the conspiracy who guessed the truth.

But what could he do? He no longer had Caracalla to report to. Indeed, there was currently no Emperor, no one in charge of the vast Roman Empire. No good would come of him proclaiming his suspicions to the army without evidence – Macrinus would have him executed immediately. Silus suspected that Sempronius would wait to see who took control and attempt to maintain his grip on his position by cosying up to the new Emperor, whoever that was. Still, Silus couldn't help but think the devious eunuch still had another trick up his sleeve.

Caracalla's funeral took place that afternoon. In that heat, flies were already swarming over the body, laying their eggs, and by sundown the corpse would be bloated and writhing with maggots. With all the solemnity and ceremony that an army on the march could provide in the middle of a foreign country many miles from the nearest city, Caracalla was burnt on a huge pyre, Macrinus leading the ceremony and acting as the chief mourner. After, he collected the bones into a large urn, and gave them to Oclatinius for safekeeping.

He then declared that the army should rest and mourn in whatever way they saw fit for the rest of the day. But the next day they must be ready to march to battle, for Artabanus and his army was nearly upon them.

No cheers followed Macrinus' announcement, just murmurs of ill-ease, discontent, and mutterings about bad omens and looming disasters. Macrinus gave them no encouraging words but retired to his tent.

Chapter XV

The following dawn saw the efficient, professional army breaking down the marching camp, and getting themselves ready to set off. Whatever the personal feelings and misgivings of the individual soldiers, the ingrained habits of army life, and the rigid discipline imparted by the junior officers, kept everything moving, even though the legions and the Empire were currently leaderless.

The conspirators met in Macrinus' tent as the sun was rising. At first, Macrinus would not get out of his bed, crying that he should be left alone, and hiding under his blankets, until Oclatinius gave him a kick on the backside, and told him to get on his feet if he didn't want to swiftly follow Caracalla. Oclatinius' harsh words did the trick, and soon Macrinus had joined the others. All the major conspirators were present, the two praetorian prefects, Ulpius Julianus and Julianus Nestor, Agrippa and Triccianus, and Silus, all seated on folding chairs in a small circle. Sempronius probably wondered why he was excluded, furthering his suspicions, but he was the least of their concerns at that moment.

Macrinus slumped down on a chair and stared despondently at the floor. 'It's a disaster. All is lost. How could it come to this?'

'What are you talking about?' demanded Agrippa. 'We got what we wanted, didn't we? The tyrant is dead.'

'The tyrant was the only one who could lead us to victory against the Parthians,' said Triccianus. Macrinus glared at him but did not dispute the words.

'We must sue for peace,' said Nestor firmly. He was gripping a cup of water from which he kept sipping, more in nervous habit than to quench a thirst.

'Are you mad?' demanded Agrippa. 'To surrender with an army this size still intact, without even offering a fight? The soldiers would mutiny in an instant.'

'Besides,' said Oclatinius, 'Artabanus would never accept. Though he and his daughter survived the massacre, he lost his wife and his other children. Not to mention the terrible insult to him and to the honour of Parthia. This is personal for him. There will be a battle.'

Macrinus buried his face in his hands, and Silus thought he might be weeping. Oclatinius pursed his lips in irritation but did his best to speak encouraging words.

'This is still a battle we can win. Whatever we may think of Caracalla, he has gathered a highly trained, highly experienced army, well led by its centurions, tribunes and legates. They will fight, and they will hold. They only need to be told what to do.'

'I don't know what to do,' cried out Macrinus piteously, and Silus hoped they were not being overheard. 'I am a lawyer, not a soldier.'

'That may be true,' said Oclatinius. 'But I have spent my whole life working in or with the military forces of the Empire. I have been a close confidante of both Caracalla and his father and have long been privy to the decisions of war. I will be by your side, Macrinus, and I will guide you.'

The look Macrinus gave Oclatinius was pathetically grateful.

'Nevertheless, we must try for peace,' said Macrinus, ignoring the glare from Agrippa. 'We should send emissaries offering to return our prisoners and pay him some financial compensation.'

'If you must,' said Oclatinius, 'but I advise you to prepare for battle nevertheless.'

'So, you still intend to succeed Caracalla?' asked Agrippa tentatively.

Macrinus swivelled his focus to the fleet commander. 'Why would I not?'

Agrippa spread his hands. 'You just seem… less certain about the prospect than before.'

Now Macrinus managed to summon a few ounces of iron to strengthen his voice.

'I will be Emperor, and I will rule this Empire of ours wisely, strongly and fairly.'

'Of course,' said Agrippa. 'I didn't mean any disrespect. I just wanted to make sure you were still… set on the course.'

Macrinus stood up, straightened his back and his shoulders. 'Are there any others who doubt my desire and ability to lead?'

No one else spoke, and after Macrinus had given them each a challenging stare, he sat back down. 'It's settled. I will summon the senators and have them pronounce me Imperator before the army.'

'Might I suggest,' said Oclatinius, 'that we wait a day or two?'

'Why?' demanded Macrinus.

'If we too hastily announce you as Caracalla's successor, people might start to ask questions. Given how loyal the army were to Caracalla, if they have the slightest suspicion that you were involved in his murder, it would go very badly for you. At least until you have consolidated your grip on power.'

'He's right,' said Triccianus. 'Give it a couple of days. You and Oclatinius can lead the army together until then, like the consuls of old used to, without the need for an Emperor.'

'But you will need to be acclaimed before the battle,' said Oclatinius. 'The men will need to know they have a single, strong, competent and confident commander to lead them. And that being the case, may I suggest you attend to your appearance before you leave the tent.'

Macrinus looked down at his dishevelled tunic, then ran a hand through his tangled hair and beard.

'Very well. Are there any other matters to attend to?'

'What is to become of the Leones?' asked Triccianus.

'They must be disbanded of course. They are Caracalla fanatics. I couldn't trust them, especially if they became suspicious of my part in Caracalla's demise. It will be easy to justify – they failed in their sole task of preserving the life of the Emperor.'

'I would recommend waiting until after the battle, though,' said Oclatinius. 'The Leones are a formidable fighting force, and we will need every advantage in the coming days.'

'Good point,' said Macrinus. 'In fact, maybe throwing them into the front line of the battle might be prudent.'

'And then what becomes of me?' asked Triccianus, a little plaintively.

'Don't worry,' said Macrinus. 'You will be rewarded for your help when the Leones are no more. A governorship somewhere. How does Pannonia sound?'

Triccianus beamed. 'It sounds excellent.'

'Now, what else?'

'The army will look after itself up until the point of contact with the enemy,' said Oclatinius, 'as long as you tell them when to march and when to halt. But we need some intelligence on exactly how far away the Parthians are, and what their strength is.'

'Aren't the speculatores already out there scouting?'

'They are,' conceded Oclatinius. 'But their reports are partial and contradictory. I want someone we know and trust to give us a definitive report of what we are facing.'

All eyes turned to Silus.

'Wait, no. I'm finished. My part in this is over.'

'Not yet it isn't,' said Macrinus.

'I have to get back to Rome. Urgently. Oclatinius, you know why.'

Oclatinius sighed. 'There is time for that. Rome is a very long way. We aren't going to send news of Caracalla's death until after the battle. We will give you a head start, so you can get there first, and do what you need to do.'

Silus looked at him uncertainly. 'You know what is at stake.'

'I do,' said Oclatinius. 'The life of a young girl. And the fate of an entire Empire.'

—

Tituria sighed.

'What's wrong, little one?' asked Juik, her personal slave. The two of them had become closer since she had moved into the household of Titus Petellius Facilis and become his ward.

'Nothing.' She sat at her dressing table and stared morosely into the bronze mirror.

'I know you well enough to know that isn't true.' Juik picked up the tresses of her long, black hair and began to plait them. 'You can tell me.'

'It's just that I had my sixteenth birthday a few days ago.'

'Didn't you enjoy your party?' asked Juik. 'I thought the master threw a wonderful celebration for you. Dancing girls, feasting, musicians, jesters and acrobats.'

'Yes, of course. I'm not ungrateful, for all the kindnesses Titus Petellius shows me. It's just, I am a woman now. Facilis will be looking to marry me off soon.'

'What an exciting prospect.'

'Maybe. But I am not his daughter. He won't gain much from marrying me to the son of a senator or even an equestrian. The best I can hope for is some rich, fat, divorced merchant who wants a young bride.'

Juik laughed. 'You think too deeply, little one.'

'Why isn't there more to life for a woman than marrying and raising a family anyway? If my father was alive, I'm sure he would only want the best for me. He wouldn't make me marry someone if I didn't want to.'

'Your father sounded like a wonderful man, who loved you very much, little one,' said Juik. Tituria had opened up to Juik enough to talk about her family, although not of course their deaths at the hands of Silus and his comrades. 'But Facilis loves you too, and he will make sure you find a suitable husband who is kind to you.'

She pursed her lips. Was a kind husband the best she could hope for?

She felt a cold, wetness press against her ankle and looked down to see Issa. She picked up the ancient little dog and held her in front of her face. The terrier's eyes were clouded with cataracts, she could hear little, and she walked stiffly. And her breath still smelled like it flowed straight from the Cloaca Maxima. But she was a constant comfort to Tituria, her companion in her exile. And besides, she was her connection to Silus, the man she ought to hate, but whom she loved more than anyone else alive.

She cuddled Issa close. Oh, Silus, when are you coming home?

—

'I just feel so fucking useless,' said Atius, lying in Soaemias' bed and stroking his fingers down her naked back.

'I wouldn't say useless,' said Soaemias. 'Not bad at all in fact. But if you like, I can give you some pointers to refine your technique.'

'I don't mean in bed,' he snapped irritably. 'Wait a minute, what do you mean, pointers?'

'Oh, sorry, lover. Forget I said anything. What were you talking about?'

Atius gave her a sideways glance, then said, 'I mean, out there, Silus is facing Christos knows what dangers, maybe giving his life, to rid us of Caracalla, and make you and Avitus safe. And I just sit here, eating the food and drinking the wine that the villagers can sell us, and making love to you.'

'I admit, the most basic of pleasures can get a bit wearing over time...'

'I should be out there, by his side, fighting with him, enduring whatever he is going through.'

He got up abruptly. Soaemias held onto his hand, but he kissed it, then let it go.

'It's time for another trip to Emesa. Oclatinius may have sent word.'

Soaemias looked concerned. 'Be careful. Please don't leave me here with just Gannys for my comfort.'

Atius felt a twinge of jealousy, though he knew he had nothing to fear from Gannys with regards to Soaemias' affections – that relationship had long turned from a passionate one, to one of mutual utility. 'I'll be back before you know it.'

He shrugged on a light tunic and went outside. Avitus was sitting in the sand, cross-legged, eyes closed, palms on his knees, lips moving in some ritual or prayer. He was thirteen now, or thereabouts, and looking more like he was on the edge of manhood. Was that a little fluff on his upper lip?

Atius didn't disturb his meditations and mounted his horse.

In Emesa, he visited the Arcani agent whom Oclatinius had stationed there to act as a conduit for messages from the spymaster. And unlike his previous visits, there was a message from Oclatinius. A small piece of rolled papyrus. He read it carefully.

'By the time you receive this message, there will likely have been some great changes in the Empire. Proceed at once to Antioch and await orders.'

Atius pocketed the message for later safe disposal. Time to say goodbye to Soaemias, at least for now. She wasn't going to like that!

–

Silus rode Delicatus through the hills of the Mons Masius, keeping up a steady pace eastwards in search of the main Parthian force. More than once he had had to hide from Parthian scouts and skirmishers, and on one occasion it was only Delicatus' speed in a straight race that had saved him from a pair of Parthian scouts.

He crested a low ridge and reined in Delicatus to an abrupt halt. Despite the heat, he felt a chill run through him and suppressed a shiver.

Below him was the biggest army he had ever seen arrayed in one place.

For a long moment, he could do nothing but stare in awe. What had Caracalla been thinking? Even the vast force that Caracalla had gathered, led by the great general himself, could surely be no match for this concentrated mass of military power. And to think that they now had Macrinus to lead them into battle...

He shook his head firmly to rid himself of his stupor. Come on Silus, he told himself. Do your job and get out of here.

There was no question of him attempting any sort of accurate count of the Parthian manpower. The best he could do was make a wild estimate of numbers and the approximate proportions of light and heavy infantry and cavalry. He put a hand to his brow to shield his eyes from the high sun, and his lips moved as he methodically worked his way across the enemy forces, committing what he saw to memory.

The most striking thing after the sheer size of the army was the preponderance of the mounted forces. It shouldn't have been a surprise – the Parthians were famed for their cavalry, but seeing it laid out across the plain below him in all its glory was terrifying. The heavy cavalry consisted of cataphracts. A good proportion of the mounts were actually camels, taller than the horses, heavier, and firmer of foot in the sandy, arid conditions, though harder to control and far less dextrous.

Both the cataphract mounts and the riders were massively armoured. A dismounted cataphract rider was vulnerable because his weighty armour made movement slow, so armouring the mounts reduced the chance the rider would find himself in that situation. A charge from cataphracts was hard to counter because of the weight of the front line as it impacted the enemy defence, and the thick armour deflecting the spears that were usually employed to break a cavalry charge. Silus saw now the wisdom and logic of Caracalla's decision to form and train a Macedonian phalanx with their long pikes. Though the late Emperor had been mocked, with most believing it was just another example of his obsession with Alexander the Great, Silus realised that the forward-thinking strategist had come up with a way to counter these formidable opponents. He would have to make sure Macrinus used the phalanx to maximum effect, rather than dismiss it as a pointless vanity project.

As well as the cataphracts, which could be launched at the enemy with the same effect as a shower of massive catapult stones, the Parthians boasted a vast number of light cavalry consisting mainly of mounted archers. Although less intimidating to behold than their heavy counterparts, Silus knew that it was these units that had been responsible for the defeat of Crassus at Carrhae. Fast, agile and supremely skilled, they could launch volley after volley of arrows into the ranks of their opponents and wheel away before they could be countered, only to return moments later like the incessant waves wearing away at the solid rocks on a shore.

Proportionately fewer, but still present in enormous numbers were the foot soldiers, again in light and heavy units. Silus tried to mentally divide them up into chunks, guess how many men were in each chunk, then multiply up to get an estimate of the size of the force, but neither his eyesight at this distance, nor his arithmetic ability were up to the task, and he decided his report would use phrases such as more than the stars in the sky, and the grains of sand on the beach.

Delicatus' ears went back, then the proud horse shifted its weight from foot to foot. Silus leant forward to chide him for his indiscipline.

He heard the whistle of the arrow through the air a fraction of a heartbeat before the missile tore through the cloth of his tunic over his shoulder, lightly scoring his skin as it whizzed past. He spun round.

Two Parthian horsemen had approached quietly up the hill behind him, and one had loosed when they thought they couldn't miss. Only Delicatus' sharp hearing and Silus' lucky movement had saved him from an arrow in the centre of his spine. Silus yanked on the reins, and Delicatus responded instantly, dancing in a tight circle to face the newcomers.

Silus took the briefest moment to calculate his options. The Parthian scouts, no doubt on the look-out for spies such as him, were between him and the route home, roughly twenty yards away. At his back now was the huge Parthian army. The scouts were clearly by far the lesser of two evils.

He dug his heels into Delicatus' flanks, urging him forward with a cry and drawing a javelin from his saddle bag. The other scout had an arrow nocked, and let it fly as Silus charged. But Silus' sudden response had taken him by surprise, and the shot was overly hasty and poorly aimed. The arrow flew high and wide. Silus' javelin, on the other hand, flew true, plunging deep into the chest of the Parthian's horse. The horse reared, tossing its rider to the ground, then fell sideways, trapping and crushing the Parthian's legs, the cries of the rider mingling with the distressed whinnies of his mount.

The other scout had another arrow nocked and was in the process of drawing the string back. But Silus was already upon him, spatha drawn, and as Delicatus galloped past, Silus lashed out, slashing the extended arm holding the bow, making the Parthian drop the weapon with a yelp.

Silus wheeled Delicatus back round, expecting the fight to be over. But the remaining Parthian had drawn his spear with his good arm and driven his horse into a gallop. With a yell of angry, incomprehensible barbarian words, the Parthian raced towards Silus. Silus flapped the reins and Delicatus once again raced forward. The two horses, evenly matched in size, charged towards each other, heading for a disastrous collision that would likely break the necks of both beasts.

It was Delicatus that swerved first, but the cunning horse knew what he was doing. Just before impact, he took a neat sidestep, and nudged his opponent in the shoulder. The Parthian horse stumbled, and the Parthian's spear thrust, aimed at Silus' chest, went wide. By contrast Silus, after many months in his saddle finally getting used to his horse's ways, was ready for the manoeuvre. He gripped Delicatus tight with his knees to keep his balance and stabbed sideways. The sword bit deep into the Parthian's neck, and Silus felt it grind against the neck bones before he pulled it free. The Parthian toppled to the ground, clutching hopelessly at the huge rent that was gouting blood. Moments later he was dead.

Silus reined in Delicatus and looked back at the remaining scout, injured and pinned beneath his dead horse. He contemplated finishing him off, but at that moment he heard a shout. A party of more Parthian scouts, a dozen strong, rode into view from the direction of the Parthian army to the east. Their mounts were no doubt fresher than Delicatus, and maybe were as quick. He needed all the head start he could get.

'Come on you little bugger, let's get out of here.'

Delicatus ears went back, and Silus wondered if he had offended him with the use of the word bugger. But if he had, Delicatus didn't let it affect his obedience to his master. Kicking up sandy dirt from beneath his hooves, he bore Silus westwards at a speed that had his rider gripping on for dear life. Before long, they had left the Parthian party far behind, and Silus eased him back to a trot. They continued back towards the Roman encampment, while Silus went over his report in his head. He hoped that Macrinus had learnt enough lessons from Caracalla's generalship, or at least would listen to others who had, to avoid disaster when these two Empires clashed.

But he wasn't confident.

Chapter XVI

Macrinus stood before his gathered army, the praetorians in the front ranks in pride of place. He was guarded by several Leones, including Thrax, Skylurus, and Silus, who had delivered his report that morning. As well as the very approximate numbers and composition of the opposing forces, Silus had also estimated that the two armies would meet the following day. Macrinus had therefore decided it was time to settle the question of the succession with immediate effect.

He had gone to every effort to cut an imposing figure, wearing his full praetorian prefect uniform, buffed and polished so every button and medal gleamed in the sunshine. His beard was neatly trimmed, his hair washed and oiled. He was even wearing his finest earrings, gold studs with embedded diamonds.

Macrinus was flanked by Oclatinius and Triccianus, with Agrippa, Julianus Nestor, Ulpius Julianus and Sempronius Rufus close behind. Between him and the army, seated on folding chairs, were the Roman nobility and military leadership – the legates and tribunes, the senators and most influential equestrians that had accompanied Caracalla on his expedition.

Macrinus spoke primarily to the most important men before him, but he raised his voice to ensure as many of the soldiers could hear him as possible. He didn't have

Caracalla's deep, booming tone, nor was he as imposing physically, but his words were relayed so all present had a more or less accurate sense of what he said, and all listened patiently and respectfully.

'Our Empire has suffered a grievous loss. Our beloved Emperor is no more, dead at the hands of a cowardly assassin. And yet we have little time to grieve. The Parthian army marches on us, and we must meet them. Though I sent them emissaries, asking for a period of grace to pay respects to our fallen leader, and even offered to return prisoners to them in exchange for a period of peace, they refused my entreaties, and declared that they were for war.

'I do not fear the Parthians, and I have no doubt we will defeat them decisively when we meet them. But to do that, we must appoint a successor to Antoninus. Though it would be ideal to delay this decision until the Senate can meet in Rome, we do not have that luxury. And the Senate is represented by many fine members of that body who are here before me today. So we can create a new Emperor, on this very day, who can then lead us to victory on the morrow. And might I suggest, you could do no better than a man who has served Rome loyally for many years and has risen to the rank of praetorian prefect because of his proven talents and abilities.'

Macrinus looked expectantly across the ranks of senators, army officers and the ranks of legionaries. For a moment, no one spoke.

Then, from somewhere among the praetorians, a loud voice rang out.

'Oclatinius!'

Macrinus looked startled. Then he regained his composure, and ignoring the voice, spoke directly to the senators.

'Who should we elevate to the purple, noble fathers?'

'Marcus Oclatinius Adventus!' came a shout from the praetorians, a different one this time. The shout was taken up by others, more and more, until it became a chant, roared out by thousands of voices, recognition of a modest man who had served the Senate and people of Rome loyally, who had worked his way up through the ranks from legionary to praetorian prefect, who had proven his talents and abilities time and again.

Macrinus stared at the arrayed faces crying out the name of their chosen Emperor, and Silus saw in his face the crumbling of his dreams as he came to terms with the fact that the name on their lips was not his.

The senators could see which way the wind was blowing and were not foolish enough to oppose the will of the soldiers – that way lay violent death. They too stood and called out for the elevation of Oclatinius, stretching their arms towards the old man in supplication that he answer their appeal.

Silus looked at Oclatinius and almost laughed out loud at the expression on his face. The old man could not have looked more shocked if Caracalla had risen from the earth and begged him too to succeed him. It was clear to all that the head of the Arcani had not sought this position, and that made them want him more.

Oclatinius took two steps forward, and Silus noticed how he exaggerated his age and infirmity, limping heavily, back bowed. He raised his hands high in the air and made motions for quiet. It took a while, but eventually the acclamation died down enough for him to be heard. He was not used to speaking in public, but his voice carried well enough, although Silus thought he added a tremulous note for effect.

'Noble senators and equestrians. Legates and tribunes. Centurions and legionaries and auxiliaries. You praise me beyond all merit. I cannot say how honoured I am that you consider me, a man of humble background who has only ever wished to serve, worthy of stepping into the shoes of a man like Antoninus.'

Yells of approbation rang out, and he waited a moment before continuing.

'But I cannot accept.'

Now there were cries of anguish and disapproval. He motioned for quiet.

'I am an old man. I have seen seventy winters. My joints are crippled with arthritis, my sight is failing. Maybe my wits will soon follow. If I was a younger man, it would have been a prize beyond all imagining to be elected to lead you, noble men of Rome. But my time has passed, and it is for a man in his prime to be the one to rule over you.'

More shouts of denial, but he waved them away.

'It's true. I am older than Galba, Nerva, even Pertinax, when they ascended to the purple. My duty is to serve your next Emperor to the best of my ability, as long as my heart holds out. And I could commend no greater leader to you than the man by my side, my co-praetorian prefect, Marcus Opellius Macrinus.'

The look that Macrinus gave Oclatinius combined disbelief that Oclatinius had turned down the gift of ultimate power, with profound gratitude. The gathered troops were silent for a moment, contemplating this turn of events. Then Cassius Dio, from the front of the gathered senators, called out 'Macrinus for Emperor!' and the other senators quickly and enthusiastically took up the chant. Silus doubted they had genuine respect for the man. After all, he would be the first Emperor not to have come from the senatorial class. But at least if they demonstrated that he was their choice, they would retain some semblance of authority over the succession, and also gain favour with the new ruler.

The soldiers, easily swayed as usual, also acclaimed Macrinus, who stepped forward, embraced Oclatinius, then waved to the soldiers, beaming from ear to ear. The cheering crescendoed to a peak, and Macrinus lapped it up like an actor taking the plaudits at the end of a play.

After some time of milking the moment, shaking hands with senior nobles and officers, as well as some of the ordinary legionaries – Silus noted that he had obviously learnt something from Caracalla, such as flattering the common soldier – he stood before them to speak.

'I accept this honour that you have thrust upon me so unexpectedly,' he said, and Silus had to turn a guffaw into a cough. 'We are still grieving for the loss of a ruler and fellow-soldier, and we shall always remember his noble achievements and immortal glory. But now we have honoured his memory, we must look to our own welfare. Artabanus is advancing upon us with all the power of the East, and he seems to have just cause to quarrel with us. After all, we were the aggressors, we broke the treaty, and made war upon him in the middle of peace.

'But now, the whole Roman Empire relies upon your courage and faithfulness. We are not in dispute about boundaries or rivers. A mighty king comes against us, to extract revenge for the murder of his children and relatives, who he says were unjustly massacred.

279

'Therefore I say to you, keep to your ranks, as Roman discipline dictates. The barbarians are an unformed multitude, and their very numbers will hinder them, while your order and military skill will give you a great advantage. So take heart, behave as Romans, as you always have. And if we vanquish the barbarians, not only will you have earned great glory, you will have proven to the world that you can beat them without treachery and surprise, but with valour and force of arms!'

It was a good speech, Silus admitted, maybe as befitted a man more used to declaiming in the courts than fighting wars, and the legions thought so too, calling out Macrinus' name, acclaiming him as Augustus and Imperator. The senators hurried to congratulate him, bowing and shaking his hand and clapping him on the back, and Macrinus delighted in every moment.

Silus glanced at Oclatinius, who had stepped back into the midst of the Leones, content that he was no longer the centre of attention. But Silus could see the doubts in his eyes, which were mirrored in Silus' own heart. How would Macrinus perform when battle was joined? Silus knew one thing. He was no Caracalla.

—

It was the third day before the Ides of Aprilis, in the year 970 ad urbe condita, the year reckoned from the founding of Rome. Silus sat astride Delicatus, one of the Leones who were still guarding the Emperor Macrinus, though their presence was leavened with numerous praetorians who Macrinus thought more loyal. Also present were the new Emperor's military advisors, Oclatinius, Agrippa and Triccianus. They were on a low hill from which they could survey their forces, and the battle that was about to commence. Nearby, but not in sight, was Nisibis, an ancient city that had been ruled over the centuries by Arameans, Assyrians, Babylonians, Persians, Greeks, Romans and the current occupants, the Parthians. To the east was a mountain range, the highest peak of which was Mount Judi, the place if Silus recalled Atius' stories correctly, that the boat that had survived the great flood in the Christian and Jewish mythology had come to rest.

The plain in front of them looked like it had suffered a new inundation, this time of men. The two vast armies confronted each other, and Silus could well imagine the emotions swirling around – tension and excitement, fear of the battle warring with impatience to be started. He had experienced them all himself too often to count.

The Parthian army was as he had surveyed it, with the forces divided into five large groups, each of which had heavy cavalry to the centre and fore, with wings of mounted archers. There had been a minor clash the day before, when some light cavalry from both sides had clashed at a water supply, but it had been inconclusive, and gave no indication as to which force was superior. That question would soon be settled.

The Romans were drawn up in a typical orderly fashion. Macrinus had organised the Macedonian phalanx into hollow oblongs at the front, ready to repel a cavalry charge, while in between the phalangeal sections were gaps through which infantry sallies could be made. The heavy infantry made up the first rank, the lighter infantry the second rank, and the cavalry were on the wings. Oclatinius had expressed some concern about the form-ation at their battle council that morning, fearing that they could be outflanked. But Macrinus, with an apparent new-found confidence now he was Emperor, dismissed Oclatinius' worries, stating that he had read Arrian and Plutarch and that he well understood the Alexandrian tactics that Caracalla had intended to employ. Silus didn't know enough to express an opinion, even if he had dared, but he would have trusted Oclatinius over Macrinus any day, and so shared the old man's disquiet.

But it was too late to make changes now. Trumpets rang out across the wide plain from the Parthian side, and immediately the Parthian cavalry charged. To the uneducated eye, they looked disorganised, ragged in their attack. But Silus knew better than to underestimate them, and the Parthians did indeed know what they were doing.

As the riders neared, the soldiers of the phalanx braced, two hands gripping their long pikes, the butts wedged into the ground, the points at the end of long poles extending well beyond the reach of any cavalryman's sword. But the Parthians were not foolish enough to throw themselves onto the spines of the porcupine. Instead the archers mounted on horses and camels raced to within bowshot of the Roman line, then wheeled away, loosing a volley of arrows over their shoulders, and Silus was privileged to watch the perfect execution of a thousand men performing the Parthian shot.

The men in the Roman front line were unlikely to be so appreciative, as the hailstorm of missiles hit home. Gripping their pikes two handed, the men in the phalanx could not protect themselves with shields, and the arrows caused devastation among the vulnerable men, with dozens falling to the first volley, injured, dying or dead. Cheers, cries and screams echoed around the plains, and Silus winced at the punishment inflicted.

A volley of javelins and arrows flew out towards the Parthians, but few hit home, and the Parthians were soon out of range. They instantly turned though, nocked new arrows, and charged back at the Roman ranks, repeating the tactic, to similar effect.

Macrinus looked agitated and turned to Oclatinius. 'They are massacring us,' he said. 'What do we do?'

'Hold fast, Augustus,' said Oclatinius. 'This is merely the beginning. It looks bad, but our losses are a mere flesh wound, when you take into account the numbers we have.'

'How can you say that? Our men are dying down there, and we are not replying. We must send in the cavalry.'

Silus felt a stab of concern. Was their new Emperor panicking already? That self-confidence hadn't lasted long. He just hoped that Macrinus would heed the wisdom of those around him with experience of war.

'I would advise against it,' said Oclatinius. But Macrinus was already turning to his buccinator.

'Sound the cavalry charge.' The buccinator instantly played the notes ordering the charge, which was relayed with more trumpets and hand signals to the cavalry reserve. Silus pursed his lips. This was looking bad.

This time, as the Parthians raced back in, the Roman cavalry converged on the mounted archers in a pincer movement from each flank. The Parthians whirled and fled back towards their own lines, and the Romans cheered as the enemy were chased away.

But the relief was short-lived. The Parthians had seen the Roman cavalry attack, and already their heavily armoured cataphracts were on the move. The two sets of heavy cavalry crashed with a sound like thunder rolling in from the mountains, and the heavily armoured cavalrymen hacked and slashed at each other.

Initially, both sides were evenly matched, the Parthian superiority in numbers being checked by the bravery and discipline of the Romans, mainly skilled German and Moorish auxiliaries. But then the Parthians began to target the Roman horses. Unlike the Parthian cataphracts, in the Roman cavalry only the men were armoured, and so the vulnerable horses started to fall like swatted flies. The Romans could not apply the same tactics to the iron-clad Parthian mounts, and soon the Parthians were in the ascendancy, massacring every dismounted Roman with ease.

'Augustus,' said Oclatinius urgently. 'Send in the club-bers.'

Macrinus, who had been watching the disaster unfold with dismay, looked at Oclatinius with incomprehension. Oclatinius pointed out the unit of soldiers that Caracalla had trained and armed specifically to deal with the cataphracts. Although they were lightly armoured foot soldiers, and had been intended to complement the phalanx in a defensive position, they were the only force they had that could counter the cataphracts.

Macrinus nodded. Oclatinius gave the order himself, and Silus saw the foot soldiers break into a run. They were about a hundred yards from the skirmish, but lightly armoured as they were, they covered the ground quickly. Within moments, they were in among the cataphracts, laying about them with their heavy maces and clubs, aiming at the cataphracts' mounts, breaking legs and caving in skulls. Though they took many casualties them-selves, the Parthians had no appetite to stay and have their precious horses maimed and crippled in this way, nor did they wish to be dismounted and forced to fight on foot like the Romans. The retreat sounded, and the Parthians broke off, leaving the remains of the Roman cavalry and clubbers to make their way back to their own lines.

There was a pause in the battle now, as both sides took stock, dragged the wounded away, and took the opportunity to drink from waterskins, as the sun and the temperature rose higher.

Triccianus, without consulting Macrinus, sent orders to adjust the positioning of the scorpions and ballistae so they could target the enemy cavalry on the next charge. They would have limited effectiveness against a fast moving, loose formation, but at least the Romans would see that some reply was being made to the Parthian attacks. Oclatinius also sent a messenger down to the cavalry, with orders that Silus didn't hear.

The next attack didn't take long, and the Parthians had no reason to change a winning tactic. The mounted archers came forward once more, and though the vicious heavy bolts of the scorpions and ballistae took down a handful of horses and riders, they came on with minimal losses.

The battered and demoralised Roman cavalry galloped out once more, loosing arrows and waving their swords threateningly, and once more the Parthian archers retreated, with the cataphracts coming forward. This time, however, the Roman cavalry fled before the fearsome Parthian horsemen. Silus noticed the Romans were throwing something behind them as they retreated, and for a moment was puzzled. Then he saw the cataphract mounts suddenly pulling up, becoming lame, or going down completely, and at the same time Silus noticed that the hooves of the Roman mounts were gleaming in the sunlight. He realised what the cunning Oclatinius had organised. The Roman horses were wearing metal slippers, and their riders had tossed out caltrops – small pieces of twisted metal crafted so that whichever way they landed, a sharp spike pointed upwards.

The cataphract charge broke up in disarray, and as it did so, the praetorians and clubbers rushed through the gaps in the phalanx and set among the Parthians. In hand-to-hand fighting, Roman infantry could not be bettered by any soldiers in the world, and they inflicted heavy casualties on the Parthian cataphracts, before they were able to extricate themselves and retreat.

Both sides broke apart, and went back to their own lines, panting like boxers between rounds, glaring at each other and nursing their injuries. Then, when the Parthians had recovered, they came forward again.

And so the day went on. Wave after wave of attacks from the Parthians were countered by the Roman defences, pikemen preventing the cavalry charge from breaking the Roman lines, cavalry doing just enough to stop the Parthian mounted archers from attacking with impunity, Roman artillery peppering the Parthians, slowly but surely taking a toll on their numbers. And before the Roman lines, bodies, most still, some moving feebly and crying, began to pile up.

When dusk fell, the Parthian attacks ceased. Macrinus disappeared to his tent, and before Oclatinius followed him, he sent Silus down to the front to assess the damage. Silus trotted Delicatus down the hill, passing lines of legionaries and auxiliaries tramping in the other direction to the relative safety of their marching camp, with its stockade and fortifications to defend them against a surprise night attack. Not that that eventuality was likely.

Attacking in the dark would not favour the Parthian mounted archers which were their main strength.

Silus looked at their faces as they tramped along, dirty, sweat-streaked, despondent. They had fought the Parthians off, and inflicted major losses, but their own losses, too, had been grievous, and they knew that nothing was yet decided, and they would have to do it all again the next day. Silus was relieved it wasn't him standing in a line, holding a pointy stick while arrows rained all around, forbidden from advancing, facing execution if he retreated. Every instinct would be telling them to fight or flee, and they could do neither.

At the site of the battle, Silus could see for himself the awful number of casualties on both sides. Legionaries, auxiliaries, pikemen and cavalry littered the ground on the Roman side, and in front of the Roman lines, in the no man's land between the two armies was a horde of fallen Parthians, camels, horses and cavalry men.

Many of the fallen were still alive, crying feebly and plaintively for help, for water, for the gods or their mothers. Some of the stricken mounts still lived too, breathing heavily, or trying to drag themselves away on broken legs. Medics and stretcher-bearers scurried back and forth, carrying away those that could be saved, and in a number of cases, speeding the passing of those that clearly could not. Delicatus' ears flicked back and forth, and his eyes were wide, the smell of blood and the noises from the dying, unsettling the usually unperturbable beast.

There were few scavengers on the field, human or animal. This was still an active battlefield, with patrols from both sides passing back and forth, sometimes leading to skirmishes, although more often the opponents kept well clear of each other, having no desire to rush into a fight that they hadn't been ordered into.

Silus did his best to assess the losses on both sides, though with the failing light, and given the size of the battlefield, it was an impossible task. He guessed that the Parthian casualties were worse than the Romans, but they also had a larger force to start with, so whether the Roman strength compared to the Parthians was relatively stronger or weaker by the end of the first day, he wasn't sure.

Delicatus started, and Silus looked down to see a young soldier had grabbed the horse's leg. Delicatus freed himself and the soldier flopped onto his back with a despairing groan. Silus looked back towards the Roman camp, then shook his head, sighed, and slid off Delicatus' back. He knelt down beside the soldier, undid the leather strap beneath his helmet and eased it off. Silus thought the youngster was not much more than a boy, his beard fluffy, his face pimpled. He had close-cropped, curly brown hair and his features seemed to Silus to be Greek. There was a long pike abandoned nearby, and Silus guessed that this was a member of the phalanx, probably recruited recently from Greece or Macedonia.

'Water,' whispered the lad, and Silus hastily took out his waterskin, and cradling the boy's head in his lap he dribbled some liquid gently into his mouth. The boy swallowed, coughed and swallowed again. Silus looked down to see what injury had disabled him. There was a hole in his mail tunic, the chain links buckled and ruptured and the underlying woollen tunic soaked through with blood. There was no arrow, so a spear or long sword must have penetrated at some point. Maybe the boy had broken ranks and been run down, or one of the Parthian cataphracts had maybe got in among the pikemen.

Gently, Silus lifted up the mail shirt and the tunic, and pursed his lips as he saw the wound. His belly was torn open, and loops of gut were protruding through the rent. At least one of those loops was ruptured, brown contents smelling of shit oozing out. Silus knew from experience that the injury was unsurvivable, even with the best care, which this poor boy was certainly not going to get among the multitude of other casualties, in a battlefield hospital.

'Where are you from, boy?' asked Silus.

'Pella,' he mumbled.

'Birthplace of Alexander,' said Silus. 'You would have been favoured by Caracalla, if he had known this of you.'

The boy gave a half smile. 'I suppose I will soon be joining the Emperor in Hades?'

'Don't talk like a madman,' said Silus. 'It's just a nick. You'll be back on the front line next week.'

The boy closed his eyes, not even bothering to make a pretence of believing the lie.

'You have family back home?'

'A father.'

'Would you like me to get a message to him? Just some news, while you are recovering?'

The boy nodded, then tensed as pain washed over him. When the spasm had passed, he said, 'My father's name is Agapetos. He is a cobbler. Tell him that his son Kassandros fought bravely, and that he hopes he made him proud.'

'I will,' said Silus, committing the names to memory. 'And when you are recovered, he can tell you himself how proud he is of you.'

Tears sprung at the corners of Kassandros' eyes, then he gasped as pain shot through him once more.

'You have an arrow head in your groin,' said Silus.

'Really,' said Kassandros. 'I didn't feel it.'

289

'I have to dig it out. It will only sting for a moment. It will help.'

The boy closed his eyes, not protesting. When Silus pressed his knife into the inside of the boy's thigh, and slid the point in, he grimaced but made no noise. Silus took the blade away, and there was a rush of hot blood from the large artery that he had severed.

'Oh,' said the boy. 'I think I wet myself. I'm sorry.'

'No, no,' said Silus. 'It's just a little blood from the wound. Nothing to be embarrassed about.'

'Good,' said the boy, and lay back in Silus' arms. Silus held him, watching the colour vanish from his face, his breathing becoming shallower, the pulse in his neck getting faster and weaker, then stutter, slow and stop. A final sigh left the boy's lungs, and he went limp, and now he did release his bladder, soaking Silus' legs.

Silus held him for a long moment, jaw clenched. Then he laid him down, pressed a coin into his mouth, and remounted Delicatus who had been waiting patiently. He gave Kassandros one last glance. Then, ignoring the hundreds of others he could have helped the same way, if only he had hundreds of hours to spare, he made his way back to report to Oclatinius.

Silus' eyes stung and his head ached. He wanted to lie down, but instead was back in position as part of the Emperor's bodyguard. Sleep was hard to come by, given the noises of camp, and the emotions swirling inside him, sadness, anxiety, and uncertainty about the future. He couldn't imagine how fatigued the soldiers below him on the plain must be.

It was the third day of the battle. The previous day had gone much the same as the first, with multiple waves of missile cavalry being countered by the Roman cavalry, which was becoming increasingly mauled by the cataphracts, which in turn were taking losses from the caltrops and the infantry counterattacks with clubs and maces. One grisly effect of the slaughter which was of benefit to the Roman defenders was the ever-heightening pile of bodies before the Roman front line. They had become so numerous that they were acting like ramparts, breaking up the cavalry charge, and providing shelter for the front-line troops from the continuing deluge of arrows.

But it had still been a horrific day for the Romans, and if dusk, and the cessation of the Parthian attacks, had come any later, the Romans may have broken. As it was, the centurions had had to use their vine sticks liberally to whip their men out of camp and back into line for yet another day of slaughter in the stifling heat.

Macrinus was ever more agitated too, his eyes red, with dark bags beneath them. Oclatinius was tight-lipped, giving advice where he could, whether or not he thought it would be heeded. Triccianus and Agrippa, too, chipped in with suggestions and comments, though Silus noticed them exchanging exasperated glances when Macrinus ignored them.

The day began as the previous two had, cavalry charges which were repelled with heavy losses on both sides. Macrinus looked out at the remnants of the Roman mounted forces and chewed his fingernails anxiously.

'They surely can't take much more of this. They are nearly spent.'

'They have no choice,' said Triccianus. 'They must endure.'

'No,' said Macrinus. 'The next attack might break them completely. Bring them in from the flanks and put them in the centre of the infantry squares where they are protected.'

'Augustus,' said Agrippa. 'What good are they there?'

'They are needed to protect the flanks from encirclement,' said Triccianus.

'Who is in charge here?' cried Macrinus, his voice high-pitched and squeaky. 'Do as I command!'

Triccianus gave the order for the cavalry to withdraw to relative safety behind the front ranks of the infantry, though they were still within range of arrows shot by mounted archers prepared to approach the Roman lines more closely. The Parthians did not initially do anything different after the withdrawal of the Roman cavalry, making another attack with horse archers, and following up with a cataphract charge. But the sheer number of dead bodies, human, equine and camelid, greatly reduced the effectiveness of the attack, and the phalanges, the clubmen, and the heavy infantry who made occasional forays forward to get in close among the Parthians, held the enemy back.

It was nearing noon when the Parthians decided to change tactics. Instead of attacking the centre, as they had done repeatedly, they extended their focus outwards, targeting the wings. Here the fighting was more diffuse, though no less bloody as the Romans fought desperately to keep the Parthians at bay. But the Parthian superior numbers and highly manoeuvrable cavalry allowed them to extend out further than the Roman lines, and with no Roman cavalry to counter them, they began to threaten the vulnerable flanks.

'Bring up the reserves,' commanded Macrinus. 'Extend our front lines to stop them coming round the sides.'

'Augustus,' said Oclatinius tentatively. 'Extending our line to prevent encirclement only works if you can reach a natural barrier on each side, like a river or forest or cliff. We are on a wide open plain, and they outnumber us. We can't extend far enough to prevent them...'

'Do as I say!' screamed Macrinus. Silus was no military strategist, but he understood Oclatinius' point, and knew that the correct tactic in the circumstances would be to form squares that were defended on all sides. But he saw that Macrinus was near panic, any semblance of listening to reason now completely vanished.

The reserves, legionaries and auxiliaries, were hurried out to the wings at a run to force back the Parthian assaults. But it was futile. No matter how long the Roman front line grew, the faster and larger Parthian forces could get round them. Macrinus threw the remnants of the Roman cavalry back into the fight to try to hold back the Parthian tide, and for some time they were successful, bravery and naked aggression keeping them at bay.

Then the inevitable happened. Two large forces of Parthian cavalry, one on either side, rounded the Roman wings, and thundered towards the Roman rear. Macrinus turned pale as he realised that the Parthians were now coming straight for them. And with the reserves committed to the front in the failed attempt to prevent what was in fact happening, there were no organised Roman forces to stop them.

'We're lost!' cried Macrinus. 'Run for your lives!' And he wheeled his horse and rode away, galloping west away from the oncoming Parthians.

Everyone on the low hill stared in disbelief at the fleeing Emperor. Then two of the Leones, somewhat reluctantly, set off after him, mindful of their duty to protect him, whatever they thought of him personally.

Silus looked back to the oncoming Parthians. There were a good thousand coming towards them on each side in a pincer movement. Between the hill on which he and the other military advisors were stationed and the Parthians was the Roman camp, a ditch and a low palisade, behind which was the baggage and supplies, manned only by a few score armed guards, and a number of non-combatant baggage handlers.

'What do we do?' asked Triccianus. 'Do we follow him?'

Agrippa was shaking his head, looking from the Parthian charge to the retreating Macrinus indecisively.

'Silus,' said Oclatinius. 'Do you think you could rally a defence from what you have there?'

Silus wasn't a legate or a tribune. His rank was centurion, but that was largely honorary – he had rarely had men under his command. But who else was there? And what choice? If the Parthians took the camp and all its supplies, the Romans were finished. It would be a disaster worse than Cannae or Carrhae.

'I'll do what I can.'

He spurred Delicatus forward and galloped down the hill and into the encampment.

'Who is in charge here?' he yelled, and a centurion, grey-haired and with a grim expression on his lined face, stepped forward.

'Centurion Varinius, sir. Who are you?'

'Centurion Silus, of the Leones. I'm taking command. How many men do you have?'

'Two centuries, not full strength.'

'Any walking wounded?'

Varinius glanced to an area where a large number of men lay or sat, attended by a small number of medics. 'Some who can still hold a sword I suppose.'

'Get them armed and on their feet. Anyone who can stand must fight.'

And now Silus looked at the non-combatants, a motley selection of slaves of all shapes, sizes and races, numbering in the hundreds. They had gathered round, and were watching him with consternation, well aware that when the Parthians arrived they would be cut down.

'All you slaves,' called out Silus. 'If you fight for Rome now, you will be granted your freedom. If you lay down like cowards, you will die. What do you say? Will you fight?'

The slaves looked at each other doubtfully. One called out, 'If we are freed, we will have no money to live and no one to feed us.'

'Every slave who fights will be rewarded with a sum of gold to start a new life as a Roman citizen,' said Silus. He hoped that Macrinus would honour his promise.

At this the slaves cheered enthusiastically.

'Arm yourselves from the supplies, anything you think you can wield, and then man the palisade. Go, quickly now. The Parthians are almost upon us.'

And indeed the Parthian cavalry had nearly covered the space between the Roman wings and the encampment. Silus had just enough time to organise the two centuries behind the palisade and ditch before the Parthian assault began.

If Macrinus had not committed his reserves, this could have been a great blunder by the Parthians. The Roman rear could have retreated and crushed the Parthians between themselves and the stockade. But there was no such threat to the Parthians, so they were free to launch waves of arrows at the defenders.

Fortunately, the ditch broke the momentum of the Parthian charge, and the palisade provided at least some protection against the missiles. The legionaries were able to counter with volleys of javelins, which were in plentiful supply given the soldiers' proximity to the stores.

But there were too few legionaries to defend the entire length of the palisade, even though their number had been almost doubled by the wounded, and Silus saw that at both ends, Parthians had tossed ropes over the points of the stakes and were hauling them down. Quickly, they made large holes in the defences, and as soon as the gaps were wide enough, the Parthians poured in, fast, light horses, their riders armed with spears and bows, bearing down on the Roman foot soldiers.

At that moment there was a roar from behind Silus, and he turned to see a flood of slaves charging forward. They brandished an assortment of weaponry – spears, long and short swords, clubs and even tools such as shovels and hammers. With astonishing bravery, they threw themselves in among the Parthian cavalry, hacking at the horse's legs, stabbing at the riders, grabbing the Parthians and hauling them off their mounts, where they viciously speared and clubbed the fallen easterners.

Silus drew his spatha and urged Delicatus into the fight, choosing the flank with the heaviest fighting, and one of the centuries followed him, the other heading for the opposite side. Immediately, he was in combat, parrying and thrusting, while Delicatus dodged and weaved, the smart horse seeming to enjoy every moment.

A Parthian thrust his spear towards Silus' face, but he batted it away and countered with a thrust of his sword that bit into the rider's shoulder. He wheeled away and retreated, holding his reins in one arm, blood flowing freely down the other.

Two more riders converged on him, spears held out like lances, ready to spit him from both sides. He raced towards one, narrowing the gap so they at least did not arrive simultaneously, and hacked at the out-thrust weapon. Delicatus charged his opponent's horse, which broke off rather than take the impact, presenting Silus with the exposed side of the rider. He thrust his sword deep, and with a cry, the Parthian fell.

Silus whirled, conscious that the other rider would be upon him, bracing for the impact he was sure was coming. But two slaves, a slight, pale, long-haired northerner and a dark-skinned African grabbed the rider as he passed and hauled him off his horse to the floor, where they proceeded to kick him in the kidneys and head, while the Parthian curled up and tried to protect himself with his hands.

The remaining Parthians broke at the same time. Too many had fallen and were continuing to fall at the hands of the brave legionaries, wounded and whole, and the ferocious baggage handlers who appeared to be taking out lifetimes of oppression on the invaders. Silus reined in Delicatus and slid out of the saddle. They had held them off, for now. But for how much longer? Surely, the next day would be the last for which the Romans could resist.

He walked over to where the two slaves were still assaulting the prone Parthian.

'Stop,' he ordered, and reluctantly they stepped back. 'Thank you,' he said to them. 'You saved my life. You have earned your freedom.'

They dipped their heads in gratitude. Silus turned to the man on the floor, who was groaning feebly. He grabbed him by the shoulders and lifted him into a sitting position, which brought cries of protest. Looking at the way he held himself, Silus thought he probably had broken ribs and a bruised skull, but nothing more serious.

'What's your name?' asked Silus in Greek, hoping the man spoke that language. He did, at least well enough that they could converse.

'Frahata.'

'Can you walk, Frahata?'

The Parthian shrugged sullenly.

'I'm going to take you back to my commander for questioning. Do I need to bind you?'

'You need to kill me before I tell you anything, Roman snake.'

Silus sighed and took out a length of rope, forcing the Parthian's hands behind his back to tie them, which caused him to hiss with pain.

'If you think this hurts,' said Silus, 'wait until my commander starts working on you. You will answer any question he cares to ask then.'

'All you need to know, treacherous invader, is that no Parthian will stop fighting until the betrayer Caracalla is dead.'

Silus stopped abruptly and stared at him.

'You mean, you don't know?'

The Parthian glared back sullenly. 'Know what?'

'Caracalla is already dead. He was murdered before the battle started.'

Frahata's jaw dropped. 'You mean, all this fighting, this death. It's for nothing?'

The enemies stared at each other, as realisation dawned on them both. Artabanus was leading his men into a battle that was resulting in carnage for both sides, all for vengeance against a man who was already dead.

'You must get a message to the King of Kings,' said Frahata. 'Please. We can have peace, while there are still some left alive to value it.'

Silus nodded, then cut the ropes binding Frahata's wrists. He held out his hand, and gently helped the Parthian to his feet.

'Come with me. I will take you to the Emperor Macrinus, and you can tell him what you told me.' If, thought Silus, the coward wasn't already halfway to Rome.

–

Silus approached the Parthian lines at dawn on the fourth day of the battle, as the easterners drew themselves up, ready to begin the slaughter once again. He held an olive branch high in the air, praying to every god of every religion he could think of that they would recognise the sign of peace in the dim morning light, and not greet him with a shower of arrows. Beside him, wincing each time his horse stumbled on uneven ground, rode Frahata.

He had been nominated to go to Artabanus with the message from Macrinus, because who else? Macrinus, who had slunk inconspicuously into the camp after his flight, hoping no one had noticed his cowardice, had first suggested Agrippa or Triccianus, but they had said they were needed to lead their men in case there was another attack. Then he had asked Julianus Nestor and Ulpius Julianus, but they had demurred, saying that it had to be someone from the military in order to command respect from the Parthian King of Kings. That was when Sempronius Rufus, with a sly look on his face, had suggested Silus go.

'After all, it was him that brought this news to our attention, and he can describe his conversation with this Frahata. Moreover, if we need them to believe Caracalla is dead in order for them to make peace, who better to convince them than a man who was there when he was murdered?'

'He could take this Frahata with him as a sign of good faith,' put in Nestor.

So here Silus was, hoping a stick and some green leaves, an injured prisoner and the goodwill of the gods would provide him with sufficient protection for him to reach Artabanus alive and relay his message.

When he was a couple of hundred yards from the Parthian lines, half a dozen riders came out to meet him, quickly surrounding him, three holding spears, three holding bows with arrows nocked, strings half drawn. Delicatus trotted on, just a flicking of his ears betraying his disquiet. Silus hoped that he seemed as cool.

'What do you want, Roman?' asked the lead Parthian in passable Greek.

'I have a message for King Artabanus from our Emperor.'

'The King of Kings is in no mood for peace.'

'Maybe he will change his mind when he hears the message.'

'Tell it to me. I will decide.'

'It is for his ears. And believe me, he will want to hear it. Your comrade Frahata here assures me of this.'

The Parthian peered at Frahata.

'Never heard of you.'

It was a slim chance, Silus realised. He got the impression that Frahata was a relatively senior officer of some description, but the Parthian army was so vast, he was sure that even those high up the chain of command would not be known by all. The man before him hadn't heard of Frahata, which weakened Silus' position. But Frahata then spoke up, still talking Greek so Silus could understand.

'I am the nephew of Apama, senior wife of Trdat, King of Gordyene.'

The Parthian leader looked doubtful, but one of the spearmen muttered something in the Parthian language, and the leader nodded.

'It seems you are known, Frahata. My apologies. I am sure your aunt will be delighted to know you still live. I'm sure you have a tale to tell us.'

'Later,' said Frahata. 'Time is short. Take this man to the King of Kings. It is vital, and urgent.'

The Parthian looked around at his men, then shrugged. 'Very well, I will escort you, though I cannot guarantee he will grant you an audience. He is rather busy.'

Silus breathed a sigh of relief. He was over the first hurdle – they hadn't cut him down on the spot. Now he had to hope that Artabanus would see him, listen to him, and that it would be enough to end the conflict. If not, the Romans would be annihilated, but not until they had inflicted grievous losses on the Parthians, a Pyrrhic victory for the easterners.

Artabanus did deign to see Silus, maybe curious, maybe persuaded by the presence of Frahata. Silus was searched, then dragged forward at spear point and forced to prostrate himself before the King of King's throne, face down, nose pressed into the dirt. There he stayed, Artabanus waiting for long enough to ensure that Silus was thoroughly humiliated, before allowing him to get to his knees.

Silus looked up at the King of Kings, clad in long flowing robes of purple-dyed silk, laden with heavy and intricate gold jewellery, necklaces, anklets, bracelets and rings. A spear point jabbed into his neck, and a voice growled, 'Avert your eyes.' Silus bowed his head, looking down at his own dusty knees.

'Speak, Roman,' said Artabanus. 'My patience is short. And if you think bearing an olive branch guarantees your safety, then you forget the treacherous behaviour of your Emperor.'

'King of Kings,' said Silus, trying to address him correctly in the way Oclatinius had coached him. 'Most high ruler of the East, of Parthia and Armenia and all the territories between the Syria and the Indus river. I humbly submit to deliver to you a message from the Emperor of Rome.'

'You may speak, but do not expect me to believe anything that originated from the mouth of that viper you call Caracalla.'

'O great king,' said Silus. 'I bring you greetings from the Emperor Macrinus.'

Confused murmurs came from the entourage around Artabanus, which stopped abruptly, presumably, though Silus could not see this, at a gesture from their king.

'Macrinus. I know the name. But he is one of your, what do you call them, praetorian prefects, isn't that so? Why do you call him Emperor?'

'Because Caracalla is dead.'

Now there were overt gasps and cries of shock from all those gathered to hear Silus' words.

'Emperor Antoninus died in battle? I heard no such reports.'

'No, high king. He died three days before the battle started.'

Now there was a stunned silence, as the import of Silus' message sunk in.

'You lie,' spat Artabanus.

'King of Kings, ruler of my body, my heart and my soul,' put in Frahata. 'May I be permitted to speak?'

'Go on,' said Artabanus.

'I am Frahata, nephew of Apama, first wife of Trdat. I can tell you that this man speaks the truth. I have met Macrinus. The message this man bears is truly from the new Emperor of Rome.'

'How did he die?' asked Artabanus.

'He was murdered,' said Silus. 'By one of his own men. I was there, I witnessed the fact, and I can swear on all that I hold dear and sacred this is the truth.' The fact that it was Silus' own blade that had finished Caracalla off did not make his statement less true – after all, Silus was one of Caracalla's own men.

For a moment, all Silus could hear was the heavy breathing of Artabanus. Then the King of Kings said, 'Give me your message.'

Silus recited from memory. 'To Artabanus, ruler of the Parthian Empire, King of Kings, greetings, from Marcus Opellius Macrinus Augustus, Emperor of Rome. I implore you that we put aside our differences, and make peace, for the sake of both our peoples. I understand you have just cause for grievance with us, but the devious and treacherous acts against you were perpetrated by our former Emperor, Antoninus, who is now dead. I beg that you do not use his actions to perpetuate the conflict against one who is innocent of his crimes, to the detriment of Parthia and Rome.

'But I recognise that Rome has wronged you, and for this reason, I will free all Parthian prisoners, and donate to your treasury the sum of two hundred million sesterces.'

More gasps of astonishment came from the listening Parthians. This was a truly enormous sum, as much as a hundred thousand donkeys could carry. Silus risked a glance up at the King of Kings and saw that a thoughtful expression had come over his face. No one chastised him for daring to gaze upon Artabanus' visage – everyone was too stunned.

Finally, Artabanus spoke.

'Very well. Go back to your new Emperor and tell him I agree his terms. He may have his peace.'

—

When Macrinus bade Silus to enter his tent, it was near midnight, but the Emperor was still awake, pacing back and forth and biting the nails on one hand. Similarly agitated were Julianus Nestor and Ulpius Julianus, standing still but fidgeting and shifting from foot to foot as if they needed to relieve their bladders. Triccianus and Agrippa weren't present, maybe taking the opportunity to sleep in the event of battle being rejoined the next day. Oclatinius was there though, reading some document written in ink on papyrus by the flickering oil light, and so was Sempronius Rufus, slouching in a chair, legs stretched out and feet crossed, eyes closed.

Macrinus hurried up to Silus and grabbed him by the shoulders, staring earnestly and desperately into his eyes.

He looked on the verge of panic, and Silus wondered if he had borne bad news whether he would have attempted to flee again.

'Tell me. Quick. What did he say?'

Silus was tempted to draw out the tension, to tease this unimpressive man. Macrinus had none of Caracalla's qualities — bravery, physical strength, a finely honed military mind. He hoped that Macrinus had none of his faults, the temper, the treachery, the capacity for terrible cruelty if it suited his purposes. After all, if Macrinus turned out to be worse than Caracalla, Silus only had himself to blame, since it was largely by his hand that Macrinus had acceded to the throne.

But he was tired, and had no heart for games, after all the suffering of the last few days.

'It's peace,' he said.

'Truly?' Macrinus couldn't seem to quite believe it.

'Artabanus accepts your terms.'

The sighs of relief around the tent seemed hard enough to puff out the door flaps. Macrinus sank into a chair and put his head in his hands for a long while, and from the movements of his shoulders, Silus thought he was silently weeping. The council members clapped him and each other on the back. Even Oclatinius was smiling.

Eventually, Macrinus looked up, and wiped his eyes with the back of his hand.

'So, it's over. And my position as Emperor is safe. I suppose now begins the work of running the Empire and undoing the mess that Caracalla has made. There are conflicts to resolve, and the treasury is all but empty.

'But it is important that I honour his memory. The soldiers still love him. I'll take the name Severus, and my son I will name Caesar and Antoninus. The legions and people will be pleased.'

'This is work for tomorrow,' said Julianus Nestor. 'You should rest now. It has been an exhausting few days.'

'It has,' agreed Macrinus. 'You're right. I can begin to address these problems when I have slept. But one thing we should do without further delay. I must send a message to Rome, to the urban prefect Flavius Maternianus and the Senate, informing them of the death of Caracalla and my proclamation as Emperor, so they can confirm me without delay.'

'Augustus,' said Sempronius Rufus. 'Forgive me, but I have already done so.'

'You did what, Rufus?' asked Macrinus, eyes narrowed.

'I dispatched a messenger to Rome, to inform them of the sad demise of the Emperor Antoninus, and the glorious news of your accession.'

And Rufus turned to look directly at Silus, just as the import of what he had said was sinking in. Silus' mouth dropped open, and Rufus smiled. He knew! He knew about the assassin Juik in Tituria's household. He knew about Caracalla's orders. Maybe it had been him that put the whole thing in place. And here was his revenge for failing to prevent the plot against Caracalla from succeeding, fuelled by pure malice.

'When did you send this messenger?' asked Macrinus.

'Just before battle commenced.'

Three days! The messenger had a three-day head start on Silus!

'And why did you not tell me?'

'I did not want to distract you from your command of the army at such a perilous time. But I thought it important that Rome knew as soon as possible.'

'Well,' said Macrinus. 'I suppose there is no harm in it. In future, though, do not take such decisions without my permission.'

'Of course, Augustus. Apologies if I caused any offence.'

Macrinus waved the apology away.

'Now I will retire. You are all dismissed. Goodnight.'

They filed out of the tent one by one, Ulpius Julianus and Julianus Nestor, stumbling away together, leaving Silus, Rufus and Oclatinius. As soon as the three of them were alone, Silus turned on Rufus.

'You did this on purpose. You know about Tituria!'

Rufus spread his hands. 'I don't know what you are talking about. I merely did my duty as I saw it.'

Silus' hand shot out and he grabbed Rufus by the throat, squeezing hard.

'What route did you send him by. What transport?'

Rufus' eyes opened wide, and he choked out, 'Over land. Fast horse.'

'Using the cursus publicus?'

'Of course.'

Silus let the eunuch spy go, and he stepped back, rubbing his neck but grinning maliciously. Silus turned to Oclatinius.

'You said we had time. You said I would get to her first.'

'I'm sorry,' said Oclatinius. 'I didn't account for this weasel here.'

'Have a care, Oclatinius,' said Rufus. 'We don't yet know which of us will find the most favour with the new Emperor. You may have assisted him in his grab for power, but he won't have been pleased with the soldiers attempting to acclaim you. You're a threat to him now.'

Oclatinius ignored him and took hold of Silus' arm. 'Listen to me. There might be a way. Travelling at a standard speed over land using the horse relay of the cursus publicus from here to Rome would take approximately seventeen days, all being in the rider's favour. But you can cut some time off that if you go by sea.'

'Sea? We are hundreds of miles from the coast.'

'Don't be stupid. Ride from here to Antioch, you can collect Atius there – he will help. Speak to Julia Domna and get her authority to commandeer two ships, one to cross the Bosporus at Byzantium, the other across the Mare Adriaticum from Dyrrhachium to Brundisium. You could make up the three days that way, though you would have to ride night and day.'

Silus looked doubtful. 'What if I'm too late?'

'I have faith in you,' said Oclatinius. 'And more importantly, so does Tituria. Now, you must leave, immediately.'

Silus took a deep breath and nodded. Then he punched Sempronius Rufus hard in the centre of his smirking face.

Chapter XVII

Silus and Atius entered Rome to find the city in uproar. They had ridden up the Via Latina, ignorant of whether they had arrived ahead of Rufus' messenger. Since they had travelled by a different route from the messenger, no one they encountered knew about Caracalla's death, and it wasn't until they reached Rome itself that they found out. Then, it was obvious.

As soon as they reached the junction of the Via Latina and the Via Appia, they encountered a riot. A group of citizens were attempting to break into a fine-looking town house, and a dozen legionaries of the Urban Cohorts were wading in among them with clubs and sticks, cracking heads and breaking bones.

Silus reined in his panting horse and shouted down to a pair of old men who were standing back with arms folded, enjoying the spectacle.

'What's going on?' he asked.

One of the old men spat a gob of mucus from his gummy mouth before replying. 'They say that house belongs to a senator who made a speech in praise of the new Emperor. The people don't like that. They think Macrinus must have murdered Caracalla to take the throne.'

'Fuck,' he said to Atius. 'We're too late.'

'When did the news of Caracalla's death arrive in Rome?' asked Atius.

'Why, this very morning. Surely not more than two hours.'

So close! All this way, and to be just two hours behind the message. All the moments where he could have made up that time flashed through his head. If he had spent a little less time consoling Julia Domna after he had informed her of Caracalla's death. If he had had to waste less time convincing the captain of the ship in Dyrrhacium that his authority from Domna was genuine. If he had snatched a little less sleep, although any less and he doubted he would have been able to stay in the saddle. If only...

'Silus, we may still be in time. Maybe she didn't carry out her orders immediately. Come on.'

Silus nodded, not believing it. He had looked into Juik's eyes and had seen no sign of doubt or hesitancy. Nevertheless, he spurred his horse into a canter, the fastest pace he could manage along the crowded, uneven streets. They skirted the city centre, the region of the fora, which were crowded on any normal day, and no doubt would be rammed with unsettled Romans, protesting, or taking advantage of the disorder to loot, mug and steal. Instead, they cut across the Caelian hill to the Esquiline. Everywhere the streets were full of anxious and angry people, with Urban Cohort legionaries and vigiles out in force, attempting to keep order, but they were able to avoid trouble where necessary by riding fast at any one in their way while waving their swords and shouting. Silus wished Delicatus had been able to make the journey, but he was too fatigued after the battle, and, besides, Silus would have had to abandon him at the first station of the cursus publicus when he swapped mounts. Oclatinius, with an indulgent smile, had promised to take care of the horse that Silus had become surprisingly attached to.

As they approached the domus of Titus Petellius Facilis, Silus tried to steal himself for what he was about to find. There had been so much loss in his life, he didn't know how he could bear any more. If he turned around now, if he rode away, took a ship to Britannia, then he would not have to confront her murder. In his mind, Tituria could be forever alive.

But if there was the slightest chance, he had to try. And if she was dead, well, he had to know.

They leapt off their horses and ran straight past the bemused porter and into the atrium. A slave who had been dusting a statue yelped as they burst in, toppling the statue so the marble smashed apart on the mosaic flooring.

'Where is Tituria?' demanded Silus, sword drawn. 'Where is Juik?'

'N... not here, master,' gasped the slave, a young Greek lad.

'Then where?'

'They left, for the master's villa in Baiae. A few days ago. They always go to the coast at this time of year to escape the heat.'

Silus looked at Atius, a glimmer of hope rising from deep within. He squashed it down. Hope could be painful. If he let himself believe she might be alive, and then found the opposite, it might break him. So he told himself he was going to avenge her, and to bury her.

'Tell me exactly where to find Facilis' villa.'

–

Baiae had been a tourist resort for three centuries, a place where the Roman upper strata could visit to escape the crowds, smells and heat of the city. The richest had built villas here, and many emperors had spent considerable amounts of time there, including Augustus, Nero and Caracalla's own father Septimius Severus. The Emperor Hadrian had even died in his villa there, nearly a century before. The concentration of wealth had caused the town to acquire a reputation for luxury, decadence and general debauched living, and it had been condemned by poets and philosophers such as Propertius and Seneca. But that only added to the pull for the young libertines of Roman society, attracted by the all-night beach parties, the drinking and the sexual licentiousness associated with the town.

Facilis' villa was on a hill a short ride from the centre of Baiae, still commanding beautiful views of the Campanian coast and to the east, across the bay, the ruined peak of the volcano, Vesuvius, that had destroyed Pompeii. No doubt, Facilis would claim that he had bought a holiday home in this location to avoid the noise and disturbance from the parties in the town centre, though Silus suspected that financial reasons were more important.

The two of them leapt off their horses before they had fully come to rest and raced straight inside the villa. The steward of the property emerged to greet them, but before he could open his mouth, Silus was on him.

'Where is Tituria? Answer me.'

'Tituria?' The steward was clearly stunned by the sudden appearance of these dirty, armed men, and expecting to be robbed, the enquiry after the young ward had taken him aback.

'Yes, Tituria,' shouted Silus, drawing his sword back, the tip pointing towards the steward's throat. 'Speak!'

'I... I don't know, master.'

'What is all this fuss?' came a voice, and Silus turned to see Facilis emerging from his study. 'Wait, I know you. Silus, isn't it?'

'Facilis. Where is Tituria? I need to know, now.'

'I don't know, exactly. She went for a walk along the beach I believe. She has been gone quite a while, now you mention it.'

Silus' heart sank. 'And Juik? Your slave?'

Facilis frowned. 'Why would I know that?' He turned to the steward. 'Do you have any idea where Juik is?'

The steward, still attempting to recover his equilibrium, said, 'She left, not long ago. She said she had an errand to run in town. Just after that message arrived.'

'What message?' asked Silus.

'Why,' said Facilis, 'the message that the Emperor Caracalla is dead. Haven't you heard? Now look, what is this all about?'

Silus looked at Atius, anguish in his eyes. Atius reached out to grasp his arm. 'We can find her,' he said. 'Don't despair. Let's split up, it will be quicker.'

Silus wanted to sit down on the ground and howl, but that tiny spark of hope, the one he had tried to extinguish, still glowed faintly inside. 'Come on,' he said. 'And please, pray to your Christos that we find her in time.'

–

The Gulf of Napoli sported a rocky, cliff-bordered coastline interspersed with sandy beaches. Facilis' villa did not have easy access to one of the luxurious beaches that the super-rich frequented, but it was a short walk from a pebble shore. Atius had gone east and Silus west in their desperate search for Tituria. Silus found himself scrambling over slippery, seaweed-covered rocks, cursing his sandals, entirely unsuitable footwear for the terrain.

He slid, scraping his ankle on the rough barnacle- and limpet-coated surface, his foot landing in a rockpool and disappearing into something squidgy at the bottom. He cursed, even as he reflected how strange it was that things as trivial as a graze or a wet foot could matter when the life of someone he cared about was in danger. He scrambled up, working his way further west, and cresting a large outcrop, he found he was looking down into a small cove. Waves lapped gently against the pebble and sand beach. A low, craggy cliff encircled the cove, dotted with nooks, crannies and little caves. Gulls wheeled overhead, crying out raucously.

And sitting on a rock with her feet in the warm sea, letting the waves lap her shins, and occasionally stooping down to splash water at the little dog standing on the beach behind her, was a tall young girl.

It had been three years since Silus left Rome. Three years since he said goodbye to Tituria. Enough time to transform a child into an adolescent on the cusp of womanhood. Her hair had grown longer and fuller, she had slimmed down, and she must have been the best part of a foot taller. But he had no doubt who he was looking at.

He stared, barely daring to breathe, unable to move, unable to take his eyes off her, scared it was a dream, a vision, and if he blinked it would disappear.

But this was real. She was here. She was alive. Gingerly, he made his way down the rock and walked slowly towards her.

It was Issa who saw him first. Maybe she had caught his scent on the wind, or maybe her hearing was still sharp despite her advanced age. The tiny, elderly terrier turned to Silus and started yapping, and the sharp, jarring sound was like the sweetest flute music to Silus' ears.

Tituria put her hand to her brow to shield her eyes from the bright blue sky. She tensed as she saw the strange man approaching. Then she gave a girlish squeal of delight.

'Silus!' She ran to him and threw her arms around him, hugging him tightly, and Silus hugged her back, squeezing his eyes shut, tears of relief in the corners of his eyes. Issa put her front paws against Silus' legs and started to lick the salty sweat from his calves.

It was over. She was safe. Caracalla was dead, and Tituria was under his protection, and no one would ever threaten her again.

Issa suddenly started to yap again.

Silus whirled just as the knife descended towards his back. His quick motion prevented the blow from being instantly fatal, but the blade still plunged deep into his shoulder, just beneath the scapula, and he grunted in pain and shock.

From somewhere among the rocks, Juik, moments behind Silus in her search for Tituria, had crept up on the two of them, and gone straight for the biggest threat. She had nearly succeeded and might yet. Silus' sword was still in its sheath at his waist, and when he reached for it, he found his right arm wasn't responding. The blade had done some damage to the sinews or nerves, and the arm hung useless and numb. What's more, he could feel blood pouring down his back, and knew he was badly hurt.

Juik advanced on him once more, holding the knife low, eyes locked on his. Silus knew then that she was not just any slave, tasked with cutting Tituria's throat in the night should it become necessary. This woman was a trained killer, probably one of Rufus' assassins, and maybe every bit as good as Silus.

And Silus was wounded, unable to use his sword arm. He took a step back and fumbled for the hilt of his gladius with his left hand. Juik lunged at him, an upward thrust that if it had struck home would have sliced up through his liver and into his chest. Silus leapt back and the point of the knife whizzed up in an arc that nearly took the tip off his wonky nose. He took the opportunity to pull out the sword, and he held it before him, keeping Juik in front of him and Tituria behind him. The assassin slave circled, looking for an opening.

Silus could fight left-handed if he needed to. Sometimes he wielded a sword in one hand and a dagger in the other. But it was his weaker, less dextrous arm. And more than that, he was starting to feel light-headed. His back was soaked now with his own blood, and the sword felt much heavier than it should. Juik clearly knew this, and was in no hurry to finish him, content to let the haemorrhage do its work.

Silus knew he had to press the attack, while he still had the strength. He stepped forward, lunged, thrust with his spatha. But it was a clumsy move, obvious that it was coming, and poorly executed. Juik danced out of the way, and actually laughed at his attempt. He felt a flush come to his face, and anger surged through him, lending him a little more energy. He used it to his advantage, feinting with a side swing. Then, when Juik stepped neatly to one side, he stabbed forward, all his weight behind the thrust.

It would have skewered most opponents and ended the fight there and then. But as he had suspected, Juik was good. She twisted, and the sword grazed her side, the slightest slice in her skin, and as she moved, she struck downwards, the blade biting deep into his left forearm. His fingers flew open, and the sword fell to the ground, clattering on the pebbles. Juik spun on the spot in a blisteringly fast turn and kicked him full in the chest with her heel. He flew over backward, hitting the wet beach hard enough to knock the wind out of him.

He looked upwards into the blue sky, and saw Juik's face looking down at him, smiling as she stroked the tip of her knife across his neck, gentle as a lover's kiss. Silus fumbled for his sword, even as he knew it was hopeless. He had failed. He had been careless, let his emotions overcome his caution, his training. He would die now, and soon after, so would Tituria. It had all been for nothing.

He closed his eyes and waited for the slash across his throat.

There was a thud.

He opened his eyes again. Juik had a strange, faraway look in her eyes. As he watched, her pupils drifted upwards, and she sunk to her knees, then toppled sideways. Silus could now see that behind her, with a large, blood-stained stone in her hands, stood Tituria.

Juik groaned, rolled onto her back, looked up at Tituria, and laughed.

Tituria brought the stone down again, into the middle of Juik's face, and carried on smashing it into her until Silus managed to regain his feet, and gently put his arms around her, pulling her away. They leant against each other, and Tituria wept aloud as Silus patted her hair.

He felt his knees give, and he clutched at Tituria to stop himself from falling. Suddenly remembering his wound, she helped him to the ground, and ripped two lengths of cloth from her dress, using one to bandage his arm, and balling the other in a vain attempt to staunch the flow of blood from the back of his shoulder. When she had done what she could, she put an arm under him and tried to get him upright. He pushed on his legs, but they were too weak for his weight, and he sunk back down, lying with his back to a rock.

'Go,' he said. 'Get back to the villa.'

She looked at him uncertainly. 'I don't want to leave you.'

'You must. I need to know you are safe. Then you can send help for me.'

She hesitated, then kissed his forehead and ran off with light feet in the direction of Facilis' villa.

Issa nuzzled his left hand, and Silus moved his fingers through her fur. He could feel darkness closing in on him and knew he would not last much longer.

'What a journey, old girl,' he whispered. 'Five years. I've seen the world. I've seen... too much.'

He tried to take a deep breath, but a stab of pain from the knife wound limited how much air he could take in. He fussed Issa's ear, and she wriggled her body closer to him.

'Just you and me, old girl,' he whispered. 'In the end, just you and me.'

Issa curled herself up against him and closed her eyes.

And that was how Atius found them, Silus looking as if he was asleep. With a cry of despair, he ran over to Silus, and lifted him into his arms.

'No, please, old friend. Don't go.'

He hugged his still, limp body to him as he wept.

Epilogue I

'Please eat, sister,' said Julia Maesa. 'He would not have wanted this for you.'

'How do you know what he would have wanted for me? He showed me little enough regard in the end.'

'He loved you, don't doubt that.'

Domna looked out across the garden, and for a moment watched a red-and-black butterfly with its wings outstretched, sunning itself. Her relationship with Caracalla was too complex for words like love. Son of her husband. Lover. Best friend. Killer of her only child.

After Silus had delivered her the news of his death, as soon as she was alone, she had screamed, torn her hair, and beat her breasts, rupturing the tumour there, so blood and oozing fluid spattered her stola. She had been in constant pain since then and knew that the cancer was spreading faster than ever.

Maesa held out a bowl of dates towards her sister, but Domna knocked them angrily out of her hand, so the fruits rolled across the dirt. Maesa pursed her lips and bent down to pick them up one by one.

'Macrinus came to see me.'

'Yes, sister, I know.' Domna's state of illness and starvation was starting to affect her memory and reasoning, so she kept repeating herself.

'He was very respectful, that horrible little man. But he is so base. Not even senatorial rank. How can one such as that think to replace my Antoninus?'

'The Senate in Rome have acclaimed him. I think they have held their noses and accepted him, just because he isn't Antoninus, for all that he isn't one of them either.'

'Ingrates,' spat Domna, then coughed. She patted her handkerchief to her lips, and when she took it away she saw there were drops of blood on it. She folded it carefully and tucked it away.

'He told me that I must leave Antioch. That I must become a private citizen.'

'Yes, you told me.'

'I, Julia Domna, Augusta, wife and mother of Emperor. To become a nobody.'

'You will never be a nobody, sister. You ruled this Empire just as much as Severus or Antoninus ever did.'

'I will not go,' said Domna, her voice steely despite its weakness. 'I will leave here on my own terms.'

'You should not despair so. Our family is still very powerful. We have vast wealth, and much influence in the East. And the soldiers love Avitus. They think he is Antoninus' son.'

But Domna wasn't listening. She was looking up, her eyes following the gentle drifting clouds.

'I could have saved him, you know. But should I have? Would Rome be better off with or without him?' Then she turned to Maesa, and a single tear rolled down her cheek. 'He didn't want me any more.'

Maesa took her hand and squeezed it in her own. Domna knew she wouldn't be in this world much longer. After that, who knew? As far as earthly matters went, her younger sister was clearly not yet finished. She was more than a match for Macrinus, especially with her fiery daughter Soaemias by her side. And she had two young grandsons that she could mould into shape, to follow whatever path she decreed for them.

And for Domna herself? She had no idea where she would end up, despite the many years she had spent in the company of the Empire's finest minds, debating religion and philosophy. Would Severus be there, waiting for her? And Antoninus? And Geta? That could all be very awkward. She managed a wry chuckle at the thought, then lay back. She closed her eyes, and let the sun warm her face.

Her breast hurt. But it wouldn't be for much longer now.

Epilogue II

Oclatinius picked up a report scratched into a wax tablet and read through it, lips moving as he tried to decipher the scrawled script. He really should make his agents take handwriting lessons he thought. He supposed it reduced the need for code, if the message was illegible, although that made it just as useless to him.

Life had just become much simpler for him. Macrinus had dispatched him to Rome with Caracalla's ashes to arrange for them to be buried with all due honours. He had also been given the unpleasant task of arranging the execution of Flavius Maternianus. The urban prefect had done no real wrong except showing loyalty to Caracalla by alerting him to a possible (and as it turned out real) threat to the Emperor from Macrinus. Unfortunately, he had also let it be widely known that he believed Macrinus was behind Caracalla's death. So Macrinus appointed Oclatinius urban prefect in Maternianus' place, and then ensured his first duty was to have Maternianus beheaded in the forum.

That appointment had not lasted long, however. Despite Oclatinius' dramatic refusal of the throne, Macrinus was wary of the power Oclatinius wielded, and so had quickly replaced him as urban prefect with a respected senator and historian named Marius Maximus whose loyalty he wished to strengthen. Oclatinius had been given the promise of a consulship for the following year in recompense, performing which duty Oclatinius intended to spend the least time possible.

Moreover, Ulpius Julianus and Julianus Nestor had been appointed the new praetorian prefects, instead of Oclatinius and Macrinus. That left Oclatinius only responsible for the Arcani, a state of affairs he was well content with. He much preferred to be thought of as the bumbling old man who had felt unable to become Emperor, than the truth, which was that he was the commander of the most effective and fearsome intelligence agency in the Empire.

Of course, Sempronius Rufus, the Commander of the Sacred Bedchamber, might disagree with that assessment. He had somehow clung onto his position and persuaded Macrinus that he was loyal to the new administration. Oclatinius could foresee trouble from that decision. But then, he could foresee trouble from many directions, not least Syria, where the female relatives of Caracalla were restless. And they wielded great influence and power, not to mention wealth, despite the passing of Julia Domna, news that Oclatinius had been sad to receive. Her ashes had been interred in the mausoleum of Augustus at Macrinus' insistence, separating her from her husband and stepson who were laid to rest in the mausoleum of Hadrian by the Tiber. Macrinus clearly wanted to separate the remnants of the Severan dynasty from the emperors to help delegitimise any claim they may have.

He re-read the scrawl on the tablet. Something about the sentiment of the legions in Antioch, but he couldn't work out from this message whether they were content with the change of ruler, or unhappy. Fortunately, he didn't have only a single source to rely on. He picked up another message, this one ink on papyrus, and much more legible.

There was a knock on his door.

'Enter.'

A young girl came in. She was tall, slight in stature, with long, night black hair and thick, dark eyebrows. She stood before his desk, straight-backed and after glancing around the room, looked him straight in the eyes.

'Tituria,' said Oclatinius. 'It has been a while. You've grown.'

'I think maybe you have shrunk a little, Oclatinius Adventus.'

Oclatinius gave a small involuntary chuckle. 'Most Roman ladies at your stage of life would be sitting at home, spinning and dyeing and waiting for their father or guardian to arrange a suitable match for them.'

'I found that I wanted something other for my life.'

Oclatinius regarded her. 'How old are you now?'

'I've just passed my sixteenth birthday.'

'Not old enough. It was lovely to see you again, Tituria, but I am busy. Send my best wishes to Facilis. Good day.'

He looked down at the papyrus, then back up at her when she didn't move.

'You're still here.'

'Train me. I'm old enough to begin. And young enough that you can bend and shape me into a weapon that will serve Rome. Someone who will be worthy of the Arcani, of its history, and all who served in it.' There was a tremor in her voice, and a fervour in her eyes. Oclatinius wasn't looking for idealists. He wanted cynical, old realists. Still, after what she had been through in her life, all she had lost, he had to admit she had shown strength of resolve and character. Even being in front of him like this took courage.

He sighed, stroked his beard, then looked to the figure who had been seated quietly in the corner. He had a nose that had been broken several times and through which air moved with a whistle. He cradled his right arm in his lap, occasionally clenching his fist as if relieving a cramp. His tired eyes looked Tituria up and down.

'Well?' asked Oclatinius. 'What do you think?'

There was a long pause. Then he said, 'I think she will do.'

Tituria smiled.

The little old dog by the man's side suddenly woke up, tottered over to Tituria, and gave her leg a nuzzle.

'It looks like you have the approval of both Silus and Issa,' said Oclatinius. 'Welcome to the Arcani.' He looked back at Silus. 'So, over to you to start her training.'

'Me?' asked Silus in surprise.

'Of course. I'm an old man. I can't run the Arcani for much longer. Soon it will be time to hand the reins over to someone else.'

'You have someone in mind?'

Oclatinius gave Silus a long, hard stare.

'Indeed I do.'

Author's Note

So was Caracalla the worst of all emperors, the common enemy of mankind as Gibbon dubbed him? Some modern commentators consider him a psychopath, while others think him a military genius whose ruthless streak and contempt for the traditions and norms of warfare allowed him to gain great victories for far less loss of Roman life than would otherwise be the case. I have portrayed him as a flawed man, with a capacity for both love and cruelty, much like most other Roman emperors, and indeed most people. For me personally, writing the Alexandrian massacre made it hard to continue to portray him in a sympathetic light, and for him to retain Silus' loyalty. Before that scene, it had been my intention to have Silus on his side until the end, attempting to foil his assassination and failing. Afterwards, I couldn't believe Silus would condone, even reluctantly, such an appalling act.

The motivations behind the massacre in Alexandria remain a mystery, and the sparse contemporary information we have helps only a little. All his previous and subsequent massacres and betrayals, such as against the Parthians and Alemanni, and his possible attempt to kill the Caledonian chiefs at the peace conference with his father, had a military justification. To murder vast numbers of the denizens of a city simply because they had made racy jokes at his expense seems like overkill, and unlikely for this calculating ruler. I suspect that the massacre came about because of either rioting among the ever-combustible Alexandrian populace, punishment for the city taking part in a conspiracy against Caracalla, or possibly concern that Alexandria may rebel while he was in the East, and so, as with the other campaigns against the threats from the barbarians at the borders of the Empire, he decided to pre-emptively pacify it.

The event tarnished Caracalla's reign more than any other. Even the murder of his brother could be justified if it was true that Geta planned Caracalla's death so he could be sole ruler. Without it, he would probably have been thought no worse in his actions than Julius Caesar, Augustus, Tiberius or Constantine. But neither modern nor ancient sensibilities tolerate the massacre of your own unarmed civilians.

Julia Domna, in contrast, seemed a thoughtful and strong woman, who for much of Caracalla's reign, attended to the civilian administration of the Empire while Caracalla was away on campaign. Although wealthy women who had personal tutors or engaged in philosophy were disparaged and mocked at that time, Domna ignored this and surrounded herself with literary men and philosophers. Suggested members of her intellectual circle included one of the future emperors, Gordian I or II, Oppian the poet, lawyers such as Papinianus and Ulpianus, Cassius Dio and Marius Maximus the historians, Philostratus the philosopher and biographer, and possibly most renowned of all, Galen of Pergamum, the most famous physician besides Hippocrates in antiquity, whose works were still being studied and utilised for more than a thousand years, until the 1500s and 1600s when his theories on human anatomy (which had been based on monkeys since human dissection was forbidden) and later human physiology were disproven.

I have discussed the controversy previously as to whether Domna was Caracalla's mother or stepmother, but there seems to be enough doubt over the facts that it is reasonable to make her his stepmother for the purposes of these novels. She died as described, from starvation after the death of Caracalla and a demotion to a private citizen by Macrinus, although her breast cancer may not have given her long to live in any case.

Many of the minor characters in this series of novels are real people from history, even if I have had to almost entirely reconstruct them from a name and a line in a history or on a tombstone. For example, the centurion who resisted the first riot in Alexandria is known from an inscription found near Rome, dedicated by Caius Cassius, commander of the Legio II Parthica Antoniniana, who was thanking Jupiter Optimus Maxinus for the well-being and return of Antoninus, and for, when Cassius was acting as centurion and standing firm in danger, he was saved through the help of the god, and therefore set up this dedication in fulfilment of his vow (see ostia-antica.org/caracalla/travels/egypt-alexandria.htm). Other characters that have appeared in the novel series that are drawn from the historical sources include Festus, Sempronius Rufus, Caracalla's inner council, the future Emperor Maximinus Thrax (who was indeed a member of the Leones before quitting when he realised Macrinus was behind Caracalla's murder, and according to contemporary sources was eight feet tall, undoubtedly an exaggeration but surely a very tall man nonetheless) and of course Oclatinius himself, whose career as praetorian prefect, consul and briefly Prefect of

Rome was all as described, only his leadership of the Arcani being fictional (although he was supposed to have had a previous career as a spy and assassin).

Julius Martialis was a member of Caracalla's bodyguard, although whether he was one of the Leones or something else is unclear. It is not even clear whether he was in fact responsible for Caracalla's death or was just the fall guy. Dio Cassius and Herodian are contradictory on this, as they are regarding his motives. Dio Cassius says his post was one of the evocati, and his motive was the failure of Caracalla to promote him to centurion, whereas Herodian says he was already a centurion in Caracalla's bodyguard who was angry because Caracalla had executed his brother. I chose to make him a praetorian and gave him both motives!

The political situation in Armenia and Parthia was complicated, and again the sources are confusing and confused. Caracalla seems to have timed his invasion to coincide with a civil war between Artabanus and Vologaesus. Vologaesus was defeated by Artabanus in 215 and then retreated to Ctesiphon near modern-day Baghdad. Artabanus put Khosrov on the throne of Armenia, against the accepted precedent, which gave Caracalla his casus belli. However, Artabanus was clearly amenable to a peace settlement, possibly to enable him to finish his war against Vologaesus, given his agreement to let Caracalla marry his daughter (naive given Caracalla's track record in these sort of situations).

It is controversial who won the battle of Nisibis. Would it have been a clear victory for Caracalla if he had been in command? We will never know, but he would certainly have had the advantage of having spent years planning for the moment, while Macrinus could only guess at

Caracalla's tactics. Macrinus seemed to have made some tactical errors, unsurprising given his military inexperience. But who did actually win?

The *Encyclopedia Iranica* states that Macrinus was 'decisively defeated', while the *Encyclopedia Britannica* says that result was inconclusive, although the treaty agreed was unfavourable to Rome. The contemporary sources Herodian and Cassius Dio don't express an opinion one way or the other.

But regardless of who was declared the winner on the day, neither of the rulers profited in the longer term. In 224 AD, the four-hundred-year-old Parthian Empire, weakened by civil war and the Roman incursions, fell to the Sasanians, with Artabanus being killed at the Battle of Hormozdgan. The Sasanian Empire proved to be an even more formidable foe than the Parthians they succeeded in Persia, and within fifteen years they had recommenced hostilities against the Romans, leading to the defeat and capture of the Roman Emperor Valerian, who became a slave of the Sasanian King of Kings Shapur, who used the poor old Valerian as a footstool for mounting his horse.

As for Macrinus, his reign lasted little more than a year. He was defeated at the Battle of Immae, near Antioch, by a force led by no other than the former tutor of Avitus and the former lover of Soaemias, Gannys. Macrinus and his son were both executed, and the Imperial throne passed to possibly the most controversial and scandalous of all the Roman emperors, (in, let's face it a crowded field), the teenage boy Varius Avitus Bassianus, better known to posterity as Elagabalus or Heliogabalus.

In previous books in this series I have included the full content of the relevant passages from the contemporary sources, Herodian and Cassius Dio, but the material pertaining to the period in this book is too extensive, so I refer the interested reader to Herodian Chs 4.8.6 to 4.15.9 which can be found at https://www.livius.org/sources/content/herodian-s-roman-history/ and Cassius Dio books 78 and 79 which can be found at https://penelope.uchicago.edu/Thayer/E/Roman/Texts/Cassius_Dio/78*.html.

For information about forthcoming books and general chatter about Roman history and historical fiction, follow me on Facebook, Alex Gough author, Twitter @romanfiction, or check out my website, www.romanfiction.com.

Bibliography and Further Reading

As this is the last book of the series I have tried to be more comprehensive about the texts I have consulted, though this is still only a selection of the most important. However, I must pay particular tribute to *Caracalla: A Military Biography*, by Ilkka Syvänne, which has been my constant companion through this series. Its detail about Caracalla's military accomplishments as well as his political and personal life has been invaluable, and while I may not agree with every conclusion, the arguments developed in the book allow a much more nuanced version of Caracalla to emerge than simply the 'Common enemy of mankind' that Gibbons describes in his *Decline and Fall of the Roman Empire*.

Adkins, L. & Adkins, R. A. (1994) *Handbook to Life in Ancient Rome*, Oxford University Press, New York

Ball, W. (2016) *Rome in the East, the Transformation of an Empire*, 2nd edition, Routledge, London

Beard, M. (2015) *SPQR, A History of Ancient Rome*, Profile Books Ltd, London

Birley, A. (1971) *Septimius Severus, the African Emperor*, Eyre & Spottiswoode, London

Bouchier, E. S. (2019) *Syria as a Roman Province*, Blackwell, Oxford

Bowman, A. K., Garnsey, P. & Cameron, A. (2005) *The Cambridge Ancient History: Volume XII, the Crisis of Empire AD 193–337*, 2nd edition, Cambridge University Press, Cambridge

Butcher, K. (2003) *Roman Syria and the Near East*, British Museum Press Ltd, London

Capponi, L. (2011) *Roman Egypt*, Bristol Classical Press, London

Carandini, A. (2012) *The Atlas of Ancient Rome*, Princeton University Press, Princeton

Carroll, M. (2001) *Romans, Celts and Germans, the German Provinces of Rome*, Tempus, Stroud

Cary, M. & Scullared, H. H. (1975) *A History of Rome*, 3rd edition, Macmillan Press Ltd, Basingstoke

Casson, L. (1974) *Travel in the Ancient World*, John Hopkins University Press, Baltimore

Casson, L. (1994) *Ships and Seafaring in Ancient Times*, British Museum Press Ltd, London

Cornell, T. & Matthews, J. (1982) *Atlas of the Roman World*, Facts on Filoe, New York

Cunliffe, B. (1975) *Rome and the Barbarians*, The Bodley Head, London

Dando-Collins, S. (2010) *Legions of Rome*, Quercus, London

De Giorgi, A. U. & Eger, A. A. (2021) *Antioch: A History*, Routledge, Abingdon

Dickey, E. (2017) *Stories of Daily Life from the Roman World, Extracts from the Ancient Colloquia*, Cambridge University Press, Cambridge

Ellis, S. P. (2000) *Roman Housing*, Duckworth, London

Everitt, A. & Ashworth, R. (2014) *SPQR, A Roman Miscellany*, Head of Zeus, London

Falx, M. S. & Toner, J. (2016) *Release your Inner Roman*, Profile Books Ltd, London

Freisenbruch, A. (2010) *The First Ladies of Rome*, Jonathan Cape, London

Goldsworthy, A. (2010) *The Roman Army at War*, Clarendon Paperbacks, Oxford

Goldsworthy, A. (2011) *The Complete Roman Army*, Thames & Hudson, London

Grant, M. (1996) *The Severans: The Changed Roman Empire*, Routledge, Abingdon

Grant, M. (1999) *Roman Cookery*, Serif, London

Harries, J. (2007) *Law and Crime in the Roman World*, Cambridge University Press, Cambridge

Hartnett, J. (2017) *The Roman Street*, Cambridge University Press, Cambridge

Hunink, V. (2011) *Oh Happy Place! Pompeii in 1000 Graffiti*, Apeiron, Sant'Oreste

Icks, M. (2011) *The Crimes of Elagabalus*, Tauris & Co Ltd, London

Laurence, R. (2008) *Traveller's Guide to the Ancient World*, Quid Publishing, Hove

Lendering, J. & Bosman, A. (2012) *Edge of Empire*, Karwansaray, Rotterdam

Lewis, N. (1983) *Life in Egypt Under Roman Rule*, Oxford University Press, London

Lindsay, J. (1963) *Daily Life in Roman Egypt*, Frederick Muller Ltd, London

Lindsay, J. (1965) *Leisure and Pleasure in Roman Egypt*, Frederick Muller Ltd, London

Matyszak, P. (2009) *Classical Compendium*, Thames & Hudson, London

Matyszak, P. (2009) *Legionary*, Thames & Hudson, London

Matyszak, P. (2017) *24 Hours in Ancient Rome*, Michael O'Mara Books Ltd, London

Matyszak, P. (2020) *Forgotten Peoples of the Ancient World*, Thames & Hudson, London

McKeown, J. C. (2010) *A Cabinet of Roman Curiosities*, Oxford University Press, New York

Pollard, J. & Reid, H. (2006) *The Rise and Fall of Alexandria*, Penguin, London

Raven, S. (1969) *Rome in Africa*, Evans Brothers Ltd, London

Sidebottom, H. (2022) *The Mad Emperor: Heliogabalus and the Decadence of Rome*, Oneworld Publications, London

Southern, P. (2001) *The Roman Empire from Severus to Constantine*, Routledge, Abingdon

Swain, S., Harrison, S. & Elsner, J. (2007) *Severan Culture*, Cambridge University Press, Cambridge

Sylvänne, I. (2017) *Caracalla: A Military Biography*, Pen & Sword Military, Barnsley

Williams, D. (1998) *Romans and Barbarians*, Constable & Company Ltd, London

Acknowledgements

Thanks to Nome, Abbie and the rest of my family. Thanks to Michael Bhaskar and Kit Nevile from Canelo. Thanks to my agent Ed Wilson from Johnson and Alcock. Thanks to Simon Turney for encouragement throughout my historical fiction writing career, as well as to all the other authors who offered help and friendship along the way, including but not limited to (in no particular order): Alison Morton; Ruth Downie; Gordon Doherty; L. J. Trafford; Caroline Lawrence; Harry Sidebottom; Ben Kane; Nancy Jardine. And thanks of course to all the readers who accompanied Silus on his journeys this far.